a
good
family

a
good
family

A.H. Kim

GRAYDON
HOUSE

GRAYDON HOUSE®

ISBN-13: 978-1-525-80458-8

A Good Family

This edition published by arrangement with Harlequin Books S.A.

Graydon House
22 Adelaide St. West, 40th Floor
Toronto, Ontario M5H 4E3, Canada
www.GraydonHouseBooks.com
www.BookClubbish.com

Printed in U.S.A.

Recycling programs for this product may not exist in your area.

For Ope

a
good
family

hannah

one

They're all drunk as usual. It's the final night of the annual Lindstrom family reunion, the official end of summer, and the last time we'll be together for a while. Everyone's indulged in a few too many Moscow mules and dirty martinis. The kitchen stool behind the Carrara marble counter provides a mezzanine view of the assembled cast.

Sam's the one dozing on the couch, his handsome head tilted back, his mouth slightly agape. There's a tiny trickle of drool snaking toward his perfect chin. Gazing at my younger brother takes me back forty years to when he was a baby sleeping peacefully in his crib: the gentle curves of his eyelids, his long lashes fluttering in rhythm with his dreams, his warm moist breath smelling sweetly of mother's milk. Like me, Sam isn't a Lindstrom by blood but at least he's one by marriage.

Eva's leaning on Sam and appears to be asleep as well, but

it's an act. Eva's a drunk—a high-functioning drunk, but a drunk nonetheless. Five or six drinks aren't nearly enough to knock Eva out for the night, but it's enough to quiet the voices in her head, the voices that remind her she's the older sister, the smart one (read: not the pretty one), the woman who squeezed out three ten-pound babies within a six-year span and has the flabby belly and sexless marriage to prove it. Five or six drinks are just enough to make Eva think she can seduce her younger sister's husband even though he has zero attraction to her and is pretty much unconscious to boot.

My sister-in-law, Beth, is the drunkest of them all, but she has reason to be. This is Beth's last taste of freedom before the dreaded road trip—the road trip no one dares talk about to her flawless face but everyone discusses sotto voce in the tastefully appointed guest rooms, countless pantries and book-lined hallways of the Sunday *New York Times*–featured weekend retreat that Beth painstakingly designed and pretentiously named Le Refuge. Beth is lying on her back on the fluffy white flokati rug, making faux snow angels and staring up at the ceiling lights while singing "Silent Night" over and over again. Never mind that it's the end of August. She apparently only knows the first verse.

The rest of the adults already went to bed. These family reunions aren't exactly relaxing: a marathon of daily activities and simmering resentments. It's not easy having to keep up with the Lindstroms when it comes to drinking, darts, Scrabble or any other pastime that can be turned into a cutthroat competition.

Eva nuzzles closer to Sam, continuing to feign sleep, her hand slipping down toward his crotch. It's outrageous. Sam's her sister's husband. Then again, the poor guy deserves to get a little action. It's the family's worst-kept secret that Beth has been frigid ever since she gave birth to their first baby over five years ago, and it got worse when their second arrived two years later. Sam's bent my ear for countless hours complaining how sexually frustrated he is, how many times he's had to jack off in the shower, how convinced he is that his testicles are going to fall off because Beth refuses to put out or go down on him. It's not polite sibling conversation but also not worth making a fuss about. After all, he's got to talk to someone, and better me than one of the guys at the club.

You have to hand it to Beth: she thought of everything when she designed Le Refuge, filling the home with all the must-have amenities and high-end appliances showcased in the interior design porn magazines she reads so voraciously. You can just imagine a real estate agent giving prospective buyers a tour of the property, making sure to highlight each envy-inducing feature. The main house has a light-filled great room complete with fully stocked wet bar (top-shelf booze only) and climate-controlled wine cellar. Adjacent to the great room is the open-concept chef's kitchen with a six-burner Wolf range, dual Sub-Zero refrigerators and walk-in butler's pantry.

Just across the grassy lawn from the main house is the barn-like dorm, outfitted with four sets of matching bunk beds and deluxe memory foam mattresses and every amusement the Lindstrom children could ever want: pinball, foosball, air hockey, Ping-Pong, pool table, giant plasma TV with Net-flix and an Xbox 360. The glass-front fridge is filled with a dizzying array of Izze sodas and organic yogurt tubes, and the snack pantry is stocked with jumbo-size cartons of whole-wheat Goldfish, non-GMO puffed cheese balls and five-pound plastic jars of Red Vines.

My cell phone buzzes to remind me to go and check on the children. Everyone says it's unnecessary—after all, what could go wrong out here at Le Refuge?—but it's my nightly habit. There's an unseasonable chill in the air tonight. The amber

light of the dorm's windows always reminds me of the glowing lanterns in a Japanese woodblock that my professor spent
an entire lecture discussing in my Harvard freshman seminar.
A brown bat swoops in the distance, and a shooting star blazes
across the sky. The recycled barnwood floorboards creak on
my way up to the dorm's main level. The little girls are already
asleep, but the older Lindstrom cousins are piled together like
tired puppies on the oversize sectional and watching something on the TV. The movie is *Superbad*, totally inappropriate
for the tween-aged girls, but it's hard to muster the guts to be
the uncool aunt and tell them to turn it off.

Standing there, unnoticed by the four children, it's magical
to observe their unguarded faces. Max, the one male cousin—
technically, a stepcousin—had been a funny-looking boy, all
stuck-out ears and snub nose and sharp elbows, but he's grown
into a quirkily handsome young man with wavy ginger hair
and softly freckled skin. Meanwhile, the girl cousins have in-
herited the Lindstrom family's classic beauty: long blond hair,
blue eyes and graceful ballet figures.

Everyone is cuddled under a cozy king-size comforter, but
even with the camouflage of baffle-stitched six-hundred-fill
hypoallergenic goose down, it's obvious that things are not
all innocent. Max rests his head on one arm of the sectional,
and Stevie, the oldest of the girls, rests hers on the opposite
arm, with quite a bit of overlapping in between. This past year,
Stevie's blossomed from girl to woman—something about
her reminds me of the farmstand peaches now in season—
which hasn't gone unnoticed by Max. Oh, to be young again
and overflowing with hormones, feeling the exhilaration of
rubbing your long, lithe limbs against a member of the opposite sex.

"Stop that, you're related," my long-dead mother repri-
mands the children in my head. But really, what's the fuss?

The two kids are stepcousins. It's not like they share any blood. Isn't that what matters?

Suddenly, I feel old. At forty-nine, I'm the oldest person at the Lindstrom family reunion and the only unmarried adult. Descending the steps of the dorm and crossing the expansive lawn, my feet feel ice-cold and slippery against my slip-on shoes. Looking up at the crescent moon shining in the evening sky, my eyes are dazzled by the delicate dusting of stars. Being a city girl, it's a special treat to see so many twinkling lights. ("Hoboken doesn't count as the city, Hannah," my brother, Sam, always teases.) It's hard to remember a time when the sky was so dark and so bright at the same time.

I close my eyes and feel the gentle breeze wafting in from the shore. I take a deep breath, savoring the briny scent of the Chesapeake. I focus my energies on gratitude, on appreciating all the wonderful things in my life rather than the difficult challenges that await us tomorrow and in the days ahead. As I slowly open my eyes, I hear an owl hooting in the distance. I look upward. And there on the second floor of the main house, backlit by one of the extravagantly perfumed candles that Beth purchases by the case, I see my brother, Sam, desperately humping Eva in the upstairs guest bathroom.

two

Morning comes too soon. The adults and older kids are still in bed, but the little girls are noisily rummaging around the kitchen and looking for something to eat. I change out of my nightgown and head downstairs to take care of them. Starting today, Sam and Beth's girls will need a lot of care.

Seeing my nieces always brings me joy. This morning, the girls are dressed in matching pink-and-purple-striped pajamas, but that's where the resemblance ends. Claire is tall for her age, chubby and, as foretold by the old wives' tale, the firstborn takes after her father's side of the family, the Korean side: dark hair, dark eyes and full, round cheekbones. Meanwhile, little sister Ally is Claire's opposite: petite and small-boned, her delicate features and fair coloring reflecting Beth's Scandinavian heritage, her wide-set almond-shaped eyes serving as Sam's only apparent contribution to the pixie-child. "My fairy-tale princess," Sam calls her. Yet despite their physical differences, the two girls are inseparable, best of friends, two peas in a pod.

Joining Claire and Ally this morning are the two youngest Lindstrom cousins, who look like juvenile versions of Botticelli's *Venus* with their cascading golden curls and soft hazel eyes. Their long white sleeping gowns evoke the goddess's alabaster skin, but instead of emerging from a scallop shell, they're wearing floppy SpongeBob SquarePants slippers.

"You make the best Mickey Mouse pancakes, Auntie Hannah," Claire says. The other girls nod and murmur in agreement.

"Oldest first," the taller Botticelli says when the pancakes are ready. She holds her plate closest to me, inciting whiny protests from the other three.

"Yes, oldest first," Sam says, appearing out of nowhere and grabbing the first pancake straight from my spatula. "Bacon and chocolate chip, my favorite!" he exclaims. He folds the pancake into quarters and wolfs it down whole.

"Dad!"

"Uncle Sam!" the girls scream in outrage. "No fair!"

"Yeah, Sam, no fair," I say. "The girls have been patiently waiting. You cut the line."

Sam leans in to give me a peck on the cheek.

"My bad," Sam apologizes unconvincingly. He grabs another pancake from the griddle and skitters out of the kitchen.

I rub the greasy kiss with the back of my hand. No one ever gets mad at Sam—or at least no one ever stays mad at him. Ever since he was a boy, Sam's had the ability to simultaneously outrage and charm everyone around him. It isn't just his good looks either. In fact, when we were growing up in suburban Buffalo, people didn't quite know what to make of his looks. My brother wasn't the fair-haired Adonis that most people thought of as handsome, but he wasn't hard on the eyes either. It wasn't until high school, when Sam got contact lenses and started working out, that people began to take real notice. Today, Sam can't walk down the street without someone coming up to him and saying, "Hey, aren't you that guy from *Lost*?" or "You remind me of that Asian dude who won *Survivor*, but even better looking."

I make sure the girls get settled at the dining table, which has already been set with utensils, fresh fruit and a pitcher of cold milk. "Don't get chocolate on your pajamas," I warn the girls.

"We won't, I promise!" Claire says.

My stern look is quickly replaced with a smile. I have a terrible poker face.

I shuffle back to the kitchen, pour a cup of Italian roast with two lumps of sugar and walk over to my brother on the living room couch.

"Here you go," I say. "Just the way you like it."

"Thanks, Hannah," Sam replies absently. He takes a long sip and groans in almost erotic pleasure. "Ah, just what I needed. What would I do without you?"

I don't bother to answer.

"How did it go last night?" I ask.

"What do you mean?"

"How did Beth sleep?"

"Oh, that," Sam says. "Not so good. I don't think she got much sleep. I went by her room around one in the morning, and her light was still on."

It's always struck me as odd that a married couple like Sam and Beth sleep in separate bedrooms. Sam complained to me about it when Beth was designing Le Refuge but seems to have accepted the arrangement.

"I walked in and saw she was up," Sam says, "sitting in her bed and going through all her precious photo albums."

Beth is famous for making Shutterfly photo albums for every occasion in their life: Claire's and Ally's birthday parties, their fabulous vacations to Paris and Martha's Vineyard and Hawaii, the Lindstrom family reunions.

"I told her to take an Ativan and Ambien and go to sleep," Sam says.

Ativan and Ambien. I am well acquainted with the combination.

"She was still sleeping when I got up this morning," Sam says. "And don't worry, I made sure she was breathing."

Sam's offhand remark makes me wonder: *In Beth's situation, would death by sleeping pills be better than what lies ahead?*

"Auntie Hannah," the girls shout, "can we have seconds?"

There, in an instant, is my answer. Beth has two young girls to live for. Everything else pales in comparison.

My poor hips feel stiff getting up from the deep-cushioned couch. Nothing about this day is going to be easy.

"No more Mickey Mouse pancakes," I say. "Who'll help me make silver dollars?"

When the girls finish breakfast, they run laughing across the lawn to wake their older cousins, leaving me alone in the kitchen to clean up. I'm stacking the leftover pancakes on a cooling rack when Sam walks in.

"You can throw those in the garbage," Sam says. "We're leaving in an hour anyway."

"Claire and Ally can eat them in the car," I respond. It's hard to imagine throwing away perfectly good pancakes. My parents grew up hungry in postwar South Korea and taught me it was a sin to waste food. Anyway, the girls will need a snack for the long drive back to Princeton.

"Well, after you're done, can you go upstairs and check on Beth?" Sam asks. "I need to take a shower and get myself ready." Sam makes a hasty exit. His feelings are clear to me, and they have nothing to do with his ablutions. He doesn't want to be the one to wake Beth in case she's still asleep.

When Sam was a young boy, one of my responsibilities was to get him up for school. Entering his bedroom every morning and seeing his wiry body curled up like a fiddlehead, I'd take a moment to wonder: *Where is he now? What exotic world is he exploring? What exciting adventure is he having?* With a heavy heart, I'd nudge him awake to face the cold light of day.

I walk upstairs and knock on Beth's bedroom door. When no one answers, I slowly turn the doorknob and peer into the empty room. The sound of the shower comes through the en suite bathroom door. It's only the second or third time I've set foot in Beth's room. It feels a bit like entering the Pearly Gates. The walls are painted the palest blue. The king-size bed is a mass of cumulus comforters and Egyptian cotton linens. The air is redolent of honeysuckle and roses.

The sheets are still warm when I peel back the covers to make the bed. "C'mon, Hannah, what's the point?" I imagine Sam complaining. "Maria's just going to strip the bed and throw the sheets in the washing machine anyway." But I can't help myself. There's something about an unmade bed that makes me uneasy.

Beth's photo albums are scattered all over the bed and floor. I return them to their place on the built-in shelves on the other side of the bedroom. Conspicuous on Beth's nightstand are two amber plastic prescription bottles. I peek at the labels and stuff them into my pants pocket. Beth can't bring them where she's going, and it never hurts to have an extra stash.

"Hannah, is it you?" Beth says. My sister-in-law emerges from the bathroom with a white towel wrapped around her head like a turban. She is otherwise completely naked. Beth betrays no self-consciousness, and I try not to stare at her supple skin and pert pink nipples. Beth picks up a frosted glass jar with an ornate golden lid. She unscrews the lid, scoops out a small handful of thick cream and slowly smooths the emollient over her arms, her shoulders, her breasts. The heady scent of tuberose nearly causes me to faint.

Everyone gathers in the great room getting ready to depart. They're all lined up along the front wall, fair-haired and blue-eyed, reminding me of the Von Trapp children introducing themselves to Fräulein Maria. Despite their eagerness to get home, none of the Lindstroms want to leave—not yet, not until they've watched the pivotal scene of the Lifetime network family melodrama that is their new life.

"Are you ready to go, Claire and Ally?" Karen asks.

"Mommy, I don't want to go with Auntie Karen," Claire cries. "I want to go with you and Daddy." Claire runs to Beth and holds tight to her legs. Little sister Ally follows suit, nodding in agreement, not understanding anything that's going on.

"Girls, remember I told you," Beth says gently. "Auntie Karen is going to drive you to our Princeton house, and Daddy and Auntie Hannah are going to drive Mommy to camp. Don't you remember I told you?"

It was my idea to tell the girls that Mommy was going away to camp. I loved the fact that it was both true and misleading at the same time. Like a good law librarian, I made sure to do my research. In the US Bureau of Prisons hierarchy, the facilities with the least security are called federal prison camps, or camps for short. In contrast with the medium-security federal correctional institutions or high-security federal penitentiaries, camps like Alderson don't have guard towers or barbed wire fences or even locked cells. If you squint hard enough at the grainy Google Maps image, Alderson looks like it could be one of the Seven Sisters all-women colleges, only with fewer lesbians and more dental problems.

Now I feel ashamed. I've been spending too much time with lawyers and gotten used to using precision with words as a way to avoid harsh truths. To what purpose? To trick a five-year-old into believing that her mother is going to sleep-away camp instead of prison?

"You're going to miss my first day of kindergarten," Claire says. As her eyes fill with tears, the adults avert their gazes.

We all know Beth will be missing much more than that.

three

Beth dozes in the passenger seat of the BMW SUV, unable to shake off her Ativan and Ambien cocktail from the night before. Sam has the music turned up loud to keep himself awake. The AC is cranked high, but the car interior still smells stale and slightly sour. Reaching between the smooth leather seats from the back, I offer Sam an Altoid before slipping one into my mouth.

"Does my breath smell that bad?" Sam jokes. I laugh along politely, but it does. It stinks of this morning's coffee, day-old booze and the cheesy garlic bread and pasta puttanesca Beth had delivered last night as her "last meal." We need to work on Sam's oral hygiene.

Sam explores the channels on the Sirius XM system, having tired of the endless loop of Led Zeppelin, Pink Floyd and the Rolling Stones on the classic rock station we've been listening to all day. He stops when he hears Madonna singing "Holiday."

"Oh my God," Sam says, "I almost forgot. Happy birthday, Hannah."

At that moment, I'm glad to be sitting in the back seat. What would my face reveal? Disappointment that no one at the Lindstrom family reunion remembered? Resignation that, at the age of forty-nine, there's unlikely to be anyone in my life for whom my birthday would be a special occasion? Or gratitude that my forty-one-year-old brother—the one person in the world who matters the most to me—always remembers, although sometimes a day or two late?

I lean back in my seat and look out the window at the rolling hills rushing past. I reach up to finger the diamond studs in my ears and think back to when Sam gave them to me. It was my fortieth birthday—my last milestone birthday.

Nine years ago, Beth and Sam had been dating for several years but weren't married yet. They rented a gorgeous vacation home for a week in the Hamptons and invited a group of their equally gorgeous friends and family for an end-of-summer bacchanal, the precursor to the now-annual Lindstrom family reunion. Beth and Sam's parties weren't my cup of tea—their lavish lifestyle looked straight out of a Ralph Lauren ad—but I suffered through them. There weren't many other chances to spend time with Sam.

It's getting dark, and everyone is huddled around the outdoor fire pit sipping drinks when Sam starts tapping a spoon against his beer bottle and calls the crowd to attention.

"Friends, countrymen, lend me your ears," he shouts, "because tonight is a very special night. It's not only the end of summer, the end of our one-week bender, it's also my older sister Hannah's fortieth birthday." Several people turn around to find me tucked near the back of the party. They encourage me to come closer to the fire pit and stand next to Sam. I've always hated being the center of attention, even on my birthday, but I take comfort in knowing Sam's speech won't be about me. It'll be about him. It's always about him.

"In honor of Hannah's birthday," Sam says, slurring his words slightly, "I want to tell you all the story of how I came to be conceived." Chuckles ripple through the crowd.

"Everyone already knows the story, you drunk motherfucker!" a male voice heckles amiably. The group erupts in laughter. It's true: Sam has a repertoire of stories, much as an actor has a repertoire of roles. "How Sam was conceived" is his *Hamlet*.

"My parents moved to the US from South Korea so my father could get his PhD in linguistics," Sam continues undeterred. "Like the good, healthy, horny young people that they were, my parents quickly and easily conceived Hannah, their firstborn, who grew into a smart and hardworking little girl, every immigrant parent's dream." This line gets a lot of hoots and hollers. I'm pretty sure the crowd's enthusiasm is for the horny parents, not the hardworking little girl.

"When she started kindergarten, Hannah jumped out of bed every morning, eager to go to school and learn. But one day a couple months into the school year, Hannah complained of a stomachache and refused to leave her bed. The next day, Hannah did the same thing. My mom was baffled."

Even though most people at the party have heard this story countless times, they're quiet, paying close attention, listening as if they didn't already know the ending. That's the power of my brother's personality.

"Finally, my mom forced Hannah to go to school, and then she hid in the bushes during recess to see what would happen. And there she was, Hannah, their perfect daughter, sitting by herself on the playground bench, the only Asian child in a sea of white faces." I look around at Sam and Beth's friends, the sea of white faces, and wonder if any of them see the irony. I'm sure Sam doesn't.

"My mom decided then and there she would have another child so Hannah wouldn't be so lonely. Only this time, it wasn't as easy for the young couple, and it took them several years of concerted fucking to conceive me." More hoots and hollers confirm it's the horny parents and not the hardworking little girl who are the crowd-pleasers.

"So, in honor of your fortieth birthday, my dear big sister and lifelong friend, the pride of my parents and the precious diamond of the Min family, I present to you this modest token of my affection, my adoration and my appreciation." Sam hands me an instantly recognizable Tiffany blue gift bag to a chorus of oohs and aahs. Inside is a small velvet-lined box containing the most beautiful diamond stud earrings. I stand on my tippy-toes to hug Sam, who wraps his strong arms around me, and it feels like home. I take in a deep breath of Sam's familiar woodsy cologne. His friends and family all applaud.

It's the happiest moment of my life.

Welcome to Alderson, West Virginia, reads the sign at the town's border, Voted Best Fourth of July Celebration. Sam drives the car along the riverbank and across a stone bridge, past a patchy green field with a lonely brown mare and along a gently curving driveway marked by a government-issued sign that announces you're entering a federal prison camp.

It's almost 5:00 p.m., and the Alderson Prison parking lot is empty. We shouldn't have stopped for lunch on the road. The letter from the Bureau of Prisons made it clear Beth had to self-surrender during business hours today or risk additional punishment. There's a black cast-iron call box next to the single-arm gate, and Sam lifts the receiver.

"Do you remember the code to dial?" Sam asks. Beth gives a mild shrug. I reach into my purse—a well-worn leather satchel found among my mom's things after she died—and begin to sort through a thick sheaf of papers when a white sedan approaches from the opposite direction, exiting the prison through another single-arm gate.

"Is she self-surrendering?" a Tipper Gore look-alike asks. She points to me sitting in the back seat. Sam and Beth don't say anything.

"No, I'm not the one. She is." I gesture toward Beth, feeling like a narc.

"Okay," Tipper replies, "dial 313 and tell them the name of the inmate. Then pull over into the parking lot, and they'll be out to get you." With that, she drives away.

Sam does as he's told. We wait in the parking lot for what feels like a lifetime before a white van drives up. The three of us get out of the car.

"You the one self-surrendering?" the guard asks, looking at me.

"No," I say quickly. My voice is louder this time.

"I'm the one," Beth says. "I'm the one self-surrendering." The guard ogles Beth up and down.

"You'll have to leave that behind," the guard says. She points to Beth's right hand. Beth is still wearing the ring Sam got her for their fifth anniversary—everyone in the family calls it her Bling Ring—comprised of five rows of pavé diamonds in a platinum setting. Beth never wears a ring on her left hand. "I like to keep people guessing," she always says.

"My lawyer said I could wear my wedding band," Beth protests.

I stifle a groan. *If you had read the Alderson inmate orientation handbook that I emailed you, you would know about the Bureau of Prisons's jewelry policy—"Inmates may have a plain wedding band*

and an appropriate religious medallion and chain without stones."
The Bling Ring is anything but plain.

"Here, take this," I say. I unclasp the thin chain around my neck, pull the simple gold ring off and hand it to Beth.

"Oh no, I couldn't," Beth says. "That belonged to your mother."

"It's okay, she'd have wanted you to have it," I say. I'm lying. My mother died years before Sam met Beth, but she wouldn't have liked her. Beth is too American, too materialistic and too domineering for my traditional Korean mother—not to mention too felonious.

"It doesn't fit," Beth says. She passes the simple band back to me. "Anyway, I'm afraid I might lose it." I return the ring to the gold chain, and Beth passes me her Bling Ring, which I slip onto my finger. The weight of the diamonds feels surprisingly nice.

"Okay, that's enough. You're already late. Time to say goodbye," the guard barks. We stand there awkwardly, not sure what to do next.

"I don't know what to say, Hannah," Beth murmurs. She takes a step forward and hugs me hard. I can feel Beth's heart beating against my chest. "Thank you for coming all this way. I'm glad Sam won't have to drive all the way home by himself. Be sure to take good care of the girls."

Beth releases me and turns to Sam. She holds his hands and leans her head into his broad shoulder. Sam buries his face in her thick hair.

"I'm so sorry, Beth," he whispers.

"Stop it," Beth says.

"It should be me."

"What's done is done."

Sam lifts his head, and Beth kisses him lightly on the lips.

"Just don't screw up again," Beth says. Then she pushes him away.

Beth looks pale as she gets into the white van. I watch as the van makes its way through the one-armed gate and into the prison compound. I linger until the van is no longer visible, but Sam just climbs back into his car. He seems eager to get away from Alderson as fast as possible.

It's past 2:00 a.m. by the time we pull up to Sam and Beth's Princeton home. The lights are all off in the house, which means Karen must have gone to bed. It feels so long ago that we said goodbye to her and the girls at Le Refuge, but it's been less than a day.

Sam and Beth's Princeton home is much more formal than Le Refuge. The grand foyer has polished marble floors and a curved walnut staircase leading to the second level. The large living room showcases rich Oriental carpets and framed Picasso prints, and the paneled dining room features a breathtaking crystal chandelier and Queen Anne–style cabinet displaying Beth's collection of antique fine bone china. There's even a library like you'd see in an elegant English manor, with built-in floor-to-ceiling bookshelves and moiré silk wallcoverings.

We carry our bags into the pitch-dark house and make our way blindly into the kitchen. Sam turns on the pendant light over the center island and opens the stainless steel refrigerator door to pull out a bottle of beer.

"You want one?" he offers. "Oh, wait, you prefer wine, right?" Sam reaches for an opened bottle of French Chablis, pours it into a Riedel wineglass, and hands it to me. I'm grateful for the hospitality. I'd normally be asleep at this hour but got a second wind around midnight. It'll take some time for me to decompress.

"Wanna play a match?" Sam asks.

"Sure," I say, happy to oblige. We grab our drinks and head downstairs to the rec room to play Ping-Pong. It's one of the few activities we have in common.

When Sam was young, my parents bought a used Ping-Pong table from an ad in the local *Pennysaver* and set it up in our unfinished basement. We needed something to burn off Sam's excess boy energy, especially during the endless Buffalo winters. Unlike me, a natural-born nerd, Sam struggled with school. My parents were at their wits' end with his terrible report cards until I read an article in *Parents* magazine that made me realize Sam is a kinesthetic learner—he processes information through physical movement. From the time he was six until he went to college, Sam and I spent countless hours in the basement playing Ping-Pong, with me drilling him on everything from multiplication tables to state capitals to French vocab words.

I've barely had time to set down my wineglass and pick up my paddle before Sam serves the first ball. "Hey, no fair," I protest, feigning outrage. "I wasn't ready yet."

"You'll never be ready for me," he teases. He pulls a second ball out of his pocket.

We've had this exact exchange innumerable times. It's our own personal liturgy. Looking across the room, I'm reminded of Sam as a gawky kid, grinning mischievously, the light from a bare bulb glinting off his metal braces. Sam serves again, and I miss badly.

"You've gotten rusty," Sam says. He finishes off his beer and walks to the carved oak bar. He returns to the Ping-Pong table with a cut-crystal tumbler of something dark brown on the rocks, takes a sip, puts the glass down and waits.

"Are you doing okay?" I ask.

"Of course," Sam replies. He answers my high-bouncing serve with a decisive smash. "Why wouldn't I be okay?"

I decide to give him his space. We play in silence for a while. When Sam goes back to the bar to refill his glass, I think about Sam and Beth's goodbye at the prison, their last moments together. "It should be me," he had said.

"Sam, I hope you're not still blaming yourself for what happened."

"It all came down to the deposition," Sam replies. "Beth wouldn't be in prison right now if it hadn't been for the damn deposition."

"It's not your fault, Sam. You have to believe that it's not your fault."

"Then whose fault is it?" he asks. His tone is irritable, perhaps even bitter. Sam lifts the tumbler to his lips and empties the contents in one swallow before resuming the match. He serves the ball so hard it barely misses my head. It bounces off the wall and knocks over my wineglass, sending it shattering to the floor.

"Sorry 'bout that," he mumbles as he drops his paddle and heads upstairs. I get down on my knees to pick up the shards.

lise

From the deposition of Lise Danielsson in *United States of America et al. v. God Hälsa AB, Andreas Magnusson and Elizabeth Lindstrom*

Q: Tell us about the first time you met Ms. Lindstrom.

A: I was sixteen, just arrived in America from Sweden.

Q: Did Ms. Lindstrom pick you up at the airport?

A: No, she sent Jorge.

Q: Who is Jorge?

A: Jorge is Beth's driver. Also the gardener and all-around handyman. A supersweet man. He's married to Maria.

Q: And who is Maria?

A: Maria's the cook and housekeeper. Jorge and Maria, they're like part of the Lindstrom family. Almost like a grandpa and grandma, you know?

Q: Okay, so after Jorge picked you up from the airport, what happened next?

A: We drove straight to the house.

Q: Which house: the Princeton house or the St. Michaels house?

A: The Princeton house. The St. Michaels house wasn't built yet.

Q: Was Ms. Lindstrom waiting for you at the house?

A: No, only Maria. Oh, and Claire of course. Claire was just a baby then. She was so cute with her chubby cheeks and big brown eyes. She was like a living doll, you know?

Q: Did you meet Ms. Lindstrom later that day?

A: Um, no, not that day. I don't think we met until a couple days later.

Q: You didn't meet Ms. Lindstrom until a couple days after you arrived?

A: Yeah, that's right.

Q: Did you find that strange?

A: Find what strange?

Q: Did you find it strange that you traveled all the way from Sweden to be her au pair but she wasn't there to welcome you?

A: Well, now that you mention it, I guess it was a little strange. But, you know, I'd never been an au pair before, and I'd never been to America either. I didn't know what to expect. Anyway, Beth is just different.

Q: What do you mean: Beth is just different?

A: I mean Beth's not like most women. She doesn't cook, clean, that kind of stuff. She's all fancy, you know? She grew up in the Swedish Embassy with her own cook and driver.

Q: So you're telling us that Ms. Lindstrom had a privileged life. Is that what you mean by "being different"?

A: You don't know Beth, do you? My God, she's different in so many ways.

beth

four

I stare at the van's passenger-side mirror as we leave the parking lot and cross over to the other side—the federally restricted side—of the one-armed gate.

"Objects in mirror are closer than they appear," I read in the etched glass surface. Hannah stands in the same spot that I left her, waving pathetically, while Sam climbs back into the car, his face impassive.

It's gonna be a long trip home.

I check out my new surroundings. To the naked eye, Alderson doesn't look too bad. Colonial-style brick buildings, neatly trimmed lawns, leafy trees. I half expect to see someone driving a golf cart or giving a campus walking tour.

Up the grassy hill, I spot a line of khaki-clad women exiting a building and walking down a path. Headed to dinner, maybe? They appear to be on their own, no guard in sight.

Except for my van driver, I don't see any guards at all. No razor wire either. The only thing separating me from freedom is that lousy one-armed gate.

"You're late," the guard mutters.

"Sorry," I say, not sorry at all.

"Did ya come far?"

"Pretty far."

"Ya married to that Chinese guy?"

"He's Korean. And yes."

"No offense. I can't tell 'em apart."

Seriously? I have no words.

We pull up in front of a boxy brick building.

"Well, here we are," the guard says, "R&D."

"R&D?" I ask. In my line of business, *R&D* stands for research and development, but I doubt there's much of that going on around here.

"Receiving and discharge."

The guard gets out of the van. I follow her up the steps of the building into an empty room with cheap vinyl floors and buzzing fluorescent lights. I can practically feel my soul getting sucked out of me.

"Wait here," the guard says. She points to a plastic bench along the wall and leaves.

As I sit and wait, I slip off my Chanel espadrilles and admire my toenails. Royal blue, red, gray, with a French tip of white. New York Giants colors. I had them done yesterday. I figure the gel polish will last a month if I'm careful.

One month down, one hundred—plus or minus—more to go.

"You here to self-surrender?" someone says.

I look up. Another guard. Male this time.

"Yeah," I say, slipping my shoes back on.

"You're late," he says. "Last admission is at five o'clock."

He points at the plain white clock on the wall. It reads 5:15.

"Great, I'll just get out of your way, then," I'm tempted to wisecrack. Instead, I just nod.

"You have your IDs?" he asks.

I walk over and hand him my Social Security card and driver's license.

He starts filling out one of those government-issue forms, the kind with the white top page and the pink and goldenrod carbons. He holds up my driver's license and compares my face to the photo, like a bartender checking a fake ID.

That's right, I'm trying to sneak my way into prison.

Fucking idiot.

"Okay, this way," he says.

He walks me over to a smaller room where I see the original guard—the one who drove me in the van. She closes the door and tells me to strip.

I feel like the star of some low-budget porno flick. I strip down to my underwear and bra while the guard watches. She can't take her eyes off me.

"All your clothes," she says.

I obey.

"Run your fingers through your hair."

"Really?" I ask.

I take it from the guard's scowl that she's not in the mood for questions.

What's next, I wonder. *Lick my lips and pout?*

"Okay," she says, "now open your mouth and lift your tongue."

As I follow the guard's orders, I can feel my nipples getting hard from the window air conditioner set to Arctic. I hope she doesn't take it as a compliment. I'm not sure why I need to be stark naked while she inspects the inside of my mouth. I feel like a goddamn cow at the Iowa State Fair.

"Now squat and cough," she says.

Damn, just when I thought it couldn't get any more humiliating. I wonder if anyone has ever just shit on the spot, leaving a big pile of steaming feces on the floor as an FU to the whole US criminal injustice system.

"Stand and lift your arms."

After she makes sure I haven't concealed any assault weapons in my pits, the guard hands me a small bundle of clothes.

"I'll give you a minute to get dressed," she says. She opens the door to leave.

Now she's giving me privacy?

I slip into my new wardrobe of khaki polyester-blend separates and canvas slip-ons. The elastic-waistband slacks are super flattering. I haven't worn tube socks since middle school gym.

There's a knock on the door.

"Ready?" the guard asks, peeking through the crack in the door.

"Ready as I'll ever be," I say.

"Want your clothes sent home?"

"What are my options?"

"Send 'em home or destroy 'em."

I look at the pile of clothes on the floor and imagine Sam's confused reaction when they arrive in the mail. Sam's not good at figuring things out on his own.

"We pay for shipping," she says. As if that's the reason for my hesitation.

"Just destroy them," I finally say.

We head down a hallway to an area that looks like a nursing station at a hospital. There's a group of three guards drinking coffee in foam cups and shooting the shit. When they see us approaching, they stop talking. Two of them walk away, like they've got something they need to get back to. Maybe a box of stale donuts.

"Late admission, self-surrender," my guard says, handing over my paperwork.

The clerk at the nursing station looks annoyed. I just ruined her day by making her do her job. After reading through my pile of forms, she turns to her computer—some crappy circa-2000 Compaq with Post-it notes all over the monitor—and logs in. Based on her Post-its, I'd guess her password is ILoveKitty. I wonder if that's her cat or her girlfriend.

"Give me your hand," the clerk orders.

She grabs my hand, rolls each finger on a spongy cushion of ink and then rolls them on a piece of paper. When we're through, the clerk pulls a premoistened wipe from a nearby pop-up container and gives it to me. The baby powder fragrance reminds me of Ally.

"Okay, stand over there, by the wall."

I look over at the wall opposite the nursing station. It's white and completely blank except for a neon-green Post-it that says "Stand Here."

There's a camera bolted to the nursing station. The clerk looks through the eyepiece and adjusts the camera angle.

I stand in front of the Post-it and look straight at the camera. No smile. No smirk. I don't want to look smug, just in case TMZ gets my mug shot.

A machine on the nursing station ejects a bright red plastic card. The clerk looks at it, loops on a black lanyard and hands it over to me.

"Federal Bureau of Prisons—INMATE," it says in large black type. In case my all-khaki ensemble doesn't give me away.

Elisabeth Lindstrom, 88299-050.

At least they got the spelling right.

The next few hours are a blur of mindless interviews and bureaucratic bullshit. As I'm led from room to room, I push my shoulders back, stand tall and stare straight ahead. I'm not gonna let this experience get me down.

"Okay, Lindstrom, you're good to go," my van-driving guard finally says.

"Now what?" I ask.

"Unit A2." The guard walks me out of R&D and points uphill toward a cluster of buildings.

"Are you coming with me?"

She shakes her head. "I got stuff to do down here. Just head up the hill. A Building's on your right. Ya can't miss it." With that, she goes back inside, leaving me alone.

After all we've been through, I thought we had something special.

I'm a little out of breath when I get to the top of the hill. At least I'll be able to get into shape while I'm in prison.

A group of women wearing white T-shirts and heather-gray shorts stands in the middle of the quad-like lawn, chatting and laughing. They all stop talking and stare at me. I often have that effect on people.

"Hey, Blondie, ya lookin' for A or B?" one of them shouts.

"A," I shout back.

"Over there," she says, pointing to the nearest building.

I nod in thanks, and the women return to their chatter.

Entering A Building, I suddenly feel like a real inmate. The prison looks pretty much like what I've seen in movies. Cinder block walls painted institutional white. More cheap vinyl floors and buzzing fluorescent lights. Up front is a guards' station manned by uniformed officers. And everywhere, women of all shapes, races and sizes—mostly XL and XXL—rush by in a khaki-clad stream of humanity.

"Lindstrom?" a female officer asks as I approach the guards' station.

"Yeah."

"You're late."

"Sorry," I say, still not sorry.

"Next count's in thirty minutes, and lights-out at ten o'clock," she says. She reaches into a cabinet and hands me a big pile of stuff. A dark gray, scratchy-wool blanket. Two threadbare sheets. A sad, flat fiberfill pillow. A clear plastic bag with motel-size soap, toothbrush and mini-tube of toothpaste.

"Count?" I ask. I follow the woman down a corridor lined on either side with identical cinder block sleeping compartments.

"Ask Flores, she'll teach you the ropes," she says, stopping in front of a compartment. She motions to the raven-haired woman sitting on the bottom bunk, who's got her nose deep in a pulp paperback.

"Flores, this is Lindstrom, your new bunkie," the officer says. As she leaves, I hear the echoes of her heavy black boots making their way back to the guards' station.

"Hey, I'm Lindstrom. Beth Lindstrom."

I sound like James Fucking Bond.

"Juanita Flores," she replies. She puts her book facedown on the mattress, wriggles out of her bunk and shakes my hand. I notice she's got an awesome manicure.

"Nice nails," I say. "Gel?"

Juanita looks pleased.

"No, it's regular polish. But, like, three thin coats and a shiny topcoat. The girls here are fricking mani-pedi geniuses. And they're not even Vietnamese."

"So, what're you reading?" I ask. I point to the paperback on her bunk.

"*Murder on the Orient Express*," she says. "I've probably read it a million times, but I can never get enough of mysteries. You read it?"

"No, but I saw the movie. A long time ago."

"Movies are never as good as the book," she says. "I'll show you how to make your bed." She reaches over to grab the sheets from my pile of stuff.

"How hard can it be to make a bed?" I want to ask—although now that I think about it, I can't actually remember the last time I did.

"Six times a day, we have count, which means you need to be at your bunk," Juanita says. "Every morning by first count, your bed needs to be inspection ready. If your bed's not perfect, you get a shot."

"A shot?" I ask.

"Yeah, it's kinda like a speeding ticket. You get enough shots, you lose TV privileges, get more time, whatever. So, whatcha do is make the bed all perfect and sleep on top."

Juanita secures the sheet on the mattress with hospital corners, drapes it partway down, then folds it back up.

"Gimme the blanket," she says.

She tucks the blanket into the foot of the bed, draws it up to the head and then folds the sheet over the edge. In a few deft moves, Juanita's created the appearance of a perfectly made bed with just one sheet—the same way we used to short-sheet our counselors' bunks at summer camp.

"Light's out every night at ten o'clock," Juanita continues. "When you're ready to go to sleep, you spread the second sheet on top of the blanket and lie on it. These sheets are crappy, but at least they're better than the horse blankets, which are itchy as shit."

Juanita pulls a colorful granny-square afghan from her footlocker. "It gets cold at night. You can borrow this 'til you get your own stuff." She folds the afghan neatly in thirds and places it at the foot of my bed.

Everyone will tell you: I'm no softie. But in that moment, I'm close to tears.

"So, does everyone do this?" I ask.

"Do what?"

"Sleep on top of their bed?"

"Yup."

"No one actually sleeps under the blanket?"

"Nope."

"And the guards don't know?"

"Of course, they know."

"But they never check? They never look under the covers?"

Juanita eyes me up and down and smiles.

"You should know, *chica*," she says. "The only thing anyone cares about is how things look. No one gives a shit about what's real."

hannah

five

After spending three weeks with Sam and the girls, it's hard coming back to my empty one-bedroom condo in Hoboken. There's a pile of legal research assignments waiting for me at the law firm, which lifts my spirits a little, but my normal life suddenly feels small and boring. So when I see the Alderson return address on the plain white envelope in my mailbox, it provides a welcome bit of excitement.

"I know I'm asking a lot," Beth writes, "but could you come visit me soon? I really need to talk to someone, and you're the one person I know who'll listen without judgment."

Beth's letter combines both guilt and flattery, an intoxicating mix. It breaks my heart to think about Beth having to be separated from Sam and the girls for nearly ten years, but it also warms my heart to think that Beth—the beautiful and powerful Elisabeth Lindstrom with her 1,001 Facebook friends—would seek out my company above all others.

That weekend, I rent a car and wake before dawn to make the seven-hour-plus drive to Alderson. Pulling into the prison parking lot, a song comes on the radio that I haven't heard in decades, the falsetto voices singing something about love and money. The digital display scrolls the name Bronski Beat, a band that was popular my freshman year in college. It's tempting to sit and listen through to the end of the song, but the dashboard clock shows it's already getting late. I take a deep breath, pull the Ziploc bag out of my purse and turn off the engine. I walk up the pathway to the visitors' building, where a uniformed female guard sits at the reception desk. She motions for me to enter.

"Step forward," the guard orders.

"I'm here to visit Elisabeth Lindstrom."

"Do you have your form?" she asks. "Because if you don't have a form, you'll have to go back outside and fill one out." Having done my research, I hand the guard a Bureau of Prisons visitors' form, neatly filled out in ink with Beth's full name and federal inmate number and my identification information. The guard looks the form over and checks my driver's license, then makes me turn out my pockets to prove I'm not smuggling in anything.

"Okay, then," the guard says. "Sign your name in the register and wait for your inmate." At the end of the reception desk is a large ledger along with one of those ballpoint pens on a chain that you only ever see at the post office or bank.

The visiting room is so crowded, there's hardly a place to sit. All the inmates are dressed in identical khaki shirts and pants. A few women sit one-on-one with their husbands or boyfriends; others are surrounded by small groups of friends or family. In the far corner, a pimply but pretty inmate holds a sleeping toddler and talks to an older woman visitor while picking at a bag of nacho-flavor Doritos. Crossing the room to an empty chair, I suddenly feel self-conscious of my gallon-size bag of coins. Beth had told me to bring plenty of change to buy snacks from the overpriced vending machines, so I dutifully went to the local bank branch office and asked the bored-looking teller for a hundred dollars in quarters. I had no idea just how heavy that much change would be. Here, inside the walls of the Alderson visitors' building, I feel like I'm flaunting my wealth in twenty-five-cent increments.

An unmarked door behind the reception desk opens, and a strikingly beautiful African American woman emerges. An adorable little girl with deep dimples and two tightly wrapped braids jumps from the lap of a weary-faced woman and calls out, "Mommy, Mommy, Mommy!" The younger woman scoops up her daughter and bursts into sobs, and I'm on the verge of tears myself even though the mother and child are complete strangers to me.

About ten minutes later, the slender figure of Beth appears in the window. She strides down the hill toward the visitors' building and disappears through a side door. A few minutes pass until Beth enters the visiting room through the unmarked door. She surprises me again with the intensity of her embrace.

"Hannah, I'm so glad to see you," Beth says.

"It's nice to see you, too."

"Let's go sit in the back," Beth suggests, scanning the crowded room. "We should have more privacy there."

As Beth leads the way past the vending machines and into the back room, I'm struck by her confidence. Despite being new to Alderson, Beth walks the visitors' building with such grace and ease. Then again, Beth has always moved with grace and ease. I guess it's what comes from a lifetime of privilege.

In the back of the visitors' building is a large room with

padded vinyl chairs, a couple microwaves and a gray metal cabinet filled with board games and jigsaw puzzles. Distracted by the library cart of Alcoholics Anonymous booklets, I bump into a muscular man pulling a burger out of the microwave. His arms are tattooed up and down.

"Pardon me, ma'am," the man says. He holds my elbow to gently steer me away from the open microwave door. He closes the door, grabs a pile of dirt-brown paper towels from a nearby dispenser and walks over to a grandmotherly-looking inmate who takes the hamburger from him and starts gobbling like she hasn't eaten in weeks. It's humbling. I was the one at fault and yet this man—someone I would have been afraid to meet in a dark alley and probably dismissed as poor white trash if I met him in a Walmart—exhibits more gallantry than my brother or any of his country-club friends have ever shown me.

I walk over to Beth, who has located two chairs in a quiet corner.

"Is this okay with you?" Beth asks, gesturing to the seats.

"You sound like the hostess at some fancy hot spot," I say. "Next thing, you're going to ask me if I want still or sparkling." We both laugh. It feels good to laugh with Beth.

"Speaking of which, I'm dying for a Diet Coke," Beth says.

"Oh, of course," I say. I reach into my Ziploc and offer her a handful of quarters. Beth shrinks back as if the coins were made of kryptonite.

"Oh my God, I'm so sorry," I say. My new surroundings had me so flustered that I forgot the cardinal rule of prison visitation: inmates aren't allowed to touch money. I look around to see if any of the guards saw me.

"That's okay," Beth reassures me. "Let's go together." Beth spreads her fleece jacket on the chairs to reserve them, and we walk over together to the vending machine room. We buy two Diet Cokes, a small package of Chicken of the Sea tuna with Ritz crackers and a bag of Life Savers Gummies.

"Thank you for taking time to come all this way," Beth says. She settles into her chair and scoots closer to me. "I know you don't like to drive by yourself, and it's a long way from New York to here." I'm touched by Beth's acknowledgment of my sacrifice and her pretense that I live in New York rather than Hoboken.

"You look good, Beth. Honestly, you look a lot better than I thought you would." Beth's fair skin looks dewy fresh, her long lashes are tastefully accented with mascara and her lips are softly enhanced with matte pink lipstick.

"Thanks," Beth replies with the casual tone of a woman used to accepting compliments. "It was hard the first week, but I adjusted pretty quickly. You'd be amazed how much less stress you feel when you don't have to worry about taking care of two young children, holding down a full-time job and fighting off creditors, all at the same time."

You mean like my poor brother has to do? I think. Then I feel guilty. Beth doesn't deserve any more judgment. After all, she's in prison.

"How's your cellmate?" I ask.

"My bunkie? She's great. Her name's Juanita, and she's smart as a whip. I've learned a lot from her already."

We spend the next couple hours chatting. I fill Beth in on Claire's and Ally's activities, and Beth describes the colorful characters that make up Alderson's population: Meatloaf Mary, Deb the Destroyer and Runaround Sue. Time passes quickly.

"Hannah, we've only got a few more minutes before visiting hours end," Beth says, "so I should explain why I asked you here."

"Okay," I say, trying to keep the edge of disappointment

out of my voice. I thought Beth just wanted someone to talk to; I didn't realize there was a reason Beth asked me here.

"Over the past few months," Beth says, "even before I got to Alderson, I've spent a lot of time thinking about Lise."

Just hearing Lise's name makes my blood pressure spike. Lise was a sweet teenager from a small town in Sweden when Beth hired her several years ago to be Claire's au pair. After Ally was born a couple years later, Lise became even more integrated into Beth and Sam's life. Lise did everything, went everywhere, with them. She was practically a member of their family. Then last year, Lise filed a whistle-blower lawsuit against Beth and her pharmaceutical company. Lise provided hours of testimony in depositions about the details of Beth's personal and professional life. Lise gave the federal prosecutors all the evidence they needed to prove Beth was personally responsible for the fraudulent marketing activities that netted her company billions of dollars in ill-gotten gains.

"What about Lise?" I ask.

"Well, Lise was a sweet girl," Beth says, "but you know as well as I do—she wasn't very bright. I've been talking to Juanita about my case, and there's one thing neither of us can figure out. How in the world did someone like Lise—a foreigner with barely a high school education—even get the idea to file a whistle-blower lawsuit?"

That's a good question. I can't believe I didn't think of it myself.

"The only answer we could come up with," Beth says, leaning into me, "is that someone—or maybe someones—must have put her up to it. And, Hannah, I need you to help me figure out who it is."

"Hey, you two, not so close," the guard barks at us.

I quickly pull myself away from Beth. My cheeks feel flushed.

"Why?" I ask.

"Why would someone want to send me to prison?" Beth asks. "You tell me. Jealousy? The multimillion-dollar reward? Who knows?"

"No, I mean…your case is closed. You can't undo your plea. So what does it matter?"

"You're right—the government's case against me is closed," Beth says, "but remember that girl in California? The one who died?"

How could I forget about the girl in California—a fresh-faced teenager from a town outside Bakersfield who died of anorexia, allegedly caused by the drugs that Beth's company manufactured and sold. How could anyone forget? The girl's grieving parents have become regular fixtures on cable news, sharing their unthinkable loss in front of a phalanx of cameras.

"My lawyers are worried they're going to file a wrongful death lawsuit against me," Beth says, "and that they'll find a witness who'll corroborate their claims."

I know from my work at the law firm that private lawsuits for wrongful death have a lower standard of proof than criminal prosecutions—preponderance of evidence rather than beyond a reasonable doubt—and California's liberal juries are infamous for granting huge damage awards. A jury verdict could wipe out whatever is left of Beth and Sam's savings. It could ruin them forever.

"What's the statute of limitations on wrongful death?" I ask.

"In California, two years from the date of death," Beth says, "which means there's still over a year on the clock for the girl's family to file suit. Over a year for them to find a witness who'll testify against me."

"Do you think Lise would testify?" I ask.

"They can't force her to testify, and she has no reason to do it. Lise's already gotten her millions in whistle-blower reward and hightailed it back to Sweden. I'm not worried about her. I'm worried she had an accomplice."

"But why ask me? I'm not a lawyer."

"I don't need a lawyer. I need someone to help me find Lise's accomplice so I can get to them before the other side's lawyers do."

"I'm not a detective either."

"Hannah, let me be blunt. Based on the government's case against me, I'm pretty sure someone very close to me convinced Lise to blow the whistle. Whoever that person is, I need to get to them first, before the girl's family in California does, so I can convince them not to testify. All I'm asking is that you keep an eye out and let me know if anyone acts suspicious."

"Five minutes," the guard calls out.

The other inmates start saying goodbye to their guests. There's a flurry of activity all around. I try to stand up to leave, but Beth won't let me.

"Hannah," she says, "there's no one else I can ask. Will you help me?"

"I don't get it," Tracy says. "Who'd want to send your sister-in-law to prison?"

Tracy is the assistant librarian at my law firm and one of my few friends at work. I don't usually talk about my personal life with my coworkers, but Tracy's curiosity was piqued by my back-to-back vacations. I've never taken so much time off from work before. Tracy kept poking and prodding until I finally had to confess about Beth being in prison.

"Shh, please be quiet," I say. "I don't want it to get around the office."

"Why not?" Tracy asks. "It's not like *you* did anything wrong. Besides, people are totally fascinated by prison these days. Think about Martha Stewart and that Real Housewife from New Jersey. Not to mention all the shows on HBO and Netflix. And here you are, with a front-row view of the action. It must be kinda exciting."

"There's still a stigma to having a felon in the family," I say. "I don't want people at the firm to know about this. Seriously, Tracy, promise me you won't tell anyone."

"Oh, all right," Tracy agrees. "I won't tell a soul." Just when I think the matter's settled, Tracy whispers, "But you can't deny me a little curiosity. Who do you think ratted on her?"

"Well," I sigh, "the whistle-blower lawsuit was filed by Beth's au pair, Lise."

"Her au pair?" Tracy interrupts. "How does an au pair even know about whistle-blower lawsuits?" Tracy never ceases to impress me. Even though she only has a two-year associate's degree in library science from some online university, Tracy is quicker than most of the Harvard Law School–educated lawyers who join Drinker, Barker and Horne every fall.

"Beth asked the same thing," I say. "She thinks someone conspired with Lise."

"A conspiracy? Now that's interesting. A real-life whodunit."

"I wouldn't get so excited," I say. "Beth doesn't have evidence that anyone conspired with Lise. I think she's probably got too much time on her hands and is letting her imagination go wild."

"In the movies, it's usually the husband," Tracy says, ignoring me.

"It wasn't Sam."

"How can you be so sure?"

"I just am."

"Love can sometimes blind you to the truth," Tracy says.

"What would Sam have to gain by sending his wife to prison?" I ask, appealing to her reason. "Beth was the primary breadwinner in the family. The legal defense costs have nearly wiped out their savings. Not to mention that Sam is madly in love with Beth. It makes no sense for Sam to have conspired with Lise."

"Okay, let's set Sam aside for now," Tracy says. "But who else could it be? Did Beth give you any ideas? Who's on the top of her most-wanted list?"

I stand up and start rearranging the books on the library cart. The mindlessness of the task helps me to think.

"Beth thinks it might have been someone close to her, maybe someone in the family, but I think it could just as easily have been one of her colleagues at God Hälsa." God Hälsa is the Swedish pharmaceutical corporation that Beth worked for, the company accused of engaging in misleading marketing practices and bilking the federal Medicare and Medicaid system of billions of dollars.

"Let's think about this logically," Tracy says. "We know Lise was the whistle-blower. So the obvious question is who had access to Lise? And who had a motive to put Beth away?"

My mind flashes through a series of images: the gorgeous guests at Sam and Beth's extravagant Hamptons summer soirees; the cutthroat competitions at the annual Lindstrom family reunions; the hundreds of pictures in Beth's meticulously curated photo albums.

"Well," I say, "a few names do come to mind."

beth

six

Charlotte Von Maur and I met almost twenty years ago on our first day of work at God Hälsa. That day—with its Power-Point presentations and catered spa meals—was a far cry from today, which I'm sure will be crappy.

Literally.

I've been in Alderson for a little over a week, and I just found out I've been assigned to be a cottage maintenance worker. That's the BOP's way of saying I'm a janitor. My entire life, I've been leaving messes for other people to deal with, and now I'm supposed to clean up after petty thieves and drug addicts.

The irony is rich.

"Meet your crew at the bus stop tomorrow at 7:00 a.m.," the corrections officer told me on the last day of prison orientation classes.

The bus stop is the cluster of beds right in front of the guards' station. It's where the inmates who've gotten in trouble have to sleep. Being sent to the bus stop is kind of like being sent to detention in high school, but instead of getting caught smoking weed or cutting class, bus stop residents are more likely to have gotten caught with a bottle of moonshine—old-timers call it White Thunder—or running an underground gambling ring.

"Hey, Blondie, listen up," the janitorial crew lead yells at me. My bunkie, Juanita, told me the crew lead's name is Deb, who's known around camp as Deb the Destroyer. It's Deb's third time in prison, she can bench-press two hundred pounds without breaking a sweat, and everyone's been staying the hell out of her way since her longtime girlfriend back in Ohio died of an overdose. The rumor is that she did it on purpose.

"Three times a day, we clean the toilets, sinks and showers," Deb yells, "and morning shift is usually the worst. Especially if dinner the night before was three-bean chili or kung pao chicken."

The other crew members laugh out loud. They're a lovely bunch: a collection of bad dye jobs and crumbling gray teeth. The biggest gals quickly grab a mop bucket and roll them down toward the bathroom. The others pick up industrial-size laundry bags of rags and spray bottles of bleach solution. The only equipment left is a plastic caddy holding a well-used toilet brush, black rubber plunger and extra large canister of Ajax.

"Whatcha waiting for, Blondie?" Deb yells.

I pick up the toilet caddy, which smells of shit and bleach.

"Do we get rubber gloves?" I ask.

"Nah, they kept getting stolen by the gals for making hooch or sticking up their cooches, so the warden got rid of them."

I take a moment to check my reflection in the mirror by the bus stop.

"Let's get moving, Blondie," she says. "We ain't payin' ya to look pretty."

I used to get paid for looking pretty. In fact, that was the chief qualification for my first job out of college. Like most pharma companies, God Hälsa trolls the college circuit every year for pretty young things willing to suffer twelve-hour days in four-inch heels, size two suits in one-hundred-degree temps and enough full-on hair and makeup to make a drag queen wince.

It's my first day of employee orientation at God Hälsa. The windowless conference room reeks of cheap perfume and Final Net hair spray. I notice several girls show up wearing the same St. John knockoff suit featured in the window displays of every Ann Taylor store in America.

Two clueless coeds enter the conference room wearing nothing on their legs but cheap chemical self-tanner. They look like fucking Oompa Loompas.

I spot one particularly pathetic hopeful who wears her ambitions—as well as the 50 percent silk-blend label—on her proverbial and literal sleeve. The poor girl is politely but firmly told to seek her fortunes elsewhere before the first day even ends.

At midday, we're herded like kitten-heeled cattle into the executive dining room for a light luncheon and official welcome.

"Iced tea, miss?" the white-jacketed server asks.

"Please," I murmur. I stifle my sigh at the limp iceberg salad.

"Is this seat taken?" a voice asks.

I look up and see a green-eyed beauty. Her God Hälsa identification badge identifies her as Charlotte. The badge dangles from a lanyard and nestles in her creamy cleavage.

I move my Prada handbag off the next chair and onto the floor.

"Iced tea, miss?" the server asks after giving Charlotte a moment to settle in. She rests her Gucci handbag on the empty chair next to her.

I notice that Charlotte nods in the same polite but distant way I did.

I hate when people are overly solicitous of waitstaff. It betrays a false humility, a deceptive democratic sensibility, a kind of modern-day noblesse oblige.

"Could I bother you for a refill?" they simper.

It's not a bother, for God's sake; it's their fucking job.

Especially, as here, when the server is so clearly in command of his role, an older black gentleman wearing a crisp white jacket embroidered with his name—Isaiah—beneath the God Hälsa corporate logo, the most respectful thing to do is to allow him to pursue his vocation as he has clearly been trained: impeccably and unobtrusively.

"I noticed you earlier today. Wolford?" Charlotte asks.

"Mais oui," I answer. I extend my legs to acknowledge her appreciation of my hosiery.

"It's nice to find a kindred spirit," Charlotte says. She takes a bite of her timid, tasteless salad. "I fear the local CVS will have to scramble to restock its now-empty pantyhose aisle."

"Someone should tell these girls that CoverGirl ivory foundation doesn't go with suntan L'eggs," I say. "Nude would have been a better choice."

"Yes," Charlotte concurs, "the collars should match the cuffs."

"Mon Dieu," I reply, "are we already speculating about their pubes?"

Charlotte laughs so hard she nearly spits out her iced tea.

"Elisabeth Lindstrom."

"Charlotte Von Maur."

"Of the department store Von Maurs?"

"You must be from the Midwest," Charlotte mutters. I sense she is suddenly disappointed by her luncheon date.

"No, New York, DC and Stockholm," I say. "Father spent his career in the Foreign Service. I've always had a peculiar fondness for family-owned department stores: Bergdorf's, Garfinckel's, Åhléns. Each has its own history and distinctive character. Too bad they're all going out of business or, worse, becoming Macy's."

Charlotte pauses a moment while her social register recalibrates.

"Where'd you go to school?" Charlotte asks.

"Barnard," I reply. I don't bother to return the question. If she went to a decent school, she'll volunteer the information; if not, she'll move on.

"I almost went there," she says, "but chose Smith instead. You know, hundreds of years of family tradition and all that."

I nod and chew. I'm not going to take the bait. Let her come to me.

"Did you know Harper St. James?" Charlotte asks. "I think she went to Barnard. She and I were classmates at Miss Porter's."

"That sounds familiar. Did she go by the name James and smoke a pipe? I'm afraid I wasn't terribly social with girls from outside the city. I mostly hung around with my friends from Brearley."

I can practically hear the click-click-clicking in Charlotte's brain.

"So, what's a nice girl like you doing in a place like this?" Charlotte asks. Her chilly reserve is replaced with sudden warmth.

I hesitate. Do I trust her? After all, she's my competition. Then I figure it can't hurt to talk. It's my first day on the job, and I could use an ally.

I give Charlotte the CliffsNotes version of my life: I wanted to go to med school like my older sister, but my grades sucked and I bombed the MCATs. Twice.

I had the choice of joining the Peace Corps and trying again in a couple years, or ditching med school entirely and coming up with another career plan. I like the comforts of civilization way too much to risk being sent to Mali or Malawi or even Maui for an extended period of time, so I chose option B.

"How about you?" I ask.

"Same story, different details," Charlotte says.

Charlotte grew up wanting to become Von Maur's first female CEO. The only problem was her father never did a decent day's worth of work and ended up drinking and divorcing his trust fund away. Given this unfortunate history, Charlotte's great-uncle was reluctant to let her into the family business. He told Charlotte he'd consider her for a job if she got a top-tier MBA.

"Alas, the apple doesn't fall far from the tree," Charlotte says. "Let's just say my GPA and GMAT weren't nearly industrious enough for Wharton or appetizing enough for Kellogg, so here I am."

Charlotte and I continue chatting through the salad and main courses until our dessert-and-coffee conversation is interrupted by a man standing at the podium in front of the room.

"Good dog," the man says. His greeting sends tiny ripples of confusion among the young women before him. Are they expected to fetch? To heel?

"That means good day in Swedish," he explains. "As God Hälsa's VP of Talent, it is my honor to welcome you to one of Sweden's finest and most esteemed corporations."

As Talent Man drones on, the white-jacketed server sets down a small shot glass of clear liquid before each of us.

I arch my eyebrow in curiosity.

"Aquavit," the server explains.

"And so, on behalf of God Hälsa," Talent Man concludes, "I bid you all *välkommen* and *skål!*" He raises his glass to the uncomprehending crowd.

"*Skål*," Charlotte and I say in unison, clinking our glasses together.

Maybe it's the aquavit. Maybe it's the repartee. Whatever it is, I don't waste much time before confirming that Charlotte's collars and cuffs match.

She's a true strawberry blonde.

I've always been sexually adventurous, but nothing compared to Charlotte. She can both read my mind about things I want and blow my mind with things I've never even imagined. In beauty, smarts and ambition, Charlotte and I are a perfect match. My older sister, Eva, tells me that being with Charlotte is as close as I can get to having sex with myself.

After finishing employee orientation, Charlotte and I move into a one-bedroom apartment near the God Hälsa headquarters in Princeton. It's common practice for young female drug reps to live together. We work long hours and spend weeks on the road, so we're rarely home at the same time. Our meager salaries are barely enough to live on, and we haven't yet built the client base to earn much in the way of commissions.

Right off the bat, Charlotte is assigned to rep one of God Hälsa's newest and most highly anticipated drugs. Brand-named Lycka, it's an SSRI antidepressant shown in Phase III clinical trials to have fewer sexual side effects than competitors such as Zoloft and Prozac.

Stealing a line from Hair Club president Sy Sperling, Charlotte's killer sales pitch is "I'm not just a Lycka representative, I'm also a customer." Just one glance at Charlotte would convince anyone that Lycka doesn't have any adverse sexual side effects—unless you consider turning on every human being within a one-hundred-foot radius to be an adverse sexual side effect.

Meanwhile, I'm assigned to Metamin, a very late entrant into the category of stimulants that includes Ritalin and Adderall. Metamin is one of God Hälsa's least successful products. By the time Metamin got FDA approval, Ritalin and Adderall were already well-established brands. Parents desperate for relief from their hyperactive boys—Metamin's patient profile is almost entirely male—know to ask for those other drugs by name. It's the rare doctor who's willing to prescribe Metamin rather than one of the better-known and equally efficacious alternatives.

I have little success with Metamin during my sales visits despite my sheer determination and even sheerer blouses. Week after week, I come home to an empty apartment to find a pile of FedEx boxes from Saks Fifth Avenue and Neiman Marcus waiting for Charlotte. We soon run out of places to store her growing collection of Louis Vuittons and Louboutins. We think about using the oven, but the heat from the pilot light isn't good for the ultrasoft leather.

"I never see you anymore," I say to Charlotte on one of the rare weekends we're home together. I hate myself for sounding so needy.

"C'mon, Beth," Charlotte sighs. She pulls me closer to her and unbuttons my blouse. "That's not fair and you know it. We went to Bermuda with your brother and his girlfriend last month, and we're going to France this spring. You agreed that it's not the quantity of our time together, it's the quality."

Charlotte slips off her emerald green silk dress. Wearing my favorite bustier—the sheer black lace one with matching black satin garter belt from Agent Provocateur—Charlotte looks like some crazy-sexy hybrid of Marlene Dietrich in *Blue Angel* and Kathy Ireland in the *Sports Illustrated* swimsuit poster that my brother, Martin, had hanging on his wall as a teenager.

"But it seems like you're choosing to spend time away from me," I say as Charlotte takes my right nipple into her mouth. "You're always taking every meeting that comes your way even though there are plenty of other girls on your team who'd be happy to take up the slack."

"You know the drill," Charlotte says. She shifts to my left nipple. She's an excellent multitasker. Her sharp incisors bite gently into the tender pink, and I feel a rush of endorphins.

"You're only as good as your latest sales figures," she says. "Sometimes you're up, sometimes you're down. We've got to take advantage of every opportunity we're given before some-one else gets to it first. It's eat or be eaten."

With that, Charlotte's magic mouth works its way down my body. Her pearly white teeth are deployed once again, this time expertly pulling down my moist panties, and Charlotte starts to do what Charlotte does so well.

I lie back and give in.

Who am I to argue? It's Charlotte's time to eat.

By the time Deb the Destroyer and I join the rest of the crew, someone's already set up the sign announcing the bath-room is closed for maintenance. The other gals are standing around and talking, waiting for us to arrive.

"Okay, Blondie," Deb says, "start with the first stall to the left. There's twelve stalls in this row and another twelve around the corner."

The other janitors chuckle as I make my way to the first stall.

I push open the door to the first stall, which reeks to high heaven. The toilet is filled with the most disgusting mix of crap, diarrhea, piss and menstrual fluid. On the tile wall behind the toilet, someone's used a tampon to scrawl "Welcome to the Shit Show."

I was expecting this. Anytime you get a group of people together like this, you're going to have a hazing process. It's natural selection. You have to separate the strong from the weak, the winners from the losers.

I know what I am.

Wearing my government-issued prison work boots, I use my foot to flush the toilet. It starts to back up. As the foul contents begin to overflow the toilet bowl, I scream, "Oh shit."

The chuckling turns into full-on laughter.

"Cut the crap," I hear someone say.

I turn around and see Deb standing there.

"Seriously, just cut the crap," she says. Then she pulls me out of the stall.

I watch as Deb bends down to twist the silver knob under the toilet, grabs the plunger from my caddy and uses the wooden handle to chop the fecal logs into small chunks. Without hesitating, she turns the plunger around, holds the shit-covered handle and plunges up and down until the noxious brew starts gurgling down the pipes. Finally, she reaches down, twists the silver knob again and flushes the rest of the crap away.

I notice my crewmates aren't laughing anymore.

Deb strides over to a sink and turns the hot and cold taps on full blast. She grabs the Ajax from my caddy and uses it to scrub her hands like a doctor preparing for surgery.

"I learned that trick from my baby brother, who's doing life in Quentin for murder," Deb says to no one in particular. "He learned the hard way that a plunger handle has a lotta surprising uses."

Deb turns off the taps and walks over to one of the crew members holding a bag of rags. Deb plucks a clean rag from the bag and calmly dries her hands.

"Yeah, there's lotsa ways a-makin' things right in prison," Deb continues. "'Specially if you don't care about gettin' your hands dirty."

Deb's boots have left footprints on the bathroom floor. She walks over and grabs a mop from the biggest, baddest-looking member of the crew, uses it to swab her boots clean and hands the dirty mop back to the gape-mouthed woman.

"Cleanup in aisle one," Deb whispers, causing the woman to scurry away. Deb gives me a nod as I return to work.

hannah

seven

Hey, Hannah, Sam texts, can you take Friday off from work and help me with Claire's birthday this weekend? I look at the calendar over my desk. It's been barely a month since we were all together for the Lindstrom family reunion. I'm not used to seeing Sam and the girls so often, but I guess things will be different from now on.

"Claire, your ride's here," the after-school monitor calls out. I carefully pull Sam's SUV to the front of the pickup line. It's not hard to spot my niece in the schoolyard. Claire stands nearly a full head taller than her fellow kindergarteners at the Princeton Country Day School, and she's one of very few nonwhite faces. Claire says goodbye to her friends, grabs her backpack and climbs into the back seat next to her napping little sister.

Back at Sam's house, I lay Ally down on the family room

couch, surround her with throw pillows in case she rolls over and head to the kitchen, where Claire is setting up to do homework at the breakfast table.

"Can I fix you a snack?" I say. "Maybe some cut-up apples and cheese?"

"No, I'm okay," Claire says. She pops the top of a can of Diet Coke and takes a sip before letting out an impressive belch.

"You shouldn't be drinking Diet Coke," I say. "It's full of chemicals. How 'bout I get you a glass of milk instead?"

"Mommy tells me to have Diet Coke when I feel hungry. That way I won't get fat."

"You're not fat, sweetie."

"Mommy says Auntie Eva used to be fat, so I should be careful."

Claire pulls a poster board from her backpack. She places a sixty-four-count Crayola box on one corner, a *Frozen* plastic pencil case on another and some library books on the other two corners, but the poster board keeps rolling up like an old-fashioned window shade.

"Here, let me help you." I take the uncooperative poster board and roll it in the opposite direction. When it unrolls, the board lies perfectly flat.

"Wow," Claire exclaims, "Mommy always says you're smart, and you really are."

"Your mommy thinks I'm smart?"

"Yeah, she says you went to Harvard, but Daddy only went to Princeton."

I can't help but laugh. Perhaps Beth wasn't praising me as much as she was teasing Sam. Never mind that I transferred from Harvard after freshman year, and Sam didn't graduate from college at all.

"So, what're you working on?" I ask.

"It's a family tree. I have to write everyone's names and paste in everyone's picture."

"That sounds fun," I say. I've always loved school projects.

"First is me," Claire says. She prints her name in neat capital letters.

"Good, and next to your name, you should put Ally's name."

"*A-L-L-Y,*" Claire spells aloud as she writes.

"Up above your names, you should put your mom's and dad's names. Be sure to leave some space so that we can fit in pictures later."

"Daddy is *S-A-M*, and Mommy is *B-E-T-H*."

Claire's spelling ability seems advanced for a new kindergartener. She must get that from me. Sam was always an abysmal speller.

"Next to your mom," I say, "you should put Uncle Martin and his wife, Auntie Karen, and then Auntie Eva and her husband, Uncle Alex. And under your aunts and uncles, you have to put all your cousins."

"Could you help me with their names?" Claire asks.

"Wait a minute while I find a piece of paper."

There's a thick pile of mail sitting on the kitchen counter. I sort through the pile, noticing several letters from expensive New York law firms. Sam told me he still owes a ton of money for Beth's legal fees. It's tempting to peek into the envelopes, but I've taken a vow to stop meddling in Sam and Beth's personal business. I pluck a piece of junk mail out of the pile and write down all the names for Claire to copy. Soon, the right half of the poster board is filled with the names from the Lindstrom side of the family.

"Oh dear," I say, "we still need to include Grandma and Grandpa Lindstrom, but we've run out of room up in that corner. Maybe we should turn the poster board over and start again?"

Claire shakes her head. "No, I don't need to include them. They're dead. I only need to include alive people."

"Okay, then," I reply, letting Claire's words sink in. There is a vast empty space on the Min family side of the poster board.

"Then I guess I'm the only one left. Next to your daddy, put my name: *H-A-N-N-A-H*."

The next day is Saturday, and we're hosting Claire's sixth birthday party at a cavernous gymnastics studio just outside town. The space smells of dirty socks and pine-scented Lysol.

"I have a wedgie," Claire announces. She takes a break from jumping on the trampoline and tugs at her faded pink leotard.

"What's a wedgie?" Ally asks. She's clinging to my side, too shy and scared of Claire's kindergarten friends to join in the birthday party fun.

Claire shows her backside to her little sister. It's probably just the leotard, which is a year old and two sizes too small, but Claire does have a pretty bad wedgie. She also looks a bit chubbier than usual. I hear Beth's voice in my head, warning Claire not to get fat.

"Okay, girls," the gym teacher calls out. "Time to have cake and ice cream!"

The teacher leads the girls up to the party room, which has already been set up with Mylar balloon bouquets, paper tablecloths, plates, napkins and jewel-encrusted plastic tiaras, all in Cinderella Sparkle motif.

Last month, Claire, Ally and I made a trip to the Princeton Party Superstore to pick out the birthday decorations. "Why don't we get Hello Kitty?" I suggested. "Hello Kitty is really cute. Or maybe Curious George? You used to love that movie." Meanwhile, I silently cursed the lack of diversity: Where's that Mulan when you need her?

"No," Claire insisted, "I want Cinderella Sparkle. I love Cinderella Sparkle."

As a girl, I loved Cinderella, too. Her blond hair done up in an elegant bun; her vacant sky blue eyes; her porcelain complexion and perfect, upturned nose. It was my secret wish as a girl to grow up to look like Cinderella. I was devastated when I realized it could never happen.

Gazing at the glittery pink spectacle, I wonder what's going on in my young niece's mind. Does she also hope to look like Cinderella someday? How does it feel to have a mother who looks like a real-life Cinderella, only with Jennifer Aniston's hair and Michelle Obama's wardrobe?

Claire blows her party horn, eliciting laughter from her fair-haired guests. I quickly light the candles on the cake— six candles for six years plus an extra one for good luck—and motion for Sam to stop staring at his phone. As Sam carries the cake out to the table, I run to my purse and grab my own phone, imagining Beth's delight when she gets the photos in my next weekly letter.

"Happy birthday to you," I begin singing. The party guests soon join in. Ensconced in her bejeweled birthday throne and softly illuminated by the candles, Claire is the picture of child-like joy. The singing ends and everyone waits.

"Hurry, Claire," I say urgently. "Close your eyes and make a wish."

Back at home, the girls have just finished taking their evening bubble bath. Claire and Ally stand on the pink bath mat, dripping wet and smelling of lavender and vanilla soap. Looking at their naked little bodies, I notice Claire's Mongolian spot is starting to fade but Ally's is still prominent. Sam never tires of teasing me about my panicked reaction years ago when I changed Claire's diaper for the first time and saw the pale blue blotches on my niece's rear.

"Call 911!" I yelled. I held Claire tight in my arms and ran to Sam and Beth in the living room. Beth had to spend nearly fifteen minutes, including online consultations with WebMD and MayoClinic.com, to convince me that the bruise-like coloration on Claire's bottom was a normal developmental condition among babies of Asian ancestry and not an omen of imminent death.

"Girls, come downstairs, it's Mommy!" Sam bellows from downstairs. The words barely have time to register in my ears, but Claire reacts instantly. Before I can stop her, Claire runs naked down the rear stairs. I wrap Ally burrito-style in a towel and carry her downstairs like a wiggly sack of potatoes.

"Where's Mommy?" Claire asks Sam breathlessly. Her eyes scan the living room. Sam holds out his cell phone, and I understand what Claire doesn't.

"Where's Mommy?" Claire asks again. She continues to look around the room for her mother. I wrap Claire in the extra towel, take the phone from Sam and say gently but clearly, "Claire, it's your mommy on the phone." Claire's face has a blank expression as she accepts the phone from me.

"Mommy?" she asks tentatively.

"Claire, it's Mommy. Can you hear me, sweetie?"

"I can hear you!" Claire shouts. "Where are you, Mommy?"

Ally starts jumping up and down, and the bath towel tumbles into a pile at her feet. I try to rewrap my little burrito, but she runs out of reach.

"Mommy, Mommy, Mommy," Ally babbles. She tries to grab the phone from Claire.

"Shut up!" Claire yells, "Shut up, Ally! I can't hear Mommy!"

I reach over to extract the phone from Claire and am struck by the strength of the little girl's resistance. A beeping sound and recorded message come over the line, but I can't hear it for the commotion.

"Claire, let me put the phone on speaker so we can all hear your mommy." I look her in the eye so she understands I'm not taking her mommy away from her. I press the speaker button and place the phone on the ottoman so both girls can hear.

Beth's voice comes over the speakerphone. "Girls? Can you hear me, girls?"

"We can hear you, Mommy," Claire says. "Where are you?"

"Yeah, where are you?" Ally parrots.

"Remember, girls, I told you I was going to camp," Beth replies. The word *camp* reverberates in my head, reminding me of my once-clever play on words. Now it just seems cruel.

"When are you coming home?" Claire asks.

"I don't know," Beth answers.

"Will it be before Christmas?" Claire asks.

"No, I'm afraid not."

"Then who'll get us presents?"

"Don't worry, sweetie. I'll make sure Santa gets you presents."

"Will you be back by Easter?" Claire presses. "That's really far away."

"No, probably not."

"You'll be back before my next birthday, right? That's a whole year away!"

"No, sorry, baby, I won't," Beth says.

"How about the birthday after that?"

There's a pause.

"No, Claire," Beth replies, "but you can come visit me."

I look over at Sam, desperate to nip this conversation in the bud. As if reading my mind, Claire grabs the phone from the ottoman, out of my reach, and retreats to the corner of the room. She holds the phone close to her face.

"Mommy," she whispers, "will I still be a girl when you come back?"

Beth clears her throat, but her voice sounds hoarse anyway. "Yes, you'll still be a girl," she manages to respond. Claire's face has a far-off expression.

"Happy birthday, baby," Beth says.

And then the line goes dead.

beth

eight

I'm roughly one month into my prison sentence, and Juanita and I are standing in Pill Line to get our daily dose of drugs. Estrogen and Zoloft for her; Lexapro and birth control for me. We've been waiting for over an hour, and there's still a dozen women ahead of us.

I've got my face buried in the latest *Town & Country*, which Hannah sent me with her most recent weekly letter. There's a six-page photo spread on the International Debutante Ball, and I recognize a classmate from Brearley. When did I become old enough to have friends with debutante daughters?

The daughter looks just awful, poor thing. All the designer tulle in the world can't hide those tragically chubby arms. They stick out like pale Vienna sausages.

I hear a commotion ahead but ignore it. There's always some ruckus or another going on at Alderson. Juanita looks up from her book—*And Then There Were None*—and says, "Watch out, here comes Meatloaf."

Meatloaf Mary was a ninety-five-pound heroin addict when she arrived in prison eighteen months ago. She got her nickname the first week after she got out of detox, when she ate an entire meatloaf in one sitting. Now she's over two hundred pounds and a key player in Alderson's shadowy drug trade.

"Whatcha gettin' today, Blondie?" Meatloaf asks me.

"Same old, same old," I reply.

"Fuck that Lexapro," she says. "Ya want an antidepressant, ya gotta get the doc to put ya on the good stuff. Like Wellbutrin. Or even better, Seroquel. Oh yeah, Suzy Q's the way to go. Grind that baby up, and it's just as good as heroin. I can get ya top dollar for that."

"Thanks but no thanks," I say, not looking up from my magazine.

Meatloaf Mary won't leave.

"Whatcha need birth control for anyway?" she asks. "Ya doin' a CO on the side?"

I can't imagine ever getting desperate enough to hook up with a corrections officer. All the ones I've met are either dumb as a box of rocks or have man-boobs the size of Big Macs.

"Bad periods," I say.

"Ya know, if it gets bad enough, ya can always ask the doc for Vicodin. Or else Percocet. Too bad they stopped givin' out Tylenol with codeine—that was the shit."

"Good to know."

Juanita and I are almost at the front of Pill Line now.

"Hey, Meat, get the hell away from here," the CO guarding the nurse yells.

"My name's Mary," she says, giving him the finger before slinking away.

It's Juanita's turn to take her meds from the nurse. With her dark hair and serious face, Juanita looks like a nun receiving Holy Communion. The nurse waits for Juanita to sip water from a pleated white paper cup, swallow and open her mouth in proof.

I'm next.

"Here you go, Lindstrom," the nurse says.

"Are you sure you don't have any of the brand-name stuff?" I ask.

"The generic's just as good, and you know it."

"I'm not so sure," I say. "I'm having trouble sleeping."

The nurse motions to the long Pill Line as if to say, "Shut your trap and hurry up."

I take the two pills at once, swallow them down with water and open my mouth wide. The nurse cocks her head sideways for me to move along. The tablets leave a bitter, gritty taste in my mouth. I miss the minty glow of my Lexapro oral suspension.

I fucking hate generics.

Generics are the bane of the pharmaceutical business. It can take years, decades even, and hundreds of millions in R&D dollars to bring a new drug to market. Even though the government usually provides twenty years of patent protection, with the long lead times needed for clinical trials and FDA approval, it's often a race against the clock to sell as much brand-name medication as possible before cheaper generics enter the market.

That's why so many drug reps are hustling for business like there's no tomorrow.

About two years after our God Hälsa new-employee orientation, Charlotte was away at a psychiatry conference in San Francisco with a bunch of other fun-loving drug reps while

I was spending another Friday night alone in our too-small apartment.

I try to entertain myself by sitting in front of the TV eating a movie-theater-size bag of Sour Patch Kids and watching *Sex and the City*. There's something about the chewy candy that I find comforting and addictive.

I reach into the bag and realize I've mindlessly eaten the entire contents before Carrie even types that episode's "I can't help but wonder" question on her computer. That's when I have my eureka moment.

The following Monday, I make a beeline to Dr. Stanley, God Hälsa's director of Product Development, who I happened to befriend in the company cafeteria one day and who I'm quite sure is in love with me.

"How hard would it be to reformulate Metamin into a chewable compound?" I ask. I rip open a bag of gummy colas and offer it to him for inspiration. Dr. Stanley reaches into the bag and takes a handful. He chews as he listens to my pitch.

"One of the things that always comes up during my sales visits," I continue, "is just how much parents hate making their boys swallow the pills. And to make matters worse, they have to do it two or three times a day. These parents say they would do anything, pay anything, to avoid the daily battle. So, my question to you is this—what if we made it so that boys actually want to take their Metamin?"

Dr. Stanley swallows hard. I see his prominent Adam's apple bob up and down. A new drug formulation triggers a new period of exclusivity. It basically resets the clock for making money and gives the drug company another slug of time without competition from generics.

We look at one another and feel the electricity between us. It's better than sex.

We've just invented gummy Ritalin.

It takes a couple years to develop and bring to market, but the new formulation quickly becomes a top seller. We turn pharmaceutical straw into honest-to-God twenty-four-karat gold. Marketed globally as Metamin-G and offered in such mouthwatering flavors as blue raspberry, root beer and wild cherry, the groundbreaking drug is the darling of the pharma industry and the savior of parents everywhere.

Overactive boys who used to hate taking their ADHD medicine are now begging for it. Even better, what was initially troubling for God Hälsa's executives—namely, that in order to accommodate the gelatin, cornstarch, sweetener and artificial flavoring and coloring for the gummy compound, the new formulation contains less active ingredient per unit—unexpectedly turns into an added benefit. A bottle of Metamin-G remains competitively priced with a bottle of Ritalin or Adderall, but the actual profitability is higher because patients have to take twice as many Metamin-G units per day as its competitor brands.

I'm soon promoted to vice president of Marketing. I get a spacious window office in God Hälsa's gleaming corporate tower, my own trusty executive assistant, a shiny black town car with a dull white driver and a bottomless expense account.

The first year or two after Metamin-G's debut is a complete whirlwind of activity. My Outlook calendar is filled with back-to-back requests for press interviews, photo shoots and keynote addresses at medical and pharmaceutical conventions around the world.

My pointillist portrait is featured prominently on the front page of the *Wall Street Journal* under the bold-faced headline "God Hälsa's Marketing Goddess." *Fortune* includes me in their annual issue profiling 40 Under 40. (I'm number seven.)

Esquire wants to do a Women We Love feature about me, but God Hälsa's corporate overlords get cold feet after they see the photo that the magazine's brilliant art director wants to accompany the article: a full-page spread of me in the nude, lying in a sea of brightly colored Metamin-G gummies with the clever caption "American Booty." I'm pissed when the uptight SVP of Public Relations nixes the photo on "poor taste" grounds, but I ask *Esquire*'s art director for a full-size copy. I figure I'll look at it when I'm old and gray and need to remind myself of what a complete babe I once was.

Meanwhile, Charlotte's star goes into free fall. God Hälsa's bean counters in Accounting discover she's been putting her wardrobe on her expense account, and HR puts her on six months probation. She's stripped of the profitable Lycka account and assigned to an extra strength stool softener called Flöde.

"What were you thinking?" I ask when she tells me the news. Charlotte's a smart cookie; I'm surprised she could fuck up so badly.

"What do you mean, what was I thinking?" Charlotte asks. "I looked it up on IRS.gov. Clothing costs are legitimate business expenses if they meet two criteria—you have to wear the clothes as a condition of employment, and the clothes can't be suitable for everyday activities. Everything I expensed qualified."

"That makes sense to me," I say. "What did HR say?"

"They said there's a difference between what I can take as a deduction on my personal taxes and what I can submit for reimbursement under company policy. So then I said to them, 'Show me where in the employee handbook it says that clothing isn't a reimbursable business expense,' and they couldn't do it. But that didn't stop the fuckers from putting me on probation. Like a common criminal or something."

"You couldn't be common if you tried," I say. "Criminal or otherwise."

"Trust me," Charlotte says, "I did everything by the book. I uploaded the invoices from my stylist for reimbursement, and my manager approved them. All the receipts were right there in the accounting system, plain as day."

Charlotte takes a small scoop of Crème de la Mer and massages it gently on my face and down my neck. She kisses the hollow where my throat meets my collarbone and then chuckles darkly.

"It's not my fault no one bothered to actually read them."

Suffice it to say my meteoric success and Charlotte's nearly simultaneous downfall affect our relationship in a major way. While I'm flying first-class to meet with investors in Zurich, London and Amsterdam, Charlotte's sitting home alone with Messrs. Ben & Jerry. While I'm taking meetings with senior executives in Stockholm to discuss my brilliant marketing ideas, Charlotte's taking shit from entry-level accountants in Uppsala to find her missing cab receipts.

These superficial changes are nothing compared to the one-eighty-degree change in expectations regarding my personal life. As a mere drug rep, I was permitted—even encouraged—to share an apartment with my female colleague. As VP of Marketing, I'm expected to have my own home, preferably pre-furnished with a handsome husband and 2.3 cherubic children.

As a drug rep, I was rewarded for exploiting my womanly wiles. As a corporate officer, I'm required to take annual sexual harassment and diversity sensitivity training to ensure that any semblance of personality and humor are stripped from my interactions.

It's Charlotte who convinces me to move into my own place, a tasteful three-bedroom midcentury modern on the edge of town, far from the prying eyes of our colleagues and bosses. To keep up appearances, Charlotte keeps the one-bedroom in downtown Princeton, although we use it more like a very large walk-in closet than an actual residence. It's also convenient for the occasional midday tryst. The risk of getting caught just adds to the thrill.

Like any couple, we have our good days and our bad ones. We break up a few times—I'm a Sagittarius, Charlotte's an Aquarius, so we're destined to have some personal drama—but we manage to remain together, to maintain both our privacy and our passion, to extinguish the rumors while fanning the flames.

Is it easy? Of course not.

Is it worth it? Absolutely.

Everything seems to be going fine until that fateful day, when I come back from the doctor's office, walk into our bedroom and announce:

"Charlotte, I'm pregnant."

hannah

nine

When Sam told me Beth was pregnant, I have to admit to being surprised. Sam and Beth had been together for years, but something about their relationship felt strange—even false. Beth was a high-powered executive and Sam was just a golf instructor. I didn't get what Beth saw in him. It feels terrible to say that, but it's the truth. Sure, Sam was attractive and charming, but that didn't seem like enough for someone as ambitious and accomplished as Beth. I didn't think the two of them would last. I guess they proved me wrong.

My niece Claire has been full of surprises ever since her conception. And now here she is, surprising me again as the opening act of Princeton Country Day School's annual Indigenous People's Day celebration.

"Indigenous People's Day?" I asked when Sam called me.

"Yeah, it's like Columbus Day, but the PC version," Sam explained.

"Is this assembly a big deal?"

"Claire would really like you to come," Sam said.

It was an invitation I couldn't refuse.

The school auditorium is packed. We're lucky to have found two seats together in the fifth row. Looking around at the well-dressed audience makes me wonder: *Don't any of these people have jobs?* I had to take a whole vacation day from work to attend.

"Why do you send Claire here, Sam? It must cost a fortune."

"We can afford it," Sam says unconvincingly. "Anyway, Claire's thriving here."

"Claire?" Ally interrupts. "Where's Claire? I wanna see Claire."

"You really love your big sister, don't you?" I say.

Ally nods excitedly.

"You know the only thing better than a big sister?" I ask.

Ally waits, her bright eyes gleaming.

"A little sister," I say, giving her hand a squeeze.

The auditorium goes dark, and the heavy velvet curtains open. Claire stands in the middle of the stage, all alone, illuminated by a spotlight. Wearing her hair in two long braids and dressed in a faux buckskin outfit, Claire makes a convincing Sacagawea. From backstage, a piano starts playing a familiar tune. It's "Day by Day" from *Godspell*.

"State by state," Claire starts singing. "State by state. Here we go, we can't be late."

Claire's voice is clear and true. She seems completely comfortable in the limelight, with not a hint of stage fright. Soon, Claire is surrounded by a group of pint-size Indigenous people who join her in song. I edge my way to the front of the auditorium to take some photos to include in my next weekly letter to Beth. After the song ends, Claire and her classmates clasp hands and bow like regular Broadway veterans.

Next up, it's the first graders, who'll be doing a rendition of Patsy Cline's "Crazy" in honor of Crazy Horse. I look down at the program. It's going to be a long time until the eighth graders get onstage to sing their version of "Seasons of Love" for Leonard Peltier. Thankfully, after the third graders finish singing, we get a break for intermission. Everyone shuffles out of the stuffy auditorium for some coffee, juice and cookies in the school library. A pack of parents sneaks off toward the exit. Sam looks desperate to join them.

"Hey, Sam," someone says, slapping my brother on the back.

We turn and see Beth's older brother, Martin, and his wife, Karen. Martin's wearing a navy blazer with gold buttons and fancy silk pocket square, his silver-streaked hair slicked back like a diplomat's. Karen's formfitting wrap dress accentuates her freckled cleavage and tanned, toned calves. The two of them give off a glamorous, almost golden gleam, like Hollywood celebrities or European royalty. Everything about them looks expensive.

"Hey, Martin, glad you could make it," Sam says. He grabs Martin's hand and bumps shoulders in the way I imagine frat brothers greet one another. "And, Karen, you look simply spectacular." Sam gives Karen a kiss on the cheek.

"Of course we're here," Martin replies. "It's not every day that your niece invites you to be her honored guests at her first school performance." He glances over at me with mild interest. "Oh, I see Hannah's here, too."

"Hannah, it's so good to see you," Karen says warmly. "And, Ally, my gosh, you've grown so big since the summer!" Ally ignores her aunt and asks me for help poking the straw into her juice box. Karen grabs a handful of cookies from the reception table. The gold bangles on her wrist make a pretty tinkling sound as she wraps the cookies in a paper napkin and sticks them in her designer handbag.

"Ally, I saw a really fun-looking swing set out back," Karen says. "How 'bout the three of us go outside to play instead of going back to the show?" Ally agrees right away.

"What about Sam and Martin?" I ask as Karen leads us toward the exit. I glance over at the two men engaged in serious conversation. Sam doesn't look happy. In fact, he looks almost angry.

"Oh, let's leave them alone," Karen says with false cheer. "Boys will be boys, you know? Anyway, I think they have some business they need to discuss."

"Business? What business?"

Karen purses her perfectly glossed lips.

"I'm not sure I should have said anything," she says.

"Karen, please. We're family." The words feel strange coming out of my mouth. Looking at us from the outside—a statuesque, strawberry blonde beauty and a short, middle-aged Korean woman—no one would suspect we're related.

"Please don't tell Sam I told you," Karen says.

"Of course," I assure her.

"You obviously don't know, Hannah," she says, "but Sam owes us quite a lot of money."

My face flushes with shame. Sam has never been good with finances, but I didn't realize he had gotten to the point of owing money to Beth's brother. Before I have a chance to ask Karen for details, Ally runs out the door and to the schoolyard.

"Help me, Auntie Hannah!" Ally shouts from the swing set.

Karen and I walk over to Ally. I lift my niece onto the swing, tell her to hold on tight and push her high. She squeals in pure joy.

"The girls seem to be doing well," Karen says, changing the subject.

"Yes," I reply, "they are. It's strange—except for that first phone call with Beth, the girls don't even seem to notice that their mother is missing." There's a catch in my voice, a surprising lump in my throat. Even worse than going to prison, it seems to me, would be to go to prison and not be missed.

"Well, Beth was always working late or traveling," Karen explains, "so the girls are used to being apart from her. They cry when she leaves but soon get over it. Out of sight, out of mind. That's how children are."

I think about Karen's statement and wonder: *Are adults any different?* Sam seems to be unaffected by Beth's absence. The day after dropping her off at Alderson, Sam was back at the country club giving private golf lessons to his executive clients by day and sipping cocktails with them at night. Then again, what choice does he have? The Princeton Country Club is unlikely to offer leave for spousal incarceration.

"Young children don't have a great sense of time," Karen says. "An hour seems like an eternity, two weeks go by like nothing. As long as you keep the rest of their routine in place—school, nanny, friends—they should be fine. At least for a while." We both watch as Ally pumps her little legs, swinging her body higher and higher toward the cloudless blue sky.

"Thankfully they're both young," Karen continues. "Ally's only three. She won't even remember these years when she grows up." Karen's casual observation causes me to wonder: *Time and memory are so mysterious; what is it we choose to remember, and what is it we simply forget?*

My earliest memory is of going grocery shopping with my mom when I was just around Ally's age. I distinctly remember blinking at the overhead fluorescent lights and being transfixed by the colorful jars of baby food as they clinked their way down the bouncy black conveyer belt. I also remember the kindly grocer with the white hair, who smiled as he gave us two bright red helium balloons knotted with red-and-white-striped cotton string. My mom tied one to the shopping cart and gave me the other to hold. When we left the supermarket, my mom untied the balloon from the shopping cart, and a gust of wind blew it out of her hand. As we watched the balloon drift out of reach and into the sky, I let go of the balloon in my own hand.

I remember thinking the two balloons belonged together.

It's past six o'clock by the time I get home from Princeton. While I wait for my Lean Cuisine dinner to heat up in the microwave, I start my due diligence on Martin. Sitting at the dining table, I open my laptop and Google Martin's name. The first hit is the website for some business called EMC Partners. Martin's listed as one of two cofounders; the other is a light-skinned black man with a broad smile. I peruse the site, but it's oddly devoid of substantive content. When I click the tabs labeled "Our Clients" and "Our Services," they just say "Under Construction."

Going back to the search results, I find several Federal Election Commission reports of Martin's donations to various congressional candidates, all of them Republican. The amounts are generous but not outrageous. There are photos of Martin with those same congressmen (they all seem to be men) at golf tournaments, gala charity fund-raisers, the occasional self-promotional book signing. The microwave beeps. I go back into the kitchen, transfer the food onto a plate and pour myself a glass of wine.

More search results provide more details into Martin's life. His LinkedIn profile reveals he went to Dartmouth College and St. Albans Prep in DC. His Facebook page is a veritable brag book of his photogenic family: Martin and Karen's two blonde daughters performing in the local production of *The*

Nutcracker; Karen's son, Max, bodychecking a burly opponent on the lacrosse field; the entire family wearing matching red-and-green outfits and posing for their Christmas card photo. A Blockshopper listing of their Colonial house in Alexandria says it was built in 1846, remodeled in 2010 and appraised at over four million dollars last year. As I scroll through the professional photographs of their designer-decorated rooms, I imagine Martin and Karen with their three perfect children living their perfect all-American lives.

The remaining pages of search results are useless, filled with articles about other Martin Lindstroms in other cities and countries. I close the search window and click the Corr-Links icon—the special email service I had to set up and pay a monthly fee to email Beth in prison—and start writing. I write about Claire's star turn as Sacagawea, Ally's adventures on the swing set, the delicious lunch Maria prepared for the family. My hands hover over the keyboard as I remember the rest of the day. The cursor blinks at me expectantly.

Do you know why Sam would owe Martin money? I type.

And then I delete the question. There's no reason to give Beth more reason to worry.

lise

From the deposition of Lise Danielsson in *United States of America et al. v. God Hälsa AB, Andreas Magnusson and Elizabeth Lindstrom*

Q: You testified earlier that Ms. Lindstrom didn't meet you until a few days after your arrival in the US.

A: Yeah, that's right. Beth's away from home a lot.

Q: When did you first meet her husband, Mr. Min?

A: Sam? I met him that first night.

Q: The first night you arrived in the US?

A: Yeah, that's right.

Q: Did the driver and cook…

A: Jorge and Maria?

Q: Yes, did the two of them stay with you that night?

A: Oh no, Jorge and Maria have their own house.

Q: So it was just you and Mr. Min in the Princeton house that first night?

A: And Claire.

Q: Yes, the two of you and the baby.

A: Yeah, that's right.

Q: Did that make you nervous?

A: Nervous? Why would it make me nervous?

Q: You were sixteen, newly arrived from a foreign country, spending the night alone with a strange man.

A: Well, I wouldn't put it that way exactly.

Q: How would you put it then?

A: First of all, Sam isn't a strange man. I mean, he's really nice. And superhot. He kinda looks like that guy from *The Fast and the Furious*, you know?

Q: No, I'm not familiar with that film. So did you or did you not spend that first night alone with Mr. Min?

A: Absolutely not.

Q: But earlier you testified…

A: Sam and I just talked that first night. We didn't spend the night together until at least a whole month later.

beth

ten

It's late October, and Alderson's having a heat wave. Indian summer, we used to call it growing up. I wonder if people say that anymore or if it's one of those newly forbidden phrases like "getting gypped" and "that's so lame."

At God Hälsa, the senior director of Diversity and Inclusion always made sure to tell me whenever I said anything that could offend anyone.

What a bitch.

Juanita and I are at the beach. That's what everyone calls the upper part of the Alderson compound where inmates go to sunbathe. Juanita told me the BOP has rules about the approved attire for sunbathing. Of course. The BOP has rules about frickin' everything.

Per the BOP, the minimum clothing required is a sleeveless T-shirt and shorts. T-shirts can be rolled up to expose the lower back and stomach area. Shorts should completely cover the ass and upper thigh. Underwear must be worn at all times and can't be visibly exposed. Inmates have to keep a respectful distance from one another. No physical contact is allowed.

Looking around the beach, I'm struck by the complete lack of vanity among my fellow federal campers. Cellulite be damned, these women are putting all their assets on full display. A group of especially raucous ladies from B Unit—the Ghetto, everyone calls it—are singing "Baby Got Back" by Sir Mix-a-Lot and shaking their ample asses.

"Aren't you hot in that long-sleeve shirt?" Juanita asks. Even from four feet away, I can smell the cocoa butter she's slathered on her tawny skin.

"I'm Scandinavian," I say. "I don't just freckle—I metastasize."

I press my pointer finger against my thigh. Damn, I'm already turning pink. I reach for the Banana Boat SPF 50 and apply another coat.

"Hey, *chica*, check that out," Juanita says, pointing down the hill.

Deb the Destroyer is walking toward the beach. I almost don't recognize her at first. I've only ever seen her in her prison uniform, which is unflattering for most women but especially for plus-size women like her.

"Deb never comes out to the beach," Juanita says.

"Who knew she had such nice tits?" I say.

"Watch what you say," Juanita whispers. "Word from the Ghetto is that Deb's looking for a new girlfriend. You don't want to get in her line of vision."

"How could I not be in her line of vision?"

"Ay, *mierda*, she's headed this way," Juanita says.

Deb saunters over to the spot where Juanita and I have staked a claim.

"Okay if I sit here?" Deb asks.

Without waiting for a response, Deb lays down a threadbare white towel and squeezes between me and Juanita. So much for our respectful distance. Deb rolls up the sleeves of her plain white T-shirt and hikes up her shorts. Deb's body is covered in tattoos; some look professional, but most look prison.

"Like your artwork," I say.

"Thanks," Deb replies. She stretches out her arms and legs to give me a better view.

Deb walks me through the story of her life as told in body graffiti. A Pokémon character for a twelve-year-old nephew who got shot in a drive-by walking home from school. A pink ribbon for a female cousin who died of breast cancer. Hand-stenciled initials and numbers to commemorate friends and family lost to the toxic stew of drugs, crime and poverty.

"And this," she says, pointing to her inner thigh, "this is for my girl."

There's a crudely drawn 3-D square etched into Deb's skin. The tattoo appears to be new; it's still red in some spots, scabbing over in others.

"Nice," I lie. "What is it?"

"A sugar cube," she says. "Her name was Sugar. We were bunkies for almost five years before she got out last spring. And now she's dead."

"Sorry to hear it."

Deb shakes her head.

"Fucking drugs," she says. "D'you know more people die every year from legal drugs than illegal ones? You wouldn't know that from looking at the folks doing time, but it's true."

"You don't say," I reply.

Juanita gives me the side-eye. She's the only person at Alderson I've talked to about what I did before prison. About what got me into prison.

"Fuck, it's hot out here," Deb says. "Can one of you rub that shit on my backside?" She points to the tube of Banana Boat in my hand and lies down on her belly.

By now, the entire beach is staring in our direction. I smile and wave to the crowd like the goddamn Queen of England. I flip open the cap on the Banana Boat, squeeze out a generous dollop on the backs of Deb's thighs and massage it in.

Some rules were just meant to be broken.

Seeing Deb strut her way onto the beach reminds me of the day Sam literally splashed his way onto the Princeton social scene. It was almost twelve years ago, soon after I was made VP of Marketing. God Hälsa was hosting a lavish but tasteful summer party at the country club for our key clients, and I made sure everything was perfect.

Cloudless skies.

Aquamarine pool.

Open bar.

It was your standard guest list. White-haired men sipping G&Ts in candy-colored golf shirts and seersucker Bermuda shorts. Young female drug reps dressed to kill and showing off their wares. Trophy wives keeping their husbands close and their talons sharp.

Charlotte and I are sipping chardonnay and picking at the shrimp cocktail on the patio buffet when Andreas Magnusson, CEO of God Hälsa, and his coral-lipsticked wife walk over.

"Elisabeth, great party," Magnusson says. "And I just heard the latest sales figures. That makes how many record-setting quarters in a row—three? four?"

"Five, actually, but who's counting?" I say, laughing lightly.

"I thought you said you had a metrics meeting every morning," Charlotte says.

We exchange faux dirty looks.

"You look lovely today, Charlotte," Magnusson says admiringly.

That's an understatement. Charlotte's seafoam-green charmeuse satin dress clings to her every wicked curve. It's apparent to everyone at the party—most especially me—that Charlotte isn't wearing a stitch underneath that gossamer gown.

"Have we met?" Magnusson's wife asks Charlotte coldly.

"Let me introduce you to Charlotte Von Maur," I say.

"Your friend?" Magnusson's wife asks me.

"Oh no," Charlotte interrupts, "we're more than friends."

Charlotte sneaks a mischievous look at me, and I flash a "don't you dare" look back.

I can see Magnusson's wife getting ready to dig further when I'm saved by a commotion in the distance. We hear peals of laughter as a tipsy young drug rep pushes a man into the deep end of the pool, creating a huge splash and showering a dozen nearby people with water. The tipsy girl apes horror, as if it were all an accident, while everyone else laughs.

The man swims toward the shallow end of the pool and stands. His wet shirt clings to his toned physique as he climbs up the pool stairs.

The trophy wives stop and take notice. The female drug reps cease their mindless chatter. The white-haired men feel their balls shrink.

"What a fucking showboat," Charlotte says.

"Pot calling the kettle black," I say.

Sam walks over to me, dripping. He leans in.

"I'm going to change," he says.

"Don't change too much," I reply, giving him a kiss. It's short enough for a work party but long enough to be noticed.

By everyone.

All eyes watch as Sam disappears into the clubhouse.

"Kudos to you for snagging the club pro," Magnusson says to me. "The town's most eligible bachelor."

"Well, Sam and I have only just started to date," I demur.

I notice Charlotte cringing at the word *date*.

So does Magnusson.

"Perhaps, but take some advice from me, Elisabeth," Magnusson says. "I know you're an ambitious young woman. But don't become one of those bitter career women who put ambition before everything else." Magnusson's eyes are on me but his meaty paw is on Charlotte's ass.

"Look around this crowd, Elisabeth," he says, gesturing with his other hand. "God Hälsa may be an international corporation, but here in Princeton, we're more like a family company. We don't just work together. We play together. Vacation together. We send our children to the same schools and clubs together."

Magnusson wraps his arms around me and Charlotte and pulls us close, like a python squeezing his prey. "Trust me, Elisabeth," he says, "getting married and having a family won't hinder your career. To the contrary, it'll enhance it."

"Darling, isn't that the CEO of Mercy Medical?" Magnusson's wife interrupts. In an instant, Magnusson releases me and Charlotte and slithers over to the other side of the pool.

"You two ladies look like you could use another drink," Sam says from behind me and Charlotte. He's changed into a pale mint golf shirt and pressed khaki linen shorts. He holds out two full glasses of chardonnay. Charlotte and I each take one.

"At least he's good at taking orders," Charlotte mutters.

"That's why I like him," I reply.

Before I met Sam, I had a Filofax full of men that I could call upon whenever I needed a date to a God Hälsa corporate event. Unfortunately, they all suffered from one of two fatal flaws: either they're so obviously gay that it fuels speculation about the true nature of my "friendship" with Charlotte, or they're such assholes that, at the end of the evening, they all but refuse to accept no as an answer.

Sam's different. Like the farm boy Westley in my all-time favorite movie, *The Princess Bride*—I remember the young Robin Wright as Princess Buttercup was my first-ever girl crush—Sam does whatever I say.

From that splashy debut at the country club and for the next five-plus years, Sam is my constant companion at God Hälsa corporate events: the summer pool party and winter ball, the annual board dinners and gala charity fund-raisers. Like Magnusson said, the God Hälsa social calendar extends beyond just work. We vacation with other God Hälsa couples: summers in the Hamptons, winters at Stowe and Killington.

It's a win-win arrangement. Sam and I enjoy one another's company. Having him on my arm makes me look both powerful and open-minded. I introduce him to business executives, all eager to throw money in his direction to improve their golf game.

Sure, I'll admit the relationship isn't always strictly business. Sam and I hook up from time to time—usually, when Charlotte and I have a fight and are "on a break"—and even then, Sam follows my lead and keeps things cool. No drama. No emotional hang-ups.

Everything's working perfectly until that pivotal moment when I tell Charlotte that I'm thinking about starting a family.

"Why do you want to ruin what we have by bringing a baby into it?" Charlotte asks. "We both work like crazy. We barely have time to see one another as it is. Why do you want to make life even more complicated?"

"I don't know. Maybe it's my biological clock. I'm going to turn thirty-five next year. They say it's a lot harder to get pregnant after thirty-five. I don't want to be one of those women who wakes up one day and realizes she forgot to have children."

"You just want to leave your superior genetic mark on the world."

Maybe Charlotte's right, but what's wrong with that? What's wrong with wanting to have children who will outlive you? Isn't that part of being human?

I spend countless hours at my work computer researching sperm banks and artificial insemination. I find the whole process way too complicated. And I don't love the idea of a dozen or more other children out there with the same genes as my baby.

That's when it occurs to me: Sam would be the perfect sperm donor. I won't even need to go to a clinic. I know Charlotte isn't thrilled by the idea of starting a family, but I figure I should act now and beg for forgiveness later. After all, my eggs aren't getting any fresher.

As I click through my Google research, I come across an article about a lesbian couple who had their sperm donor sign a waiver of his parental rights, only to have the donor change his mind and get partial custody. The article suggests two ways to avoid a similar outcome: have the sperm transfer done under a doctor's supervision, or make a financial payment to the donor as "consideration" for the sperm.

"Let me get this straight," Sam says, "you want to pay me to have sex with you?"

"Well, yes," I reply, "but not for the sex. For the sperm."

"Because, you know, the sex is totally worth paying for."

"It's just your sperm I want. The sex is just a necessary delivery mechanism."

"Thanks, Beth, nice way to boost a man's ego."

"I'm serious, Sam. This is business, not personal."

"I'm not going to seek custody of the baby," Sam assures

me. "I'm more than happy to share my sperm with you as many times as you want. No strings attached."

"If you really mean that, then you won't mind signing this."

I hand him a twenty-page contract and cashier's check. Sam examines them both and frowns.

"There's something wrong here," Sam says.

I don't know what the going rate is for sperm donation, but I thought ten thousand dollars sounded like fair consideration. Maybe Sam is getting greedy. Maybe he wants more.

"You forgot to put 'for sperm' on the memo line," Sam jokes. When I don't laugh along, he quickly signs the contract and endorses the check before taking off his shirt and reaching over to unbutton mine.

"Are you ready for your first insemination, Ms. Lindstrom?" Sam says.

Sam certainly gives me my money's worth. A couple months later, I'm pregnant. When I come back from the doctor's office and deliver the news to Charlotte, she doesn't react the way I hoped.

"What about 'no' didn't you understand?" Charlotte says. "I told you I didn't want a baby, and I certainly don't want to be in a relationship with someone who'd lie to me the way you have."

I try to explain, but Charlotte won't listen.

"Good luck being a single mother," she says. "Let's see how that works out for you."

With that, Charlotte walks out.

It's hard being alone and pregnant. Harder than I expected.

Once I start showing, everyone assumes the baby is Sam's. After all, Sam and I have "been together" for over five years. The big question on everyone's lips is: "When are the two of you lovebirds going to get married?"

With Charlotte out of the picture, I actually start to envision a life with Sam. He's a good guy, and he tries hard to take care of me. He brings me my favorite Panda Express take-out (hey, don't judge—everyone's entitled to a guilty pleasure) when I'm working late. He holds my hair back as I'm retching from morning sickness. He tells me I'm beautiful even when I'm as big as a cow. He speeds me to the hospital when my water breaks.

"Why are you doing this?" I ask as Sam grips my hand.

"Why am I doing what?" Sam says.

"Why are you here, in this room, as I push out this bowling ball of a baby?"

Sam waits while I scream out in pain.

"Because I love you, Beth," he says. "And I want to marry you."

"I thought I was very clear in my instructions," I respond. I'm trying hard to rest between contractions. "This was a business transaction. You were not to fall in love with me. Hard stop. Period. End of sentence."

"Sorry, I've done everything you asked, but on this one, I failed."

"You know, at some point, I'm going to get back together with Charlotte," I warn him. "It's just destined to be."

"We'll see. I'm betting you'll fall in love with me. You know, most people find me very charming. And if you and Charlotte do get back together, I'm sure we can work it out. I'm good at sharing. Just ask my big sister."

I'm momentarily speechless as another contraction takes over my body.

"If we get married," I whisper, "you'll need to do as you're told. Take care of the kids. Make sure the help gets paid on time. Ignore the redheaded interloper in the woods."

And like Westley from *The Princess Bride*, Sam leans over me, his perfectly coiffed hair falling over his eye, and replies:

"As you wish."

hannah

eleven

It's been many years since I've celebrated a real Halloween. My Hoboken condo building doesn't seem to have any children—it's mostly young professionals who commute into the city—but that doesn't stop me from buying a bag of Hershey's Miniatures every year just in case. I'd hate for a child to be turned away disappointed. The only time anyone ever knocked on my door on Halloween, it was a couple drunk young men looking for the "Drink or Treat" party up in apartment 302. I gave them a handful of Krackel and Mr. Goodbars anyway.

It's always crazy at work on Halloween, and this year is no exception. Old Man Barker walks down the hallway of my white-shoe law firm wearing a purple velvet suit and matching top hat. He uses his walking stick to lightly whack Alice in Wonderland on the rear while the Mad Hatter chuckles by her side.

"Willy Wonka's on the prowl," I warn Tracy. She's wearing a tight black leotard, racy leopard-print skirt and cat's-eye glasses. It's hard to tell whether she's in costume or just retro-chic. Tracy has a way of looking effortlessly stylish.

"Shit, I thought he was supposed to be Prince," Tracy replies. "No wonder he looked at me funny when I said, 'I would die for you.'"

"Don't worry about it. He was probably flattered. He loves people who give as good as they get. Who knows, you might even get a promotion out of it."

A pair of third-year associates enter the library dressed like Dr. Seuss characters. The fat one was editor-in-chief of the *Yale Law Journal*; the skinny one clerked for Justice Sotomayor. They're co-lead counsel on a high-profile death-row appeal the firm is handling pro bono, but right now they're a distant fourth place in the firm's annual Halloween contest, *The Amazing Res Ipsa Loquitur*.

"Dearest Hannah," Thing 1 says in a plummy British accent, "what query hast thou?"

Thing 1 is from South Bend, Indiana, but he's an ardent Anglophile. He's the only other person I know who's watched every Hugh Grant movie ever made, including *Mickey Blue Eyes*. Thing 2 stands there panting, having climbed the one flight of stairs connecting the lower and upper floors of the law library. He's twenty-nine years old and almost three hundred pounds. The poor guy's a heart attack waiting to happen.

I reach into my bottom desk drawer and pull out a bright yellow envelope.

"'The attorney-client privilege is recognized in every jurisdiction,'" I read aloud, "'but other privileges vary by state. Which of the following is not a recognized legal privilege in any state? A. Spousal privilege. B. Sibling privilege. C. Parent-child privilege. D. Pharmacist-customer privilege. Or E. Accountant-taxpayer privilege?'"

Things 1 and 2 stand there thinking.

"C'mon, dude," Thing 2 says, "you're the freaking Supreme Court clerk."

"We handled complex Constitutional conundrums, not elementary evidentiary motions," Thing 1 responds snootily.

"Well, don't look at me," Thing 2 says. "I went to Yale."

The two Things nod at one another to indicate "Enough said."

"The last two sound the most implausible, so they must be real," Thing 1 reasons.

"And I read about the spousal privilege while studying for the bar," Thing 2 says.

"The first or second time?" Thing 1 asks.

Thing 2 makes an obscene gesture.

"Five more seconds," I say.

"When in doubt," Thing 1 begins.

"Always pick C," Thing 2 concludes.

The Things look at me.

"You picked C, the parent-child privilege," I say. "Is that your final answer?"

"Yes," Thing 1 and 2 say in unison.

"I'm sorry, gentlemen, but you are incorrect. The answer is B, the sibling privilege."

"Damn, I knew it," Thing 2 says. "You can never trust a sibling."

"You knew it," Thing 1 says bitterly. "Pish-posh."

"Gentlemen, you'll need to re-shelve this cart of books before you can proceed to the next station," I say. "Tracy will follow behind you for quality assurance."

Tracy grins as the Things check the spine of the first book and roll the cart down toward the federal law section of the library. As I scan the cart, I have to smile. It's taken me years to train Tracy to arrange the books on the library carts in such a way that maximizes the efficiency of re-shelving. Only someone who knows the library as well as Tracy does could produce a cart of volumes so completely in disarray.

Hours later, drunken whoops erupt from the appropriately named Drinker Conference Room, where *The Amazing Res Ipsa Loquitur* awards are being handed out. I exchange a few pleasantries in Spanish with the night janitor before he starts vacuuming the library stacks.

"What did you say your sister-in-law's name was again?" Tracy asks. She peers over her cat's-eye glasses at the computer screen. Her long nails make a clicking noise on her keyboard. The sound reminds me of my beloved Smith Corona typewriter from college days.

"Elisabeth Lindstrom, spelled with an *s* instead of a *z*," I say.

"That's what I put in," Tracy mutters, "but I'm coming up empty."

"What are you looking up?" I ask.

"The government's witness list."

"For what?"

"*United States v. Elisabeth Lindstrom,*" Tracy answers. "Geez, for someone who's taken a blood vow to avenge her sister-in-law, you don't seem to be making much of an effort. You're like the O.J. Simpson of whistle-blower lawsuits."

"Why are you looking for the witness list?"

"I figure the prosecution's witness list is the best source of info on who might've conspired with the au pair."

"What client code are you using?" I ask. At my law firm, you can't run a search on any database without first putting in a client code, and it's against the firm's rules to misuse client codes for personal use. I'm a stickler for rules.

"I'm not using a client code."

"Then how are you running that search?"

Tracy doesn't answer. She clicks the mouse in a rapid barrage as document after document flashes across the screen. It's giving me a mild case of seasickness.

"What site are you using? That doesn't look like PACER." PACER is the federal court system's database of pleadings and decisions.

"PACER sucks," Tracy says.

"Yeah, well, unfortunately, PACER is the only game in town."

"Not anymore," Tracy replies. She pauses her clicking to move the cursor to the top of the computer screen and draws my attention to the URL name.

"It's called PacerSux.com," she says. "It's a free website for federal court documents."

"I've never heard of it."

"A friend told me about it. It's still in development. It's crowd-sourced like Wikipedia. You can get almost all of the recent cases because people are uploading those real-time, but it's hit-and-miss with the older stuff."

"Is that legal?"

"More legal than PACER. The government isn't supposed to charge money for public documents, but they get away with it because they're the government."

I close my eyes to relieve the nagging nausea, but I can still hear the clicking of Tracy's mouse. I'm momentarily transported back to the dorm, watching Sam playing some depraved postapocalyptic shooter game on the Xbox 360, his hands working the controller so vigorously it seems almost sexual.

"Bingo," Tracy says, "the fuckers spelled it with a *z*." Tracy stops clicking, takes off her glasses and leans in closer to the screen.

"Oh shit," she mutters.

Reading over Tracy's shoulder, I see the federal government's preliminary witness list for Beth's case. The prosecution's proposed witnesses included God Hälsa executives, medical and scientific experts, and over a dozen aggrieved customers, but there, in the middle of the list, one name stands out.

Dr. Eva Lindstrom-Larsen.

"You don't think Beth's own sister would've testified against her, do you?" Tracy says.

"I don't know that she would've had much choice," I say. "When the feds come calling, you can't turn them away. Not unless you have a privilege."

Tracy rubs her eyes in tiredness. It's been a long day.

"Too bad she isn't an accountant," Tracy jokes before turning off her computer.

lise

From the deposition of Lise Danielsson in *United States of America et al. v. God Hälsa AB, Andreas Magnusson and Elizabeth Lindstrom*

Q: Earlier in your deposition, you admitted to having an affair with Mr. Min.

A: It wasn't an affair.

Q: Excuse me?

A: I said, it wasn't an affair.

Q: But you admitted to sleeping...

A: Beth told me an affair is when you're doing it in secret. Sam and I weren't keeping it a secret from Beth.

Q: Ms. Lindstrom knew you were sleeping with her husband?

A: Yeah, sure. She pretty much suggested it.

Q: Ms. Lindstrom suggested you should sleep with her husband?

COUNSEL FOR MS. DANIELSSON: Objection, what relevance does this line of questioning have with respect to the allegations against Ms. Lindstrom?

COUNSEL FOR THE PROSECUTION: Ms. Lindstrom is accused of engaging in activities that put young women at risk of severe bodily harm. This line of questioning goes to demonstrate her complete lack of regard for young women's emotional and physical well-being.

COUNSEL FOR MS. DANIELSSON: That's a stretch, Counsel, and you know it.

COUNSEL FOR THE PROSECUTION: Your objection's been noted for the record.

[Questioning resumes.]

Q: You said you weren't keeping your relationship with Mr. Min a secret from Ms. Lindstrom. Was it widely known that you were engaging in sexual relations with Mr. Min?

A: Of course not. Beth told me it's not the kind of thing most people would understand.

Q: So, besides your employer, Ms. Lindstrom, did anyone know about your relationship with Mr. Min?

A: Yes.

Q: Who?

A: [Unintelligible.]

Q: I'm sorry, Ms. Danielsson, but could you please speak more loudly?

A: I said, Eva.

Q: Dr. Eva Lindstrom-Larsen? Ms. Lindstrom's sister?

A: Yes.

Q: And did Dr. Lindstrom-Larsen condone this behavior?

A: What does that mean?

Q: Did Ms. Lindstrom's sister think it's acceptable for a grown man to be having an affair with a sixteen-year-old girl?

A: I told you—it wasn't an affair.

Q: Let me put it a different way. Did Dr. Lindstrom-Larsen ever express concern that a sixteen-year-old girl would be engaging in sexual relations with a grown man?

A: Well, Eva didn't find out about it until I was older. Maybe eighteen or nineteen. But yeah, Eva was really upset.

Q: What did Dr. Lindstrom-Larsen do when she found out?

A: She got really angry with Beth. Said all this stuff about Beth's past that I didn't understand. And then here's the weird part—Eva asked me to forgive her.

Q: Dr. Lindstrom-Larsen asked you to forgive her?

A: Yeah, Eva begged me to forgive her. She said it was all her fault.

hannah

twelve

The hallways of Drinker, Barker and Horne are quiet. It's the day before Thanksgiving, which is technically a workday, but you wouldn't know it by looking around the empty offices. It's practically a ghost town. I usually like to work over the holidays. It's nice to have the office to myself and not be constantly pestered by first-year associates who make twice as much money as me but have a tenth as much legal knowledge. It's nice to slip off my shoes while sitting at my desk without having to worry that Old Man Barker will creep up behind me and reminisce about the "little ladies" who walked barefoot on his back during his business trips to Bangkok. It's nice to come into the city and do something productive rather than sit in my quiet condo and stare at the walls.

This year feels different. After spending so much time with Sam and the girls, I realize what it feels like to be part of a family, and I miss it. I miss it viscerally. Sam invited me to join them for Thanksgiving, but after the weeklong Lindstrom family reunion, my two-week stay in Princeton to help the girls adjust to life without Mommy, and my trips to visit Beth in prison and watch Claire in her school performance, I've blown through most of my allotment of vacation days. I need to work over Thanksgiving if I want to spend Christmas and New Year's with the family.

I walk up and down the hallways at work to see if anyone needs help. The few secretaries sitting in their cubicles are playing Solitaire on their computers and don't even bother to look up from their screens. The handful of associates who haven't made their minimum billable hours for the year sit morosely in their offices, hoping to eke out enough work to merit a decent year-end bonus. The only partner who seems to have come in today is the brilliant but eccentric head of the firm's tax practice, who always likes to use holidays to catch up on his backlog of USTC Advance Sheets. Back at the library, I pull my cell phone out of my purse and click the FaceTime icon. There's only one number in the cache.

"Hello? Hello?" a child's voice says. Claire's face fills the small screen. "Who is it?"

"It's me, Claire. It's Auntie Hannah."

"Oh, hi, Auntie Hannah," Claire says. "Where are you?"

"I'm at work. Remember I told you I had to work this weekend?"

"Oh yeah," Claire says. Her eyes dart to the side, distracted by something going on outside of my screen view. "I remember. Is it really busy there?"

"No, actually, it's not busy at all." I want to explain the concept of vacation days to Claire, for her to understand that my absence from the family Thanksgiving celebration has everything to do with needing to earn a living and nothing to do with my desire to spend time with her and Ally. Before I can say another word, though, Claire erupts in a fit of giggles.

"Stop it, stop it, I'm on base," she screams. "I told you I'm on base."

The screen image jostles about as Claire struggles to hold on to the phone while getting mercilessly tickled by her older cousins. Claire seems to have accidentally pressed the reverse image button, so I can see what's going on all around her at Le Refuge. Martin and Karen sit on the couch engaged in what appears to be serious conversation. Eva's husband, Alex, lounges in a nearby chair and peruses a glossy home design magazine. Eva stands by the wet bar wearing Beth's luxurious gray cashmere robe, tipping back the last drops from a large wineglass.

"Sam, where's my refill?" Eva yells.

Sam emerges from the wine cellar with a magnum bottle.

"Hey, everyone," Sam calls out, "look what I found! Château Margaux '99. The last of the case we brought back from France. Remember that trip, Martin? What was the name of the guy who came with us?"

"I can't remember," Martin says. "He was the senior senator from Nebraska or Iowa or one of those flyover states. Complete waste of money bringing him on that trip—he got voted out of office the next year."

"Claire?" I say into the phone, but Claire is giggling so hard she doesn't hear me. She drops the phone to the ground. I stand by for a full minute, staring at the image of the pure white flokati rug on my screen, waiting for someone to pick up. No one ever does.

It was nice of Tracy to invite me over for Thanksgiving. Tracy shares a brownstone in Brooklyn with an ever-changing number of housemates all under the age of thirty. The apartment is filled with pieces of furniture that look like they were abandoned on a street corner somewhere, but Tracy's stylistic influence is apparent in the brightly painted ceramics and ethnic textiles that somehow tie everything together into a bohemian-chic space.

The Thanksgiving meal is similarly eclectic. Tofu turkey and quinoa stuffing are joined by a HoneyBaked spiral-cut ham, a family-size aluminum tray of Stouffer's mac and cheese, and several boxes of take-out pizza. The white cast-iron clawfoot tub is filled with plastic bags of ice and cans of Pabst Blue Ribbon. I set my two freshly baked pumpkin pies onto the Mexican-oilcloth-covered sideboard, next to the clear plastic containers of store-bought cookies.

"Everyone, this is Hannah, my boss" is how Tracy introduces me. Although she says it with genuine warmth and kindness, it makes me feel awkward, as if she had been forced to invite me over, as if her year-end review and bonus depended upon it. Tracy's introduction also draws attention to the substantial age difference between me and everyone else at the party. I could be some of these kids' mother, and not even a teenage mother at that.

I circumnavigate the buffet table and spoon a morsel of everything on my Chinet paper plate, taking care not to offend anyone by not trying their dish. Entering the living room to find a place to sit, I notice the floral-patterned papasan in the corner is empty. I sit down and nibble at my food. There's a group of millennials nearby, sitting cross-legged on the worn Oriental carpet around a faded and chipped Thomas the Tank Engine play table repurposed as a coffee table. It's hard to tell if the table is meant to be ironic or simply economic.

"It's bullshit," proclaims a mixed-race young man. He's got disturbingly large ear gauges that make me wince just looking at them. "I mean, all she did was cop a few prescription pads at work. It was her shit-for-brains boyfriend who wrote all the fake scrips."

"It's a complete travesty of justice," a pretty girl seated next to him concurs. By her body language, I suspect she's either the young man's lover or desperately wants to be. "It's like going to prison for stealing fucking Post-its. I take Post-its from the supply room at work all the time. That doesn't make me a criminal, does it? Right, am I right?"

Everyone nods. She's right.

"I totally agree," another young woman chimes in. She has short-cropped fuchsia hair and piercings through her left eyebrow and nasal septum. "But I have to admit I find this whole 'going to prison' thing sort of fascinating." She uses her fingers to make air quotes even though there's no need for them. "Ever since I heard about your mother going to prison, I've been binge-watching *Orange Is the New Black*. And *Wentworth*. And *Prison Break*." Everyone nods again. There's been a lot of binge-watching going on.

"I doubt that real prison is like those shows," the wannabe girlfriend says. "Like, I'm sure the guards would never let all that girl-on-girl action take place under their noses."

Fuchsia Girl looks disappointed. My heart starts racing. I'm tempted to join in their conversation and share some of Beth's stories about life at Alderson. I imagine the look of shock on their faces when Ms. Prim-and-Proper Librarian Lady reveals she has a relative in federal prison. Fuchsia Girl's eyes will pop when I tell her that "gay for the stay" is a real thing. I won't even use air quotes. The wannabe girlfriend will watch her handsome companion jealously as he turns his attentions to me and asks questions about his poor mother's heartbreaking situation that only someone "who's been there" can answer. I imagine myself sitting on the papasan surrounded by the circle of engrossed listeners, the Hans Christian Andersen of prison tales, with *Chained Heat* taking the place of "The Little Match Girl." But before I can gather up the courage to utter a word, the young man speaks up.

"I'm tired of talking about my mom and her fucked-up life. Can you believe that crazy game last night?" The group quickly shifts conversation topics, and I have no idea what game he's talking about. Quietly, I negotiate my way back around Thomas the Tank Engine to return to the buffet table, hoping there's still some tofu turkey left.

After what seems an appropriate period of time, I track down Tracy to say my farewells. She's standing barefoot in the hall, a Solo cup in one hand and a joint in the other, surrounded by a group of mostly bearded guys in plaid. It looks like a lumberjack convention.

"Are you leaving so soon?" Tracy asks. She passes the joint to the Paul Bunyan next to her and escorts me down the hallway so we can talk quietly.

"Yeah, I've gotta catch the train back to Hoboken," I reply, stepping over a Chinet plate heaped with chicken bones and pizza crusts. It takes all of my self-control not to pick up the dirty paper plates and beer cans littering Tracy's apartment, but the festivities are still going strong, and no one likes a party pooper.

"Have you heard from Beth lately?" Tracy asks. "What did she say about us finding Eva's name on the witness list?" The front door bursts open, and I shiver as a group of last-minute guests enters.

"Actually, I haven't told Beth about that yet."

Tracy squints at me. I can't tell if she's surprised or disappointed, maybe both.

"Beth says her emails and letters are all being monitored," I explain. "She doesn't want the feds to know she's got me digging around for Lise's accomplice."

"Why not? I mean, what would the feds care about it?"

"I don't know, but Beth made it clear she doesn't want me putting that kind of stuff down in writing. She said she's paranoid about getting herself or the family in more trouble."

Tracy wrinkles her brow.

"To be continued, then?" I say. I pull on my knit cap and give Tracy a quick hug.

"To be continued," Tracy concurs.

I thank Tracy one more time for the nice Thanksgiving and then reach into my purse to find my set of keys, which I weave in between my fingers. They say Brooklyn is safe, but you can never be too careful.

When I get to the station, it's surprisingly crowded as I wait for the PATH train to take me home. The sound of distant trains echoes in the white-tiled space. I sit down on the concrete bench and pull out my cell phone to kill time. My mood brightens upon seeing the red dot on the CorrLinks icon indicating I've got an email from Beth.

Dear Hannah,

Happy Thanksgiving. Sam told me that you had to work this week and couldn't join the family at Le Refuge, but I hope you are enjoying a delicious holiday meal with your friends. I myself just polished off an embarrassingly huge plate of turkey, stuffing, mashed potatoes and gravy, cranberry dressing, green bean casserole and two kinds of pie—pumpkin and apple—before falling into a three-hour food coma. I'm going to have to take spinning and Zumba tomorrow to work it all off.

We've got the rest of the weekend free so I don't have to work and can just snuggle in bed and read the pile of magazines on my nightstand. Thank you for the subscriptions to the *New Yorker* and *Bon Appetit* and for your latest weekly letter with the photos of the girls from Halloween. The other ladies in my unit are pea green with envy—the poor things don't get much support from the outside—but I've gradually won them over by sharing my embarrassment of riches. *People* and *Us* and the latest James Patterson thrillers are in particularly high demand.

I would write more, but my bunkie just came to remind me that the game is about to start. If I don't get to the TV room soon, all the good seats will be filled by Cowboys fans. Everyone here already knows what a Giants fanatic I am, so I'm sure someone will save me a seat, but I don't want to cause a prison riot...!

You know, it's funny: while I wouldn't wish this experience on my very worst enemy, I must say that this Thanksgiving has made me feel grateful for all that I have, including you.

Love, Beth

P.S. I know you're busy, but when can you come visit again? I'm dying to hear what you've found out about my "special assignment"!

I stare at the screen, thinking how to respond. My mind is a blank, so I click off the cell phone and decide to reply later. When I look up, the platform is empty. The train must have come and gone while I was reading.

beth

thirteen

It's late November, and the West Virginia days are growing short. I hate this time of year. I can already feel the cloud of depression starting to descend. To make matters worse, I haven't been able to get a good night's sleep ever since I stepped foot in Alderson. I just can't seem to quiet my brain. What I wouldn't give for one of my old Ativan and Ambien cocktails.

I recently started getting up before sunrise and going to work before everyone else. That way, I can finish work early and enjoy the rest of my day. It's against BOP regulations, but I get away with it. I've always had a knack for getting what I want.

This morning, I'm cleaning the last toilet in the bathroom when Deb and the rest of the janitorial crew show up for the first shift.

"Done?" Deb asks.

"Almost," I say.

"Ya look tired," Deb says. "Still can't sleep?"

"Nope."

"Sugar had that problem for a long time."

"Yeah, 'cause she was a freaking cokehead," Meatloaf Mary says. "That's why they called her Sugar, you know."

"Were we talkin' to you, Meat?" Deb asks. She pulls the plunger from my caddy and wields the handle menacingly under Mary's chin. Like she's looking for an excuse to shove it into Mary's brain stem.

"I was just tryin' ta make conversation," Mary says, shrinking back—as much as a two-hundred-pound woman can shrink.

"Anyway, turns out it was her meds," Deb continues. "They had her on some kind of speed. It helped smooth out some of her craziness but fucked up her sleep."

"Metamin," Mary says. "Sugar was on Metamin. Cheap-ass shit. The drug company was selling it for next to nothin' so BOP bought it by the truckload."

"Sugar was on Metamin?" I ask.

"Yeah, you heard of it?" Deb asks.

"I've seen the ads," I say.

I don't know if I'm being paranoid, but I don't like the way Deb's eyeing me.

I can't believe people are still using Metamin. Once Metamin-G came out, you couldn't give the original Metamin away. Believe me, we tried. God Hälsa dropped prices for the original Metamin to rock bottom just to deplete the inventory. We figured pennies on the dollar was still real money.

The only people who wanted the original Metamin were hard-core speed freaks who ground up the bitter white tablets and snorted it like coke. We heard rumors that junkies were digging through dumpsters behind suburban elementary schools, searching for half-used bottles of Metamin that school nurses threw away once all their students switched to Metamin-G.

"So anyway," I say, changing the subject, "can I go? It's Tuesday, remember?"

"Get outta here," Deb says.

"What da fuck?" Mary protests. "It's still work hours. Why you always givin' Blondie here special treatment?"

"Meat, feel free to show up before sunrise," Deb says, "and I'll be happy to give you the special treatment, too." Deb puts the plunger handle between her legs like a dildo and fake-fucks Mary. The crew laughs while Mary scampers away.

Tuesdays are my designated day to visit commissary—or FedMart as we locals call it. My first couple months in prison, I quickly blew through my allowed commissary limit stocking up on the essentials: workout gear, toiletries and makeup, MP3 player and earphones. Before I got here, I wouldn't have been caught dead in a Champion sweatshirt and sweatpants combo or pair of granny-white Reeboks, but now I wear them like they're the latest from Atelier Versace.

Today, I need to stock up on groceries. I pull Juanita's handwritten shopping list from my pants pocket: Fritos, refried beans, jalapeños and Cheez Whiz (for tongue-tingling tamales), shrimp-flavored ramen, peanut butter, honey-roasted peanuts and sriracha (for prison pad thai), and chocolate pudding cups, Oreos, mini-Snickers and a can of Coke (for an out-of-this-world molten lava cake). Juanita doesn't get any financial support from the outside, so I promised I'd get the ingredients if she'd do the cooking. We plan to invite some of the gals in our unit over for an evening of international cuisine and Texas Hold'em.

I hand the shopping list over to my friend Sandy, the commissary clerk, who collects the items from the storeroom shelves and piles them on the counter.

"You sure you can handle all that?" Sandy asks.

"Yeah, I'm cool," I say. I take off my sweatshirt, put my purchases inside and tie the sleeves together. The bundle looks like Santa's bag of presents.

"Is that all for today?" she asks. "Sorry we don't have any new stuff right now."

I look up at the display case of items behind the Plexiglas. My eye catches on a clear glass bottle with a shiny golden cap. It's Maybelline Kissing Potion—something I haven't seen since the 1980s.

I lick my lips just remembering.

It was a gorgeous autumn afternoon. One of those impossibly perfect days you see in college admissions brochures. Gold leaves, blue sky, the whole package.

I'm sitting by myself in the top row of bleachers. St. Albans is playing Sidwell Friends in the last game of the season. I hear someone in the row below say that Coach Adrian has come to watch the star forward even though underclassmen never make varsity.

I see my sister, Eva, headed toward the St. Albans side of the field with a swarm of her National Cathedral School girl-friends. They've changed out of their school uniform of white polo shirts and plaid kilts into their after-school uniform of ripped sweatshirts and acid-washed jeans. It's the era of *Flash-dance* fashion.

Eva pulls a clear glass bottle of Strawberry Swirl Kissing Po-tion from her back pocket and pouts while she rubs the slick roller ball around her pencil-thin lips. I can smell the sicken-ing sweetness from fifty feet away.

Eva passes the Kissing Potion to the girl on her right, who

rolls it over her own lips before passing the bottle to the next girl. And so on and so on.

Gross, I think.

Eva and her girlfriends sit two rows below me. Most of the girls have feathered blond hair, but one girl in particular stands out: a perfect Heather Locklear clone with an L.L.Bean canvas tote monogrammed with her initials in lime-green script. She's clearly the alpha girl, the queen bee of the swarm.

Alpha Heather pulls out a six-pack of Tab from her tote and offers them to her friends. The fluorescent pink cans are quickly dispersed and shared. I sneak down to the far edge of the NCS contingent but don't dare get too close.

"You're Evie's little sister, aren't you?" the girl nearest me asks. Unlike the rest of the swarm, she's more Demi Moore than Heather Locklear. I notice her black nail polish is chipped around the edges.

I smile and nod, delighted to be noticed.

"You're adorable," she says, giving me an appraising once-over.

She offers me her can of soda. I see a glistening circle of Kissing Potion around the stay-tab opening. I'm simultaneously frightened and thrilled. I put my mouth to the cold metal and take a sip. It tastes bitter and strange. I pass the can back to the girl and smile, my lips sticky and smelling faintly of strawberry.

I keep my eyes fixed on the soccer field but don't see a thing. My heart is beating with the excitement of sitting among these heavenly creatures who know things and do things I can't even imagine. I pretend to watch the game and strain to hear the conversations around me. All the girls are fixated on St. Albans's star forward.

"He looks like that guy from *The Blue Lagoon*," one girl says.

"Did you actually see it?" Eva asks. "Wasn't it rated R?"

"Oh my God, Evie," Alpha Heather says. "It's on cable!"

"Speaking of which," she continues, "I found a stash of pornos in my dad's dresser the other day. I'll invite you all to watch when my parents leave for Bermuda."

The swarm buzzes over this news.

"Evie, don't hold out on us," Alpha Heather says. "Is Golden Boy as delicious naked as he looks in those soccer shorts?" She sticks out her pink, wet tongue and swirls it around.

The other girls start giggling.

"Come on, you guys, don't get gross," Eva protests.

I'm smiling with the rest of the girls when Eva spots me sitting there at the end of her row. I feel like a deer in the crosshairs. I wonder if she can smell the Kissing Potion on my lips.

"Elisabeth Lindstrom, what are you doing here?" Eva yells.

My face flushes with a mixture of anger and shame. I avoid making eye contact with my Tab-sharing seatmate as I slink back up two rows to sit by myself.

Like a wolf pack that bonds more tightly after ejecting its weakest member, Eva and her friends seem to close ranks after my departure.

Alpha Heather reaches into her bag, pulls out a pack of Fruit Stripe gum, takes one for herself and passes the pack along. The girls crumple up the wrappers and toss them through the cracks of the bleachers to the ground below. A swift wind picks up the wrappers and blows them away like tiny tumbleweeds.

I sit glumly by myself. I pout my lips so I can smell the hint of strawberry.

I return to watching the game on the field. Soon, everyone is standing up and cheering Golden Boy as he breaks away from the rest of the field and scores another goal just under the buzzer, giving him a hat trick for the game and St. Albans's first league championship in a decade.

The crowd is jumping up and down as Golden Boy strides over

to the St. Albans side of the field and looks up into the bleach-ers. He makes eye contact with one lucky girl and motions for her to join him, and she runs down the bleachers and jumps into his waiting arms. It's a prep school mash-up of Bruce Spring-steen's "Dancing in the Dark" video and the closing scene from *An Officer and a Gentleman.*

Golden Boy and his chosen girl are surrounded by ecstatic St. Albans teammates as they parade around the field in vic-tory. Eva and the other NCS girls start packing up to leave, but their stolen glances tell a different story. What they wouldn't give to be that lucky girl. In boys, envy can transform into ambition and even inspire greatness, but in girls, it almost al-ways spirals into insecurity and petty jealousy.

I see that jealousy in Eva's eyes as I sit beaming atop Golden Boy's wide shoulders. The cheering of the crowds is nothing; it's the hateful silence from Eva that's deafening.

What can I do? I'm eight years old and completely in love. No one could be cooler, more heroic or handsome, than Golden Boy.

And best of all, he's my brother.

When I get back to our cube from commissary, Juanita's wiping down our footlockers with soapy water. She always keeps our place spotless, but she's particularly meticulous when she's getting ready to cook. Juanita reminds me of my beloved housekeeper, Maria, in that way.

"Back already?" she asks.

"The line wasn't too bad today." I toss my Santa bag of junk food on Juanita's bunk and help her dry the lockers with maxi-pads.

"Yeah, women usually hold back this time of year," Jua-nita says. "Not everyone has your megabucks. They're saving up for the Christmas stuff that comes in after Thanksgiving."

"What Christmas stuff?" I ask, throwing the used maxi-pads in the garbage.

"Last year, the warden let us have turkey jerky, tinned oysters, Dove ice cream bars, mint-flavored Oreos, even Little Debbie Christmas Tree Cakes. And that's just the food part. You should've seen the fancy soaps and lotions and sparkly nail polishes on offer. It was like a regular Avon lady party."

When Juanita's done cleaning, I unknot the sleeves of my sweatshirt and dump out the contents on her bunk.

"*Chica*, you must have spent a fortune!" Juanita cries out.

"Nothing's too good for my brilliant bunkie," I reply.

Juanita crawls onto her bunk, shoves the rest of the junk food over to the side and opens the bag of mini-Snickers. She gestures for me to join her.

"You heard from your sister-in-law lately?" she asks. She nibbles on a chocolate and offers me the bag. I decline.

"She still sends me her weekly letters," I say, "but she hasn't sent any emails lately—ever since I told her about the BOP monitoring all my communications. After all, she wouldn't want to do anything that could get me or my family in more trouble."

"Some things are better said in person," Juanita agrees. We both laugh.

"We're a good pair, I think," Juanita says, leaning up against me.

"The best," I say, pulling the bottle of Kissing Potion from my pocket and savoring the artificial sweetness.

hannah

fourteen

The temperature gauge on the dashboard reads forty-five degrees, but it feels colder. The weak December sun is barely visible behind the mist-shrouded mountains. The trees that were so full of rich color the last time I visited are now barren and lifeless, black sticks against gray sky. The SUV is moving fast, and the Alderson Prison Camp sign passes in a blur.

"Hey, I think that's a bad word," Claire shouts from the back seat.

"What's a bad word?" Ally asks.

"Prison," Claire whispers.

Claire's kindergarten teacher reported to Sam and me at our first parent-teacher meeting that Claire is reading two years above grade level. I stare out the car window and pretend I didn't hear the girls' exchange. It's uncharacteristic of me, normally so encouraging and attentive to my nieces, to ignore

Claire's observation. As Sam pulls the car into the parking lot, I think to myself that nothing about today will be normal.

"Hurry, girls," he says, "there's already a line."

I get out of the passenger side and unbuckle the girls from their booster seats. I cautioned Claire and Ally in advance that there are lots of rules at Mommy's camp. Claire eagerly chimed in, "There are lots of rules at my school, too. No nuts. No bad words. No touching other people if they don't want to be touched." I'm pretty sure the opposites of those things are true at Alderson.

"Hurry up, girls!" Sam repeats.

I pull out my Ziploc bag of change—still heavy with ninety-two dollars' worth of quarters and dimes—and make sure I have the BOP forms and my driver's license before joining Sam and the girls at the end of a long line of people eager to spend time with their beloved sister, mother, daughter or wife before Christmas. When we finally get to the front of the visitors' building and wait to be called in by the guard, Claire looks up at Sam.

"Daddy, oh my God, I almost forgot," she says, "did you remember your driver's license? Because if you didn't, they'll make you go back to the car."

Sam smiles at his bright little girl and nods, showing her his license as proof.

"You don't have any scrunched-up tissues or mints in your pockets, do you?" Claire asks. "Because if you do, they'll make you go back to the car."

Sam shakes his head no and pulls his pant pockets inside out to show her.

"Did you remember to put your license plate number on the form?"

Sam shows Claire the form before he leans over to me and

whispers, "I think you scared the pants off our Claire here." I shrug in apology.

After we enter the visitors' building and complete the security routine, the guard at the front desk says, "Go ahead and sign in, but you'll have to wait awhile for your inmate. The place is on lockdown."

"Lockdown?" I ask. The guard ignores my question and gestures for us to move along. Sam heads to the bathroom—he drank a lot of Red Bull during the drive—while I lead the girls to the back room to snag one of the big tables.

"Is this really Mommy's camp?" Ally whispers to Claire, who doesn't answer. For once, Claire doesn't know any more than her little sister. My heart aches seeing my young nieces take in their new surroundings. I know what they must be thinking: *This doesn't look like any camp we've ever been to. Where is the beading table? The paint easels? The camp counselors ready to lead us in a round of I-Spy or the Chicken Dance?*

"Who wants to get a treat from the bending machines?" I call out. When Claire was just three, she mispronounced the phrase "vending machine" during a family trip, and the term has become part of the Min-Lindstrom lexicon. Claire and Ally jump up and down with excitement, reminding me how easily young children can get distracted: "Woe is me… Oh, look, a butterfly!"

"This bending machine has hamburgers, cheeseburgers, breakfast sandwiches and fried-chicken sandwiches," I say, "and this one has candy, chips and cookies."

"Oh, I want M&M's!" Claire says, "Definitely M&M's."

"Me, too," Ally agrees.

"But wait, girls, there are two more machines on the other side of the room."

"I want M&M's," Claire whines.

"Me, too," Ally echoes.

My first impulse is to force the girls to look at the other machines, which contain yogurt and string cheese and pieces of prison-grade pie. How can the girls possibly make an informed decision if they don't know what all their options are? Then again, what does it matter? With ninety-two dollars' worth of change and four hours to kill, Claire and Ally could do several circuits of the vending machines. Anyway, what kind of kid would choose string cheese over M&M's?

I put five quarters into each of the girls' sweaty little palms and then lift them up, one by one, so they can insert the coins into the vending machine slot and push the buttons. Claire and Ally squeal in amazement as they watch the silvery metal spiral slowly turn and eject a bag of M&M's into the waiting hopper. The second time is apparently no less thrilling than the first.

We wait anxiously for over an hour before we finally see Beth walking down the hill. Claire stands up and screams, "Mommy!" Claire and Ally run to the front window and eagerly press their noses against the glass. Beth flashes a brilliant smile to her daughters, and the three of them are nearly face-to-face, separated only by a pane of glass, when Beth turns and disappears behind an unmarked door.

"Where did Mommy go?" Claire asks, her face panicked.

"Let me show you," I say. Claire and Ally follow me to the front room of the visitors' building. "This is where your mommy will come out," I explain. The three of us sit on the two hard plastic chairs near the unmarked inmate entrance door: Ally in my lap, Claire in her own chair. When Beth emerges from the door, the girls are ecstatic. Beth gives her daughters a warm embrace, but she looks shaken.

"Is something wrong?" I ask.

Beth glances over at the girls and says, "We can talk later."

"Mommy," Claire says, tugging on Beth's shirt for attention, "if you want a Diet Coke or anything, just let me know and I'll get it for you because you're not allowed to touch money. It's against camp rules." Beth smiles over at me, appearing grateful that I prepared the girls yet chagrined that such preparation should be necessary.

"Now that you mention it, Claire," Beth says, "I would really love a Diet Coke. Would you and Auntie Hannah go get one for me?" Claire is delighted to be of service to her mother, and Ally is equally delighted to be her sister's shadow. I have no problem serving as the girls' chaperone—I'm used to it by now—but can't help but feel disappointed. I had hoped that Beth, having been separated from her young daughters for over three months, would want to go to the vending machines with them, to share in their thrill of putting the coins in the slot and pressing the buttons, to savor every precious minute they have together. Instead, Beth seems content to sit and be served. It makes me wonder whether prison has changed her at all.

After a couple hours of catching up, a uniformed guard enters the visiting room and announces that the Children's Room is open for the day. The Children's Room is in the farthest back section of the visitors' building and looks like an elementary school classroom. There's a cozy reading nook with upholstered armchairs and a shelf full of books ranging from classics like *Green Eggs and Ham* to more unusual selections such as *Visiting Day* and *The Night Dad Went to Jail*. There's a play kitchen area and a selection of wooden puzzles and board games.

The most popular spot in the Children's Room is the craft counter, which is staffed by volunteer Alderson inmates and offers a selection of seasonal projects for visiting children to make and take home: construction paper jack-o'-lanterns decorated with markers and glitter; construction paper Christmas trees decorated with markers and glitter; construction paper

Easter eggs decorated with markers and glitter. Claire and Ally are amazed by their good fortune.

The inmate in charge of the craft counter is Miss Sally. According to Beth's letters, Miss Sally is a former meth addict from a defunct mining town outside Wheeling, West Virginia. Prison is the best thing to ever happen to Miss Sally. It's given her a new set of teeth, free antidepressants and three course credits shy of a GED. It's also given her the gift of true love with another member of the Alderson Christian Fellowship. Miss Sally and Runaround Sue found each other at the same time they found Jesus.

"Why, Lordy me, look at these little angels," she says. "You, little missy, look like a Precious Moment." Miss Sally pokes Ally in the tummy as if she were the Pillsbury Doughboy.

"And you," she says, looking at Claire, "you look like a plus-size Dora the Explorer."

Miss Sally cackles like a crone, taking pleasure in her own wit.

"So, which project would you like to make?" Miss Sally asks after she has a moment to regain her composure. There are a dozen choices displayed on the craft counter sample board. "Baby Jesus in his manger? Santa in his sleigh? Or maybe the Three Wise Men?"

"The menorah," Claire replies. She points to the construction paper sample decorated with glitter-covered candles. "Definitely the menorah."

After finishing their craft projects and taking in a couple more rounds of the vending machines, Claire and Ally grow restless. Sam takes the girls outside to play on the swing set. Beth and I watch through the window as Sam pushes Ally in the little-kid swing. Claire sits in the big-kid swing, pumping her legs as hard as she can and soaring almost level with the top bar.

"Finally, a quiet moment together, just the two of us," Beth says.

"Yes, finally," I say. "So tell me—what's going on? When we got here, the guard said the place was on lockdown."

"Mary is dead."

"Meatloaf Mary?"

"Yeah, when she didn't show up for work this morning, Deb went to her bunk. And that's when she found her lying cold, unconscious and covered in vomit."

"Oh my God," I say. Even though I've never met Meatloaf Mary, Beth has told me so much about her that it's shocking to hear that she's dead. "How did she die?"

"We don't know. The COs put the place on lockdown while they took Mary's body away. And then they started pulling people one by one for questioning."

"Did they pull you?" I ask.

"No, but they questioned Deb for a really long time."

Despite Deb's fearsome reputation, Beth seems to have become friends with her. It's hard for me to imagine what the two of them have in common.

"Do you think Deb did it?" I ask.

"I don't know what to think."

For the first time, I start to worry about Beth's safety. Even though Alderson has a reputation for being a cushy prison— Camp Cupcake, some people call it—it's still prison.

"Anyway, we're running out of time," Beth says. "I'm sorry to make you come all the way out here to talk in person. You must think I'm being paranoid."

"I don't mind," I say. "It gives me a good excuse to bring the girls to visit. And you've got every reason to be cautious. The people who post on PrisonTalk say the BOP monitors all calls, emails and letters that go in or out of prison. Like the managing partner at my firm always says—don't write anything down that you don't want to see on the front page of the *New York Times*."

"Yeah, I've learned the hard way that emails can bite you in the butt. So, quick, before Sam and the girls come back, what have you found out so far?"

"Well, my assistant librarian, Tracy, was able to find a lot of the case documents online. The docket card includes hundreds of items."

"Yeah, the prosecution went balls-to-the-wall on my case. Depositions, document requests, motions, objections, you name it. No taxpayer expense spared to bring me down."

"We found the government's preliminary witness list," I say, "which had a few dozen names on it, most of them unremarkable." There's a catch in my voice.

"But…" Beth says, prompting me.

"Well, I hate to ask this, but did you know Eva was on the witness list? That they planned to call her to testify against you?"

Beth smiles. "Yeah, I know. The feds pretty much copy-and-pasted my entire Rolodex. The final witness list included the whole family—Eva and Alex, Martin and Karen, even Sam. The prosecutors were ready to haul everyone into the courtroom. My lawyers said they do that to rattle us into settling. And in my case, I guess it worked. What else did you find?"

"There were a number of exhibits referenced in the pleadings, but we haven't been able to find those online yet. They all seem to be marked confidential."

"I've seen the exhibits," Beth says. "Photographs mostly. We got the prosecutors to keep them confidential because they have minor children in them."

"Minor children?"

"Nothing scandalous," Beth assures me. "We just didn't want the photos becoming part of the public record. What else have you found?"

"Well, um, that's all so far," I answer. "Tracy and I scoured all the documents we could find online, but we still haven't been able to find anything to suggest Lise had a conspirator."

"Never mind the official documents," Beth replies, "I already know about those. What I want to know is what's going on outside these walls. Is anyone acting strangely since I went to prison? Like Eva? Or Alex?"

Eva and Alex always seem strange to me, but I'm not going to tell Beth that. They're her family after all. It makes me sad that Beth suspects her own older sister. Then again, I can't help remembering that last night at Le Refuge before Beth left for Alderson, the silhouette of Sam and Eva in the upstairs window.

"Hey, babe, could you do me?" Sam says.

Beth and I look up at the same time, surprised by the interruption. Sam's holding out a Band-Aid and an exposed elbow, which appears to be badly scraped up.

"I fell on the stupid walkway," he explains.

"Go to the bathroom and wash it with soap and water," I say, taking the Band-Aid from Sam. "Make sure to dry it well with paper towels. And I'll take care of you when you get back."

Sam does as he's told. Meanwhile, Claire runs in, grabs the Ziploc bag of change and runs off toward the vending machines, Ally chasing behind her. I look apologetically at Beth. Minutes ago, she was so eager to hear more about my sleuthing, but the moment seems to have passed.

"Don't worry," Beth says. "I can wait. Besides, I have all the time in the world."

It's a long drive from Alderson to Le Refuge. As soon as we arrive, Sam makes a beeline for the wet bar and pours himself a double shot of Macallan to take the edge off the road buzz.

I unbuckle a sleeping Ally from her booster seat, get Claire to grab Ally's favorite stuffy, Olaf, and head into the house. Claire and I walk upstairs and lay Ally down on her bed. We strip off Ally's wrinkled dress and dirty tights, and we cover her up with the soft pink comforter. Claire makes sure to tuck Olaf under the covers next to Ally. As Claire and I walk down the stairs, we run into Sam coming up.

"I'm going to bed, girls. I'm beat," he mumbles.

"Good night, Daddy," Claire replies sweetly. She tilts her face up to get a kiss, but Sam walks past her.

"Your daddy's so exhausted he can't even see straight," I say. I give Claire a kiss on the top of her head as a consolation prize.

"You must be tired yourself," I say. The two of us walk down the stairs and settle on the great room couch. "You want me to help you get ready for bed, or do you want me to fix you a snack first?"

"No, Auntie Hannah, I'm not even the least bit tired," Claire insists. "Let's get the suitcases out of the car and unpack."

"Oh, sweetie," I say, "I'm too tired to drag in all of our suitcases. Let's just leave our stuff in the car overnight and your daddy will bring them in tomorrow morning."

"But Christmas is almost here," Claire cries, "and I want to wrap the gift I made for Daddy. I want it to be a surprise."

"What gift?" I ask.

"You know, the one I made with Miss Sally."

Claire and I run outside to grab our stuff from the car. Back in the house, Claire looks proudly at her construction paper menorah festively decorated with construction paper candles and gold-glittered flames.

"Let's go up to the wrapping room," Claire suggests, "so I can wrap Daddy's present."

"The wrapping room? What's the wrapping room?"

Claire leads me upstairs, into Beth's bedroom and the adjacent bathroom and past the sleek Swedish steam shower. Claire pushes open a door I've never seen before—could it actually be another pantry?—and reveals a room that takes my breath away.

The wrapping room is a large walk-in closet but instead of storing clothes, it's outfitted with floor-to-ceiling shelves laden with rolls of luxurious wrapping paper and spools of ribbon in a rainbow of colors. In the corner of the room is a custom-built cabinet with dozens of individual cubbies. I open them to discover loads of tiny treasures: jingle bells, silk flowers, ceramic candy canes. There is an expensive-looking desk and high-backed chair, and inside the desk drawers are boxes upon boxes of personalized, embossed vellum stationery.

Claire opens a tall armoire that nearly overflows with handled shopping bags and stiff cardboard boxes emblazoned with the names and logos of high-end department stores and luxury goods purveyors.

"Can you get me that one, please? The pretty blue one?" Claire asks, pointing up.

"This one?" I ask, indicating the top box in the pile.

"Yes, that one."

I pull down a flat, rectangular Tiffany box and set it down on the desk. I lift the lid off the box and discover, nestled in the pristine white tissue paper, the sterling silver frame I gave Sam and Beth last year for Christmas, the one I used my annual bonus to buy. It's a three-part frame. On each side are two smaller photographs—one of me holding Sam on my lap when he was a baby, the other of Beth, Martin and Eva as young children standing in front of a Christmas tree—flanking the larger central photograph of Sam, Beth and the girls from a recent Lindstrom family summer reunion.

"It's perfect," Claire declares. She carefully sets the silver frame aside and tucks her construction paper menorah inside the box. "It's just the right size. Now, what wrapping paper do you think I should use?"

I go through the motions of examining the different options with my niece, but my mind is racing with questions. Is there something about the Tiffany frame that Beth found distasteful, or do Sam and Beth have so much stuff they don't even notice when someone gives them a gift? I think with bitter irony about the unopened boxes of embossed stationery tucked away in the desk drawers and remember that I never received a thank-you note from Sam and Beth.

Not for the silver frame. Not ever.

beth

fifteen

It's almost midnight on Christmas Eve. I'm bent double over a toilet scrubbing the bowl with Ajax. It's usually noisy in the bathroom, the tiled surfaces magnifying every little sound, but it's dead quiet tonight.

"I know you like to get to work early, but this is crazy," Deb says. Her voice is deep and booming.

"Shit, you scared the hell out of me," I say, startled.

I turn around to find Deb leaning against the sinks and watching me. I can't say I blame her; it's the best view in the house.

"Insomnia, no appetite and now paranoia, too?" Deb says.

"Yeah, I'm a frickin' train wreck," I say.

I flush and move my caddy to the next stall.

"You talk to the doc about your meds?" Deb asks.

"I can't get in to see him for another six months."

"Ya goin' through the change? 'Cause that'll screw you up royally."

"I don't think so," I say. "I'm still getting my visits from Aunt Flo."

"Ha," Deb snorts. "Haven't heard that one in a while."

We're quiet for a while.

Another flush, another stall.

"How about you?" I ask to fill the silence.

"Whaddabout me?"

"How are you doing?"

"Happy as a clam. Actually, my clam's never been happier."

"Oh yeah? What's your secret?"

"Testosterone."

"Testosterone?"

"I'm not trans or nothin'," Deb is quick to say. "I was just havin' the worst hot flashes. Sweating through my sheets every night. The shit they gave me didn't work, so the doc got me on this clinical trial."

"A clinical trial?" I ask.

"Yeah."

"Phase III?"

Deb looks at me again in that way, like she either wants to fuck me or kill me. Or both.

"You sure know a lot about this pharma shit," Deb finally says. "Almost as much as Meatloaf did."

"My sister's a doctor," I reply.

"I saw you with your girls in visitation last week," Deb says. "Must suck being apart from them at Christmas."

"Yeah, it does," I say. "You don't have kids, do you?"

"Nope, got my ovaries yanked as soon as I could. Right after my third abortion."

"I didn't know you did guys back then."

"Guys did me" is how Deb responds.

Deb moves her ass off the sinks and walks over to me. She's so close I can smell her pits. I look out the chain-link-covered window. A few snowflakes drift against the ink-blue sky.

"It's starting to snow," I say.

Deb stops staring at me and looks out the window, too.

The fluorescent lights overhead flash on and off.

"Five more minutes 'til lights-out," a male voice announces over the PA system. "Merry Christmas, ladies."

"Merry Christmas, Deb," I say.

And then I get back to work.

I've always loved the first snowfall of the season. When I was growing up in the Swedish Ambassador's Residence in DC, the first snow usually arrived in early December, right around my birthday.

It was late afternoon. Eva and I were on break from school and cranky from being cooped inside all day. The first snow-flakes of the season began to drift outside the window.

"Do you think I'll get a Småland dollhouse for my birth-day this year?" I ask.

"It's too expensive," Eva says. "Anyway, dollhouses are for babies."

"I'm not a baby. I'm ten today."

"If you want a dollhouse, then you're a baby."

"Shut up," I say.

"You shut up," Eva replies.

I run to the kitchen to find my mother and tattle on Eva. She's not there. I wander around the house looking for her. I find myself standing outside my parents' bedroom upstairs. The door is closed. Mother says I should never bother her when her bedroom door is closed.

I press my ear to the door and listen. I hear murmurs but

can't make out anything more. I stand there for a long time, my head against the polished walnut.

I muster up the courage to knock. Not loudly, but loud enough.

I wait. I open the door a crack and peer inside. And then I see Mother lying naked on her bed. Her full breasts are soft and round. Her eyes are closed and fluttering. One hand is folded behind her head, the other is touching herself between her legs, which are spread wide, a triangle of tawny tuft at the center.

Standing over her, wearing a robe and smoking a pipe, is Papa. Most people call him the Ambassador. He watches Mother wriggle and moan. It's only when Mother lets out a sharp cry, her back arching like a cat's, that Papa sets down his pipe and removes his robe. Naked, he flips Mother roughly onto her belly and enters her from behind. I can barely breathe as I watch them moving together in a reckless rhythm.

When the two of them collapse in a shuddering heap, I'm suddenly afraid of being seen. Quietly, I pull the door shut.

I stand outside the door. My heart's beating fast. There's a tingling feeling between my legs. Something I've never felt before. It's strange but nice.

Really nice.

I race down the stairs back to the living room. Eva is sitting in the window seat and looking outside. By now, the drifting snowflakes have accumulated into a blanket of white.

"Eva," I say breathlessly, "I went looking for Mother…"

"You know you're not supposed to bother Mother while she's working."

"She was in the bedroom. And Papa was with her."

Eva pauses, looks at my face.

"Hey, how about we go outside?" she says.

It's dark outside. The pure white snowflakes are striking

against the dark sky. Eva grabs her coat and slips on her boots, but I don't bother. I follow her in my stocking feet.

"I love the first snowfall of the year, don't you?" Eva says, falling back into the downy layer of snow. She starts making snow angels. I do the same.

"You won't learn about this in school until next year," Eva says, "when you're in the fifth grade. But I think you're ready to know."

I keep quiet, signaling for Eva to keep talking.

"Do you know where babies come from?" she asks.

"Not really," I whisper.

And so she explains. As Eva talks, my mind's eye returns to the scene I just witnessed in my parents' bedroom. I try to make sense of what I saw, what I felt, but I can't. Suddenly, I want Eva to stop talking, but she keeps going on and on. I wish she'd just shut up.

"Silent night," I start singing. "Holy night. All is calm, all is bright."

"God, you're such a baby," Eva says, annoyed. She brushes the snow off herself and marches into the house. I stay outside and continue singing until my lips turn blue.

After dinner, Mother brings out the almond-flavored princess cake she always makes for my birthday. When I finish blowing out the candles, she gives me a large, beautifully wrapped present: a Småland dollhouse, complete with all the accessories. I see the pleasure in Mother's face as I admire the finely detailed pieces. And in the corner of my eye, I see Eva standing in the shadows, her face dark with jealousy.

Four years later, Mother dies. Her untimely passing rips a hole in the fabric of our family. Each of us deals with the loss in our own way. Father drowns himself in drink. Martin looks for comfort in the beds of countless women. Eva does everything she can to keep up her perfect facade. Only I know that she's an out-of-control bulimic.

And me? I put on a good face, but it's not easy. We move from DC to New York, and I try hard to adjust to my new school. Martin has his own apartment and Eva's in college, so it's just me and Father left at home. With Father passed out drunk most of the time, I might as well be alone.

"Eva, can you come over this weekend?" I ask over the phone. "Maybe we could hang out, go to a movie or something." Father and I have a nice apartment on Park Aveue, but Eva rarely leaves her dorm at Columbia to visit us.

"I've got to study all weekend," Eva says.

"You're always studying," I reply.

"If I don't keep a straight-A average, I could lose my scholarship. And I definitely won't be able to get into medical school."

"There's more to life than grades."

"That's what the stupid girls in high school used to say to make themselves feel better."

Eva's comment stings, mostly because I know it's true.

"And what did the fat girls say to make themselves feel better?" I say, trying to get even. "Or can you even understand one another with your fingers shoved down your throats?"

The silence on the line speaks volumes.

"Smart women can be anything they want," Eva says. "But pretty women can only be two things—a wife or a whore."

Eva pauses to let her words sink in.

"I'm going to be a doctor," she says. "What do you think you'll be, Beth?"

hannah

sixteen

Christmas has always been my favorite holiday, but spending it with my beloved nieces makes it even more special this year. Everything is warm and fragrant inside Le Refuge. The marble kitchen counters are covered with racks of freshly baked Christmas treats: rich butter cookies decorated with colorful sprinkles, broadly smiling gingerbread people and snowball-like Russian tea cakes. I look around the kitchen in quiet satisfaction. The pea gravel makes a familiar rumbling sound as Eva's Volvo station wagon pulls up into the driveway of Le Refuge.

"Claire and Ally, your auntie Eva and the girls are here," I call out. I dry my hands on the front of my apron and make my way to the foyer to wait for the guests to come in from the cold. "And Uncle Alex, too," I say as an afterthought.

"Oh, Hannah, you look tired," Eva murmurs as soon as

she enters the house. "If you make an appointment with my office, I can laser off those dark patches." Eva has never been the nicest person, but Sam insists the entire Lindstrom family gather at Le Refuge for Christmas, as if the sheer number of people will somehow prevent Claire and Ally from noticing their mother is missing.

"Oh, I'm fine," I say, trying to sound as breezy as possible. "In fact, I'm loving being a second mommy to Claire and Ally." As if on cue, Claire and Ally race into the great room, careening past me and Eva and screeching with enthusiasm upon seeing their cousins.

"Come see the dollhouse that Daddy got for us," Claire says, "it's up in my room!"

Eva's daughters toss off their candy-colored down jackets and leave them scattered on the great room floor before running with Claire and Ally up to Claire's bedroom. Their fluffy fleece boots leave large wet footprints on the floor. I take off my apron and blot up the largest puddles, and then I pick up the jackets, roll them up like down-filled sushi and tuck them into the individually labeled nooks in the adjacent mudroom.

"Alex, you've outdone yourself," Eva comments as she walks through the great room. Alex appears in the main entryway, his short-cropped hair pomaded into a Kewpie doll–like peak. He's wearing a silk ascot and crisp-pressed shirt underneath his cashmere shawl-collar sweater. Sam told me that Beth hired Alex to help design the perfect Scandinavian Christmas interior for Le Refuge. Beth and Alex spent hours poring over interior design magazines and Pinterest pages to create the understated but festive look.

The great room is dominated by four Christmas trees of varying sizes—one for each person in the family—from a special tree farm in Maine. A specially trained arborist carefully prunes each tree, almost like a bonsai, so that the individual branches are widely spaced and perfectly balanced. Guarding each tree is a large straw goat that Alex orders from Sweden each year. Alex once said the goats are handwoven by Swedish virgins, which I assumed was a joke. This year, when the enormous boxes arrived by FedEx, the invoice confirmed that the straw goats had indeed been crafted by a small cloister of nuns in a remote town in Sweden. The cost of shipping alone was more than my annual bonus.

Each tree has its own decorative theme. The largest Christmas tree is covered with wooden hearts painted glossy red. The next largest shimmers with shiny silver balls and crystal snowflakes. The third is festooned with porcelain candy canes and gingerbread men. And the smallest tree, which always reminds me of the Charlie Brown Christmas tree, features angels handwoven in straw by the same Swedish virgins who crafted the goats. Instead of electric lights, the four Christmas trees are lit with small white candles sitting in antique tin holders.

"I had to drive all over Pennsylvania Dutch country to find these," Alex explained at the first Le Refuge Christmas. "No one makes them today because they violate fire regulations, so there's a huge underground market for them."

"Isn't that dangerous?" I asked.

"Not with trees as fresh as these," Alex sniffed.

Eva surveys each tree carefully, as if looking for a flaw. She picks at some melted wax on Ally's tree. "These candles are almost burned-out," she says. "Someone needs to replace them."

Alex heads upstairs with their designer luggage, while Eva walks over to the wine pantry and pours two enormous goblets of red wine.

"How was your visit to Alderson?" Eva asks, handing a goblet to me.

"Fine," I say. "Beth seems well. And Alderson isn't nearly as bad as you might think."

"I have no interest in ever visiting," Eva says.

"How about you, Eva?" I ask, trying to lighten the mood. "How are your girls liking school?"

"Stevie just finished her first semester at Madeira and loves it." Eva beams. "She adores the equestrian program, of course. Can you believe I ran into my French teacher from my high school days? She used to teach at NCS but moved to Madeira after I graduated. She recognized me right away and said I looked like I could be in high school myself."

Eva suddenly stops talking.

"Did I say something funny?" she asks.

"Oh no, not at all," I say. My darn poker face. Our awkward conversation is interrupted when Eva's youngest daughter bursts in crying.

"What is it?" I ask. "What's wrong?"

"No one's playing with me," she wails.

I slide off the couch and get down to her level.

"Where are the other girls?" I ask.

"They're all in Auntie Beth's room with Claire and Ally."

"What are they doing in Auntie Beth's room?" I ask.

"I don't know," she cries.

"Auntie Hannah and I will come upstairs," Eva sighs, "if you'll just stop your incessant whining." When we enter Claire's bedroom, the dollhouse pieces are strewn all over the floor as if a tiny tornado just blew through.

"Oh my God, Småland," Eva says. She picks up the miniature Christmas stocking and holds it with reverence.

"How do you know Småland?" I say. I'd never heard the name before reading it on the ridiculously unhelpful instructions that accompanied the dollhouse.

"When I was young, my parents took Martin and me into Stockholm at Christmastime to see the windows of the fancy NK department store. This was before Beth was even born.

One of the windows was of a little girl's room decorated in beautiful cream-and-pink-striped silk, and in the center of the room was a Småland dollhouse with a big Christmas bow on top. I always woke on Christmas morning hoping to find a Småland dollhouse under the tree." While Eva is talking, we pick up the dollhouse accessories—a rust-orange bean-bag chair, a crusty loaf of bread—and place them carefully in their designated spots.

"It wasn't until years later," Eva continues, "when we moved to the Swedish Embassy in DC, that we finally got one. Of course, by then, I was too old to play with dollhouses."

Our conversation is interrupted by distant shrieks from Beth's bedroom. We make our way down the hallway, Eva opens the door, and the scent of tuberose hits me like a tidal wave, reminding me of the last time Beth was here. It's hard to believe her scent lingers on nearly four months later. The four girls are lying on their stomachs on Beth's bed, looking at one of Beth's Shutterfly photo albums and laughing hys-terically. Piles of other albums are strewn all over the ground and on the bed.

"What's so funny?" Eva asks.

The girls look up and start laughing even harder.

"Is this you, Auntie Eva?" Claire asks, pointing to the page.

Eva leans over to see what the girls are looking at, and her face turns a strange color. She grabs the album and screams, "You girls know better than to come in here. This bedroom is off-limits. And look what a mess you made." The girls seem unfazed, as if used to Eva's outbursts. They jump up and rush out, giggling the whole way, leaving me and Eva alone in Beth's room.

Eva's face starts to return to its normal color as she picks up the albums from the bed and floor and places them haphazardly on the bookshelf. I follow silently behind her, re-arranging the albums in their proper order.

I know the photo that the girls were laughing at, the one that made Eva so upset. It was taken during Eva's freshman year in college. She's sitting at her dorm room desk, her mousy brown hair cut into an unflattering bowl with bangs. Her thick-lensed glasses distort her eyes, and she appears considerably heavier—perhaps forty pounds heavier—than her current slim self. In the background, her roommates are casually laughing. Sam told me Beth spent weeks pulling together old photographs to compile the album for Eva's fortieth birthday present, but Eva never even acknowledged it.

It never ceases to amaze me how quickly children can create a mess. As Eva heads back downstairs, I linger awhile longer to return Beth's room to its pristine state. I line up the photo albums on the shelf, plump the goose-down pillows and smooth out the duvet.

By the time I get back to the great room, Eva's already opened another bottle of wine and poured herself a glass. She turns on the plasma TV and starts scrolling through the channels until she gets to the Food Network. It's yet another episode of *Diners, Drive-Ins and Dives*. As Guy Fieri shovels an obscenely huge burger into his mouth and compliments the juxtaposition of the fatty meat with the acidic bite of the kimchi pickles, Eva puts the TV on Mute.

"I can't stand that guy's voice," she mutters.

A commercial comes on for Tide detergent. It shows an angelic little girl walking along a sunny beach boardwalk and spilling a chocolate ice-cream cone on her pretty cotton dress. The girl erupts in tears, and her impossibly young mother comforts her. The scene cuts away to the young mother rubbing the stain with a touch of Tide, with the final scene showing the little girl blowing out her birthday candles wearing that same pretty cotton dress while her mother looks proudly on. She seems to be just as proud of her laundry skills as she is of her precious daughter.

I feel a lump in my throat.

"It breaks my heart to think of Beth being apart from Claire and Ally for so many years," I say. "Claire's just in kindergarten, and Ally's not even in preschool. Even if Beth gets time off for good behavior, Claire will be in middle school by the time she's released."

"Yeah, well," Eva says, "I guess that's the price you pay when you're a murderer."

My heart stops for a moment. Did Eva really just call her own sister a murderer?

"What do you mean?" I ask. "You don't actually believe that, do you?"

The instant the words come out of my mouth, I want to take them back. The cold look on Eva's face reminds me of something Sam once said to me in private: "Eva seems normal on the outside, but she's got some seriously fucked-up issues with Beth."

"Of course I believe it," Eva says. "Don't tell me you don't. Beth might have been able to con your poor brother into believing her 'I only pled guilty to reduce my prison time' excuse, but I can't believe someone as smart as you would buy it. Pictures don't lie."

I don't need to ask what pictures she's talking about. For a while, they were featured on every newspaper, magazine cover and cable news show in the country. They showed dozens of teenage girls suffering from anorexia after becoming addicted to Metamin-G. When news broke about the girl in California who died of Metamin-G–related anorexia, the accompanying pictures were even worse. You couldn't go a day without being bombarded by images of her wholesome friends crying at her high school memorial service, her grief-stricken parents holding on to one another at her gravesite, the girl's skeletal body in its final days.

Both Beth and God Hälsa's CEO were pilloried for allegedly promoting Metamin-G for such off-label uses as weight loss, academic performance enhancement and treatment of social anxiety. God Hälsa's once-premium stock price plummeted as the company was accused of putting personal and corporate greed before the well-being of young women prone to depression and anorexia. It was a media feeding frenzy, and Beth's telegenic face was the bait. The federal whistle-blower lawsuit against God Hälsa was not only the talk of legal and financial circles; it became top news everywhere. *People* and *Us* even did photo features on Beth's designer outfits at various court appearances. Paparazzi started stalking her like she was a Hollywood celebrity.

"Yes, I've seen the photographs," I say, "but you can't blame that poor girl's death on Beth. I mean, all drugs have side effects. When you read the litany of potential side effects for any drug, it's like a parade of horribles—dry mouth, erratic heartbeat, erections that last for hours. I haven't seen any credible evidence that Beth intended for those girls to get sick or die. I think the federal prosecutors were just playing hardball so they could get God Hälsa to settle and prove to the public that they were being tough on white-collar criminals, and Beth was unlucky enough to get caught in the cross fire."

I'm slightly breathless by the time I finish my defense of Beth. I don't know what came over me. Neither apparently does Eva, who casts a cold stare in my direction.

"I guess I underestimated you, Hannah," Eva finally says.

And then she unmutes the volume.

lise

From the deposition of Lise Danielsson in *United States of America et al. v. God Hälsa AB, Andreas Magnusson and Elizabeth Lindstrom*

Q: Are you acquainted with Mr. Martin Lindstrom?

A: Sure, that's Beth's older brother.

Q: How would you describe their relationship?

A: Beth and Martin are really close. They spend holidays together. They go on vacation together. They even have a business together.

Q: Ms. Lindstrom has a business with her brother?

A: Yeah, sure. The two of them plus a third guy.

Q: Do you know what kind of business it is?

A: Beth told me they sell stuff to the government.

Q: Do you know what role Ms. Lindstrom plays in the business? What she does?

A: Beth mostly just gives her brother money, and Martin and the other guy run the actual business.

Q: How long have Ms. Lindstrom and her brother been in business together?

A: Oh gosh, I don't know. Way before I started working for Beth.

Q: So the business must be successful?

A: Actually, no, I don't think so. Martin's always asking for more money.

Q: Why would a smart businesswoman like Ms. Lindstrom continue to invest in a failing business?

A: I don't really know. All I know is that Beth said she'd do anything for Martin. That she owes him a lot.

beth

seventeen

Christmas has come and gone, but my cube is still decorated with the cards and photos that Hannah sent me as part of her "Twelve Days of Christmas" theme.

My favorite is the photo of Claire and her ballet class as nine ladies dancing. They're all wearing matching pink leotards and fluffy tutus. I'm happy to see Claire seems to be growing out of her awkward chubby phase.

It's boring in prison. I peruse the stack of reading material piled up on my footlocker. Also part of Hannah's "Twelve Days of Christmas" campaign. The only gifts the BOP allows from the outside are books and magazines, so Hannah's always ordering me stuff she thinks I'd like.

Honestly, I'm not much of a reader. Never have been. I let the other gals in the unit have their pick of my stuff. One of my patented methods of winning friends and influencing people.

"Hey, Lindstrom," Deb calls into my cube. "Ya comin' to dinner?"

I glance at my brand-new Fitbit. My Christmas gift to myself. Commissary only had a few in stock, but I asked Sandy to set one aside for me.

It's not even five o'clock. I still can't get used to having dinner so early. Some nights, like when they're serving overcooked spaghetti noodles in soy sauce that they try to pawn off as chow mein, I don't even bother to eat. Most nights, though, I make the trek as much to kill time than anything else.

"You know what they're serving tonight?" I ask.

"How could you forget?" Deb asks. "It's pizza night."

Pizza night. One of the highlights of the Alderson social season.

I jump off my top bunk and walk with Deb from A Building to CDR.

Central Dining Room is about a five-minute walk from the living units. When we arrive, there's already a long line.

Of course. It's pizza night.

"I don't think I'm up for this," I say to Deb.

Deb struts to the front of the line and glares at the inmate.

"Thanks for saving me a spot," she tells the unsuspecting victim.

Most people at Alderson wouldn't get away with such a ballsy move, but Deb's not most people. Since Meatloaf Mary died, everyone's more afraid of Deb than ever. Even the COs are scared to give her grief.

Deb seems to revel in her growing notoriety.

"Lindstrom, whatcha waitin' for?" she calls to me.

I walk past the pairs of glaring eyes and join Deb. I know what everyone thinks: that I'm Deb's new girlfriend. Her Sugar substitute. But it's not true. I've managed to hold her off so far. I have to be careful, though. No one likes a cocktease.

"Yo, *chicas!*" Juanita calls from behind the service line. She's got her thick black hair trapped inside a white mesh net, but she still manages to look stunning. Her smile could light up a stadium.

Juanita gives Deb and me a wink as she grabs a couple double slices and puts them on our trays. The girl next to her doles out a scoop of greenish-gray string beans.

Deb and I have our pick of seats in the dining room. We grab a couple cartons of apple juice and utensils before sitting down at a table by the window.

"You and Flores seem tight," Deb says.

"Yeah, she's an awesome bunkie," I reply. "I lucked out."

"That's how me and Sugar got started. Just bunkies."

"Well, that's all we are," I say.

"Maybe you'll change your minds."

"I don't think so. She's not my type."

Deb grunts as she digs into the slice of pizza on her tray. The gal really knows how to pack it away. I take the double slice off my tray and place it on hers.

"Italian food doesn't agree with me," I say.

I've always had a love-hate relationship with Italian food. It started over twenty years ago, the summer after I graduated from high school. It was a soft summer evening in Rome's Trastevere district. Locals and tourists sat elbow to elbow in the romantic cafés that line the Piazza.

Even though it's my first time visiting Europe, I can identify the American tourists right away: they're the fat ones wearing tacky Colosseum T-shirts and gorging themselves on pizzas and pasta at five o'clock. Europeans won't be dining for at least another few hours.

My brother, Martin, is hungry and tired from a long day of sightseeing. He begs to go somewhere less busy, but I ignore him. *Let's Go Europe* says this is the place to be, and I refuse to leave the center of action just to satisfy my brother's animal urges.

I stroll around the Piazza looking for the coolest-looking café and settle on a place called Rossetti's. I ask the waitress if there's a waiting list, and she acts like she doesn't understand me. I haven't met a single goddamn Italian who speaks English. She points at the tables on the patio as if to say, "Good luck—it's every man for himself."

I check out the scene to see if anyone's likely to abandon their spot.

My pulse quickens when an elegant woman gets up as if to leave. The metal legs of her chair sound like fingernails on a blackboard as they scrape against the ancient cobblestones. But her male companion stays behind, and soon she returns with a fresh coat of scarlet lipstick. The man raises his fingers, and the waitress replaces their empty glasses with full ones.

"Fuck this," Martin grunts, "let's get out of here, Beth. I'm starving."

Martin's been a pain in the ass for most of the trip.

I know Martin's going through a tough time. He had to quit Dartmouth a semester shy of graduation when Papa refused to pay his tuition. He used his frat contacts to land a series of jobs on Wall Street but got fired from them all. Now Martin's unemployed, nearly homeless and twenty pounds overweight from a diet of fast food and beer.

I thought a trip to Europe would lift his spirits, but I was wrong. It just seemed to make him miss the comforts of home, even if the comforts consisted of nothing more than a stained twin-size futon and a four-foot tower of empty pizza boxes.

"Beth," Martin repeats, "I said let's get out of here."

I notice a sad-eyed man looking straight at me. He's sitting by himself, a nearly full glass of beer in front of him. When our eyes lock, he smiles and cocks his head to join him. I reach for Martin's arm to signal that we're together. The man smiles more broadly as if to indicate, "Yes, both of you are welcome."

Martin and I join the sad-eyed man, who seems as grateful for company as we are for seats. The waitress saunters over, and I try to sound casual as I order a negroni.

"A negroni?" Martin asks. I want to wipe the smirk off his snarky face.

I'm barely eighteen and don't have much experience with alcohol other than the occasional glass of wine at Christmas dinner. When my high school girlfriends and I manage to sneak into a bar and not get carded, my drink of choice is rum and Diet Coke.

"Hey, when in Rome," I say.

Martin orders a pizza and beer. I feel so lucky to have snagged a table that I don't give him a hard time for his American eating habits.

The sad-eyed man introduces himself as Paulo, a businessman from Brazil. His English isn't great but it's better than my Portuguese, which is nonexistent. I don't even speak Spanish.

"I can tell by the way you look at each other that you are young lovers, no?" Paulo says.

"What?" I ask.

"You are young lovers, no? On your honeymoon?"

Martin lets out a quick laugh and then drapes his arm along the back of my chair. He looks soulfully into my eyes and says in a faux Spanish accent, "Oh yes, we are young lovers. Young lovers on our honeymoon."

Paulo nods, proud of his powers of observation.

"Oh no," I say, swatting Martin's arm off the back of my chair. "We're not...what you think. He's my brother. I'm his sister."

Paulo looks at me, then Martin, then me again. We all have a good laugh.

Martin's pizza arrives, and he digs in.

"Beth, you should eat," he mumbles with his mouth full.

Instead, Paulo and I order another round of drinks. As the evening wears on, Martin orders more food, and Paulo and I order more drinks.

"Beth, it's late," Martin finally announces, patting his stomach. I notice his gut hanging over his shorts and feel ashamed for him. "I'm ready to go to bed."

"You go ahead," I say. "It's our last night in Rome, and I want to spend a little more time enjoying it."

Martin is unsure. He wants to leave but doesn't want to leave me.

Paulo smiles warmly. "Don't worry, my friend," he says, "I have a younger sister, too. I will take care of her like a brother."

Martin heads back to the hotel, and Paulo and I hang out for another hour. I tell him about living in New York and my plans to attend Barnard in the fall; he tells me about his hometown of Rio and all the beautiful women who live there.

It's almost midnight when I start to get sleepy. Martin and I got up early to see the sights, and now I can barely keep my eyes open.

"I think I better go now," I say, and Paulo nods. He summons the waitress, who brings us the bill. Shit, those drinks really add up.

I pull out the Amex that Papa gave me for emergencies, decline Paulo's half-hearted offer to pay for his beers and hope that Papa won't get the statement until after I've left for college.

Paulo offers to pay the tip, and I gladly accept. He pulls a well-worn and crumpled note from his pants pocket and leaves it on the table. I can't see how much it is, but as we leave, the waitress looks disgusted picking it up.

Paulo and I are silent as we make our way toward my hotel. Away from the bright, buzzy atmosphere of the café, we seem to have nothing to say to one another.

I stumble as my shoe gets stuck in a crack in the cobble-stones, and Paulo catches me in his beefy arms. Paulo crouches down to pull my shoe from the crevice and place it back on my foot. He looks up and smiles as if to reassure me, but his eyes don't meet mine.

He's looking up my skirt.

Paulo offers his arm, and I reluctantly accept. The negronis have kicked in, and I've completely lost my sense of balance. As we keep walking, I see the sign for a gelato shop—the same gelato shop we've already passed twice—and I realize I've also lost my sense of direction.

Paulo seems to sense my confusion.

"You are lost?" he asks.

"No, not lost," I say, "just a little turned around."

We turn onto a quiet side street, and Paulo grabs me by the waist. He takes a step closer to me, and I instinctively take a step away. It's like we're doing the tango, but Paulo won't stop advancing until my back is literally up against the cool stucco wall of a closed souvenir shop.

Paulo kisses me so deeply that I nearly gag, but I don't want to do anything that would make him angry. I moan softly, pre-tending to appreciate his affections. Encouraged by my response, Paulo shoves his hand up my skirt, his fingers into my crotch.

"No," I yell, pushing his hand away.

"Your mouth says no," Paulo hisses, "but your *cona* says yes." He puts his fingers into my mouth, chuckles at my sur-prise and then sticks them back up my pussy.

Paulo starts kissing me again, his hot breath reeking of stale beer and cigarette smoke, the thrusting of his grotesque tongue keeping rough rhythm with the thrusting of his fat fingers.

A year later, my girlfriends and I will be sitting in the Barnard Women's Health Center with a dog-eared copy of *Our Bodies, Ourselves*, inspecting our vaginas with a hand-held mirror and tasting our own fluids in a radical act of self-empowerment.

But on that steamy night in Rome, all I can taste is humiliation.

Paulo's weight is heavy against me, and I realize I'm trapped. I have a flashback to the poor frog that I did such a pathetic job of dissecting in high school biology class, its tender skin peeled away and pinned to the wax tray, revealing its delicate vital parts.

"Get your hands off my sister, you asshole!"

Martin appears out of nowhere, pulls Paulo off me and pushes him to the ground.

"Are you okay?" Martin asks.

I nod but break into tears. Martin draws me close and holds me tight. I've never loved anyone more.

"Shush," he says, "I'm here now."

Paulo suddenly stands up and punches Martin. Once, twice, three times. Martin falls to his knees and then to the ground, blood streaming from his face onto the cold, hard cobblestones.

Paulo looks at me, then at Martin, spits at us both and says, "Fuck you, you fucking Americans." Then he kicks Martin twice in the stomach for good measure.

Martin and I spend the rest of the night at the Rome American Hospital waiting for the doctors to stitch up his right eye and confirm that he doesn't have any broken ribs. In the years ahead, countless women will admire the tough sexiness of his broken nose, but I'll forever be reminded that it's my fault.

That night in the Piazza wasn't the first time Martin came to my rescue and paid a hefty personal price. As I sat there in the hospital feeling the warm blood oozing from my crotch and running down my leg, I made a vow to myself.

It would absolutely be the last.

hannah

eighteen

Two weeks straight is a long time to spend with the Lind-stroms. Christmas was just a week ago but already seems like a distant memory. Outside, the snow-covered recycling bin is overflowing with empty wine and vodka bottles. Even the kids seem hungover from too much soda and video games.

The Lindstroms are not the warmest of families, but Eva and Karen at least make an effort to make polite conversation with me, to invite me to their girls' birthdays and other family gatherings. Beth's brother, Martin, on the other hand, has spoken fewer than a hundred words to me in the many years we've known one another—maybe a thousand if you count cocktail orders. Martin always struck me as a male chauvinist, a guy's guy, someone who's most comfortable in the company of his Dartmouth frat brothers or business colleagues than anyone of the opposite sex, including his own wife and daughters. Given this history, I'm surprised when Martin invites me to have lunch with him on New Year's Eve. "A time to talk, just the two of us," he says.

"Wow, this place looks lovely," I say as we pull up to a country French restaurant just outside St. Michaels. "How in the world did you find it?"

"The senior senator from Maryland loves their food," Martin says. "He's chair of the appropriations committee, so I come here all the time. It's not great for my cholesterol levels but what can you do? Occupational hazard of the job."

The exuberant chef/owner personally greets Martin at the restaurant entrance and shows us to Martin's usual table by the geranium-bedecked windows.

"And what is it that you do, exactly?" I ask. Sam once described Martin as one of those people responsible for those solid gold military toilet seats you read about in the paper from time to time, but I never understood what that meant.

"I'm the chief customer officer at EMC Partners."

"And what does EMC Partners do?"

"EMC is one of the leading strategic sourcing companies in the Mid-Atlantic. We work with Fortune 500 companies to leverage their competitive advantages in price and quality while moving the needle on critical supplier diversity goals."

This all sounds like marketing gobbledygook to me. We pause our conversation as the waitress pours a splash of wine into Martin's glass. Martin take a sip, swishes it thoughtfully in his mouth and nods. I place my hand over the rim and shake my head when the waitress attempts to pour some wine into my glass.

"Oh, come on, Hannah, loosen up," Martin says. He reaches over to remove my hand from the glass. "For my sake. I hate to drink alone." Martin looks at me warmly, the corners of his eyes crinkling just so. My cheeks radiate heat as I compli-antly nod. The waitress deftly pours me a glass.

"To the family. And to us. Cheers," Martin says, lifting his glass for a toast.

"Cheers," I reply, hoping the wine won't go to my head.

After the salad plates have been cleared, Martin confides, "Hannah, I wanted us to have lunch so we could talk about Sam. I'm worried about him." Martin's words are as surpris-ing as they are comforting. Perhaps it's the wine, but sitting so close together, it becomes apparent to me how Martin was able to attract a lovely woman like Karen. He's wearing a fine-gauge cotton sweater in a shade of cornflower blue that matches his eyes. He smells clean but masculine like he just showered with a bar of Irish Spring. There's a slight bump in the middle of his nose from when he broke it—a boxing in-jury perhaps—which is oddly sexy in its tough imperfection.

"You know I think the world of your brother," Martin says. He stops talking and leans back as two waiters arrive with our entrees: filet mignon steak for Martin, truite aman-dine for me. The waiters stand there like the Queen's guards, one at either side of the table, and set our plates before us si-multaneously.

"As I was saying, you know I think the world of Sam," Martin continues. He sounds as if he's returning to a script. Martin doesn't touch his food, so I don't either. The buttery aroma of my trout is tantalizing but I don't want to seem ill-mannered, chomping away like a churl while Martin is try-ing to have a serious conversation.

"I remember the first time we met," Martin says. For a mo-ment, I think he means the two of us but quickly realize he's talking about him and Sam. "Beth didn't have a lot of boy-friends growing up. The guys she brought home were mostly Eurotrash who'd spend Thanksgiving with us and invite her to Gstaad or Mykonos for Christmas. Beth always had a knack for getting what she wants out of other people."

I'm mesmerized by Martin. I love the way the words *Gstaad* and *Mykonos* roll off his tongue. He reminds me of a news anchor, a hybrid of Peter Jennings and Anderson Cooper.

"Frankly, I was seriously worried that Beth played for the other team, if you know what I mean. The whole family had heard rumors about her exploits at Barnard. So we were delighted when Beth brought Sam to meet the family. Here he was, this good-looking, athletic, charming guy who was obviously smitten by Beth, and she seemed to return the feelings."

It's one of my pet peeves when people overuse the word *frankly*. It's a verbal tic that people use as empty filler or as an excuse to say something that would otherwise be offensive.

"While everyone agrees that Sam's a terrific guy, I don't think it's a secret that Beth has always been the main breadwinner in the family. These past couple years have been really rough on them financially. Beth stopped making an income. Their lawyer bills and the huge restitution payments ate through their savings."

My heart stops. This lunch isn't about family. This lunch is about money.

"Frankly, it was an uncomfortable situation. When I first convinced Beth to help form EMC Partners, I promised her that Chaz and I would do all the work—she could just be a silent partner. And for the past fifteen years, I've been true to my word."

"Chaz? Who's Chaz?"

"Charles Butterworth III. He's a fraternity brother of mine from Dartmouth and a genius with the numbers. He's the *C* in EMC Partners."

"And Beth is the *E*," I say, the picture suddenly clear.

"Yes, EMC Partners is Elisabeth, Martin and Charles. Beth

provides the cash, Chaz provides the financial acumen and I'm the customer relations interface."

"And who are your customers?"

"We work with a number of major corporations. They want to do business with the federal government, and the federal government wants to do business with them. But here's the thing, the bleeding-heart liberals have imposed certain minority quotas—what they call 'supplier diversity targets'—on every federal agency. That's where EMC comes in. We get a contract with the agency to supply the products they want, and we subcontract with the major corporations in exchange for a share of the revenues. Win-win."

I'm familiar with supplier diversity targets. At my law firm, we're always getting pressure from our corporate clients to subcontract work to minority-owned firms. The managing partner once suggested converting Tracy and me into subcontractors and counting our librarian services toward our supplier diversity targets, but Old Man Barker interceded on our behalf.

"Sorry if this sounds rude, but how is your business diverse?" I ask. The Lindstroms are perhaps the whitest family I've ever met.

"Chaz is part black, and Beth is a woman, so we're well over the 50 percent diversity threshold. When Beth got wind that she might be in legal trouble, she signed over her share of EMC to Sam. Thanks to Sam's Oriental status, we're able to maintain our diverse credentials."

I see the butter has started to congeal, the transparent sheen on the trout now taking on an unpleasant opacity.

"I don't need to tell you Beth's legal troubles have been devastating for the entire family. At one point, the prosecutors even put me on their witness list, threatening to open up EMC's business to public scrutiny. We weren't doing anything wrong, mind you, but your Average Joe doesn't have a clue how things get done in Washington. Once there's blood in the water, the media sharks will swarm in, and then it's all over. Nobody wants to do business with you again. We avoided that trouble when Beth pled guilty.

"Anyway, I've been lying low for a year because I wanted to give Sam time to get back on his feet. Now that things have settled down, we need Sam to provide some short-term cash to make payroll. That's what Beth always did when we were waiting for our bids to come through. This past year, though, Sam hasn't paid a single cent toward the business. With Chaz out on medical leave, I've had to cover all of EMC's costs.

"At last count, Sam owes the business over half a million bucks. I've asked him a couple times to pay, but he keeps putting me off. I know how much he values your opinion, and I was hoping you could talk to him about it. Frankly, I'm sorry Sam has put us both in this awkward position."

In my mind, I hear Karen at Claire's school performance. *You probably don't know, Hannah, but Sam owes us quite a lot of money.* Something clicks into place. And with that, Martin saws off a chunk of his steak and shovels it into his mouth. The red wine has stained his large, horselike teeth purplish gray. There's a heavy dusting of dandruff on his sweater, and wiry hairs and blackheads on his nose. I look out the window and notice that the geraniums are fake, made of cheap polyester and plastic. The parking lot is filled with Humvees and other gas-guzzling luxury cars. I wonder how many of the meals in the room are being paid with taxpayer dollars.

I'm not sure how long I've been lost in thought when I hear the clatter of Martin's fork and knife against his plate. He's practically inhaled his meal and is busy cleaning his top incisors with a wooden toothpick.

"Is something wrong?" the waitress asks. She points to my

untouched plate. "Would you like your meal wrapped to go?" I shake my head.

"I'm afraid I may have upset you," Martin says. He reaches over for my hand. I wait a moment—the minimum that politeness requires—before pulling it away.

"It's just…" I begin. "It's just that Sam isn't exactly in a position to be giving away money. He's been struggling to make ends meet himself."

It feels like I'm betraying Sam, admitting his weakness to Beth's older brother, but I also want to protect Sam from any further financial pressure. The corners of my mouth quiver as I struggle to contain tears. I'm embarrassed by my show of emotion.

"I know what struggling feels like," Martin murmurs. It makes me wonder: *Is this the real Martin, or the customer relations professional?* "Like I said before, I've been lying low this past year to give Sam some time to recover. But meanwhile, I haven't been able to bring home a single regular paycheck. Karen and I have eaten through our savings. We've taken out a second mortgage on our house. We haven't gone on a real vacation in over two years. Karen and I are even thinking about pulling the girls out of their school, but we hate to separate them from their friends."

I think back to that sunny morning at Le Refuge when I made Mickey Mouse pancakes with Karen and Martin's daughters. They've always been such affectionate girls, full of sweet smiles and generous hugs. They even call me Auntie Hannah, like a true blood relative. My heart aches at the thought of them suffering.

"Can I interest either of you in dessert?" the waitress asks as the busboy clears away the dishes. We both decline.

"Will you at least think about it?" Martin asks.

I nod compliantly. I feel like a fraud, but I don't know what else I can do. When the check comes, Martin insists on paying.

He puts it on his corporate card.

New Year's Eve has always been one of my least favorite holidays. It's right down there with Valentine's Day and Mother's Day—the other annual reminders of my spinsterhood—but recently, it's taken on an even worse connotation. It was New Year's Eve exactly one year ago that Sam first told me about Beth's legal troubles.

I'm sitting in my condo watching an old movie on cable when the phone rings. I know it's Sam because I programmed my home phone to play "The Entertainer" whenever he calls, although it's not like I need a musical cue. Except for telemarketers, Sam is the only one who ever calls my landline.

"Hey, stranger," I say. "What a treat to hear from you."

"Hey, Hannah. Happy New Year's Eve. Are you doing anything special tonight?"

Sam knows the answer. If it had been anyone else, the question would be cruel, but with Sam, I know he's just being lazy, making small talk.

"Nah, you know me—Little Miss Homebody. Just staying home and watching TV, the usual stuff. How about you? Don't you have a gala event or something fabulous tonight?"

"Not really. Beth and I are staying home and spending a quiet New Year's Eve with the girls. We promised Claire that she could stay up past midnight, so we're camping in the living room. Pillows and stuffed animals everywhere."

It's nice to imagine the scene. Sam and Beth had been going through a rough patch, so I'm relieved to hear they're a happy family again.

"Listen, Hannah, I have something I need to ask you," Sam says.

"Sure," I say. "What's up?"

"Are you sitting down?"

"Sam, you're scaring me. What is it?"

"Is there any way you can loan us a million dollars?"

"Ha ha, very funny," I respond—a response I instantly regret when Sam fails to say anything. "You're kidding, right?"

"I wish I were."

"What in the world do you need a million dollars for?"

"Hannah, I know you're not going to believe this, but Beth's going to prison. The feds are planning to issue a press release about it in the next couple days."

"Sam, if this is some sick joke, I don't get it."

"I wish it were a joke. Beth and her company have been talking with the feds for months. She's been accused of all sorts of crazy stuff. Beth and I were going to fight it to the end, but…well, things just started to look bad. Beth's lawyers convinced her to plead guilty. If we can raise a couple million dollars before her sentencing hearing, we might be able to reduce her time in prison."

"What are you talking about, Sam?" I ask. "What kind of crime could Beth possibly be accused of? And why in the world would Beth plead guilty?"

Sam describes the whistle-blower lawsuit. Lise, their Swedish au pair, has accused Beth and her company of illegally marketing Metamin-G for off-label uses. The Justice Department has been investigating the allegations and gotten the federal grand jury to return an indictment against both Beth and the company's CEO. It takes me a while to let Sam's words sink in.

"But companies get caught for stuff like that all the time," I say. "I've read about these cases at work. The company pays a fine, maybe a couple people lose their jobs. No one ever goes to prison."

"That's not happening here, Hannah. The government's

looking to send a message to the public, and those fuckers at God Hälsa are handing them Beth's head on a platter."

"Wait, wait, wait," I say. "This doesn't make any sense to me. Whistle-blower lawsuits don't result in prison time, just financial penalties."

"I haven't told you the worst part, Hannah. They're not just accusing Beth of fraud against the Medicaid and Medicare system. They're talking obstruction of justice. Securities fraud. Even manslaughter. Beth could face up to thirty years in prison."

"Oh my God, Sam," I say. My head starts to throb.

"Apparently, a bunch of girls became anorexic—one girl even died—while taking Metamin-G, and they're trying to say that Beth knew about the potential side effects and marketed the drug anyway."

"Come on, that's ridiculous. There's no way they could prove that."

There's silence on the line. I wonder if our connection's gone dead.

"Sam, are you still there?" I ask.

"Yeah," Sam grunts.

"What evidence could they possibly have?"

Sam refuses to answer.

"Sam, do you know what evidence they have?"

"My lawyer said the deposition was just a formality," Sam finally says. His voice is barely audible.

"Deposition? What deposition?"

"It was a disaster," Sam continues. "The lead prosecutor was this total bitch—this total manipulative, tricky bitch. She showed me some family pictures and caught me off guard with her questions. She asked me about Claire and Eva, stupid shit that Beth would sometimes say. You know Beth—she'd tease them about their weight but never meant anything by it.

She was just joking around. But the prosecutor would twist my words around—make it sound like Beth was some sort of monster. Like she was guilty."

My brain struggles to process Sam's words.

"I know I should have come to you before," Sam apologizes. "I wanted to ask for your advice as soon as we found out about the lawsuit, but—I don't know—I guess I thought I should be able to handle it on my own."

"Sam, slow down and listen to me. Didn't your lawyer tell you that you didn't have to be deposed? You're Beth's husband. You have the spousal privilege. That means they can't call you into court to testify against Beth, and they can't ask you questions in a deposition about anything the two of you talked about as a couple. You have the right to just say no."

"Yeah, I know, but they offered me immunity, Hannah."

Sam's not making sense. Why would the federal prosecutors offer him immunity? Then I realize Sam's probably just confused. He's not a lawyer. He doesn't know the difference between privilege and immunity. He doesn't know what these legal words mean.

"You don't need immunity, Sam," I say slowly. "You're not the one being prosecuted. The only reason you need immunity is if you're at risk of being prosecuted and put into prison."

"That's the whole point, Hannah," Sam says. "They said if I agreed to be deposed, then they *wouldn't* prosecute me."

As soon as the words come out of Sam's mouth, I feel a chill come over me. My poor, sweet, gullible brother. Of course he'd somehow get himself accidentally into trouble.

"Okay, Sam," I say, "what did you do?"

"It wasn't me, it was Alex," he says. Sam's defensive tone reminds me of when he was a little boy and would break a vase, a window, a promise. It was never his fault.

Sam goes on to confess his crimes.

"I can help," I say. "The lawyers at my firm used to work at the Supreme Court. They could probably find a way to challenge the admissibility of your deposition at trial. Or they could hold up Beth's case on appeal."

"It's over, Hannah," Sam says. "Beth's already pled guilty. There's nothing more to be done. Beth is going to prison. And it's all my fault."

I rack my brains for something to say. Some way to fix this broken, terrible mess.

"Hannah, believe me when I say I didn't want to testify against her," Sam says.

In the background, I can make out Claire and Ally shrieking and giggling. His voice cracking, Sam says, "But Beth told me to do it. She told me to do it for the girls."

beth

nineteen

"The New Year brings new beginnings," Juanita says. She's got her hair up in a do-rag and is scrubbing the lockers and floors with soapy water. Deb and I are sitting together on the bottom bunk, leafing through the latest *Bon Appetit* and *Southern Living* magazines and trying to stay out of Juanita's way.

"Need any help?" Deb asks.

"I could use another box of pads," Juanita says. She points to the pile of maxi-pads in the trash bin. "These things are so cheap, they fall apart as soon as they get wet."

"Not the best quality in a maxi-pad," I say.

"Hey, Lindstrom, why don't ya come with me," Deb says. She gives me a little shove as she squirms out of the bunk.

We walk together down the long hallway. Past the bus stop and the guards' desk to the storage closet by the bathrooms. As the head of cottage maintenance, Deb's literally got the keys to a lifetime supply of bleach, single-ply toilet paper and off-brand maxi-pads.

Deb opens the door, and I step inside. The storage space is stacked from floor to ceiling with brown cardboard boxes. Along the wall nearest the door is an open box filled with wooden handles. The kind you attach to a black rubber suction cup to use as a plunger. The kind Deb used to threaten Meatloaf Mary just weeks before she died.

Deb pulls the door shut behind us. The closet suddenly feels very small.

"You know, I'm not dumb," Deb says. "I know what people been sayin'."

"What do you mean?" I ask.

"About Meatloaf. About how she died."

"I thought no one knew how she died," I say.

"C'mon, you know people think I had somethin' to do with it."

It's true. Gossip and rumor spread quickly at Alderson. First, we heard the COs found a broken plunger handle in Mary's bunk. Then we heard the handle had traces of blood and shit on it. Then we heard Mary died choking on her own vomit.

With these details, everyone has a theory about how Deb killed Mary—most of them involving some type of sick sex torture.

"You and Flores—you don't believe it, do ya?" Deb asks.

"Believe what?"

"That I killed Meatloaf," Deb says.

"No, of course not," I lie.

Deb steps closer to look me in the eye. I avoid her glare by looking up.

And then I start to laugh.

"What's so funny?" Deb asks.

I reach up to the top shelf of the supply closet and pull down a brown cardboard box of maxi-pads. On the side of the box, next to the red, white and blue "Made in the USA" logo, are the words *Distributed by EMC Partners, a certified Minority Business Enterprise.*

"No wonder these things are so crappy," I say, laughing.

"Ya gotta fill me in," Deb says.

"This is my company," I say.

"So that's what got you in here? Making cheap-ass feminine hygiene products?"

"We didn't make 'em. We only distributed them."

"Wow, you're lucky you didn't get the death penalty," Deb says.

I try to play it light, but Deb looks deadly serious.

The door to the supply closet bursts open.

"Hey, whatcha doin' in there?" the CO barks. "It's not work hours. You're supposed to be in your cubes. I could give both of yous a shot."

"And happy New Year to you, too, Officer," Deb says. She hands me a box of pads and pretends to shove me out of the closet.

"We better get back before Juanita starts to wonder about us," she says.

I remember when Martin told me that EMC Partners got the contract with the Bureau of Prisons. It was over a decade ago—and over a decade after our European trip.

At that point, Martin and I are both full-grown adults trying to make our own way in the world. I've already been named VP of Marketing at God Hälsa, and Martin and his business partner are finally getting their company off the ground.

We're sitting in Martin's car. There's heavy traffic on the Chesapeake Bay Bridge.

"So, remind me what we're celebrating?" I ask.

"EMC Partners just won its first major government contract—supplying the federal prison system with paper products. Paper towels, toilet paper, stuff like that."

"Well, congratulations, Martin. It's been a long time coming."

"I know," Martin says. "I really appreciate your patience. And generosity."

"You really don't have to take me out to lunch, you know," I say, although what I really want to say is "I would've been happier to stay at my suite in the Four Seasons and order us room service."

After a week of endless meetings and negotiations with the FDA commissioner and his lackeys, I'm ready to lie back in luxury and style, but Martin wants to show off his newfound success to his younger sister, and I don't want to deny him that small victory.

"This place has a Michelin star," Martin explains as we clear the bridge and turn off the highway, "and the most amazing wine list. I've been dying to try it out. They say all the top DC power brokers go there."

It's almost 2:00 p.m. by the time we arrive at the restaurant—one of those French country-style places with white lace curtains and geraniums in the window. It looks charming, but I'm pretty sure this place isn't worth the nearly two-hour drive from Georgetown.

As we enter the main dining room, I assess the clientele. It's your typical Beltway Blend: Hermes-tied lawyer-lobbyists, congressmen with their gold lapel pins, pastel-toned Washington wives and a midlevel bureaucrat or two thrown in for good measure.

Your tax dollars at work.

The curvy waitress is wearing a clingy dress that shows off her big tits and nice ass. She greets Martin with a sexy smirk and wiggle of her hips. She reminds me a little of Karen, who was also in the service industry before she married Martin. Now that I think about it, so was his first wife. Maybe Martin has a thing for nubile, servile females.

Then again, who doesn't?

I'm reviewing the offerings on the menu when Martin leans in and whispers, "Over there, at three o'clock, is the assistant secretary of defense. God, I'd give anything for a meeting with him. Did I tell you that this place attracts all the DC power brokers?"

I couldn't care less if the POTUS himself were seated at the next table; I'm famished and dying for a drink. But I humor Martin by turning my head and nodding approvingly.

"I wonder if he's meeting with Rumsfeld," Martin says. "Both he and Cheney have places in town, you know."

"Town? What town?" All I could see on the way to the restaurant was vast open fields and flat expanses of pewter-colored water.

"St. Michaels," Martin explains. "A couple miles farther down the road. It's small and sort of touristy, but Karen and I like to pop over when we need a quick getaway from the hustle and bustle."

I try not to laugh at Martin's concept of hustle and bustle. For God's sake, he lives in Old Town Alexandria and drives a leased Lincoln.

"Speaking of quick getaways," I say, "is it true that you and Karen aren't coming to the Hamptons this summer?"

"Yeah, sorry, but Karen will be almost due by then, and it's a pain in the ass driving all the way to the Hamptons from DC in the summer. The New Jersey Turnpike is a nightmare, and don't get me started on the Parkway."

I pretend to examine the heavy leather-clad wine list, but I'm really sulking.

I remember back when I was still a struggling drug rep, sitting in that one-bedroom apartment and watching some documentary about Jacqueline Kennedy Onassis. Right after JFK was killed, Jackie created this myth of the Kennedy White House as a kind of Camelot.

Seeing those home videos of toothy-grinned Kennedys

playing football on the Hyannis Port lawn, all madras shorts and seersucker dresses and endless cocktails, I said to myself, *I want that life.*

"Last year, Eva bailed because she couldn't risk being so far from DC at nine months pregnant," I complain, "and now you and Karen are pulling the same line on me? Don't you guys have anything better to do than breed?"

"Maybe you should think about it yourself," Martin says. "After all, your eggs aren't getting any fresher."

"Fuck you very much."

"Excuse me," a blue-haired matron says. Her smile is saccharine as she leans in from the next table. "I couldn't help but overhear your conversation. If you're looking for a summer place closer to home, you really couldn't do any better than St. Michaels. We've got some lovely waterfront properties for sale."

She hands over her business card; she's a Realtor.

"Just think of the possibilities," she coos.

Maybe I'm weak from hunger, but I do start thinking. I see the tempting vision of a Camelot on the Chesapeake.

"How long a drive is it from Princeton to here?" I ask.

"Less than three hours," Martin responds. "And about two hours from DC. Really, Beth, it would be so much easier for us to get together here than in the Hamptons. Plus, if we owned a place instead of renting, we could get together every holiday and not just once a year during the summer."

I assume Martin is using the "royal we," since neither he nor Eva has the finances to buy a summer place or even go in on one with me. Martin and the Realtor talk about some lots for sale on the waterfront. They seem unusually friendly with one another.

"I forgot to mention the best part," the Realtor says.

"What's that?" I ask.

"It's also a great tax refuge," Martin finishes her thought.

hannah

twenty

January slowly gives way to February, and the freshly fallen snow on the city streets gradually turns slushy gray with salt, sand and exhaust. It's freezing cold outside but almost unbearably warm in the Grand Ballroom of the Marriott Marquis, the venue for this year's New York City Diverse Lawyers Association's awards ceremony.

The Drinker, Barker and Horne table is prominently located near the stage and populated by last-minute table fillers. The firm is winning Diversity Champion of the Year, so the partners felt compelled to buy a twenty-five-thousand-dollar Gold Sponsorship, which gets us a table for eight and a full-page color ad in the glossy program. Unfortunately, the luncheon organizers failed to realize the event conflicts with the American Bar Association's annual meeting, which is taking place this year in New Orleans and happens to coincide with both Valentine's Day and Mardi Gras. By the sparse attendance, it appears most of the city's lawyers couldn't resist the tempting trifecta of alcohol, business development and debauchery.

"What a depressing way to spend Valentine's Day," the bird-like young woman seated next to me mumbles to herself. She reminds me of a young Ruth Bader Ginsburg but by way of Mumbai rather than Brooklyn. She's a first-year litigation associate, the lowest rung on the firm's ladder, even lower than me or the head mailroom clerk, who also happens to be seated at our table. At DBH, as with most major law firms, there's roughly a one-in-twenty chance that a first-year associate will make partner. Every fall, law firms across the country bring in a new crop of associates in hopes of yielding one partner in ten years' time. As each year passes, the once-promising young lawyers buckle under from the burden of billing twenty-five hundred hours per year and repaying their massive student loans. The streets of New York are littered with JDs trying to avoid the ever-present threat of being tossed into the trash heap like yesterday's losing Lotto scratchers.

As the keynote speaker recounts her inspirational rags-to-riches tale, everyone at my table is looking down at their laps, their faces lit like a Caravaggio painting by the glow of their iPhones. In keeping with the theme of the luncheon, my firm's table looks admirably—and deceptively—diverse. The handsome African American man across the table from me is Andre, the security supervisor. The buxom Filipina next to him is the backup receptionist. I'm not sure, but I could swear the other two guys work in the firm's cafeteria. They look different without their hairnets. Except for the firm's Diversity Counsel and the Indian RBG, everyone else at our table is staff or, as most people at the firm call us, non-lawyers. That phrase has always irked me: non-lawyers. How can you define someone by what they are not? Then again, I don't really love the term "staff" either. It makes me feel like Mrs. Hughes from *Downton Abbey*.

I can't help but eavesdrop—or should I say e-drop?—on my dining neighbor's texts.

BORING!! No lawyers here. Just staff, the young lawyer writes.

Humiliating is the response.

Tell me about it.

What R U doing for V Day?

Fucking nothing. Literally.

Me 2. How long do U go w/o sex b4 U get Ur virginity back?

LMAO. I'd say the statute of limitations is 2 yrs.

Shit, wanna go out 2nite? I might get in under the wire.

The Indian RBG inserts a smiley face with a stuck-out tongue. Two years seems like a reasonable statute of limitations on virginity. By that standard, my virginity has been restored since before the senior Bush administration. No pun intended. Checking my own phone, there's a red dot on my CorrLinks icon indicating an email message from Beth. It's not like me to be so rude, but an email from Beth is too tantalizing to ignore.

Dear Hannah,
I've had the craziest day—the craziest week, actually—and it's not even over yet.

All week, my cube's been getting deliveries of Valentines and little gifts from women I hardly even know. Here's the listing of the gifts so far: two bottles of Bath & Body Works body wash (in Sensual Amber and Dark Kiss scents—don't love them but it's the thought that counts, right?), a box of Tampax Pearls (the prison provides free pads, but they're so cheap I'm sure they're filled with asbestos or something), an extra large bottle of Banana Boat SPF 50 sunblock (Eva would kill me if I let the West Virginia sun ruin my peaches and cream complexion) and several king-size chocolate bars (Almond Joy and Mounds, my favorites!).

This morning, Juanita and I got back from our Ballet Barre workout class to find a warm blueberry muffin, a crocheted heart-shaped pillow and a jar of Kiehl's Ultra Facial Cream. (Did I tell you my friend Sandy got promoted to head of commissary, and we convinced the warden to stock some quality beauty products? I told them my skin was breaking out from the nearly expired drugstore brands they usually offer, which is partly true. I think my bunkie's world-famous nachos with four-cheese topping are also to blame.) The muffin was from my awesome bunkie, who honestly has a future as the next Food Network Star: Prison Edition, the jar of Kiehl's was from Sandy and the heart-shaped pillow was from...wait for it...Deb the Destroyer.

The keynote speaker has finished, and the sparse audience breaks out into a round of applause, drowning out my gasp of surprise. Beth has written to me several times about Deb the Destroyer, the fearsome repeat convict who uses her massive bulk and terrible tongue to keep order at Alderson, but even Beth's colorful stories didn't adequately prepare me for the reality of the woman. When Beth pointed her out to me at my last trip to Alderson, both the ground and the inmates literally shook as the Destroyer entered the visitors' building.

> Apparently, Deb's secretly been taking crochet lessons from one of the old-timers. Can you believe it? I wish I could send you a photo. It's an elongated heart shape, with concentric ovals of red and pink yarn. I swear it looks like a giant clit. My bunkie's already taken to calling it the Pussy Pillow.

My cheeks flush reading Beth's words. Working among lawyers has inured me to most profanity, but words describing female genitalia still make me uncomfortable.

> They're serving a special Valentine's Day/Mardi Gras meal at CDR today. Jambalaya, corn bread, creamy coleslaw, king cake, chocolate mousse and sparkling (nonalcoholic) apple cider. God, what I would do for a glass of real champagne. I've heard that Deb makes a pretty tasty homebrewed hooch, but I don't want to press my luck by leading her on. My bunkie keeps teasing me that the Pussy Pillow could be a self-portrait. That girl is a complete laugh riot.
>
> Anyway, thanks for updating my Amazon wish list and getting me the Nora Roberts book. Most stylists charge a Pepsi six-pack for a haircut but mine won't accept anything less than the latest Nora or Danielle. I'd be tempted to find a new stylist, but the pickings around here are pretty slim, so I appreciate you keeping me looking my best. I can't be seen with dark roots, even at Alderson.
>
> Will you be able to visit me soon? I'm dying to hear what you've found out since your last trip.
>
> Have a good one.
>
> Love, Beth

After spending two hours at the Diverse Lawyers luncheon, I have to work late to get all my work done. It's past seven by the time I re-shelve the last book, neaten up the piles of legal research on my desk and shut down my computer. I decide to treat myself to a store-bought dinner instead of heating up a can of Progresso soup.

"That'll be $12.02," the clerk says, placing my salad in a large paper Whole Foods bag. Twelve dollars for a salad-bar salad? It's those darn beets. They're surprisingly heavy.

"Don't you have a smaller bag?"

"No, sorry," she responds, not looking sorry at all. I open my soft leather coin purse and remember giving my change to the homeless man sitting outside the Marriott Marquis. I felt so guilty seeing the untouched rubber chicken lunches that I couldn't just pass the man by, as if doling out $1.36 in nickels and pennies would somehow make up for the thousands of dollars in wasted food.

"All I've got is a twenty," I say. I scan the counter for a "Take a Penny, Leave a Penny" jar and show the clerk my empty coin purse.

"Okay," she says. She rings up the twenty and counts out seven dollars and ninety-eight cents in change. She apparently missed my internationally recognized gesture for "cut me a break on the two cents."

The brown paper bag rattles against the wind like a child's kite as I slowly make my way home. I gather the woolen scarf around my neck and lean into the icy draft. My neighborhood in Hoboken had been a quiet backwater when my parents helped me buy my one-bedroom condo back in the early 1990s, but like everything else in the greater New York metropolitan area, it's gotten popular and gentrified over the years. Along Washington Street, the old-school Italian red-sauce restaurants with their sticky checkered plastic tablecloths have given way to farm-to-table gastropubs with artisanal toast, and faux turn-of-the-century barbershops that cater to young men with boxy beards and waxed mustaches.

It feels good to enter my warm apartment. I turn the radio on in my kitchen. It's one of those walnut-sided Sony radios from the 1970s. I took it from my parents' home after they died. The radio dial is set to WQXR, the classical station, and Ravel's *Bolero* is playing. They always play *Bolero* on Valentine's Day. Everyone who's ever watched *The Partridge Family* knows that *Bolero* is the music of passion. I remember it from that episode where Keith tries to get lucky with a cheerleader—although it seems every episode involved Keith trying to get lucky with a cheerleader.

I neatly transfer the salad to a large white dinner plate. It's sad enough eating a salad-bar salad for Valentine's Day, but eating it straight out of the plastic container seems pathetic. I pour a glass of white wine from the shiny cardboard box in the fridge and take a sip. I'm not proud of the box wine, but *Real Simple* gave it good reviews, and I was getting self-conscious about all of the empty bottles in my trash—as if the local hoboes rummaging around for recyclables would go around bad-mouthing me.

Sitting at the dining table and flipping through the latest *New Yorker*, I can't focus on the words on the page. I keep thinking about the birdlike young woman's texts. I reach over for my laptop and start typing Owen's name, which automatically populates from the dozens of other times I've run the same Google search. I stare once again at the images of my onetime college boyfriend smiling at various Bay Area charity events. He's done quite well for himself, owning and operating several successful music venues in San Francisco: Alphaville, a gay bar and 1980s-style dance club in the Castro; Erasure, an electronic music space in SoMa with pitch-black walls and a dizzying menu of "energy drinks"; Culture Club, a café/bar/art gallery in Dogpatch featuring Blue Bottle Coffee, handcrafted cocktails and a coterie of heavily pierced and tattooed young artists. And there's his first venture, the one that made him famous: Stardust, a luxe 1920s-era speakeasy right on the San Francisco Bay featuring local and world-class jazz performers.

As I scroll through the photos, a wave of relief tinged with sadness washes over me seeing his graying hair and thickening waistline. According to a recent profile in *San Francisco* magazine, he got divorced a couple years ago and is currently single, which I'm embarrassed to admit gives me a small measure of consolation. I don't know why; it's not as if I have any chance with him now. After thirty years, I wonder if he ever thinks of me.

Owen and I met freshman fall in a class called Rhymes, Rhythms and Rhapsodies. It's one of those humanities survey courses that underclassmen take to fulfill their general education requirements and to prepare for the kind of erudite cocktail conversation expected of a Harvard graduate. Informally known as R-Cubed, the class is taught by two renowned experts in their respective fields of poetry and musicology and explores the relationship between poems and music over the centuries.

A couple years before I took the class, R-Cubed generated a swirl of controversy when the professors decided to add the then-burgeoning genre of rap music to the curriculum. For several weeks, the *New York Times* was filled with articles and op-eds bemoaning the decline and fall of classical higher education. The controversy led to a nearly fivefold increase in enrollment. R-Cubed had to be moved from a modest-size lecture hall in the music building to Harvard's imposing high Victorian Gothic cathedral of learning, Sanders Theatre.

Students were quickly made to realize they'd have to wade through volumes of Petrarch, Goethe and Auden and spend countless hours listening to Palestrina, Bach and Stravinsky before getting to hear even one verse of Afrika Bambaataa or Grandmaster Flash.

It is in the Loeb Music Library that I first meet Owen. Schubert's *Winterreise* is playing through my oversize head-phones when Owen pops his head over the carrel wall and gestures for me to remove them.

"Did you hear that?" he asks.

"Hear what?"

"Wait for it," he says. "It's oddly predictable."

I climb up on my carrel so that Owen and I are just a few inches apart. I strain to hear the mysterious noise, and then there it is: the distinctive sound of someone farting.

"It sounds like a cross between a trumpet and a tuba," he says.

"A French horn," I respond.

"Tooting his own horn?"

It's not that funny, but I'm a sucker for bad puns.

"I think it's that guy over there," he says. He looks toward a dumpy guy wearing a *Ghostbusters* T-shirt. I immediately feel sorry for him.

"It's not fair to accuse someone without proof," I say.

"I've got incriminating circumstantial evidence," Own says. "He keeps lifting his butt cheek every few minutes." Owen shifts his hip to demonstrate.

"Oh my God, that's gross."

"Let's get outta here before he busts out another one," he says. Owen jumps deftly off his carrel and extends his arm to help me off mine. Uncharacteristically, I don't hesitate to take the leap.

"Wanna get some ice cream?" he asks as we leave the building.

"Who doesn't like ice cream?" I reply. We walk from the library to Herrell's, my favorite of the nearly half dozen premium ice cream shops in Harvard Square. Each of us orders a single scoop in a cup—banana for me, coffee with Heath Bar smoosh-in for him—before heading to the register.

"I got this," Owen says, pulling out his billfold.

"Oh no," I say, "you don't have to."

"I know I don't have to—I want to." Owen pays the cashier and quietly slips a dollar in the "Leave the Change You Want to See in the World" tip jar. My heart warms at his generosity.

The normally crowded shop is quiet. We sit in the color-fully painted back room, which used to be a vault in the days when the store was a bank.

"So, how're you liking the class so far?" Owen asks.

"I love it. I've always loved poetry and classical music. How 'bout you?"

"Not so much. I took ten years of piano lessons and played way too much classical. I'm just waiting to get to the good stuff."

"I play piano, too," I say, not knowing what he means by "the good stuff."

Owen looks down at my hands. "You've got mighty small hands for a pianist," he says. He holds up his right hand. I lift my own hand and place it palm-to-palm with his. My fingers barely reach his first knuckle joints.

"You know what they say about big hands," Owen says. He takes a dramatic pause before cracking a smile. "Big gloves." We take down our hands and begin eating our now-melting ice cream in earnest.

"So, I've been sitting behind you in R-Cubed," Owen continues, "and couldn't help noticing your color-coding system for taking notes. But you never use green. Don't you like green?"

I clear my throat as a time filler. I don't know whether to be flattered or scared. Perhaps I'm a bit of both. No one has ever paid such close attention to me.

"I hope that's not too weird," Owen says. "It's just something I've been dying to ask. We four-color-pen types have to stick together." He reaches into his pants pocket and pulls out a Bic four-color pen. It's the kind with the blue barrel, medium point, just like mine.

I can feel my face flush as I stand up. Owen stands, too, as if trying to stop me from leaving. I shake my head and pull out my R-Cubed notebook. I open it up to the back pages and show him the contents: pages and pages of green ink drawings, tiny shapes and swirls that fit together like puzzle pieces. The pages are curled and rippled from the pressure of my pen point against the cheap, lined paper.

"I like to doodle when I listen to music," I say.

"Wow, they're really cool. They remind me of M. C. Escher."

Bingo—he got it on the first try. Owen looks at me with amazement, and for the first time in my life, I see myself reflected in his eyes.

All freshman year, Owen and I are inseparable. We eat together, we study together, we sleep together. No one is more surprised than me about my personal transformation. *Where did this person come from*, I wonder, *and what would my parents think if they knew?* By the time freshman year comes to an end, I can't bear the thought of returning home to my dreary life in Buffalo. More exactly, I can't bear the idea of being separated from Owen for three whole months. During our weekly calls, my parents tell me about Sam's latest run-ins with the neighbors. As usual, I feel the weight of responsibility—I should be home to help take care of him—but at the same time, I start to feel something new: a sense of independence, an impulse to run in the opposite direction.

"Stay in Cambridge with me," Owen says. We're squeezed together on the narrow mattress in Owen's dorm room. When outstretched, Owen's feet dangle over the end of the extra long bed, but he usually curls his body around mine, big *S* next to little *s*.

"I couldn't," I say.

"Why not?" he asks. "I've got a sublet in Porter Square lined up for the summer, and you can stay with me for free." It's an extremely tempting offer.

"But what would I do? I don't have a job or anything." Owen has already gotten a paid internship at a local music production company, courtesy of his father, a noted jazz musician from New York City, who called in a favor. I don't have any such connections.

"You could do anything, Hannah. You're one of the smartest people in our class—I'm sure one of your profs could help you find something to do in Boston over the summer."

Now that Owen mentions it, my R-Cubed professor did offer to put in a good word for me at one of the publishing houses in Boston if I ever wanted a summer internship. I wonder if it's too late to take her up on the offer.

"But how would I explain it to my parents?"

Owen kisses the space between my eyebrows.

"Tell them that it's a once-in-a-lifetime opportunity, and you just can't pass it up."

On Sunday morning, I call my parents and have no problem repeating Owen's explanation. After all, it was absolutely true.

beth

twenty-one

I jiggle my leg, waiting for my stylist, Erin, to call my name. The air in the dingy room is thick and smells of rotten eggs. Like in any hair salon, there's a pile of glossy magazines on the faux wood table, only most of these date back to the early 2000s.

I dump a couple months of *New Yorker*s on top of the pile. Hannah got me a five-year subscription. Not that anyone in here would read them. Hell, I can barely make it through the cartoons myself.

The Alderson hair room is worlds away from my beloved Park Avenue salon, but it isn't half-bad, especially for the price. I've got a box of L'Oréal Preference in Champagne Blonde on my lap, along with Erin's preferred form of payment—the latest Danielle Steele, also courtesy of Hannah. According to the back cover, this one's about a beautiful but damaged Eastern European princess who falls in love with a tough-as-nails NYPD homicide cop assigned to investigate the murder of her ex-husband. I didn't know they still made Eastern European princesses anymore.

The gal next to me has a faded pink streak through her yellowy bleached blond hair. Her hair is buzzed on one side, permed on the other. In her twitchy hands, she's got a couple packets of Kool-Aid, the hair dye of choice among the younger, edgier inmates. On the dusty floor by her feet is a six-pack of Diet Coke. A widely accepted form of payment. She must be seeing one of the stylists in training.

"Hey, Lindstrom," I hear someone say.

I look up and see Deb, who glares at the Kool-Aid chick.

"Move or die," Deb growls. The girl scampers like a mouse to the other side of the room, sitting as far away from Deb and me as she can.

"Move or dye, get it?" Deb says, pointing to the L'Oréal in my lap.

Who knew Deb the Destroyer liked bad puns?

"Damn, someone should clean this shit up," Deb says, riffling through the teetering pile of magazines. She glances at the date on my *New Yorker*s and sets them aside before holding up a dog-eared commemorative issue of *People* devoted to William and Kate's royal wedding and throwing it in the garbage. She pauses when she gets to an old issue of *Esquire* with Beyoncé on the cover. I recognize it right away. It's the Women We Love issue. The one I'm featured in.

"This one's from 2007, can you believe it?" Deb says.

When God Hälsa's CEO demanded that *Esquire* abandon the American Booty photo spread, the magazine almost dropped the entire idea of doing a feature on me. With a little sweet talk, I managed to convince the editors to keep the article but replace the full-page nude photo with a smaller, more tasteful headshot. God Hälsa's six-figure advertising commitment helped, too.

"I do love me some Queen B," Deb says. She starts flipping through the magazine. The feature on me starts at page ninety-four—the feature that describes in glowing detail my genius creation and marketing of Metamin-G. I think about Deb's ex-girlfriend, Sugar. Deb's never told anyone what Sugar OD'd on, but something in my gut knows the answer. Metamin was the cheapest high on the street.

As Deb flips closer to page ninety-four, I fight the urge to grab the magazine out of her hands. And then I see salvation in the form of a Trésor ad.

"Hey, is that a perfume strip?" I ask. Most perfume strips have long been torn out of the magazines at Alderson. They're one of the few luxuries available for free.

I reach over and take the magazine from Deb, rip out the perfume insert and rub it along my wrists. I don't usually wear department store perfume, but desperate times call for desperate measures.

"What do you think?" I ask. I lift my scented wrist under Deb's nose.

Before Deb can answer, my stylist, Erin, appears in the doorway.

"Beth, you're next," she says.

"Perfect timing," I reply. I quickly tuck the magazine underneath the Danielle Steele and box of L'Oréal. "See ya later, Deb."

I follow Erin into the hair room and bury the *Esquire* magazine deep inside the grungy trash bin filled with old peroxide bottles, cheap plastic gloves and hair clippings.

I sit down in the salon chair, and Erin ties the black nylon cape around my neck.

"So, what do you want today?" Erin asks.

"Surprise me," I say. "Cut it short. Change the color. What-ever you want. Starting today, I want to be unrecognizable."

"Great," Erin says, spritzing my head with a spray bottle. "I've been wanting to give you some foil highlights."

The first time I met Alex, he had the most flawless foil high-lights I'd ever seen. This was years ago, when Eva and Alex had just started dating. Alex was wearing white chino shorts, an immaculate white polo shirt underneath a white V-neck sweater with navy stripes and white Fred Perry tennis shoes that looked like they came straight out of the box. He flashed a smile so artificially white I almost expected a cartoon star-burst to go "ping."

With this as a first impression, I don't think it's unfair for me to assume this guy who's dating my sister is gay. Not that there's anything wrong with that. After all, who am I to judge?

"He's not gay," Eva says.

We're sitting at the bar of The West End and sipping rum and Diet Cokes.

"How do you know?" I ask.

"Because we've done it," she says. She looks down at her lap.

"It?" I laugh. "And what exactly is 'it'? The Jane Fonda workout?"

"Sex," she blurts. The patrons at the next table look over curiously.

"We've had sex," Eva whispers. "More than once. And it was really good."

I stifle another laugh. I don't want to be unkind. In truth, I'm happy for Eva. She's had it rough the past several years with her cruel roommates and ongoing struggles with bu-limia and depression.

Now that I'm at Barnard, just down the street from Co-lumbia, it's nice to be able to spend some time with my older sister, even if that means resisting the impulse to make fun of her gay boyfriend.

"Well, I'm glad it's good," I say. "You deserve good."

Eva looks surprised. We sit in silence sipping our drinks and listening to the music playing on the stereo.

"Remember when we used to spend Saturday afternoons dancing in the living room to *American Bandstand*?" I ask. "God, I think we wore a groove in the carpet with all the times we did the Bus Stop and Electric Slide."

The rum must be working, because the two of us laugh like we used to when we were girls. Back before things got complicated.

I look over at an older couple dancing to the music in the corner of the bar. They must be in their thirties or forties. They're laughing more than they're dancing. Something about seeing them so happy makes me feel generous.

"I'm glad you're happy," I say.

"Thank you," Eva responds. She doesn't even try to suppress her smile.

"You're welcome," I reply. "And anyway, if worse comes to worst, you can always share clothes. Those white chino shorts were simply darling."

About five or six years later, it's the late 1990s. I'm a newly minted God Hälsa drug rep and Eva's a dermatology resident. Eva just got back from her honeymoon in the British Virgin Islands, and we're catching up over oysters and champagne at Balthazar.

"So, how's the Fat Virgin?" I ask. I think it's hilarious Alex chose Virgin Gorda for their honeymoon destination. Although, Eva's not fat anymore. Or a virgin.

"It was gorgeous," Eva says. "The resort was to die for."

"It must've set Alex back a pretty penny."

"He's doing really well these days."

"Oh really," I say. "So he's stopped auditioning for *America's Next Top Male Model*?"

"He only did that once. As a joke."

"Right. So what's he doing now?"

"He's a trader," Eva says.

"A traitor?" I ask.

"Ha ha, very funny," Eva says. "A day trader."

I roll my eyes. Of course, Alex is a day trader. The dot-com bubble is at its frothiest, and everyone seems to be making a quick buck day-trading stocks. Leave it to Alex to choose a job because it's trendy.

"He's actually very good at it," Eva claims. "He makes more money as a day trader than I do as a doctor."

I stop myself from pointing out that that's a pretty low bar. As poor as I am as a drug rep, Eva's got it even worse as a medical resident. You wouldn't think it takes that much to become a dermatologist, but for some reason, Eva works crazy hours and gets paid almost zero.

"How does he know what to invest in?" I ask.

"Believe it or not, he meets a lot of really connected people on the tennis courts," Eva says. "Guys who work on Wall Street. Guys who're starting these crazy new tech businesses. Guys who are just loaded. They're always talking about what's the next hot stock."

Visions of Michael Milken and Ivan Boesky dance through my head.

Several years and life changes later, I'm in the library of our Princeton house. I've got a thick stack of statements in front of me from our brokerage account, the joint account I opened for me and Sam because that's what happily married couples are supposed to do.

"Sam, do you know why our account is down, like, fifty thousand dollars?"

Sam looks like a puppy with his tail between his legs. Almost everyone I know finds this look "completely adorable," but it makes me want to rip his head off.

"Uh, yeah, I'd been meaning to talk to you about that. Alex gave me a tip about an IPO that he promised was going to go through the roof," Sam says. "I mean, who doesn't love frozen yogurt? With mix-ins? And having it delivered to your home or office?"

"Go on," I say.

"Well, it turns out the company had some issues," Sam says. "Food safety, I think. Anyway, I decided to get out before the stock went to zero."

"How many times have I told you not to listen to Alex?" I tell Sam. "He's a poseur. A fraud. Don't you remember that fiasco with the Tiffany by Marla Maples jewelry collection he convinced you to get in on? I don't even want to think how much that disaster cost you. I'm telling you, Sam, don't listen to Alex's bullshit. Don't believe his get-rich-quick schemes. And whatever you do—don't give him another dime of our money."

As usual, Sam does as he's told. Sam doesn't listen to Alex, believe his schemes or give him any of our money. Still, Alex somehow manages to screw us over.

I should have told Sam to just keep his damn mouth shut.

hannah

twenty-two

Spring is finally upon us, providing welcome relief from the long, dark days of winter. Claire's Easter break from school falls early this year, and the girls are eager to make the drive from Princeton to Alderson to visit their mother.

"Where did you put the extra Bureau of Prisons forms I brought back last time?" I call out to Sam. I'm standing at his desk in the library of his Princeton home, rummaging through piles of paperwork and stacks of unopened mail. I want to make sure to fill out the BOP forms ahead of time so we can maximize our time with Beth.

"They're in the filing cabinet," Sam shouts back from the kitchen.

I pull open the top drawer of the filing cabinet and discover dozens of manila folders. They have neatly typed labels and are arranged in alphabetical order: AAA MEMBERSHIP,

BANKING, BIRTH CERTIFICATES, CABLE SERVICE, COUNTRY CLUB MEMBERSHIP, DENTAL RECORDS and so on. The second drawer is similarly organized, and so is the third. When I open the last drawer, there's a jumble of handwritten folders in Sam's messy scrawl: BMW service records, secret passwords, Beth's birthday gifts. There, among Sam's files, is the purple folder with the printed label BOP FORMS that I gave him last December.

As I pluck the purple folder and close the drawer, I remember that Lise was Beth's personal assistant. She must have been the one responsible for maintaining Beth's files. I think back to the last time I saw Beth in prison and what she said about the prosecution's witness list. *The final witness list included the whole family—Eva and Alex, Martin and Karen, even Sam. The prosecutors were ready to haul everyone into the courtroom. My lawyers said they do that to rattle us into settling.* I open Beth's file drawers again and scan the folder labels. No Alex or Eva or Martin or Sam, but there is a folder for Karen O'Sullivan—Martin's wife's maiden name. Why would Beth have a folder on Karen?

Inside the folder is a pile of invoices in reverse chronological order, with the most recent invoice on top. "For services rendered," they all say. Attached to each invoice is a Filofax daily schedule page, with various names and phone numbers handwritten in red ink. I recognize most of the names from the reams of documents I've read in Beth's whistle-blower case file: Andreas Magnusson, CEO of God Hälsa; Stellan Starck, Senior Vice President and General Counsel; Mark Fischer, Vice President and Head of Clinical Trials; and so forth. Most of the services last an hour, but some last ninety minutes or two hours. All are stamped in crisp, red ink: "PAID—God Hälsa Accounts Receivable."

As I skim through the invoices, there's only a single female client among the many male ones: Charlotte Von Maur, Senior Account Representative. She also seems to be the only one who isn't a vice president, senior vice president or CEO, and the only one whose name doesn't appear in any of the whistle-blower case documents. The last document in the Karen O'Sullivan file folder is a God Hälsa Corporate Security Department request form. It seeks to provide Karen with access to God Hälsa's corporate offices. Karen's title is listed as "Private Wellness Coach." In the section marked "Requested Access," someone has checked off the highest level, described as "Complete Access, including all common spaces, conference rooms, employee offices and executive suites." At the bottom of the form is Beth's signature, but it's clearly fake. Beth's signature is like her: big and bold. This signature is small and cramped. Someone's forged it.

"Did you find it?" Sam asks, walking into the study.

I close the Karen O'Sullivan folder quickly and place it under the purple BOP folder.

"Yeah, I did," I reply.

"This room is smaller than last time," Claire announces as she enters the large hotel suite. Like the rest of The Greenbrier Resort, our suite is tastefully appointed in shades of sage green and dove gray. Claire's sniffy assessment reminds me of the old Helmsley Hotel advertisements, where Leona Helmsley would point out the one flaw in an otherwise flawless room. I seem to recall that Leona ended up in women's prison, as well.

"And it's only got one bedroom," Claire says. "Where's Auntie Hannah going to sleep?"

"The couch pulls out into a bed," Sam responds. "You girls can either sleep with Auntie Hannah in the king-size bed and I'll sleep on the couch, or else Auntie Hannah can sleep on the couch and I'll sleep with you in the bed."

"Oh, Daddy, you need to sleep in the bed with us," Claire

insists, and Ally nods. I can't deny that, after spending so much time with the girls, it hurts my feelings just a little that they still prefer to sleep with their father. And at what age does it become inappropriate for a father to sleep with his daughters?

"Why didn't we get the same room as last time?" Claire asks. "It had two bedrooms and a kitchen." I resist the temptation to remind her it also had a formal living and dining room, deluxe built-in wet bar and hot stone sauna. That hotel suite was twice as large as my condo, and the daily rate was almost the same as my monthly mortgage payment.

"We have to start economizing, Claire," Sam says. I can tell by the way he's enunciating that the message is intended for me more than for the girls. I've been badgering Sam to cut back on his spending.

"What does that mean?" Claire asks. "Economizing?"

"It means we can't always stay in the Governor's Suite," Sam explains. "Sometimes we have to stay in a regular room." Sam doesn't understand that most people visiting Alderson stay at the donation-only Alderson Hospitality House or maybe the Motel 6 in the next town over.

"Speaking of economizing," I whisper to Sam. "Have you told Princeton Country Day that Claire won't be attending next year?"

"I hate to do it," Sam says. "I mean, she's really thriving there."

"Sam…" I begin.

"I was thinking of applying for a scholarship," he says. "I already downloaded the application and everything. Maybe you could help me write the essay. You're so good at that. You know that I wouldn't have even gotten an interview at Princeton without your help."

My face burns with the memory. I know I shouldn't have rewritten Sam's college admissions essay. I honestly just intended to fix his spelling errors, but before I knew what I was doing, Sam's simple story about being a three-sport varsity athlete turned into a thoughtful meditation on what it means to be an Asian American male in a country with few masculine role models.

"If she doesn't get a scholarship, I promise to pull her out," Sam says.

Sam doesn't have a great track record of keeping promises, but I don't want to ruin the night by nagging him any further. I distract myself by unpacking Claire's and Ally's suitcases and placing their clothes carefully in the drawers. At my request, Karen recently mailed us a box of hand-me-downs. Her daughters are growing like weeds, and it seems a shame to let all their nice clothes go to waste. Claire and Ally don't even know the difference.

"Are we gonna visit Mommy now?" Claire asks. She climbs onto the elegant bedspread and begins jumping up and down. Ally struggles to join her big sister on the bed, but the force of Claire's jumping catapults Ally backward and onto the floor. Ally lands with a heavy thump on her butt.

"Claire, look what you've done," Sam bellows. Claire stops jumping and starts crying. She is quickly joined by a sobbing Ally, although it isn't clear whether the younger girl's tears are due to pain, surprise or sisterly solidarity. I pull the girls' swimsuits out from the suitcases. They're part of the Karen hand-me-down collection and still have their tags on them.

"Girls," I say, "remember last time, we didn't bring your swimsuits because we didn't know they had a pool here? How about we go downstairs and swim a little bit? That way, we'll be plenty hungry for dinner and we can burn off some of that extra energy from sitting in the car all day." Plus, I think to myself, it would give Sam some time to unwind. Claire's and Ally's tears vanish as quickly as puddles on a hot summer's day.

"Did you bring your swimsuit?" Ally asks as I help her wiggle into her suit.

"Why, yes, I did," I answer. I walk over to my weekend bag and pull out a navy blue one-piece with modest scoop neck and shirring at the waist. "Flatters while hiding imperfections" was how the suit is described on the Lands' End website.

"Get naked, Auntie Hannah," Ally orders. "I want to see you naked."

I'm surprised by how my young niece's words affect me. No one has expressed interest in seeing me naked in a very long time. I think back to those nights with Owen at Harvard. It feels like a different life, a different person, altogether.

"I can't get naked here," I explain. "Your daddy's here. I'll go into the bathroom and get changed."

"I'll come with you," Ally says. "I see Mommy naked all the time."

"No, Ally, you can't come," I reply. I look over at Sam in the hopes he'll tell Ally to give me some personal space, but he's reclined on the bed, a glass tumbler in his hand and two minibar bottles of Tanqueray lying empty on the floor. He's watching a Warriors basketball game on the wide-screen TV, but his eyes are already heavy. He must be tired from a long week of work and an even longer day of driving. Claire is cuddled up by his side, her swimsuit on, watching a video on her iPad. I walk quickly toward the bathroom, but Ally follows close behind.

"Why not? Why can't I see you naked?" Ally asks.

Why not, indeed. What am I afraid of?

"Ally, I need my privacy," I say. "Adults need privacy." I dart into the bathroom and slowly close the bathroom door, taking care not to crush Ally's fingers. The lock on the door makes a distinct click.

"But mommies don't need privacy," Ally says. She's talking

into the tiny crack between the door and the door frame. I hear her panting on the other side. I look at myself in the bathroom mirror and take a deep breath. And then I let her in.

The following morning, the visitors' line is short when we pull into the Alderson parking lot just after dawn.

"I've got the money, Auntie Hannah," Claire calls out. "Don't forget your license and forms!" Claire grabs the Ziploc bag and bolts out of the car.

"Wait for me!" Ally screams as I unbuckle her seat belt. It never ceases to amaze me how quickly children adapt to change. Although they've only been to Alderson once before, Claire and Ally seem happy—even comfortable—with their new surroundings. As they take their place in line and smile sweetly at the two heavyset Latino men standing in front of them, I have to wonder: *What do they tell their friends about Beth? Do they say she's at camp? In prison? Do they understand the difference? When will their classmates stop being innocent and start being cruel? When will Claire and Ally begin to feel ashamed of their mother?*

I tick down my mental checklist for prison visitation: driver's license, BOP forms, empty pockets. The parking lot of a federal prison is probably the safest place to leave a purse in plain view, but I make sure to cover mine with Ally's favorite blanket just in case. One of the corners of the blanket is worn and gray from Ally's constant thumb sucking and rubbing. Glancing over at Sam, I notice he also looks worn and gray. I lost count of how many drinks he had last night. Now that I think about it, he didn't eat much dinner either. Lately, he seems to be getting most of his caloric intake through alcohol. We need to work on that.

"Daddy, Mommy, hurry up!" the girls shout back at us. Did the girls really just call me Mommy? It feels nice and wrong at the same time. The two Latino men have already gone into the visitors' building. It's almost our turn.

"We're coming!" I shout back, shoving Sam to get going.

Although they've only visited Alderson once before, Claire and Ally already know the visitation drill. At the guards' desk, they smile politely and turn out their pockets. They skip into the back room to reserve our favorite table by the window, then raid the Ziploc bag of change to buy a can of Diet Coke and bag of Life Savers Gummies—Beth's favorite treats. When they see Beth make her way down the hill, they run to the front room to wait in the two chairs by the unmarked door.

After a few hours, Claire and Ally complain of being bored. The coffee table is littered with the detritus of our vending machine snacks. We've played countless rounds of hangman and tic-tac-toe, Uno and gin rummy. It's raining outside, so the playground isn't an option.

"Sam, the Children's Room is just about to open. Why don't you take the girls to do an Easter project?" I suggest. "Beth and I will just stay out here, if you don't mind."

"Don't think you're fooling me," Sam responds. "I know you're just trying to get some private time together." He smiles good-naturedly and takes the girls away.

"What?" Beth asks eagerly. "Have you got any new information for me?"

"I don't really have new information—just something I discovered in your files."

"What is it?"

I tell Beth about looking through her filing cabinet to find the extra BOP forms and accidentally coming upon the Karen O'Sullivan folder.

"I know Karen didn't graduate from college," I say, "so I'm wondering what kind of services she can provide at such a high hourly rate. I mean, it's as much as my law firm charges for paralegal work."

"As much as paralegal work? And most of her clients were male?" she asks. Her face looks concerned. "And the services usually lasted an hour?"

"Yes."

"Wow, that *is* interesting," Beth says.

I don't know what I was expecting Beth's reaction to be, but this isn't it.

"Don't you already know about this, Beth?" I ask. "I mean, the invoices are in your files. Your company paid for them."

Beth looks at me wide-eyed and then bursts out laughing.

"Of course I know about them," Beth says. "Oh, Hannah, sometimes I forget just how innocent you are."

beth

twenty-three

Before I got to Alderson, I hardly ever worked out. With my busy job, traveling and the girls, I didn't have time. Thanks to the BOP, I've become a full-on exercise junkie. Most days, there's Zumba or spinning in the morning, Ballet Barre or Pilates in the afternoon, with the occasional pickup basketball game or 5K fun run on the weekend thrown in for good measure.

"You sure you want to go to the gym today?" Juanita asks. "You're looking so skinny these days. I'm getting worried about you."

"Don't worry," I say, "I'm perfectly fine. Besides, I need to work off that cheesecake we demolished last night."

Juanita's chocolate peanut butter cheesecake is epic. Her recipe calls for an entire wheel of Laughing Cow cheese and jar of Skippy peanut butter, which she spreads on a bed of crushed Oreos and margarine topped with a layer of melted Hershey's bars. How can anything so bad be so good?

Juanita and I stop by B Unit to pick Deb up on our way to the gym. Deb is practically bursting with excitement.

"Did ya hear the news?" Deb asks.

"About what?" I say.

"About Meatloaf. How she died."

"No," Juanita and I both say at the same time.

"I guess the BOP was tryin' to keep it hush-hush," Deb says, "'cause it don't look good for an inmate to die in prison, but someone in the West Virginia coroner's office leaked the info and now it's all over Twitter."

Deb dives in with the gory details.

"Remember when the COs searched our cubes a couple days before Meatloaf died?" Deb begins. Juanita nods, but honestly, I can't remember anything anymore. It's like my brain's been short-circuited.

In addition to our daily counts and inspections, guards at Alderson conduct random searches of the living units to make sure inmates don't have any contraband. Once the search begins, word spreads like wildfire. Book and magazine hoarders like Juanita and me scatter our possessions among our less well-read neighbors so we don't get caught exceeding the BOP's five books and five magazines per person limits. Meanwhile, drug dealers like Mary have to be even more ingenious. I've seen guards slice through their pillows and mattresses in search of hidden caches of drugs.

"Meatloaf knew she was just one shot away from getting sent away," Deb says. For Mary, *away* meant a high-security prison with locked cells, abusive guards and homicidal bunkies.

"Turns out, whenever there was a search, Meatloaf shoved her stockpile of pills into an old rubber glove and stuck it up her cooch," Deb says. "The broken plunger handle was what she used to get it way up there."

I see Juanita's eyes widen in horror.

"But the week she died, she was on the rag," Deb says. "When the COs started their search, she panicked and shoved the package up her ass. She was waiting until the coast was clear to pull the glove out, but before she could..."

"The glove broke," I say.

"She had over a hundred grams of drugs in her system when she died," Deb says.

The gym is almost full when the three of us show up for spinning class. Juanita and I take our usual spots in the front row, and Deb takes her usual spot directly behind me.

"Stop your yapping and get your skinny ass on the bike, Lindstrom," the instructor says. She gives the stink eye to my shorty shorts.

"*Chica*, you're just asking for trouble," Juanita warns, glancing back at Deb.

I hike up my shorts a little higher.

"C'mon," I say with a grin, "girl's gotta have a little fun."

The first thing I noticed about Karen was her ass. It's like that scene in *9½ Weeks* when Mickey Rourke describes the first time he saw Kim Basinger. Karen had this beautiful, upside-down heart of an ass. And I wanted it.

"Follow me," Karen says. She leads me into the darkened room. "Take off your clothes and slip under the covers. I'll be right back."

I quickly slip off my dress and slide between the silky smooth sheets. It feels good against my bare skin. I can't wait for Karen to return. I've heard she's incredible.

Karen opens the door. "Ready?" she whispers, her voice soft and husky.

"Yes," I murmur.

Karen closes the door and walks over to me. She lays her warm hands on my body and lets out a deep exhale, and then she slowly, gently pulls down the sheet. I feel goose bumps on my naked skin. The anticipation is intoxicating.

"How hard do you like it?" she asks.

I open my eyes and, in the dim light of the room, watch as she dips her fingers into the jar of thick, fragrant lubricant.

"Hard," I say, "the harder the better."

"I thought so, but I always like to ask. I never want to presume."

For sixty solid minutes, Karen goes harder than I've ever gone before. Hard to that delicious point where pleasure crosses into pain. By the end, I'm in nirvana—a blissed-out puddle of gratification.

Afterward, we're sitting on the sun-drenched porch, me in a terry-lined silk robe, Karen in her skintight yoga pants. We're sipping some mildly hallucinogenic herbal tea when I ask, "How in the world did you get that fucking amazing ass?"

Karen smiles and says, "I was a dancer."

"A dancer *and* a mind-blowing masseuse?"

"Watch out!" someone shouts, and a Frisbee lands just inches from my feet.

"Sorry, Beth!" Martin says, running onto the porch.

Martin looks better than he has in a very long time. Divorce has been good for him. He was so depressed when his wife left him that he stopped eating altogether; now he's almost down to his high school weight.

"And sorry, whoever you are," he says, looking over at Karen. *Smooth, Martin. Very smooth.*

"Martin, this is Karen, the amazing masseuse I told you so much about," I say by way of introduction, even though I've never mentioned her to him. "And, Karen, this is my older brother, Martin, the brilliant, soon-to-be-billionaire business-man and newly available bachelor."

"Nice to meet you, Martin," Karen says, eyeing him up and down.

"The pleasure's all mine," Martin responds, doing the same. Not quite.

For the next few years, I made sure that Karen was fully employed servicing God Hälsa's executives and most valued clients in the comfort and privacy of their own homes, of-fices or hotel suites. I told Karen to triple her normal hourly rate—God Hälsa officers get a generous perquisite for per-sonal health and fitness expenses, and people put more value on things that are expensive.

Karen was so grateful for the business that she gave me un-limited massages and ballet barre workouts for free. The mas-sages tapered off when Martin and Karen got married, but the benefits of the workouts endure. Need proof?

You should see my amazing upside-down heart of an ass.

Karen and I aren't exactly best friends, but I have to give her credit for another amazing achievement: my second brilliant Metamin-G marketing idea. It came to me on a Thanksgiv-ing weekend when we were having a "girls' night out" at the Applebee's down by the Safeway shopping center.

Hey, don't judge: their spinach and artichoke dip isn't half-bad.

That year, Eva and Alex agree to host Thanksgiving at their place in suburban Virginia. It's the Friday after Thanksgiving, and Martin, Alex and Sam stay home to watch the kids while the women go out to blow off some steam.

Applebee's is doing gangbusters business. Eva, Karen and I have just ordered our fourth round of cranberry cosmos when Karen starts complaining about her son Max's abysmal high school grades.

"All he wants to do is play *Madden* on his damn Xbox or watch Mexican wrestling videos on YouTube. It makes me wonder if something's wrong with him. Maybe we should get him tested."

Looking across the table at Karen, I notice there's something different about her. She's had some work done. Soon, I won't be able to tell Eva and Karen apart, with their Botox-smooth foreheads and collagen-plumped lips. They've even taken to dressing alike, in head-to-handbag Tory Burch. Karen, the struggling single mom and yogi, has transformed into a manicured MILF. Money will do that to you, I guess.

"Well, if it makes you feel any better," Eva says, "Stevie is just as bad. Stevie was such a good student in elementary school, but now that she's in middle school, she's always distracted. It seems like she's constantly texting her friends or checking her Instagram feed to see how many 'OMG, you're so pretty' comments she gets."

"Tell me about it," Karen sighs. "My girls are already obsessed with social media, and they're not even teenagers. It's getting out of control. Their teachers said I shouldn't have let them get their own phones so soon, but how else can I keep track of them?"

"You know what they say," Eva replies, "you pay your dues with boys when they're young, but girls cause more headaches when they're older."

The two women continue exchanging tales of teenager trouble—lost homework, sky-high data charges, cracked brand-new iPhones—as the overworked waitress brings another round of cloyingly sweet drinks. While Karen and Eva chatter away, I start chewing on a fried calamari ring and the synapses of my brain go into overdrive.

Distracted. Obsessed. Out of control.

OMG.

Thank God for fucked-up kids and their even more fucked-up parents.

hannah

twenty-four

Over the past several months, I've developed a new weekend routine: I take the 6:05 train on Friday after work to stay with Sam and the girls in Princeton, and return home to Hoboken on the second-to-last train Sunday night. This way, I can spend lots of quality time with Claire and Ally and still save up my vacation days for holidays or trips to visit Beth.

Today will be different, though. It's Sam's birthday, and I'm working just a half day in the morning and catching the 12:15 local to Princeton so we can all celebrate his special day together.

"Happy birthday, baby brother," I sing into the phone. It's barely past dawn, but I know Sam works extra early on Fridays during the spring and summer to accommodate his clients.

"Thanks, Hannah," Sam responds. He sounds gloomy.

"Is something wrong?"

"Yeah, some idiot just backed his truck into my car in the club's parking lot. The tow truck's here right now," Sam says. The clatter of metal on metal can be heard in the background.

"Oh, I'm sorry," I say. Sam loves his Z4 like it's his child. "What a bummer. And on your birthday, too. Did you get the other guy's insurance?"

"Yeah. Hey, I know it's in the opposite direction, but do you think you could swing by the club and pick me up before dinner?"

"I don't know. It's a whole two miles out of my way," I say, teasing. "But since it's your birthday, I guess I'll do you a favor."

"Thanks, Hannah."

Sam still sounds blue, which is uncharacteristic of my eternally sunny brother. I wonder if something's worrying him—something other than a wrecked car and a wife in prison.

"Buck up, buckaroo," I say. "I'll see you soon."

Maria and Jorge are waiting to pick me up from the Princeton Junction station. I always tell them they don't need to do it—after all, there are plenty of cabs at the station—but Maria and Jorge insist on picking me up anyway.

"You are family," they say, "and family don't take cabs."

In my less charitable moments, I think the two of them probably don't have anything better to do. I can't count the number of times I've told Sam that he doesn't need a full-time cook and driver, but he refuses to let them go.

As we pull up the long driveway, my spirits lift. It used to make me uncomfortable to stay at Sam and Beth's Princeton house, all that formal furniture and hard marble surfaces, but I've grown used to it. The house feels almost like home to me now.

Claire and Ally are already back from school when I enter the front doors. Grace, their part-time nanny, is also there.

They're all sitting on the couch, each staring at her own personal screen. Once I enter the room, though, Claire and Ally turn their enthusiastic attention to me. It feels like a gift.

The girls and I spend the next hour making Sam's special birthday cake. Ever since he was little, Sam's birthday cake of choice has been chocolate cake from a box mix filled with strawberry jam and iced with store-bought chocolate frosting. Beth always buys him something from a fancy bakery—marzipan-covered Princess cake, espresso-soaked tiramisu or decadent New York–style cheesecake—but Sam's face lights up whenever I bring him his tried-and-true favorite.

"Have you been practicing your golf?" I ask Claire.

I gave the girls a toy golf set for Christmas, and Claire and I got creative over Presidents' weekend and set up a three-hole mini-golf course in Sam's basement rec room.

"Yes!" Claire shouts. She shakes the multicolored sprinkles on top of the cake. I don't usually put sprinkles on Sam's cake, but Claire thought they would make it more festive.

"I've been practicing every day after school, and I'm getting really good," Claire says. Claire doesn't seem to lack confidence in any aspect of her life. I pray that never changes.

"You think you can beat Daddy?" I ask.

"I can never beat Daddy!" Claire says. "Because he cheats! Daddy is a big fat cheater. Cheater, cheater, pumpkin eater." Claire laughs as she continues to shake the sprinkles on the cake. Maybe she's had a little too much sugar today. I take the shaker away from her.

"I think that's enough, Claire."

It's almost five o'clock when I pull Sam's SUV up to the Princeton Country Club. This being early summer, the sun is still shining brightly. The valet parking guy rushes toward our car and then backs away after recognizing me and the girls. He smiles and waves. I wave back. I feel like Norm entering

Cheers. It's nice to go where everybody knows your face, if not your name.

Claire and Ally are in the back seat, watching a movie on Claire's iPad and sharing one set of earbuds between them. I can't help but think Claire will be a wonderful mother someday. She's got a generous soul.

Sam should be off duty soon, and then the birthday celebration can begin. We're going to a hip new Putt-Putt place that opened near the university. They've already gotten buzz for their bourbon-glazed chicken wings and garlic curly fries with homemade ranch dip. I double-checked their website to make sure you don't have to be over twenty-one to enter. Claire is dying to test her mini-golf skills on an actual Putt-Putt course, and I don't want her to be disappointed.

Knowing Sam's tendency toward tardiness, I debate whether to turn off the car or let it idle, when I see Sam's silhouette walking toward the parking lot. He's intercepted by a feminine figure who emerges from the clubhouse. I can't make out her face, but she is tall and curvaceous and has what Sam would crassly call a "nice rack."

The clock on the dashboard reads 5:05. I glance at the back seat to make sure the girls are still occupied and then pull out my phone to check work emails. My in-box is empty. It seems to be a quiet Friday in the office.

I click onto Facebook and see that over two hundred friends have wished Sam happy birthday. Several people have posted unflattering shots of Sam from days gone by: as a college freshman on spring break, slumped in a barstool with eyes half-closed between two very flamboyant drag queens; at a circa-2001 Princeton Country Club New Year's Eve party, hanging out with a group of men holding their golf clubs between their legs like penis proxies; at the poolside of some

glitzy resort, lying passed out facedown on a chaise while Eva's
husband, Alex, pretends to enter him sexually from behind.

It must be a generational thing to post unflattering photographs, or perhaps it's just a guy thing. I realize that, with
the exception of Alex and a couple others, I don't recognize
most of Sam's Facebook friends or the people in the posted
photos. How could it be that huge swaths of Sam's life are
unknown to me?

I scroll through the other photos on Sam's Facebook page,
the ones he posted himself. There's Sam smiling broadly next
to Jack Nicklaus, his all-time hero, at a fund-raising golf event
in Detroit. Sam and the girls making sandcastles on the pale
sand beach in Maui, with a blurry image of Lise in a white
bikini in the background. Sam and Beth on the red carpet at
a charity gala in New York City, Sam looking dapper in his
tuxedo and Beth flashing her gleaming smile and lissome legs.
My eyes well up thinking about the life he once had, the life
that's now been ruined.

As I wipe the tears away, my hands reach subconsciously
for my earrings, the diamond studs that Sam gave me for
my fortieth birthday. I give the earrings a twirl and try to
remember: What did I give Sam for his fortieth birthday?
It takes me a while to remember the set of cuff links made
from an old Buffalo Bills football. I've never seen him wear
them. It's hard to think of gifts to get for people who spare
no expense for themselves.

Beth recently wrote me about the birthday gift she arranged
for her bunkie. Alderson's shower temperatures are erratic, and
Beth told me Juanita complains endlessly about how much she
misses a scalding hot shower. It's one of the things that Beth
and Juanita first bonded over. For Juanita's birthday, Beth arranged for a "twenty-one-gun salute"—all the women in their

living unit flushed the toilets simultaneously while Juanita was taking her morning shower.

"BEST. BIRTHDAY GIFT. EVER!" Beth bragged. It puts things in perspective.

The dashboard clock reads 5:19, and the Putt-Putt place expects us at 5:30. I hate to be late, but I also hate to be rude. I hesitate before giving the horn a playful honk. Sam and the woman look up. The sun shifts ever so slightly, and I can barely make out the woman's face. The woman hands Sam a large shopping bag. They kiss each other on the cheeks, French-style, and then Sam walks to the car while the woman re-enters the clubhouse.

"Who was that?" I ask. I get out of the car and walk over to the passenger side.

"No one you know," Sam responds. He puts the shopping bag in the trunk before getting in the car and adjusting the seat and mirrors.

"I think I recognized her," I say.

"No, I don't think so," Sam grunts. He shifts the SUV out of what he calls "old lady mode" and speeds down the street. Despite Sam's denials, I'm absolutely sure I've seen the woman before. I have a good eye for faces, and even if I didn't, most people would remember her. She's drop-dead gorgeous.

"I remember meeting her at one of your Hamptons parties," I say. "I think she was talking with Karen."

Sam doesn't say anything.

"Charlotte," I say with a snap of my fingers. "Her name's Charlotte, right?"

"What's in the bag, Daddy?" Claire asks from the back seat. "Did the pretty lady give you a birthday present?"

Sam continues in silence.

"Sam, Claire asked you a question," I say quietly. Claire is an observant child. She notices when she's being ignored.

"What's with the cross-examination?" Sam barks. "Can't I just enjoy some peace and quiet on my birthday without being subjected to a game of twenty questions?"

My pulse quickens at Sam's outburst. I crane my head backward and see Claire's eyes filling with tears. She tries hard to hold it in but starts bawling, and Ally joins in solidarity.

"Sam, what's wrong?" I ask. I try to sound sympathetic, but a little anger comes through.

"Fuck this!" Sam yells. He makes a sharp right turn and pulls the car to a screeching stop on the side of the road. He gets out, slams the door and stomps away. I'm tempted to chase after Sam but can't leave the girls unattended in the car. Claire and Ally are howling now, their faces red and puffy.

"Girls, I'll drive us home now," I say calmly.

By the time we get home, the girls are so exhausted from crying that I tuck them into bed without any supper. I soak a washcloth with cool water and pat gently around their eyes. When I was young, I used to wake up after a night of hard crying and discover my eyes were practically sealed shut like a boxer after taking too many punches. I hope to spare Claire and Ally from that experience.

I go down to the kitchen and rummage through the refrigerator for some leftovers to reheat for dinner. As I sit down with the microwaved enchiladas, I wonder to myself: *What could have set Sam off? Was it something that happened at work? Something that Charlotte said? Or maybe whatever is in that shopping bag?* I head into the garage and get the shopping bag from the car trunk. Inside is a Tiffany box. I lift the box's lid and see the three-part silver frame—the one I got for Sam and Beth a couple Christmases ago, the one I spent my annual bonus to buy.

The one I last saw in the wrapping room at Le Refuge.

★ ★ ★

I'm asleep on the living room couch when the front door lock makes a loud click.

"Sam?" I call out. I check my phone and see that it's just after midnight.

"Hey," Sam replies. He walks into the living room and sits down next to me. His face looks gaunt and weary. I want to ask where he's been but don't want to trigger another twenty questions outburst. I sit up and give him a hug.

"I'm sorry about ruining your birthday plans," Sam says. "And yelling at the girls."

"I know things are hard, Sam," I say, taking care with my words. "How can I help?"

Sam leans forward and holds his head in his hands.

"I feel like I'm drowning, Hannah," he says. "Charlotte was up at Le Refuge this week and said there's a sheriff's notice on the house."

So, it was Charlotte after all. Then I remember her full name: Charlotte Von Maur. She was Beth's coworker at God Hälsa. The one woman among the many men on Karen's client list.

"A sheriff's notice?" I ask. I refrain from asking what Charlotte was doing at Le Refuge.

"Yeah, like a foreclosure notice."

"Oh," I say, knowing full well what a sheriff's notice is.

Sam told me that he and Beth took second mortgages out on Le Refuge and the Princeton house to help pay for Beth's legal bills. I always wondered how Sam could manage the payments on his limited income. Apparently, he can't.

"I called my lawyer to see if there was anything I could do," Sam says.

"And?"

"He says I can stop the foreclosure by paying the full amount due."

I grit my teeth, knowing the question that's coming next.

"Hannah, I really hate to ask this, but I have no other choice. Do you think you could float me a loan?"

"How much are we talking?"

"A couple hundred thousand."

"What? How could it be that much?"

Sam explains to me he's also delinquent on his payments for the Princeton home. It's just a matter of time before he gets the foreclosure notice for that house, as well.

"I don't have that kind of money just lying around," I say.

"How about taking a second mortgage on your condo?"

"I already did that, remember? For the restitution payment?"

"Oh yeah, I forgot," he says. "Can you take out a third mortgage?"

"I don't think so."

"How about your 401(k)?"

"Sam, that's my retirement. I'll need that to live on when I'm old. And I can't withdraw from it without incurring a penalty."

"I promise to pay it back, including the penalty."

I look at Sam, his face a combination of sincerity and desperation. He honestly believes himself when he makes these promises.

"Hannah, I need your help," Sam says.

My mind flashes back to the many times I've heard these words from his mouth. And then I imagine Claire and Ally sitting on the curb, cold and homeless.

"Okay, I'll do it," I say. "On two conditions."

"Anything."

"You start living on a budget."

"Sure thing."

"And you stop keeping secrets from me."

beth

twenty-five

It's a beautiful summer morning. One of those rare West Virginia days when the weather isn't too hot or too cold. I fantasize about the cool linen sheets and warm summer nights I used to enjoy in my bedroom at Le Refuge. It's a world away from the scratchy wool blanket and spartan cinder block cubicle at Alderson.

"You're lookin' better these days, Lindstrom," Deb says, watching me as I touch up my makeup. She's hanging out in her new favorite spot, Juanita's bottom bunk.

"Yes, more rested," Juanita concurs. She's bent over and brushing the baby powder out of her hair. It's the prison version of dry shampoo. Juanita and I are both expecting visitors, so we want to look our best.

"Deb, I forgot to tell you," I say, "you were right—it was the drugs."

"Whatcha mean?" Deb asks.

"The generic Lexapro they had me on? One of the listed side effects is insomnia," I say. "Not to mention loss of appetite, paranoia and memory loss. I finally got in to see the doc and sweet-talked him into switching me to the good stuff. My tried-and-true favorite, Lexapro oral suspension. I've been sleeping like a baby ever since."

"You got him to give you the brand name?" Deb says. "BOP docs never do that."

"Told him I was also having libido issues. Told him to check under the hood for proof."

"Is there anything you won't do to get what you want, Lindstrom?" Deb asks.

I swirl the Maybelline Kissing Potion on my lips and climb into Juanita's bunk. I lean in close next to Deb so she can smell the sticky sweetness on my lips.

"Can't think of anything," I whisper.

"Hey, don't mess up my bunk," Juanita says.

"It's almost count," Deb says, laughing. She wiggles her butt out of the bunk. "I better get outta here before I get in trouble."

After Deb leaves, I return the Kissing Potion back to my makeup kit. I stand in front of the mirror hanging on my side of the cubicle and give myself one last look-over. I have to agree with Juanita and Deb: I'm looking more like my usual gorgeous self.

"Who's visiting today?" Juanita asks.

"Hannah," I say.

"Again? Wasn't she just here?"

"Yeah, but this time she's bringing the girls."

"She's a good sister-in-law," Juanita says.

"Did you notice Deb's been especially friendly lately?" I say, changing the subject.

"I think you need to stop playing games, *chica*," Juanita says. "It's getting out of hand. And someone might get hurt."

"I'm not playing games," I say, directing my words at her face in the mirror.

Juanita gives me a stare that could rival Medusa's.

Good thing I'm looking at her reflection.

"Okay, so maybe I'm playing games a little," I admit, "but I promise I won't do anything to hurt her. Truth be told, I've gotten to really enjoy her company."

"You know what they say," Juanita warns, "when you play with fire, you have to be ready to pay the piper."

"I don't think that's a saying, Juanita."

"You know what I mean."

Yes, I do know what she means. In my experience, the world is filled with two kinds of people: those who'll do whatever it takes to get what they want, and everyone else.

I'm not everyone else.

Every quarter after Metamin-G's initial release, I make sure to personally present the latest sales figures to God Hälsa's board of directors, even though the CEO usually limits board meetings to senior VPs and higher.

After nearly five years of unprecedented growth, Metamin-G's sales curve starts to plateau. I'm able to make modest strides in sales of God Hälsa's other drugs, but Metamin-G is still the company's gold mine. If I want to keep my job or, better yet, get promoted, I need to figure out how to boost sales from flat to stratospheric.

Within months of my Applebee's outing, I'm standing in front of the God Hälsa board wearing a brand-new Armani suit I've had tailored to fit my every curve. The fine-gauge fabric has the luster of a suit of armor, and I'm a modern-day Joan of Arc ready to go into fucking battle.

"Metamin-G and its competitors have historically focused their marketing efforts on boys," I declare to the stony-faced board members. I pace slowly from one side of the room to the other like a panther surveying her territory.

"The common misconception is that only boys get ADHD. However, the reality is that girls are also at significant risk— it's just that girls exhibit symptoms at a later age than boys. In fact, a National Institute of Mental Health study released last year finds that teenage girls are almost equally as likely as teenage boys to exhibit ADHD symptoms over the course of high school and college."

Like a modern-day Don Draper, I flash my most seductive smile as I click the remote. The slides advance to unveil the arresting images for the new Metamin-G marketing strategy.

"Gentlemen, I present you with God Hälsa's newest ad campaign. 'Fit Right in with Metamin.' With this marketing strategy aimed specifically at parents of teenage girls, I won't simply increase God Hälsa's piece of the proverbial pie, I'm going to double the size of the pie itself."

Soon after my presentation, God Hälsa's CEO comes into my office to tell me that the board has approved my promotion to senior vice president of North American markets.

"You'll be the youngest senior vice president in God Hälsa's history, Elisabeth, and the first female senior executive," he intones gravely. "I want you to understand—with increased pay comes increased responsibility."

Yeah, yeah, I've seen Spider-Man. *Who do you think you are: the Swedish Uncle Ben?*

I don't say that, of course.

"I completely understand, Andreas," I say. "I know the marketing staff will look to me not only to set the strategic direction for the company but also to ensure they are rewarded for achieving our company metrics. I'm excited to demonstrate my leadership on both fronts.

"I also understand my promotion reflects the board's recognition of my contributions to the bottom line. They expect me to continue to create marketing strategies to make God Hälsa a world-leading pharmaceutical giant. I want to assure you I'll do everything in my power to make sure the board is satisfied.

"And finally, I fully recognize this achievement isn't mine alone. It's a testament to the years of mentoring, sponsorship and support you have provided. I'm grateful to have had the opportunity to learn from your example, and I promise to do everything in my power to make you proud of me."

Andreas is all smiles. He pats me on the back and congratulates me on my promotion.

Confidence and cock sucking: my patented recipe for success.

If you thought God Hälsa was big after Metamin-G was released, you should've seen the stock price after we started marketing the drug to parents of teenage girls. We're talking crazy levels of irrational exuberance. Investors go into a frenzy for God Hälsa's stock, which doubles, then triples, in price. It seems there's no limit to the money we can rake in. And for a good stretch there, we're *really* raking it in.

With our increased income, Sam and I move out of our midcentury modern house into one of those enormous mansions near the prestigious Princeton Country Day School. We take vacations to Hawaii and Paris and the Vineyard and stay at the best five-star resorts and hotels. Sam gets that BMW sports car he's always been dreaming about.

I promote Lise from au pair to personal assistant and put her on the payroll. She's come a long way from that horny Swedish teenager who used to post sex tapes of her and her boyfriend on the internet. If she's lucky, she might be able to make something out of herself.

I tell the architect to throw away his blueprints for the sweet summer cottage and instead design a luxurious family vacation compound. I think I'll even ask Alex to help me plan the interior decor. With their girls' private school tuitions, I know Eva could use the extra money, and Alex could use something to keep him out of trouble.

I'm looking at the architect's latest plans on my work computer when my executive assistant, Renee, pops her head into my office.

"Your brother's here to see you," she says.

"My brother?" Martin didn't tell me he was coming.

I walk out of my office and see Martin sitting in the waiting area.

"Martin, what are you doing here?"

"Hey, Beth, can't a guy come and check out his baby sister's new corner office?" he says. He gives Renee a smile and a wink.

I know Martin well enough to suspect he's got ulterior motives, but I give him a hug and usher him into my office anyway.

"Karen wanted to join me, but she's busy with the kids," Martin says.

"Of course," I respond. Honestly, I couldn't care less. Unless I'm stark naked and getting rubbed with essential oils, Karen is of no use to me. I think she's kind of a dolt.

"Wow, this is frickin' incredible," Martin says. He takes in the view from my floor-to-ceiling windows. "A guy could really get used to this."

"Yeah, it's pretty nice. Do you want something?" I ask. I'm standing in front of the blond wood built-in kitchenette with its gleaming silver Nespresso machine.

"Why do you always think I want something?" Martin asks. He sounds defensive.

"Do you want a drink?" I clarify. "I can make you an espresso, latte, cappuccino. Or else I've got sodas and waters in the fridge. No booze, though, sorry."

"Oh," Martin responds, "I'll take a sparkling water, if you've got one."

I open the fridge and pull out a chilled Pellegrino for Martin and a Diet Coke for myself. I hand Martin his drink and take a seat on the celadon mohair couch. Martin sits opposite me in the matching armchair, his back hunched, his elbows on his knees.

"So, seriously, it's great to see you, Martin, but do you want something?" I ask.

"Beth," he begins, "you know how much I appreciate everything you've done. For me. For us. Your support of the business has been incredible, and we're this close to scoring that new Defense Department contract." Martin holds his thumb and index finger just millimeters apart.

"Okay."

"But, you know, until the contract is signed and invoices paid, cash flow is tight."

"So, you want me to put more into the business," I say, trying to complete his thought. God, I wish people would just get to the point sometimes.

"Yes, and no. I mean, yes, we need to make this month's payroll, but even apart from that, Karen and I need…" He stops to take a sip of his Pellegrino.

"What?" I say. "What do you need?"

"Fifty thousand."

"For what?"

It takes Martin a few false starts before the full story comes out: Karen's son, Max, got caught with a backpack full of drugs.

Pot, shrooms, nothing serious, just kid stuff. The police agreed not to send him to juvie if Martin and Karen send him to a residential drug treatment facility over the summer.

"That kid's a pain in the ass, if you ask me," I warn. I walk over to my desk and pull out my checkbook from the bottom drawer.

"I know, but he's Karen's son," Martin says. "The poor kid's had it rough, with his dad running off and abandoning them when he was just a baby."

"We had it rough, too," I reply, "but you don't see us dealing drugs."

Martin looks at me. We stare at one another for a beat and then laugh.

"Well, not the illegal kind," I reply.

I write out a check for a hundred thousand dollars, made payable to Martin Lindstrom.

"Half of that's for payroll, the other half's for your stoner stepkid," I say, handing the check to Martin.

"Thanks, Beth. I really appreciate this," Martin says as he stands up. He leans forward and gives me a kiss. "This is the last time, I promise."

Yeah, that's what he always says.

I show Martin out of my office and watch as he strides to the elevator bank. His broad back straightens from Sad Sack to Master of the Universe. I make my way back into my office, eager to check out the architect's blueprints, when I have a sudden compulsion to look out my window.

In the visitors' parking lot, I see Karen leaning against a brand-new Lincoln Continental, dressed to kill and having a smoke.

hannah

twenty-six

"Thanks for doing this, Hannah," Sam says. "I owe you one." He pecks me on the cheek and carries his golf bag and week-end duffel out the front door. It's the final week of August, but the morning air is unseasonably crisp. I wrap my bath-robe tightly against my body, slip on my shoes and follow Sam outside. The Z4 flashes its lights and makes a beep noise as Sam clicks the remote and tosses his bags into the trunk. As he makes his way to the driver seat, I hand him a crisp brown paper sack.

"I packed you lunch for the plane. A ham and brie baguette, some green grapes and half a dozen chocolate chip cookies." I wasn't sure how many cookies to include. Growing up, Sam could eat practically an entire batch of chocolate chip cookies in one sitting, but I figure he's not a kid any longer.

"Thanks, Little Mommy," he says, giving me another kiss on the cheek.

I watch and wave as Sam backs the car out the long driveway. The sleek silver roadster pauses for a moment on the street, and I wonder whether Sam forgot something. Then I see him stuffing two cookies into his mouth as he puts the car into Drive and speeds away.

Shuffling back to the house, I try to calculate the number of weeks since I last visited Beth. *Thirty days has September, April, June and November*, I recite in my head. It's only been eight weeks. This is my fourth or fifth time visiting Alderson. Neither Eva nor Martin has visited Beth even once in the entire year she's been in prison.

Although I've already spent way too much time away from the office this summer, I just couldn't say no when Sam asked me to take Claire and Ally to visit Beth. The girls wanted to see their mommy before school starts in September, but Sam had committed to play at an invitational golf tournament in Pittsburgh. Sam hasn't competed in over a year, and Oakmont is one of his all-time favorite golf courses. I'm happy to make another trip out to Alderson and give Sam a welcome break from the girls.

I take a quick shower and change into comfortable clothes for the long day ahead. My suitcase and the girls' roller backpacks are already packed and loaded in the car. I just need to finish getting some healthy snacks for the trip and wake the girls.

We make good time and get to Alderson shortly before 3:00 p.m. Visiting hours don't end until 6:30 on Fridays, so we should have plenty of time to spend with Beth before we need to check into the hotel.

"They're in the middle of count," the guard says, "so it'll be a while."

"That's okay," Claire says. "We know what to do."

Claire grabs a deck of Uno cards from the front desk, and she and Ally make themselves comfortable. Meanwhile, I start flipping through the visitors' ledger out of curiosity. Beth wrote me that a former *American Idol* contestant recently checked in on a drug conviction. I'm vaguely hoping to see Kelly Clarkson, Carrie Underwood or even Adam Lambert among the list of visitors. Instead, I'm surprised to see another familiar name: Charlotte Von Maur. I check the date. Charlotte visited exactly a week ago. Something clicks in my brain. I turn the pages back one by one. It's like one of those black-and-white movies where the pages of the calendar keep flying off to show the passage of time. As I go further and further back in the visitors' ledger, I keep seeing Charlotte's name over and over again.

Charlotte Von Maur has been visiting Alderson like clockwork ever since Beth arrived.

"Count is finished," the guard comes over to tell us. "Your mommy should be down any minute."

The girls and I head back to our favorite room and start a game of Uno. "Mommy!" the girls shout when they see Beth coming down the hill. They place their Uno cards on the coffee table and run to the two chairs by the unmarked door. I stay behind, tidying up the stack of cards so their edges are straight. Several minutes later, Beth beams as she enters the back room, Claire pulling her one arm and Ally pulling the other. I stand up to give my sister-in-law a hug.

"Happy birthday, Hannah," Beth says warmly. I'm dumbfounded she remembered.

"Oh, is it your birthday today, Auntie Hannah?" Claire asks.

"Duh, Claire," Ally pipes up. "Don't you remember…"

"Of course, Claire remembers," Beth interrupts, "but she just forgot for a second."

"Yeah," Claire says agreeably. "I just forgot for a second."
I'm still shocked Beth remembered my birthday.

"Mommy, do you want us to get you a Diet Coke?" Claire asks.

"I'd love a Diet Coke, girls, but how about I go along with you and we can pick out some treats together," Beth responds. "Hannah, is there anything we can get you?"

"No, I'm fine," I say. "I'll head into the back room and see if our regular spot is free."

Claire grabs the Ziploc bag of change, and the girls pull Beth into the vending machine room. Soon, they join me in the back room with a pile of junk food: snack packages of Oreos, chocolate pudding cups, Snickers, M&M's, Twix and Beth's favorite, Life Savers Gummies. I think about the cooler full of fresh fruit in the car that has gone uneaten.

"How was the family reunion this year?" Beth asks as she rips open the bag of gummies and offers them to the girls and me. "Did you have fun with your cousins?"

The hours fly by as the girls and I talk about going to our favorite berry-picking farm up the road from Le Refuge, steaming a huge pot of Maryland blue crabs and fresh ears of corn and dumping them, hot and spicy with Old Bay Seasoning, onto the brown paper-covered table on the back porch, running around the lawn at night and catching fireflies in our hands.

The guards come by to give us the half-hour warning. We return the Monopoly set to the gray metal cabinet and throw away our pizza wrappers and soda cans. It bothers me that the BOP doesn't seem to provide a bin for recycling.

"Claire, why don't you take the extra treats back to the hotel?" Beth says.

"Okay, Mommy, good idea," Claire says cheerfully.

"You're not staying at The Greenbrier, are you?" Beth asks.

"No," I reply half-apologetically, "we're staying at the Holiday Inn Express."

"It's closer than The Greenbrier," Claire chimes in.

"And they have a pool," Ally adds.

"And free breakfast, including a make-your-own waffle machine," Claire says.

Beth smiles, first at the girls and then at me. "Wow, that sounds perfect."

The four of us make our way to the front room of the visitors' building as the guards clear the back rooms. Beth says hello casually to several other khaki-clad women.

"So, you'll come and visit me tomorrow morning, right?" Beth says. She moves to get in line for the unmarked door. She's still holding Ally on one hip, with Claire close by her side. I watch the other women go one by one through the door and back up the hill.

Ally starts to whimper and holds tight to Beth's neck. As admirably as the girls have adjusted to their new life, goodbyes are still hard. Claire reaches over to comfort her little sister but has tears in her eyes, as well. Beth tries to hand Ally over to me, and for a moment, it seems like Ally won't ever let go. And then she does.

Ally falls asleep the instant we hit the road. It takes less than thirty minutes to drive from Alderson to the Holiday Inn Express, and Ally refuses to be roused when we arrive. I must look particularly frazzled as I enter the hotel lobby carrying Ally, her floppy head on one shoulder and my oversize handbag on the other. The check-in clerk calls to a young co-worker to offer me assistance.

"You'll be in Room 211," the clerk says as I sign the registration form. "Why don't you take the lil ones up to the room and Vicki here will get your bags from the car."

I hesitate to give this stranger the keys to Sam's BMW SUV.

I worry this might be one of those small-town scams you hear about on the six o'clock news.

"I'll help Vicki," Claire offers. "I know how to push the button to open the car."

I'm about to protest when Ally suddenly wakes up crying, as if from a bad dream.

"I have to go pee-pee," she wails.

Ally only recently became potty-trained, and she still needs to wear Pull-Ups when she sleeps. I didn't think to put her in a Pull-Up when we left the prison. I remember the full can of Sprite she drank back at Alderson. In a panic, I grab the car keys out of my bag, hand them to Claire and say, "Just bring in the bags. You can leave the coolers in the car. I'll get them later."

"Don't worry, Mrs. Min," Vicki says. "I won't steal your car or your little girl."

Before I can think twice, Ally screams, "I have to go!"

We rush up to Room 211, and I plop Ally down on the toilet seat, taking care to balance her tiny bottom so she doesn't fall into the porcelain basin. I can't help but feel impressed by the amount of liquid Ally held in.

"Okay, all done?" I ask. I feel relieved on her behalf.

"No," she says. Her face reveals she has more business to transact. I glance nervously at my watch. How long can it possibly take to bring up a few bags?

By the time Ally finally completes her business, I'm already imagining Claire's cherubic face on the side of a milk carton. I'm about to leave the hotel room when I hear the electronic beeping indicating someone is about to enter.

"Happy birthday, Auntie Hannah!" Claire sings out. She's holding a small Pyrex dish filled with what appears to be chocolate cake. On top of the frosting, formed out of multi-colored M&M's, is the number fifty. Claire enters the room holding the cake in one hand and pulling her Hello Kitty roller-bag in the other. Vicki waits in the hallway with my suitcase and the girls' bags on a luggage cart.

"Oh, Vicki, I can't thank you enough," I say. I remove the bags from the cart and feel bad about ever having doubted her. I run to grab my purse, pull out my wallet and see I've only got $20 bills from my visit to the ATM. I remember the Ziploc bag. Would it be gauche to tip Vicki in quarters? I give Vicki a $20 bill and thank her for her service. I close the hotel door and look fondly at Claire and Ally, who are jumping up and down on the two queen-size beds, screaming, "Happy birthday, Auntie Hannah!"

"Where in the world did you get this cake?"

"I made it!" Claire replies breathlessly. "Mommy told me about the cake on one of our phone calls. Her bunkie, Juanita, makes it at camp all the time, and I asked her to send me the recipe in a letter. Maria and I practiced making it at home."

"You didn't make it just now, did you?" I ask.

"Yes! It's made of Oreos, pudding and Coke. I made it in the microwave downstairs," Claire explains. "Mommy says the candy bars in the middle make it extra delicious."

"Were you part of the secret?" I ask Ally incredulously.

"Yes!" Ally replies.

"No!" Claire says, giggling. "Ally didn't know about the secret. I was going to make the cake with you after dinner, but when Ally said she had to go pee-pee, I thought I would make it with Vicki and surprise you. Did I surprise you?"

"You would have surprised me either way," I respond. I hug Claire tightly. Claire rips herself away from me and runs to her Hello Kitty roller-bag.

"Wait!" she says. "I have another surprise. Close your eyes, Auntie Hannah."

Ally jumps on me and orders, "Close your eyes, close your eyes."

I sit on the edge of the bed and let Ally cover my eyes with her moist little hands. I hear the sound of unzipping zippers and rustling papers.

"Okay, open your eyes, Auntie Hannah," Claire orders. Ally takes her hands off my eyes and resumes jumping up and down on the bed.

Piled up next to Claire's chocolate cake are three birthday cards—two slightly crinkled construction paper and crayon cards from Claire and Ally, and a handcrafted origami card from Beth—along with a soft bundle wrapped in white tissue paper.

"Open it!" Claire and Ally shriek. My hands are trembling as I remove the tissue paper and uncover the treasure inside: a beautifully hand-crocheted afghan in soft hues of green and blue, my favorite colors.

"Mommy made it all by herself. She mailed it to our house, and I snuck it here in my suitcase. Do you love it, Auntie Hannah? Do you just love it?" Claire asks. Her face is beaming. Ally giggles nonstop.

My vision is blurred as I take in the bounty before me.

"I do," I say. "I love it all."

"How was your birthday weekend?" Tracy asks. She sits down at her computer and waits for it to boot up.

"Wonderful," I say. "Really wonderful." I shuffle through the bundle of periodicals that arrived in the mail and start sorting them into piles.

"Do you have a minute?" Tracy asks. "I've been doing some research on my own, and there's something I wanted to show you. It's about Beth's case."

I've been so preoccupied by Sam's financial problems and taking care of the girls that I haven't had time to work on

Beth's special assignment, but Tracy is like a dog with a bone. She won't give up.

I walk over to Tracy's desk.

"What's that?" I ask. There, on Tracy's computer screen, is a bar chart marked with tiny notations. It's true what they say about turning fifty: my near-vision is getting worse. The letters are too small for me to read.

"It's an exhibit that shows God Hälsa's stock price over the past five years," Tracy explains, "and the dates that certain events happened—when the FDA approved Metamin-G, when the board okayed the 'Fit Right In' marketing campaign, when the federal indictment was served."

Tracy clicks the magnifying glass icon so I can read the details on the screen.

"And see those red arrows?" she continues. "Those are the dates certain people bought or sold unusually large quantities of God Hälsa stock. As you can see, they seem to have timed their activities perfectly."

"Wow, that looks really bad," I say.

"Yeah, it's pretty incriminating," Tracy says. "I'm not a prosecutor, but I'd say it's a clear-cut case of insider trading."

"Where did you find this?"

"The usual. PacerSux.com."

I give Tracy a nod in recognition of her stellar research skills.

"After we read everything in Beth's case file, I thought we had reached a dead end," Tracy says. "But then I found this case citation. To another criminal prosecution."

Tracy looks at me like she's delivering a death sentence.

"Sorry, Hannah," she says, "but the case is called *United States v. Sam Min and Alexander Lindstrom-Larsen.*"

lise

From the deposition of Lise Danielsson in *United States of America v. Sam Min and Alexander Lindstrom-Larsen*

Q: Good morning, Ms. Danielsson. I'm the Assistant United States Attorney assigned to this case.

A: Wait, what happened to the other lawyer?

Q: Which other lawyer?

A: The lady lawyer. The one with the nice hair and sharp teeth.

COUNSEL FOR MS. DANIELSSON: Could we go off the record?

[Off the record.]

Q: Now, Ms. Danielsson, do you understand that you are being deposed in the case of *United States v. Sam Min and Alexander Lindstrom-Larsen*? And that this is a different case from the one you were previously deposed for?

A: Yeah, I do now. Oh my God, is Sam in trouble? No one said anything about Sam getting in trouble.

Q: Mr. Min, along with Mr. Lindstrom-Larsen, has been accused of violating federal securities laws. Specifically, it has been alleged that Mr. Min shared material, non-public information about God Hälsa with Mr. Lindstrom-Larsen, who traded on that information to their financial advantage.

A: Can you put that into regular English?

Q: Mr. Min and Mr. Lindstrom-Larsen have been accused of insider trading.

A: I still don't know what you're talking about.

Q: Ms. Danielsson, do you recall your employer, Ms. Elisabeth Lindstrom, ever talking to her husband, Mr. Sam Min, about her work at God Hälsa?

A: Yeah, I guess so. Like, isn't that normal? For people to talk about their work to their family?

COUNSEL FOR MS. DANIELSSON: I advise my client not to speculate.

A: What does that mean?

COUNSEL FOR MS. DANIELSSON: It means don't guess.

Q: More specifically, do you recall Ms. Lindstrom, about three years ago, telling Mr. Min that the US Food and Drug Administration had rejected God Hälsa's request for approval to market Metamin–G for use as a weight loss medication?

A: Uh, I don't want to…spec… What was that word again?

COUNSEL FOR MS. DANIELSSON: *Speculate.*

A: Yeah, I don't want to speculate.

Q: It's a yes or no question, Ms. Danielsson.

COUNSEL FOR MS. DANIELSSON: My client has already testified that she doesn't recall and refuses to speculate.

Q: Do you recall Ms. Lindstrom, also about three years ago, telling Mr. Min that the US Food and Drug Administration had rejected God Hälsa's request for approval to market Metamin–G for academic performance enhancement?

A: Same answer as before.

Q: And what was that answer?

A: What my lawyer said.

Q: Do you recall Ms. Lindstrom, around two years ago, telling Mr. Min that God Hälsa's board of directors had just approved a new marketing campaign for Metamin–G aimed specifically at girls?

A: Same answer as before.

Q: Do you recall Mr. Min ever speaking with Mr. Alexander Lindstrom–Larsen about any of these events I just described?

A: Same answer as before.

Q: Ms. Danielsson, I will remind you that you are under oath.

A: What does that mean?

Q: It means, when I ask you a question, you have to answer honestly or else you could go to jail.

A: Is that really true?

[Off the record.]

Q: Ms. Danielsson, could you please answer my question?

A: What was the question again?

Q: I asked do you recall Mr. Sam Min ever speaking with Mr. Alexander Lindstrom–Larsen about any of the events at God Hälsa that I just described?

[Silence.]

Q: Ms. Danielsson?

A: Do I really have to answer these questions? I don't want to get Sam in trouble.

beth

twenty-seven

The fall rains have started, and the path from A Unit to CDR is soft and muddy tonight. I walk a couple paces behind Juanita and Deb, who are engaged in lively discussion about what Juanita should make for our next gambling party. Juanita's not working tonight, which means the food at CDR won't be as good but at least we'll get to sit together.

We grab our trays of the infamous kung pao chicken, along with thick slices of banana cream pie, and sit down at our usual table by the window. While Juanita and Deb eat, I pull out a fresh legal pad and ballpoint pen that I bought from commissary earlier this week.

"Whatcha writin'?" Deb asks.

"Another letter to Hannah, I bet," Juanita says.

"Just making sure she gets the girls' back-to-school supplies," I say. "And updates my wish list on Amazon."

"Did you thank her for sending me those books on my birthday?" Juanita says.

"No need to—it's one of the fringe benefits of being my bunkie," I reply.

I notice Juanita silently pushing over her piece of pie to Deb, who's already finished up everything on her own tray.

"I'm lucky to be a friend with benefits," Juanita says.

I have to laugh at Juanita sometimes. Even though she's completely fluent, there are moments when you can tell English is her second language.

"I don't think that's what you meant," I say.

Juanita's not paying any attention to me. She uses her index finger to wipe some whipped cream off the corner of Deb's mouth and then sticks her finger in her own mouth. Neither one of them is paying any attention to me. They've only got eyes for each other.

"Hey, you two," I say. "What's going on?"

Juanita turns bright red. Deb smiles and reaches for Juanita's hand.

"Don't tell me you're surprised," Deb says. "Didn't ya notice how much time I been spendin' around ya guys? Or did ya think I was tryin' to get some insider information on Big Pharma's next hot drug?" She breaks out in a big belly laugh.

It's one of the rare occasions where I'm speechless.

"What did you just say?" I ask.

"I think you heard me," Deb says.

"So, you know I used to work for God Hälsa?"

"C'mon, Lindstrom," Deb says. "You're a celebrity. You were in *People* and on frickin' *TMZ*. Everyone around here knows what you used to do. Some gals even used to take bets on what you'd wear to court. When they heard you were coming here instead of getting sent to Danbury, they almost threw a party. They ain't been so excited since Martha left."

"And Sugar? You're not pissed at me about her?"

"Sugar was fucked up from the moment she was born to her cokehead mom and drug dealer dad. Metamin and me were the only things that kept her halfway sane. Once she got outta here and didn't have us anymore, she crawled back into her crack pipe. Freedom was what killed her. Had nothin' to do with you."

"Well, I'll be damned," I say.

"I hope you're not upset," Juanita says. "I know you thought maybe you and Deb…"

Oh. My. God. The two of them are worried about hurting my feelings.

"No, not at all," I say. "I'm just surprised, that's all."

Deb reaches over and grabs Juanita's ass, which makes Juanita blush even redder.

"Sorry, Lindstrom," Deb says, "but you're not my type. You're just too damn skinny."

It was over a year after Claire was born. The longest Charlotte and I had ever been apart. After months of my begging, Charlotte was finally willing to meet with me at the Champagne Bar in the Plaza Hotel and talk it out.

"You've gotten too skinny," she says. "I thought new moms were supposed to get fat."

"How many times do I have to tell you? I'm not like most women," I say. "And I'm not too skinny."

"I know, I know," Charlotte interrupts. "You can never be too rich or too thin."

"You know me so well," I say. I place a signature red Cartier box on the table.

"And you know me so well," Charlotte says. She can barely contain her excitement. She opens the box, and inside, there's a five-carat canary diamond ring. Platinum-set. Cushion-cut.

"I've missed you, Charlotte," I say, reaching to put the ring on her finger.

Good thing I already checked in to the suite upstairs, because we can barely wait for the waiter to arrive with the bill before we tumble over one another to rekindle the spark that never really went out. Charlotte and I get back together, just as I predicted. And true to his word, Sam is good at sharing.

We arrange it so that I spend alternating weeks in alternating homes. One week, I'm the perfectly dressed Fortune 500 executive living with her perfectly handsome hunk of a husband and two perfectly adorable children in our perfectly designer-decorated Princeton home. The next week, I'm "traveling on business" or "telecommuting" and indulging in quality time with Charlotte at Le Refuge or various five-star hotels across the globe.

It's the night of *AdWeek*'s annual Brand Genius Awards. They're the Oscars of Madison Avenue. Or maybe the Golden Globes would be more accurate. There's an open bar and plenty of top-shelf cocktails to keep the evening flowing.

I don't need any artificial stimulants. I'm buzzing from the natural high of winning Best Ad Campaign in the pharmaceutical category.

I am at the very top of my professional game. Little do I know that I'll be going to prison less than two years later. But tonight, all is good in the world.

For the first time in history, the Brand Genius Awards are swept by women. In honor of this milestone, *AdWeek* persuades Ellen DeGeneres, America's Sapphic sweetheart, to emcee the event.

"Oh my God, is that Portia de Rossi?" everyone whispers.

We all stare at the blindingly beautiful blonde in the front row. Charlotte and I are both thunderstruck. We remember seeing her for the first time as Nelle Porter in *Ally McBeal*.

Goodbye Buttercup, Hello Nelle.

For the opening sequence, *AdWeek* assembles a montage of classic female-targeted ads from the 1960s, 1970s and 1980s, including the Mystery Date board game ("when you open the door, will your date be a dream...or a dud?"), Secret deodorant ("strong enough for a man, but made for a woman"), Virginia Slims cigarettes ("you've come a long way, baby") and everyone's all-time favorite, Enjoli perfume.

I recall spying that sleek purple-helmeted bottle in the perfume counter of the Rexall pharmacy when I was young, curious to understand its magic powers while at the same time hoping to avoid any chance encounters with my classmates as my mother stocked up on Kotex maxi-pads and Summer's Eve douche.

"I can bring home the bacon, fry it up in a pan and never, ever let you forget you're a man," Ellen sings slightly off-key as the video montage finishes up. The enthusiastic audience roars in recognition.

"I don't know the Madison Avenue genius who came up with that ad campaign," Ellen continues in her charming deadpan, "but *he* sure as hell is going home empty-handed tonight."

Everyone goes wild.

After the awards ceremony, Charlotte and I are exhausted. Exhausted but exhilarated. We're both reclining on the smooth leather back seat of the limo, headed back to Princeton.

"Damn, I've got that stupid song stuck in my head," Charlotte mutters. She kicks off her five-inch Giuseppe Zanottis. I don't need to ask what song she's talking about. It's stuck in my head, too.

"I can bring home the bacon..." I start to sing.

"No," Charlotte begs. "Please don't." She leans over to kiss me.

"One stop or two?" the driver asks.

I hesitate. I know the answer, but I hesitate anyway.

"Two," Charlotte responds.

"I could tell Sam I was suddenly called away on business," I suggest.

"Oh, that'll work for sure. Sam will never see through that."

"I don't care if he sees through it," I pout.

"Beth," Charlotte cautions.

"What?"

"Be fair," she sighs.

"I don't want to be fair. I want to be with you."

"Beth, you are with me. But this is your week to spend with Sam and the girls."

"I'm tired of keeping up appearances. I never know which week I'm supposed to be with Sam and which ones I'm allowed to be with you, which weekends we're spending in Princeton and which ones we can sneak away to Le Refuge."

"Ah yes, the perils of a double life," Charlotte says dramatically.

"Speaking of Le Refuge, did you do something with that frame I usually keep on the nightstand?"

"You mean the Lindstrom family triptych?"

"Yeah, I didn't see it the last time we were there."

"I couldn't stand seeing Sam smiling at me every time we were fucking, so I put it away in your paper pantry."

"You mean the wrapping room."

"Whatever."

"Well, don't do that. Hannah gave us that frame, and I rather like it."

Charlotte turns her body away from me and looks out the car window.

"Okay, if you don't want it at Le Refuge, I'll just put it in the Princeton house," I say.

I pull Charlotte's feet onto my lap and give them a good, hard rub. Karen once told me about pressure points in the

foot that can help relieve stress and tension. I wish I could remember where they are.

"Honestly, Charlotte, I think it's time to stop with this
charade. Did you see Neil Patrick Harris in the front row tonight? He gets to have the career of his dreams *and* two beautiful kids *and* live with the person he loves."

"Darling, you're amazing, but you're no Neil Patrick Harris."

"I'm not joking," I say.

"You'd be committing career suicide," Charlotte warns.
"You're the only female senior executive in the whole company. Those chauvinist pigs are stuck in the Stone Age. They
can barely tolerate having a woman in their ranks. I don't
think they're ready for a dyke."

"Things have changed," I say. "Lipstick lesbians like us are
a dime a dozen. No one cares anymore. Hell, there are more
same-sex weddings featured in the *New York Times* style section than there are straight ones these days."

"What about the girls?" Charlotte asks. "Are they really
ready to costar in the after-school special *I Have Two Mommies*? Never mind the psychological stress of being the kid of
divorced parents. This is the whole reason I didn't want kids
in the first place. Now you have to think about them instead
of just doing what you want. You have to think about the
girls before you make any rash decisions you'll later regret."

Our car emerges from the Holland Tunnel. The bright
lights of the city are behind us, and we head into the dull gray
maze of steel and concrete that is the New Jersey Turnpike.

I close my eyes and try to think. I'm thirty-nine years old.
Next year, I'll enter my fifth decade of life. Mother died at
the age of forty-four. Would she have lived her life differently
if she'd known how little time she had?

The year is drawing to an end. Thanksgiving is just around
the corner, and then it'll be Christmas before you know it. I've

already told Alex to go ahead and order the trees from Maine and the straw goats from those enterprising Swedish nuns.

Claire and Ally were so happy when they woke up at Le Refuge last Christmas. It really was a magical winter wonderland scene. Charlotte is right: I have to think about the girls instead of just doing what I want.

But children are resilient. Everyone says so. After Christmas, one day soon in the new year, I'm going to do it. I'm going to ask Sam for a divorce.

Because I'm worth it.

hannah

twenty-eight

The days are getting shorter now. Even though summer barely ended, the cold winds and dim lighting make it feel like winter is just around the corner. It's been an unusually long week at work. Thankfully there's only one more day before the weekend. I log off my work computer and start reaching for my overcoat when my cell phone buzzes. The screen reads Sam@Home. I pick up right away.

"Auntie Hannah," Claire says, "do you know where Daddy is?"

"Claire, honey, are you okay?" It's past six o'clock. Sam usually comes home by five in the afternoon to relieve Grace, the babysitter, so she can get back to her dorm in time for dinner.

"Yeah, me and Ally are here with Grace, but Daddy didn't come home yet."

I ask Claire to put Grace on the line, apologize profusely and get her to agree to stay a couple more hours with the girls until I can get there. I don't have time to go back to Hoboken to pick up my weekend bag. Getting myself to Princeton as soon as possible is the top priority.

Where are you? The girls called so I'm headed to Princeton right now, I text Sam on my way to the train station. There's no answer. I keep checking my phone every few minutes as the train wends its way toward Princeton, as I sit in the taxicab driving me to Sam and Beth's house, even as I walk up the brick walkway to the front door. The screen remains blank.

"Auntie Hannah!" the girls cheer as I enter the foyer.

"Grace, I'm so sorry about this," I say, slipping off my shoes and reaching into my purse for my wallet. "I got here as soon as I could. There's a cab waiting outside to take you back to school. I've already prepaid him. How much do I owe you?"

Grace casts her eyes sideways to the girls at her elbows.

"Claire and Ally," I say, "hug Grace goodbye and go check the freezer to see what you want for dinner." There were at least two homemade lasagnas and a chicken tetrazzini in the freezer the last time I checked.

As soon as the girls are gone, I ask Grace if there's something wrong. She tells me this isn't the first time Sam's been late, although he usually texts or calls in advance. Sam promised to pay Grace double her ten-dollar hourly rate for anything beyond her normal working hours, but he's always been short on cash.

"Has he paid your regular wages?" I ask, dreading the answer.

"Oh yeah, that's fine," Grace says. "I get two hundred dollars automatically transferred to my bank every week. That's never been a problem."

Grace has been working for Sam and Beth for over two years, ever since she was a sophomore. Beth would've set up the automatic payment arrangement when they hired her. Sam's never been good with computers or finances; he wouldn't know how to change the arrangement even if he wanted to.

I can't help but do the mental math: two hundred dollars per week times roughly thirty or forty weeks of work in a year. It's way more than the nineteen-hundred-dollar annual IRS threshold. I can't imagine they've been withholding for Social Security and FICA or paying the required taxes.

"How much does Sam owe you for overtime?"

"I haven't been keeping super close track," Grace says. I can tell she's lying. Grace's parents own a dry-cleaning store in Pittsburgh. Grace helped out at the register every day since she was old enough to count. Grace was trained to keep super close track of money.

"Come on, Grace, tell me what Sam owes you." As our conversation drags, I think about the taxi driver in the driveway, the minutes ticking away and the waiting charges piling up.

"Like, maybe, nine hundred?" Grace says, her voice inflecting upward.

I'd been expecting to hear a hundred dollars, maybe two hundred, but nine hundred dollars takes my breath away. How many nights has Sam been coming home late? And why?

I give Grace all the money in my wallet—roughly sixty dollars—and write her a check for the remainder. Grace looks almost guilty as I make the notation in my check register and rip the check carefully from the checkbook.

"Um, this is probably a really bad time to bring this up," she says, accepting the check with both hands, Korean-style, "but I'm going to be graduating next spring." Her voice inflects upward again, as if this is a question rather than a statement.

I hadn't thought about it before, but of course we'll need to find a replacement for Grace. Sam needs someone who can pick up the girls from school and watch them until he comes home from work, and Grace can't be expected to do it forever. Normally, I'd suggest Maria or Jorge take on these additional responsibilities, but I've been urging Sam to let them go, so that's not a long-term solution.

"Oh, congratulations," I say. I'm grateful Grace is giving us so much advance notice.

"My parents say I've saved up enough money to get me through the end of the school year, so they said I could take spring semester off—you know, so I can enjoy my last semester of college?"

It takes me a moment to realize she's not taking spring semester off from school. She's taking it off from work. She's quitting.

"Can you stay with us through the end of the year?" I ask.

"Mrs. Lindstrom usually gave me December off," Grace says. "You know, to study for exams and stuff?"

"Of course, that makes sense. Can you work through the end of November?" I ask. That's just five weeks away.

"Yeah, definitely," Grace says, slipping on her jacket and heading outside.

As the cab drives away, I check my phone again, but there's no response.

"Where are you, Sam?" I say to myself.

After dinner, I give Ally a bath and zip her into footie pajamas. I've sent Sam three more texts—all unanswered—and scoured the local news websites for reports of car accidents or other calamities. I'm tempted to call the police but Sam's not even four hours late. I don't know what the minimum number of hours is to report a missing person, but I'm pretty sure it's more than four. I don't want to call and be reprimanded for wasting precious police resources.

I'm snuggling with Ally in bed, reading her a book, when Claire bursts into the room and yells, "Oh my God, Auntie

Hannah, tomorrow's my field trip to The Cheesecake Factory, and I just remembered my teacher told me that Daddy didn't turn in my permission slip."

"You're taking a field trip to The Cheesecake Factory?" I ask. "What could you possibly learn at The Cheesecake Factory?"

Claire looks at me despairingly. "Everyone says it's the best field trip of the year, Auntie Hannah. You have to help me find the permission slip or else I can't go."

Ally's delicate eyelids had been heavy with sleep just moments ago, but now she's wide-awake and eager to help her big sister with the all-important permission slip search.

"Yeah, Auntie Hannah, you have to help!" Ally insists.

I reluctantly get out of Ally's bed, and Ally jumps out to follow behind me.

"Where do you think it might be?" I ask.

"I don't know!" Claire cries. "I checked my backpack and my folder, and I looked all over my bedroom, and it's not anywhere!"

"Did you give the slip to Daddy?" I ask. "Do you think it might be in the study?"

"Oh yes!" Claire says. "Maybe it's in Daddy's study!"

When Beth and Sam first moved into their Princeton home, the room that impressed me the most—and the one room that inspired the most jealousy—was the formal library. The room has dark wood floor-to-ceiling shelves like you'd see in an English manor home, complete with a tall ladder on a railing so you can reach the top shelves. It's furnished with an antique cherrywood desk, two silk-upholstered wingback chairs and a rich green velvet lounging couch that just invites you to curl up with a good, thick novel.

Being a librarian, I was curious to see which books Sam and Beth had on their shelves. Next to thrillers by Tom Clancy and Robert Ludlum are flowery romances, literary novels, diet

books, celebrity memoirs and horticulture guides. A whole
section of the library is filled with old law school texts and
treatises, and another section is devoted to oversize art books.

"Hmm, this is an unusual selection," I commented.

"Books by the Foot," Sam responded. "Ten dollars per foot
for the regular hardbacks—upward of a hundred dollars per
foot for the fancy ones."

At first, I was shocked that Sam and Beth purchased books
solely for their decorative value, and then realized I would
have been even more shocked to learn that Sam and Beth had
purchased the books to read. The two of them never seem
to read, preferring to spend their free time watching *Breaking
Bad* and *House of Cards*.

I walk with Claire and Ally downstairs to the library. As
with the rest of the house, the library looks like it hasn't had a
good cleaning in a long time. I need to have a stern word with
Maria the next time I see her. Better yet, I'll insist that Sam
let Maria and Jorge go. He really can't afford them. But I'll
also write them a letter of recommendation and bonus check.
After all, they have been very kind to me and the girls, treat-
ing us like family.

I look at the messy pile of papers on top of Sam's desk: catalogs from Neiman Marcus and Saks and Tiffany's; appeals for
money from groups ranging from Planned Parenthood to the
Republican National Committee; dozens of business envelopes
from AT&T, BMW Financial Services, Prudential, Mutual of
Omaha and more. More than one envelope has printed on it
in red font: FINAL NOTICE.

"I found it," Claire yells.

"The permission slip?" I ask.

"No, Daddy's phone."

Claire holds up Sam's iPhone, which she's pulled out of
his gym bag.

I take the phone from Claire, hoping it'll provide me some clue of Sam's whereabouts. The phone is locked. I try Beth's birthday—1210—and the phone springs to life. I need to tell Sam to have a less predictable password.

There's the string of texts from me, and another string from Grace. As I scroll backward through the texts between Sam and Grace, there's a near-constant stream of sorry, running late and can U stay late tmrw? texts from Sam.

My curiosity gets the better of me, and I start to look at his other texts and phone calls. There's a slew of missed calls from Martin and Alex, cryptic texts from Charlotte and a series of compromising photos of Lise in various states of undress. I click the phone off, afraid of what I might discover next.

"It's here, it's here!" Claire screams. She pulls a crumpled piece of paper from a pile of worksheets, art projects and Scholastic book order forms gathered in the corner of the library.

"I remember now," Claire says. "I came here last week to give Daddy the permission slip, but he was taking a nap, and then I had to dump everything 'cause my juice pouch leaked all over the place."

Claire picks up the crushed Lunchables box that sits next to the pile of school papers, and she extracts a slightly soggy Oreo from the debris and takes a bite. I cringe while Ally begs for her sister to share.

I clear a small space on Sam's desk so I can fill out the permission slip and sign my own name; I don't feel comfortable forging Sam's signature. Claire and Ally bounce around the room doing a happy dance. I get the girls to brush their teeth and go to sleep, and then I sit down in the library waiting for Sam to come home. As I wait there on the velvet couch, I silently pray for his safety.

But a tiny part of me just wants to kill him.

It's nearly two o'clock in the morning when I hear the

garage door open. Sam stumbles into the house, reeking of gin and musk perfume.

"Where have you been?" I ask, turning on the hallway light.

"Fuck, Hannah," Sam says. "What're you doing here? Where's Grace?"

"The girls called me at six o'clock to say you were missing, so I had to rush here and relieve Grace."

"I told Grace I needed her to work late tonight," Sam says.

"That's not what Grace says," I say. Between Grace and Sam, there's no question who's a more reliable source. "And anyway, late doesn't mean two in the morning."

"I was having a couple drinks with the guys at the club and lost track of time." Sam rubs his eyes and turns off the light.

"The club bar closes at midnight," I say, turning the hallway light back on again. "And you smell like a skanky cocktail waitress."

"Okay, okay, you caught me, big sister," Sam says cheekily. He pats me on the head and leans on me for balance. "I've been moonlighting as a skanky cocktail waitress to make some extra cash. And, boy, are my feet killing me."

Sam laughs at his own joke and starts heading up the stairs. I block his way.

"What now, Hannah?" Sam whines. "I'm drunk and I'm tired and I really need to take a piss right now."

"No, what you really need to do is come with me and explain what's going on."

Sam doesn't have the energy to argue. He follows me to the study.

"Look at this," I say. I point at the towering pile of papers on Sam's desk, and he bursts out laughing.

"You really gonna give me shit for having a messy desk? What is this, fifth grade all over again?"

"Sam, this isn't funny. Grace told me about how much

money you owe her—hundreds of dollars. What possible reason do you have for coming home late night after night?"

"I'm a golf pro, Hannah. My income depends on rich white men wanting to spend time with me. I'm like a fucking whore. One or two hours of after-work drinks can turn into hundreds or thousands of extra dollars in my pocket," Sam says. "It's called sales."

"That's all well and good if you actually had hundreds or thousands of extra dollars in your pocket," I say, "but that doesn't seem to be the case. When I loaned you the money, you promised me that you'd live by a budget. You've got two little girls upstairs who depend on you. For once in your life, be a responsible adult." Even drunk, Sam knows that once his big sister gets into one of these moods, he's better off just shutting up and letting me talk.

"Okay, then, Hannah, what do you want me to do?" Sam asks. "At fucking two o'clock in the morning?"

"First of all, you need to clean up this mess," I say. I grab all of the catalogs and start throwing them into a brown paper grocery bag. "You can't think straight with all this junk."

"Wait," Sam protests, "you can't throw those away."

"I know," I reply, annoyed. "I'll put them in recycling later."

"No, not that. I mean, I send them to Beth."

"You send what to Beth?"

"I send the catalogs to Beth."

"Why in the world does Beth need catalogs in prison?"

Sam pauses. "She picks out the clothes I should buy for the girls. And for myself."

I can't believe Sam spends good money to send junk mail to Beth in prison. Sam keeps looking at me with his outstretched hand until I relent and give him the paper bag of catalogs.

"Can I at least throw away the Republican Party appeals?" I ask.

"Yeah, yeah." Sam nods. "Listen, I'm not a child. I can go through my mail myself."

"Apparently not." I toss envelope after envelope into the waiting bag.

"Wait, I might renew my subscription to *Maxim*," Sam says.

"No, you're not," I say, throwing the renewal envelope away.

Once I've gotten rid of the junk mail, I pull my handy letter opener from my purse and start slitting the business envelopes open, neatly stacking their contents into two piles: statements that don't require any action, and bills that need to be paid.

I see the tuition notice for Princeton Country Day. The bill says thirty-five thousand dollars is past due.

"Sam, why's the school still asking for tuition? You told me you'd pull Claire out of school if she didn't get a scholarship."

Sam takes the tuition envelope and sets it aside.

"The school said I missed the deadline for this year, but I could apply for next year," Sam says. "I really don't want to pull Claire out of school. She's thriving there."

"You always say that, Sam. Like that's an excuse to spend money you don't have. Claire is supersmart. She'd thrive anywhere."

"Message received, okay? If Claire doesn't get a scholarship next year, I promise to pull her out. I really mean it this time."

I let it drop for now. Looking at the pile of letters, one in particular catches my attention.

"Sam, this notice here says you're overdue paying Beth's life insurance premium."

"What's it matter?" Sam says. "It's not like she's making any money these days, or that she has any potential to make money in the future."

I put the life insurance letter into the "to be paid" pile and continue working my way through the mail. After I finish,

I turn to Sam and ask, "Sam, where's the notice for your life insurance?" Sam doesn't answer.

"Sam?"

Sam averts his eyes.

"Oh my God, Sam. Have you learned nothing in life?"

My parents emigrated from South Korea to the US so that my father could pursue his graduate degree in linguistics. My father wasn't any ordinary graduate student. He combined a brilliant and original mind with a genuine love of languages. At a time when Korea was barely emerging from two devastating wars, my father taught himself basic Latin, French, German and English, in addition to being fluent in Korean and Japanese. Being offered the opportunity to study at an American university was a dream come true for him.

When my father received the paperwork to apply for a student visa, he filled out the document in his clear, crisp hand. My parents agreed to use my father's family name, Min, as their last name and were discussing potential first names.

"They should be American, so that people can pronounce them," my father said in Korean, "and the two names should go together, so that people will remember them easily."

"Mickey and Minnie?" my mother suggested.

"I'm trying to be a respected scholar."

"George and Martha? What could be more respect-worthy than the father and mother of America?"

"Can you imagine me as George? And you as Martha?"

The young couple chuckled. Even in translation, they could never be George and Martha.

My father looked down at my mother's Korean passport. Her maiden name, Song, was printed beneath the photo of her pretty face, a playful smirk peeking out from under her official-looking stare. The word for *song* in Korean is *no-rae*; the word for *play* is *no-rah*.

My father looked over at his own photo, his black hair slicked back with Brylcreem, the sad droop in his dark eyes offset by charming crinkles of sly humor. My parents were both so happy the day they got their photos taken in preparation to go to America. They were practically drunk with joy.

"Nora," he said. "We're going to be Nick and Nora." Nick and Nora Charles were the smart and sassy, privileged and perennially drunk couple from the *Thin Man* movies, which my parents had seen at the tiny moviehouse in Seoul. To my parents, Nick and Nora were America.

Years after they immigrated, my parents died in a car crash on a highway just outside Buffalo. The roads were icy, and the other driver had gotten drunk at an office holiday party. My parents were completely sober. The other driver survived.

It was the winter of Sam's sophomore year at Princeton. I was working as an assistant librarian at a small law firm in New York City, and Sam was planning to take finals and then go back home for Christmas. I got the news of my parents' deaths by long-distance phone call, and I took the train that night to Princeton to tell my brother in person. Sam never returned to college, partly because he had no interest in academics— he was practically flunking most of his courses anyway—and partly because we couldn't afford it.

Sam and I were now impoverished. I had the Hoboken condo and some savings in the bank, but Sam had nothing. It blew my mind that my parents could be so irresponsible. Despite my mother's constant badgering on the subject, my father failed to purchase life insurance for either of them. My father had so much going on in his life, he didn't have the time.

Besides, he figured, he was much too young to die.

hannah

twenty-nine

After our parents' deaths, I did whatever I could to hold Sam and me together, to ensure we kept some semblance of a family. That first year was the hardest, with each passing holiday serving as a painful reminder of what we had lost. The first Thanksgiving without our parents, I made a Butterball turkey with all the fixings and invited over Sam's friends, mostly his Princeton classmates who weren't going home. Sam called it the orphans' Thanksgiving.

Today, as I make the long drive from Hoboken to St. Michaels, I realize this is the first real family Thanksgiving I will celebrate in over twenty years. When I arrive at Le Refuge, Eva has already put the Willie Bird farm-raised turkey into the oven. The delicious scent of the roasting turkey is making my stomach growl. Eva asks me to help her make some appetizers to take the edge off everyone's hunger.

"I can't believe this," Eva mutters. "I should've just gotten some frozen ones from IKEA or Trader Joe's. No one gives a shit if they're homemade." She cracks several eggs into a large bowl, grabs a balloon whisk and starts beating in the heavy cream.

"Excuse me?" I ask. I can barely hear Eva over the drone of the kitchen fan as I cook the onions. "Finely chopped with a full stick of butter over very low heat," as Eva directed.

"I said I can't believe I'm making Swedish meatballs," Eva says. She reaches over to turn off the fan over the range. "I hate Swedish meatballs."

Of all the foods in the world, Swedish meatballs seem to me one of the more innocuous, but I don't say anything. Eva and I rarely spend any time one-on-one, and I don't want to risk annoying her with my unsolicited opinions.

Eva takes a swig from her glass and consults the recipe. She's using a dog-eared copy of the Junior League of Washington, DC, cookbook from the early 1970s. The red wine–stained and grease-spattered Swedish meatball recipe is credited to the Embassy of Sweden. Eva adds generous pinches of salt, pepper and allspice to the liquid mixture and resumes whisking.

"Growing up," Eva explains, "we had to have Swedish meatballs with gravy and lingonberry sauce whenever the Embassy was entertaining guests." Eva unwraps the butcher-paper packages of fresh ground beef, pork and veal and plops them into the liquid. She uses her bare hands to stir the mixture. Her simple platinum wedding band is sitting in a saucer by the sink. She reaches for the large tempered-glass bowl of fresh bread cubes soaking in milk. She squeezes the milk from the softened bread and adds handful by handful to the meat mixture.

"Mother suggested that we serve something more refined on occasion—gravlax or roast venison, for example—but the

Ambassador insisted that visitors to the Swedish Embassy always expected Swedish meatballs, and it was Swedish meatballs they would get."

Eva looks over at my pan of onions. They're starting to get brown on the edges.

"Turn off the heat," she directs. "You want them soft, not bitter."

I comply. We wait for the onions to cool.

Eva goes to the farmhouse sink and washes her hands. She opens another bottle of wine, fills her glass and tops off mine, which I've barely taken a sip from.

Eva scrapes the onions into the bowl and gives the mixture one more kneading before walking with the bowl over to the kitchen table, where she's already laid out an array of sheet pans covered in crisp white parchment paper. It reminds me of the clean paper on the examining table at the doctor's office. Sam told me Eva's fancy dermatology practice caters to politicians' wives in suburban Virginia. I wonder whether she has a good bedside manner.

We sit down at the table together, our glasses of wine within reach. Each of us has a stainless steel scoop with which we measure out the meatball mixture. We shape the mixture into round balls and place the meatballs onto the parchment. I can't help but notice that Eva works fast, and her meatballs are just as perfect as mine.

"This reminds me of making Korean dumplings with my mother when I was little," I say. The meatball mixture is nearly the same consistency as the dumpling filling. "We always made dumplings for the lunar new year."

"It must have been cold growing up in Buffalo," Eva says.

"I guess so, but when you're a kid, you don't really notice," I reply. "You assume everything about your life is normal. You don't know any better."

My thoughts turn to Claire and Ally and whether they think going to visit their mother in prison is normal. For many children, visiting a loved one in prison seems to be all too common. As I contemplate the sorry state of our criminal justice system, I lose sight of what's in front of me. It takes me a minute to realize that Eva is crying.

"I'm sorry," I say, "did I say something wrong?"

Eva shakes her head as if embarrassed. I quietly resume scooping the meat mixture and placing them in neat rows on the parchment, not knowing what else to do.

"Growing up, Mother wanted only the best for us," Eva says. "She insisted we go to the best schools and wear the nicest clothes. To the outside world, our lives looked perfect. But all of that came at a cost."

Eva goes on to describe her parents' lives and the sacrifices they made: leaving a land they loved, moving away from their parents and their siblings, in pursuit of greater opportunities for their children. They had to become fluent in a new language, which isn't easy to do as adults, and to learn the customs of a new country. And in the end, they both died early—too early to see the fruits of their labor.

The story of Eva's parents sounds a lot like my own parents' story, and I tell her so. She glances up from her work, and there's a sense of mutual understanding that is comforting and a little strange. I'm not used to feeling a sense of connection with Eva.

"Still," I say, trying to lighten the moment, "it must have been awfully nice growing up in a mansion with a cook and driver."

Eva stares at me intensely, and I'm reminded of that photo of her from freshman year of college, her eyes owl-like in their bottle-lensed magnification.

"Hannah, you know my parents were the cook and driver, don't you?"

The cold stainless steel slips from my hand.

Eva's words hit me like a thunderbolt. How could I not have known that the Lindstrom parents were the hired help? As I think back on all the times Sam described Beth's childhood, I realize he never said what her parents did, just that they lived in the Swedish Embassy. I must have filled in the rest of the details with my own imagination.

It makes me wonder what else I've misunderstood about Beth.

The Monday after Thanksgiving, I'm back at my job in New York. I decide to skip lunch and take the subway up to Tiffany's. Having berated Sam for failing to renew his life insurance policy, an oversight I made sure he corrected right away by filling out the paperwork and paying the premium myself, I feel like a hypocrite for not having a jewelry rider on my homeowner's insurance. Admittedly, I don't have much to cover: just my mother's wedding band, a Tiffany pearl bracelet that Owen gave me and, of course, the huge diamond studs from Sam. Nevertheless, I want to be covered.

Sitting across from me on the subway train is an older Mexican woman holding a plastic Gristedes grocery bag. Something about her reminds me of Maria, Sam and Beth's housekeeper. Maybe it's the soft brown eyes or the weary curve of her spine. I hope Maria and Jorge were able to find a good job after Sam let them go.

I emerge from the subway and walk up Fifth Avenue, the transcendent image reminding me of the dreamy opening credits of *Breakfast at Tiffany's*: the long shot of the classic yellow cab driving up an empty Fifth Avenue just at sunrise, the heartbreakingly melancholy strains of Henry Mancini's "Moon River," and the breathtakingly beautiful Audrey Hepburn in her Givenchy black sheath gazing longingly into the windows of the famed jeweler. I step onto the deep-pile carpeting and am almost blinded by the bright lights as they bounce off the spotless glass surfaces and shiny silver corners of the display cases. A sharply dressed man approaches and asks, "May I help you, ma'am?"

"I'm looking to have some personal items appraised," I answer. I hate being called ma'am. It makes me feel old and matronly. The man directs me to the appraisal department on the fifth floor of the store.

"Good afternoon, miss," a stately gentleman greets me on the fifth floor. Now, that's more like it. He's wearing an official-looking blazer monogrammed with the Tiffany name.

"I'm hoping you might be able to provide me with an appraisal for a few items," I reply. In the movie, the salesman at Tiffany's agrees to inscribe a toy ring found inside a Cracker Jack box for Audrey Hepburn and George Peppard. Surely, what I'm asking for isn't nearly so silly as that. I reach into my handbag and pull out the soft blue pouch containing the pearl bracelet.

"It's been many years since I received this as a gift," I say. "I saw it on your website, but the insurance company says I need an actual appraisal and not a printout."

"Ah yes," the gentleman responds, fingering the pearls delicately. "A nice little piece. It's part of our Return to Tiffany collection. It's currently valued at five hundred dollars. Most insurance policies would cover that without a special rider, but I'd be happy to fill out an appraisal if you'd like."

Despite his respectful tone, I can't help but feel a little dismissed, like my five-hundred-dollar bracelet isn't worth his time. I feel my cheeks flush, probably from the heat of the lights. I'm eager to prove myself with my next item.

"I received these as a gift, as well," I say. I pull out the signature blue jewelry box from my handbag. "When I went on your website, the largest diamond studs available were one carat total weight for both studs, and I believe these are one carat each." The diamond earrings on the website were valued at ten thousand dollars. I can only imagine how much my earrings are worth. I open the box and wait for the elegant gentleman to be dazzled. He pulls out his loupe and examines the earrings closely.

"Do you mind?" he asks. He pulls the earrings out of the box but doesn't wait for me to respond. I know diamonds are valued based on the four Cs—color, cut, clarity and carats—and I'm hoping he hasn't spotted something. As far as my untrained eye can see, these diamonds are flawless. The gentleman arranges the earrings carefully back into their box and closes the lid.

"Miss, these are lovely earrings, but I'm sorry to have to tell you—they are not from Tiffany's. And they are not diamonds."

I can barely see straight as I leave the store and take the PATH train back to Hoboken. My voice is raspy when I call in sick for the rest of the day.

They're just earrings, I think as I lie on the couch. *Are you really so materialistic that you would let something as meaningless as a pair of earrings come between you and your brother?*

I close my eyes and try to blot out the memory of that night of my fortieth birthday—but I can't. I see Sam's face, ruddy from drink and the heat of the bonfire, making such a spectacle of himself as he presents the gift to me. I hear the roar of the crowd's adulation as they recognize the signature color of the gift bag and the extravagant size of the gemstones. I smell the nauseating mix of expensive cologne and even more expensive booze that envelops me as I give Sam a grateful hug.

Why does Sam need to make it about himself all the time? Why couldn't he just have given me the earrings in a quiet moment, just the two of us, in whatever box the earrings came in? Then again, perhaps the earrings didn't even come in a box. Perhaps Sam picked them up from one of those African sidewalk vendors in the city, or from the buy-one-get-one-free rack at the Accessory Mart in the mall—the same place I purchased the hot-pink cubic zirconia necklace for Claire's sixth birthday.

I don't have any appetite. I have no interest in watching TV or reading a book. It's not even eight o'clock when I go to the bathroom, open the medicine cabinet and take a couple Ativan and Ambien. It occurs to me I haven't taken these in a long time, not since Beth left for Alderson. I've been trying to be good for the girls.

"I just want this day to be over," I say to my reflection in the mirror. I'm disturbed by the image I see. When did I turn into my mother?

I can feel the drugs working to relax my tightly wound mind.

"The earrings don't matter, they really don't matter," I keep saying to myself.

If I say it enough times, maybe I'll finally believe it.

hannah

thirty

It's the morning after my trip to Tiffany's, and I still can't think straight.

"I'm not feeling well," I say into the law firm's voice mail system. "I need to take one more day off, but I should be in the office tomorrow."

I turn off my phone and lie in bed, my head dizzy from the drugs and consumed by my memories. I reach over the nightstand and pour the pearl bracelet out of the soft blue pouch and into my palm. I distinctly remember the day Owen gave it to me to celebrate our six-month anniversary. As my fingers caress the smooth orbs, I feel like a nun saying the rosary.

My mind floats back to that summer in Cambridge after my freshman year when Owen and I were sharing an apartment in Porter Square. I felt like we'd been playacting as adults all summer. We'd ride the Red Line into Boston, where we'd get off together and kiss goodbye at Park Street. I'd walk up-hill past the grand State House to the laughably picturesque Beacon Hill brownstone that houses the publishing company where I had an unpaid internship. On weekends, Owen and I would run errands and go grocery shopping at the nearby Stop & Shop, checking items off my to-do lists. Owen some-how managed to get me to join him at the hole-in-the-wall jazz clubs in Inman Square and frenetic dance clubs in Boston.

It's been sweltering all week, and I've got the windows wide-open in the bedroom. I'm drifting in and out of sleep, my glasses still on my face, when I hear the sound of Owen's voice. He's half whistling, half singing a song. I recognize the melody as Hoagy Carmichael's jazz standard, "Stardust." I can't tell if I'm dreaming.

I get up and look out the window, but Owen is gone. I hear Owen's footsteps as he makes his way up the creaky wooden stairs to our second-floor flat. As Owen reaches the door of our apartment, I'm startled by the sound of the phone ring-ing. I glance at the clock. It's 12:25 a.m. My heart clenches; no one ever calls at this hour with good news.

"Your brother is in the hospital," my father says.

"What happened?" I ask.

"He jumped off the roof."

"Oh my God, is he okay?"

"He has some broken bones and concussion, but the doc-tors say he'll be fine. It's lucky he's young. Ten-year-olds heal quickly."

"What was he thinking?"

"He was trying to be a superhero."

Of course. Sam the superhero. Why wouldn't he think he could fly?

"And Umma?" I ask.

"You know Umma," my father says.

"I'll get on the first flight out," I say.

The next morning, my father picks me up at the Buffalo Niagara International Airport, his face drawn and his eyes deeply shadowed from lack of sleep.

"How was your flight?" he asks as he takes my bag and puts it in the trunk.

"Fine. How's Sam?"

"Fine. He was still sleeping when I left the hospital. The doctors say he's recovering well but they want him to stay in the hospital a few days for observation."

I don't bother to ask about Umma. I already know the answer.

As my father drives in silence to the hospital, I look out the soot-covered car window at the flat, industrial landscape, so different from the charming brick buildings of Harvard Square. Power lines and rusty warehouses pass by in a blur. My mind drifts back to just a few hours ago, watching the early-morning light slowly brightening the walls of our Porter Square apartment, the gentle summer breeze wafting through the window, the two of us curled together listening to Nat King Cole crooning "There Will Never Be Another You." I blink the memory away and return my focus to my family.

"I'll go to the cafeteria and get us some coffee," my father says as we walk into the hospital. I nod even though I don't drink coffee.

"Hannah, I've been waiting for you!" my mother shrieks in Korean. I enter the sterile hospital room, the cheap industrial curtains drawn closed and blocking the world outside. She runs over to embrace me, then falls dramatically in a heap as if completely depleted of energy, pulling my body down on the faded teal linoleum floor with her.

"Sorry to be late, Umma," I apologize.

"Sam almost died," she says, still in Korean.

"I know," I say comfortingly, although it isn't true. After my mother called 911, the paramedics arrived and asked her what happened. She couldn't answer, so they gave up trying to communicate. During the frantic but wordless race to the hospital, my mother convinced herself Sam was going to die. Even after my father spoke with the ER doctors and confirmed Sam would be fine, my mother clung to the original fiction.

"Sam almost died," she repeats over and over. "Just like before, Hannah. Remember? Just like before."

"I know," I say again, though it isn't true either. This isn't at all like before. This is just a stupid accident: my brother being foolish and acting reckless. The last time was a tragic twist of fate, an innocent life lost too soon. The two events are completely different, but I can't fault my mother for conflating them.

My mother pushes me away from her so she can look me straight in the eyes. Her face is streaked with tears, clumpy mascara running down her cheeks in gray rivulets, her coral-colored lipstick smeared. She looks like a madwoman.

"You're different, Hannah," she says. "Something about you is changed."

I feel the rush of blood to my face. I know I've changed, but can my mother really tell? The awful thought crosses my mind: Perhaps she can smell Owen's scent on me? But no, I showered before I left for the airport.

"No, Umma, I haven't changed," I reply using my little-girl voice. "I'm still your same Hannah." She continues to scan my face, unsure. After a while, my mother stands up and sits in the padded chair in the corner of the hospital room, where she urgently fingers her well-worn rosary beads, her lips moving silently in prayer.

From my vantage point on the hospital room floor, I look up at Sam sleeping peacefully, his chest rising and falling in a steady rhythm. I'm reminded of the many moments I've watched him in repose: as a tiny baby in his crib, as a toddler clutching his Power Rangers action figure, as a boy wearing his Buffalo Bills jersey and kicking off his thick fleece blankets. I think about the countless times my mother would beg me to intercede when Sam was going off the rails—throwing a tantrum, beating his skull against the headboard, refusing to open his mouth for the dentist or return a toy to a child on the playground.

I get off the floor and sit gently at the foot of Sam's bed. I glance over at my mother, who is lost in urgent prayer. I wonder where my father has gone. I can only imagine how much drama he's had to shoulder by himself in the year I've been away. It can't have been easy. For just an instant, I imagine what my life might be if I didn't have to worry about Sam anymore, if he did in fact die from the accident. And then I wipe the thought away as quickly as I can.

The week after Sam is released from the hospital, I call Harvard to ask them to transfer my credits to the University at Buffalo. And then I write Owen a long letter to say I won't be coming back to Cambridge. We continue to exchange letters for about a year, but I can't bear to talk to him by phone and I forbid him from visiting. It just hurts too much.

Just as Sam has his repertoire of stories, so, too, does my family. For a period in the mid-1980s, the most requested story among my parents' social circle is "Why Hannah Left Harvard."

To hear my mother tell it, I just couldn't bear the strain of being so far away from home. "My sweet daughter has such a soft heart," she'd explain. "She missed her family too much to stay away from us."

The local gossips don't buy it. "I hear that Hannah Min

had a nervous breakdown," they'd whisper. "She met a boy at Harvard, and he broke her heart."

My father has a more generous narrative, one he shares only with me: I returned home because my emotionally fragile mother and high-maintenance younger brother couldn't manage without me. My family needed me to take control, to make sure that everything and everyone was taken care of, because without me things had fallen apart.

"You should be proud of yourself, Hannah," my father would say in my lowest moments. "You sacrificed everything for your family."

Homesick innocent. Lovelorn victim. Dutiful control freak. Perhaps the truth lies somewhere in between.

After two days away from the office, I drag myself back in. It's not like me to wallow in misery, but something about Sam's deception cuts me to the core. I can barely focus on the legal cases I'm researching for one of the litigation partners at my firm. My mind keeps returning to the shiny surfaces of the Tiffany store, reflecting my image back at me a million times.

"Hey, are you in the middle of something?" Tracy asks.

"Not really," I say, welcoming the break.

"I have to show you something," Tracy says.

I'm puzzled as Tracy leads me out of the law library, over to the firm's elevator banks and down six floors to the supply closet on the twenty-fourth floor. It's where the law firm stores our miscellaneous junk: reams of extra letterhead, boxes of holiday decorations, opened bottles of cheap booze. Tracy turns on the light and reaches down to retrieve a white banker's box that's been tucked behind a cardboard container of firm-logo'd water bottles and fleece vests.

"Where'd you get this?" I ask. In big block letters, the box is labeled *"United States v. God Hälsa AB, Andreas Magnusson and Elizabeth Lindstrom."*

"Let's just say I called in a favor with a friend of mine at the US Attorney's Office," Tracy responds. She lifts the box out of the metal wire shelf and onto the table in the middle of the room.

"Tracy, did you get this legally?" I ask.

"The case is closed," Tracy responds. She points to the bright orange sticker that says CLOSED on it, but that doesn't answer my question. I'm still uneasy. This doesn't feel right to me.

"I met this guy at aikido who works as an Assistant US Attorney," Tracy says. "We struck up a conversation, and one thing led to another. When I first opened the door to the discovery closet, I couldn't believe my eyes. It reminded me of the final scene in *Raiders of the Lost Ark*. Or better yet, that room in *From the Mixed-Up Files of Mrs. Basil E. Frankweiler.*"

I love Tracy. For all her rule-breaking faults, she's brilliant and speaks my language.

"I couldn't very well walk out of there with a dolly full of boxes, so I chose this one," Tracy says. "I think these are the confidential exhibits we couldn't find online." She lifts off the lid of the box, which is filled with reddish-colored folders. Redwelds, they're called. She pulls out a folder and hands it over to me. I pull out a sheaf of papers on US Department of Justice letterhead. Having worked on countless litigation matters, I know to flip through the first dozen pages of legal boilerplate and get to the meat of the document.

"Please provide any and all evidence documenting (A) that God Hälsa was promoting Metamin and Metamin-G for off-label uses such as weight loss, academic performance and social anxiety; and (B) that Mrs. Min-Lindstrom was personally responsible for promoting Metamin and Metamin-G for such off-label uses."

The response simply says: *"See attached exhibits."*

The ensuing pages are color-copied advertisements from a wide range of publications: *Time, People, Ladies' Home Journal, Parents, InStyle.* All the advertisements have the same tagline: "Fit Right in with Metamin." I've seen these ads countless times before, but I turn the pages one by one and look at them with fresh eyes.

The first advertisement features a plump Hispanic girl of eight or nine wearing a too-small bright pink leotard, frowning as she stands in gymnastics class and stares into a full-length mirror, comparing her reflection to that of a petite white girl by her side. Directly behind the ad is a color copy of a photograph taken at Claire's fifth birthday party. The two photographs are nearly identical.

The second advertisement shows a bespectacled college-aged young woman sitting at a desk and surrounded by a pile of textbooks, her head in her hands as if struggling to concentrate. Directly behind is the unflattering photograph of Eva from her freshman year of college.

The final advertisement shows a sad-looking little girl sitting by herself on a playground bench, the only Asian child in a sea of happy white faces. Directly behind is a photograph of a smiling Claire standing arm in arm with her friends at her mostly white preschool.

"Do you recognize these photos?" Tracy asks.

"I do," I say. "They're from Beth's family albums." I think back to what Beth said when I asked her about the missing exhibits: *We got the prosecutors to keep them confidential because they have minor children in them.* Beth didn't mention that the minor children were her own.

"Who has access to those albums?" Tracy asks.

I think about Beth's bedroom at Le Refuge. The pale blue walls and luxurious linens accented by the soft lighting and heady floral fragrance. It's like a sanctuary—off-limits to all but the most intimate relations.

"This is it, right?" Tracy says. "The smoking gun? The proof that Beth was personally responsible for the Metamin-G ads at the heart of the whistle-blower case?"

"Yeah, it appears so."

"Hannah, I hate to say this," Tracy says, "but Lise's accomplice has to be a close family member, right? Who else would even know about these photographs?"

I look through the pile of photographs, but I can't take my eyes off the last advertisement, the one of the little girl sitting by herself on the playground. You can't blame the prosecutors for getting that one wrong. Whenever he told the story of how he was conceived, Sam made sure that everyone had a mental picture of me sitting alone in the schoolyard.

But no one was there that day to take an actual photograph.

lise

From the deposition of Lise Danielsson in *United States of America v. Sam Min and Alexander Lindstrom-Larsen*

Q: Thank you for taking the time to answer my questions today.

A: You told me I could go to jail if I didn't.

Q: Notwithstanding, I appreciate your cooperation.

A: You're welcome, I guess.

Q: You are free to go now.

A: Before I go, can I just say one more thing about Sam?

Q: Sure.

A: I don't know what you think Sam did, but he shouldn't go to jail for it. He's a really nice guy. He would never intentionally hurt anyone.

Q: Thank you for your opinion.

A: If Sam did anything wrong, it's because he's so nice. He always sees the good in everyone. I remember Sam telling me once how lucky he is. "I have a gorgeous wife, two cute girls and plenty of time and money to enjoy it all," he said. "I've led a charmed life. It's like someone's always looking out for me."

beth

thirty-one

I wait until the week after the holidays before asking Sam for a divorce. He takes it a lot harder than I thought he would.

"I've done everything you asked," Sam says.

"I know, and I'm sorry. But I'm tired of living this charade. And anyway, we weren't even supposed to end up together. Remember our deal?"

"You're not going to hold me to the contract now, are you?" Sam asks. "Not after all these years."

"I don't want to play hardball," I say. "But I will if I have to."

Sam and I agree to consult with our lawyers to see if we can work something out that minimizes the disruption for the girls. Months pass. The wheels of justice—or at least marital dissolution—turn slowly. Especially when lawyers who charge by the hour are involved.

I'm sitting at my desk at God Hälsa HQ when it all starts to fall apart.

At first, I think my assistant screwed up.

Every morning, my trusty assistant, Renee, places a clear plastic folder on my desk with a color printout of my day's meetings along with any materials needing my attention or signature. It's my regular routine, the way I operate. I wouldn't know where to go or what to do without my daily folder.

There is a thick legal document in today's folder. I'm annoyed.

My executive assistant and I have been together long enough that she knows the protocol. She's authorized to sign any administrative forms on my behalf. She sends any legal documents directly to our in-house lawyers. I shouldn't even see them.

"Renee," I yell from my desk, "come in here."

Renee scurries into my office from her nearby cubicle.

"Please take this and send it to Legal," I say, handing her the binder-clipped document.

Renee stands there blinking.

"Renee, did you hear me? Please take this and send it to Legal."

Renee's face turns cherry. "But…"

"But what, Renee?" My exasperation is showing.

"But that came from Legal."

I look more carefully at the document and sure enough it has "RECEIVED—God Hälsa Legal Department" and last Friday's date stamped on it.

"You have a 9:00 a.m. with Mr. Starck in the Mälaren Room to talk about it," Renee says. Starck is God Hälsa's general counsel. Our company's top lawyer.

I examine my daily calendar to confirm Renee's statement.

"Which one is Mälaren again?" I ask Renee for the umpteenth time. All of God Hälsa's conference rooms are named after Swedish lakes, but no one ever uses the official names, which are unpronounceable.

It's like working at fucking IKEA.

"The big conference room next to the women's bathroom," Renee answers.

Everyone calls it Flushing Meadows.

This is unusual. Legal doesn't usually need to talk to me about lawsuits. Everyone agrees such matters are below my pay grade. And Starck rarely shows up in the office. Starck sightings are usually limited to quarterly board meetings or charity fund-raisers with his spray-tanned skeleton of a wife. It must be serious if he's involved.

I check my phone for the time. Damn, I'm already late. Who schedules a meeting for 9:00 a.m. on Monday?

I know something's wrong the moment I step into the room. CEO Andreas Magnusson is sitting at the head of the table, and General Counsel Starck is at his immediate right. A phalanx of unfamiliar faces in pin-striped suits fills the rest of the table.

I resist the temptation to apologize for my lateness and instead allow the door to be my frame as I stand there looking poised and professional. I am the picture of cool.

"Sit down, Elisabeth," Starck orders. I'm put off by his rudeness but tolerate it for the moment. I sit in the chair closest to the door, directly opposite Magnusson.

"Have you read the materials I sent?" Starck asks.

"No, I just got in," I answer briskly. Never apologize, that's my motto. Along with "you can never be too rich or too thin."

"What's this about?" I ask.

"It's a qui tam lawsuit against God Hälsa that specifically names you and Andreas as codefendants."

Goddamn it, first Swedish and now Latin. What do they think I am, a freaking linguist?

"What's a qui tam lawsuit?" I ask.

"It's a lawsuit filed by a whistle-blower. It alleges that God Hälsa committed fraud against the United States government. Do you know someone named Elise Danielsson?"

"Lise? Are you talking about Lise Danielsson?" I laugh derisively. Lise was my au pair and personal assistant. She grew up in some sleepy Swedish town whose only claim to fame is making clogs.

"Lise wouldn't know the first thing about filing a whistle-blower lawsuit," I say.

"Miss Danielsson doesn't need to know anything about filing a lawsuit," Starck responds. "She hired one of the best plaintiff's law firms in the country to file it for her."

I pull the document from my daily folder, undo the binder clip and scan the contents.

United States of America et al. v. God Hälsa AB, Andreas Magnusson and Elizabeth Lindstrom.

They misspelled my name; I hate it when they misspell my name.

"This is an action to recover civil damages on behalf of the United States of America for violations of the Federal Civil False Claims Act... Plaintiffs did personally and willfully engage in marketing efforts to promote off-label uses of Metamin and Metamin-G such as the treatment of social anxiety, promotion of weight loss, enhanced academic performance, among other purposes..."

I stop reading. I've read enough.

"This is bullshit, and you know it," I say. "I've always been careful to make sure our reps stick with the official script, even though everyone knows Metamin can do so much more than what the FDA has approved it for. We can't control what doctors or patients do of their own volition. This is a free country after all."

"Elisabeth, you do realize that, if we are convicted on any of these counts, God Hälsa could be debarred?" Starck asks.

Fucking lawyers.

"Well, being disbarred would be a pity for you, Starck, but is that any reason to throw the rest of the company under the bus?"

"Debarred, Elisabeth, not disbarred," Starck says. I spy one of the snot-nosed outside lawyers smirking at his fellow toady.

I look at everyone imperiously, waiting for an explanation.

"Being debarred means that the federal government refuses to do any business with us," Starck says. "I don't need to tell you that Medicaid and Medicare pay for the lion's share of our pharmaceutical sales. If we lose the government, we lose billions in revenues. If that happens, we lose investor confidence, our stock drops, the company fails. We can't afford to risk that."

"We get these frivolous lawsuits all the time," I respond, "and we always settle out of court. You've told me before— it's just the price of doing business. What makes this one any different?"

Before Starck can answer my question, Magnusson stands up, smashes his hand on the polished glass table and growls like a roused giant.

"Because this time, Elisabeth, they've got proof."

The following months are a nightmare of revelations and recriminations. I finally face reality and agree to make a plea deal with the prosecutors. Now I've got to get my personal affairs in order.

"Sign here," the lawyer says, passing yet another document to me.

I sign on the line.

"Where do I sign?" Sam asks.

God, he's such an idiot sometimes.

"At the X, the highlighted part," the douchebag lawyer responds. He guides Sam's hand like a kindergarten teacher helping her charges with the ABCs.

I've had it up to here with lawyers. There are the lawyers that God Hälsa hired for me, the lawyers that God Hälsa hired for CEO Magnusson, the lawyers that God Hälsa hired for its board of directors, the lawyers that God Hälsa hired for itself as a corporation and the lawyers that I hired for myself and Sam because I don't trust God Hälsa's corporate lackeys to have our best interests at heart.

And then there's this guy, some Dartmouth buddy that Martin reconnected with on LinkedIn, one of those lawyer/financial consultant types that I called in to help me and Sam figure out how to manage the next ten years.

"Now that we've completed the power of attorney process, we need to think about next steps," the lawyer advises.

"Next steps?" Sam asks.

"Yes, the next steps to preserve your cash flow while Beth is…" The lawyer pauses.

"In prison," I say, finishing his sentence. "We need to talk about how to take care of Sam and the girls while I'm in prison."

"Well, finances will definitely be tight for the next several years," the lawyer continues. "However, I think Sam and the girls could possibly manage on Sam's income if you sold your homes. The equity you have in the homes might be enough to tide the family over, and there's certainly no need for you to own two homes. I'm sure the family could rent a perfectly nice house, perhaps not right here in Princeton, but nearby."

"Oh yes, I hear Trenton is quite lovely," I reply.

"And you really need to work down your monthly household expenses," the lawyer says. "For example, I don't see a need for a full-time housekeeper and gardener. My Lord, it's not like you need to keep up appearances once you're in prison."

I glare across the table at Sam.

"And finally," the lawyer continues, "you really ought to consider pulling your daughter out of private school. That should be no problem at all if you stay here in Princeton, given how strong the public schools are, although I'll admit if you move to Trenton, it could be a bit more challenging..." The lawyer's voice trails off, as if the hot air were slowly leaking out of the old windbag.

"Okay, listen to me," I say, "the most important thing—our true north—is the girls. We can't do anything that hurts them. I'm fine taking out second mortgages, but we're not selling the houses. Both the Princeton house and Le Refuge are my children's homes. Their homes. They're losing their mother—there's no way in hell they're going to lose their homes, as well.

"As for monthly expenses, go ahead and cut the nonessentials, but don't you even think about firing Maria or Jorge. This goes beyond just appearances. They're family. They've devoted their lives to taking care of me and my kids, and they deserve to be taken care of in return."

My words are directed at Sam, not the lawyer. I want Sam to understand: these things are nonnegotiable.

"And finally, Claire's not going to public school. She's been working hard all year, and she's looking forward to moving up from pre-K to kindergarten. Claire adores her teachers, and they love her. Now, more than ever, Claire's going to need their emotional support. Claire can't be pulled out of Princeton Country Day. After all, she's thriving there.

"Do you understand?" I ask Sam. "You can't let me down on this, okay?"

Sam nods.

Sam might not be the brightest bulb, but there's one thing I can say for him.

He always does as he's told.

hannah

thirty-two

"We just finished up our year-end partner meeting," Old Man Barker says. "Per-partner profits were at an all-time high this year, and our back-office costs were at an all-time low. We have you to thank for that, Hannah."

"You're welcome, Mr. Barker."

"I assume you've heard people talking about the new office?" he asks.

Indeed, the firm has been abuzz with rumors that Drinker, Barker and Horne will be acquiring a boutique litigation firm out in San Francisco. The associates are already taking bets about who'll be asked to relocate. It's considered a plum job—with high-profile clients like Twitter and Lyft and Salesforce—and the chance to fast-track your way to partner.

"Well, the rumors are true. We're making the announcement tomorrow. And, Hannah, we're hoping you'd be willing to help open the new office," he says. "We just signed a lease for three floors of a brand-new office tower just South of Market, with breathtaking views of San Francisco Bay. You'd have the title of Director of Legal Administration as well as a substantial increase in salary."

The offer is extremely flattering, and I make sure to tell him so.

"You're my top pick for the job, Hannah," he says, sensing my hesitation. "You're more than a law librarian. You're our de facto IT guru, you outshine our best paralegals and you can even handle the receptionist desk in a pinch. Simply put, you get things done. You're an asset to the firm, and I want to offer you this once-in-a-lifetime opportunity."

A once-in-a-lifetime opportunity.

How could I say no?

I've been to San Francisco just once, for a legal conference on e-discovery and document management best practices. It was a few years ago, and I stayed at one of those classic old hotels right in the heart of Union Square. The famous cable car route runs directly in front, transporting tourists up Nob Hill toward Fisherman's Wharf.

As with most conferences, the attractive location is almost irrelevant. We attendees are trapped in the hotel all day. The carpeted hallway connecting the elevators to the conference rooms is filled with vendors shilling their services, each one offering an astonishing array of company-branded swag: pens, Post-its, water bottles, coffee mugs, Koozies, hand sanitizers, lip balms, squeeze flashlights, earbuds, screen cleaners, mobile device chargers, luggage tags, tote bags, golf umbrellas.

Breakfast, lunch and dinner are all served buffet-style, the same Sterno-fueled chafing dishes of bland American food being consumed in countless windowless banquet rooms across the country. Between such scintillating sessions as "Hold Me

Closer: Litigation Holds in the Modern Corporate Environment" and "Metadata Management: A Year-End Review," we keep ourselves awake with tasteless chocolate chip cookies and vats of bitter brown liquid posing as coffee. For those attendees in search of more sugar, the vendors in the hallway offer enormous bowls of company-logo'd M&M's, carnival-striped bags of caramel corn and even a mobile frozen yogurt bar with a dizzying choice of mix-ins.

On the final afternoon of the conference, we attendees feel like children on the last day of school, eager to finally break free of our keepers. Another conference attendee and I strike up a casual friendship and decide to make our way down to Tadich Grill, the oldest restaurant in the city. We treat ourselves to steaming bowls of their world-famous cioppino, the thick tomato broth redolent of garlic and loaded with seafood. The white-jacketed waiters remind me of the famously surly servers at Durgin Park, the centuries-old restaurant in downtown Boston where Owen and I had our first dress-up date.

"God, I'm stuffed," my conference companion says. She signs her receipt and slips the customer copy into her wallet. I sneak a peek to make sure I give the same tip on my half of the bill. "Wanna go for a walk to burn off some calories?"

I'm happy to oblige. As we leave the warmth of the restaurant, the cold night air hits me hard, reminding me of the quote that may or may not have been uttered by Mark Twain. I pull the collar of my blazer up around my neck, realizing why all the tourists seem to be wearing the same cheap fleece jackets with the Golden Gate Bridge embroidered on the left breast. A foghorn sounds off moodily in the distance, and I half expect to run into Humphrey Bogart in search of the Maltese Falcon.

My conference companion and I roam aimlessly around the downtown streets, giving wide berth to the homeless men bedding down for the night on flattened cardboard boxes in the doorways of dry cleaners and Starbucks that have closed for the night. We find ourselves on the Embarcadero, the scenic walkway that hugs the waterfront. The salty scent of the air reminds me of Le Refuge.

"I think we run into Fisherman's Wharf if we keep going left," my companion says.

"Then let's go right," I respond.

We walk together in comfortable silence. After three days at the conference, it feels good to breathe fresh air and get some exercise. There's a long line of people—notably diverse in race and age, but uniformly attractive and well dressed—standing patiently behind red velvet ropes in front of a nondescript building. Up near the roofline, it says "Pier 13½" in plain large script. There is no other sign on the building to indicate the purpose for the queuing up.

"What do you think it is?" my companion asks.

"Excuse me," I ask a silver-haired woman who looks like she stepped out of an Eileen Fisher advertisement. "What are you waiting for?"

"Joshua Redman," she says. "He's playing here tonight."

"Who's Joshua Redman?" my companion whispers to me.

"He's a famous jazz musician," I answer. Truth be told, I can't remember exactly what instrument he plays, but I do remember he graduated from Harvard a few years after I would have. There was a fawning profile of him in the *New Yorker* a while ago.

"Do you like jazz?" my companion asks.

"I used to, but it's been a long time since I've been to a live jazz club."

"What's this place called?" my companion asks the Eileen Fisher model.

"Stardust," she replies.

I stop breathing for a moment. My mind's eye recalls images of Owen from the numerous Google searches I've run on him over the years.

"Joshua Redman just finished playing a fund-raiser for the San Francisco Jazz Festival," the Eileen Fisher model explains, "but the club owner just posted on Twitter that he's personally driving him here for an impromptu jam session. It's a once-in-a-lifetime opportunity."

"That sounds cool," my companion says. "A once-in-a-lifetime opportunity!"

I pull my collar even closer to my neck, but I can't seem to stop shivering.

"You wanna stay?" she asks.

"Nah," I say. "I'm freezing, and I've got an early flight tomorrow."

"Fine with me. I don't really like jazz anyway. Hey, I think that's the Ferry Building," she says. She points to the brightly lit clock tower up ahead. "I hear there's a place in there that has ice cream made with bourbon and Corn Flakes. You have room for a little dessert?"

I'm walking before she even finishes her sentence.

"Who doesn't like ice cream?" I respond.

Despite the attractive potential of moving to San Francisco, there's no way I can justify accepting the job, not with Sam and the girls. But I also can't bear to waste the opportunity; it's too good to pass up.

"What about Tracy?" I suggest.

"Tracy? Who's Tracy?" Old Man Barker asks.

"She's the stylish young woman who supports me in the library. The one who helped me come up with all the questions for *The Amazing Res Ipsa Loquitur.*"

Old Man Barker looks at me blankly.

"She's the one who helped cite-check that enormous brief we wrote for the DC Circuit last fall. She also organized that citywide scavenger hunt for the summer associates."

I can tell this isn't ringing any bells.

"She's the black girl. The one with the great legs. The one you called Whitney Houston at last year's holiday party."

"Oh, why didn't you say so," Old Man Barker says. "Of course, I remember Whitney."

"Tracy," I correct him. "Anyway, I think Tracy would be the perfect person to help set up the new San Francisco office."

Old Man Barker looks doubtful. "She'll have to submit a résumé," he says.

"Absolutely."

"And go through the normal interview process."

"I'm sure you'll find her very capable."

"We usually ask for references, but..."

"Mr. Barker, I hope you'll take my word for it. I can think of no one better than Tracy to help open the new San Francisco office."

A couple weeks later, a group of us gathers at Bombay Palace, an upscale Indian restaurant not far from the firm but far enough that everyone at Tracy's impromptu going-away celebration feels comfortable ordering several rounds of Kingfisher beer. Andre, the handsome security guy, made the mistake of telling the waitress that he liked his food spicy, and everyone is now suffering the consequences. We're all sweating like Nixon.

"When Old Man Barker called me into his office, I practically shit my pants," Tracy says, and the circle of friends around her laughs.

"Were you worried he found out about the midnight brownie deliveries?" one friend asks, reaching for another piece of naan to absorb the spiciness.

"Or the mysterious stains on the Barker Conference Room carpeting after the Summer Associates Welcome Party last year?" another friend adds.

"Hey, watch it, you guys," Tracy says, "Hannah's here."

"Oh, don't worry about Hannah," the mailroom boy says. "She's not your boss anymore. Isn't that right, Hannah?"

All eyes turn to me.

"That's right," I say, giving Tracy a warm smile. "Tracy's got no reason to worry about me anymore."

hannah

thirty-three

I haven't spoken with Sam for nearly a month since my trip to Tiffany's. Honestly, it isn't easy. Every morning, I have to remind myself: I'm mad at Sam. I'm not going to call to check in on the girls. I'm not going to see how his day is going.

At the end of the first week of silent treatment, I shoot him a quick email—I can't come to Princeton this weekend; tell the girls I'm sorry—and expect him to call to ask why. Instead, he just emails back, Okay, have a nice wknd. The same thing happens the next week. I start to wonder if Sam notices my absence from his life.

It's the week before Christmas, and I'm sitting at work when an email alert flashes in the corner of my screen. It's from Sam.

Hey, Hannah, hope you're doing okay. Could I ask a favor? Could you get the Xmas decorations set up at Le Refuge

before I get there with the girls on Thursday night? Eva
and Martin won't answer my texts, and I know I can trust
you to make sure everything is perfect. Thanks so much.
Love you, Sam.

I feel conflicted. It's almost Christmas. It's one thing to
punish my brother for his gift-giving transgression, but the
girls? Why should they suffer? They've done nothing wrong.
And besides, I miss them.

I'll leave work early on Wednesday, I type. Everything will
be ready by the time you arrive. My fingers hover over the
keyboard.

Love you, too, I write before pressing Send.

I don't know what I was thinking. It's like that children's
book I used to read to the girls, *If You Give a Moose a Muffin*.
When I stop off at the Home Depot just outside St. Michaels,
it's with the express purpose of buying one, just one, Christmas
tree. I pick out a tall noble fir, not as fresh or fragrant as the
trees Alex used to get from that specialty tree farm in Maine,
but it's perfectly fine and a fraction of the price. A nice young
man wearing a bright orange apron puts my selection on a hand
truck and starts wheeling it toward the checkout when my eyes
seize upon a tiny tree. It reminds me of Charlie Brown, which,
in turn, reminds me of Ally.

"How much for the small tree?" I ask, pointing.

"That one's ten dollars."

What a bargain. How can I pass it up? I nod to the young
man, who adds the small tree to the hand truck. But if I get
a tree for Ally, I have to get one for Claire, too, and if I go
through the bother of buying three trees, it doesn't make sense
not to buy a fourth. Otherwise, I can hear the cries of disappointment from the girls: "Where's Mommy's tree? What

happened to Mommy's tree?" Forty more dollars is a small price to pay for Claire and Ally's happiness.

"That'll be $145," the cashier announces. It's less than the cost of one of Alex's fancy designer trees. I feel a mild sense of triumph as I hand over my credit card.

"Which one's your truck, ma'am?" the young man in the bright orange apron asks.

Truck? I look out and see my subcompact rental dwarfed by the pickups and SUVs in the dimly lit lot.

"I'm sorry," I say. "I don't have a truck. I should have thought of that."

"We offer delivery service for fifty to a hundred dollars, depending on your location," the cashier says helpfully. "Our delivery guy is out on a call right now, but he should be back in an hour, if you want to wait."

I should probably just return the three smaller trees and have the young man strap the largest tree to my car roof, but in my mind's eye, I can already see the girls reveling in the magical holiday scene. Four sparkling trees, just like always.

"That would be great," I say.

The next evening, my hands are still sticky from tree sap as I clutch my coat tight around my neck, trying to ward off the icy Chesapeake wind. I dart between the clusters of happy holiday-goers strolling around St. Michaels's retail district. Most are tourists visiting for the day, taking in the Christmas decorations that festoon the four-block main street and ogling the expensive offerings in the posh shop windows. The cozy pubs and restaurants are full of boisterous patrons taking advantage of the seasonal excuse to eat and drink to excess, although, truth be told, none of them look like they've been holding themselves back the rest of the year.

I'm not tempted by the jewels or the booze. I've got more important things to do.

"'Marzipan, ginger beer and heavy whipping cream,'" I read off my shopping list as I enter St. Michaels's Gourmet Galley.

Claire and Ally loved the tiny marzipan treats I made last year, the sweet almond paste tinted and molded to look like their favorite emojis, and they were crushed when I told them I hadn't had time to make them this year. I imagine their joyful faces tomorrow morning when they dump out their Christmas stockings on the floor and see that Santa came through after all. I'm still debating whether to make a poo-shaped marzipan this year.

Martin and Karen decided to spend Christmas at their own home, but Eva and Alex begrudgingly agreed to come at the last minute. Sam has selected the nor'easter as the signature cocktail of the week, and it's a sign of how tense everyone feels that, in just one day together, we've already gone through our entire supply of ginger beer. We're still good on bourbon, however, as Sam makes sure to buy that by the case.

I can't remember exactly why we need whipping cream. And I have this nagging feeling there's something else. Something I didn't put on the list.

It's almost claustrophobically crowded in the small shop. Festive out-of-towners needing to warm up from the cold are chatting with the cheesemonger over slivers of Humboldt Fog and Neal's Yard cheddar. Regal housekeepers in their secondhand mohair coats exchange holiday greetings with red-faced butchers as they wait for their huge hunks of meat to be wrapped like presents in pure white paper. As I push my cart through the crowd, I'm still mad at Sam about the diamond earrings, although I haven't had the nerve to mention it to him. If fraudulent gift giving were a crime, the statute of limitations would have come and gone a long time ago. It's been over ten years since that fortieth birthday celebration.

I find the marzipan in the baking aisle. The two small

tubes look lonely sitting at the bottom of the oversize grocery cart. Despite my disappointment with Sam, I feel compelled to give him another chance. After all, Christmas is the season of forgiveness. Or is it? It's been a long time since I've been to church.

"Senorita Hannah," someone calls from the back corner of the shop. I turn around and see the familiar faces of Jorge and Maria, the lovely Mexican couple that has cooked, cleaned and generally taken care of Sam and Beth and the girls ever since I can remember.

I give each of them a warm hug. In a world where most people stand at least six inches taller than me, I feel a special kinship with Jorge and Maria, who are similarly short.

"Jorge, Maria, how wonderful to see you! *¿Cómo estás?*"

"We are well," Maria responds while Jorge nods and smiles.

"What are you doing here in St. Michaels?"

"We find work with another family here. But we miss *nuestros ángeles* Claire and Ally."

I smile appreciatively. Maria has always been so kind to the girls. She even encouraged them to call her *abuela*, which means a lot to me given that my nieces have no grandmothers of their own.

"We miss you, too," I say, "especially the girls. I hope our letter of recommendation helped." Out of respect for their pride, I don't mention the two-month bonus I withdrew from my own savings account to go along with the letter of recommendation I drafted for Sam to give to them. The couple looks at one another with knit brows. I can't tell whether they don't understand me or whether I've insulted them somehow.

"I'm sorry. Did I say something wrong?" I ask in Spanish.

Jorge and Maria start to argue, with Jorge whispering gently and Maria shaking her head crossly. My Spanish is rusty, but

I get the drift of their conversation. Sam didn't give them any recommendation.

"Did he give you the bonus?" I ask, although I already know the answer. The lovely couple shake their heads again. They explain Sam hadn't paid them for nearly four months, so they finally had no choice but to quit. This was months before Sam told me he had decided to let Jorge and Maria go. I think back to that night in the fall when the girls and I were searching for The Cheesecake Factory permission slip. The house had looked uncharacteristically untidy. I'm ashamed to remember I thought Maria was shirking her duties and taking unfair advantage of Sam in Beth's absence.

"Lo siento mucho," I say. I give Maria and Jorge a hug and swallow something bitter in my mouth. "I'm so very sorry." Looking down at my nearly empty cart, with Louis Armstrong's comforting voice crooning "Baby, It's Cold Outside," I suddenly remember my Sunday school stories. Christmas isn't the season of forgiveness. That's Easter.

Christmas is supposed to be the season of hope.

hannah

thirty-four

Le Refuge is dark when I get back from shopping. My heart clenches: maybe the electric company turned off service; but no, that couldn't be it. I made sure all of Sam's utilities were on auto-pay and connected to my personal bank account. It must be something else.

I fumble with the mass of keys in my purse before realizing the door's unlocked.

"Hello?" I call out, turning on the mudroom's overhead lights and stamping my boots on the dark gray water-repellent doormat. I'm relieved to see the lights all work.

"Hello?" I repeat, pulling off my boots and leaving them on the mat before slipping on my trusty wool scuffs. I place the bag of groceries on the kitchen counter and notice the light over the Wolf range is on. The lemongrass-green Dutch oven of beef stew that I left simmering on the stove emits a whisper of bubbles. I open the heavy enamel lid, breathe in the savory steam and turn the burner down a titch before flicking off the light.

Looking across the kitchen to the great room, the moonlight streams through the wall of windows, illuminating the outline of the Christmas trees. Having four trees may be excessive, but they do look magnificent, especially with the lights all aglow. Someone must have lit the candles while I was out.

Candles: that's the thing I forgot to put on the grocery list. I was so upset after talking with Maria and Jorge that I left the grocery without remembering candles. Oh well, we'll just have to make these last.

Thankfully, the handmade straw goats that I saved from last year's Christmas look none the worse for wear, at least to my untrained eye. They smelled a little musty from being in the basement all year, but I gave them a generous dousing of Beth's pine-scented essential oils, and it brought them back to life.

I spy a note in the middle of the great room coffee table, a cranberry-scented votive candle serving as a beacon. "We've gone caroling!" the note reads. I recognize Claire's neat, childlike handwriting. Red hearts and yellow stars adorn the green crayon letters. In blue ballpoint ink, Eva has written in delicate script:

> *Dear Sam and Hannah,*
> *The neighbors came by to invite us to go Christmas caroling. We'll be parked at St. Paul's Church and walking down First Street, if you want to join us. Otherwise, we'll be back in time for late dinner and one-gift opening.*
> *Eva and the girls*

When Sam and I were little, our parents let us open just one gift on Christmas Eve, saving the rest of the presents for

Christmas morning. It fills me with gratitude that our Min family tradition has been adopted by the Lindstroms.

"Sam?" I call out, wandering the darkened halls of Le Refuge. I finally find him passed out in the wrapping room amid a tangle of Target plastic shopping bags and rolls of wrapping paper, a nearly empty glass by his side.

"Sam," I say. I kneel on the floor and shake him awake.

"Wh—at?"

"The rest of the family has gone caroling in town. If we hurry, we can join them."

Sam sits up, rubs his eyes and wipes the area around his mouth and cheek for drool. For all his vaunted handsomeness, Sam looks worse than I've ever seen him. I'm reminded of those tawdry gossip magazines that litter the checkout stand with their schadenfreude-fueled covers: "Stars without Makeup!" "Beach Bodies Caught on Camera!" "You Won't Guess Who This Belongs to!" (Cue photograph of a cellulite-riddled thigh.)

"Uh, no," Sam says. "I've got to finish wrapping the girls' presents." He's surrounded by piles of plastic encased in more plastic: a pretend cash register with realistic-looking money and credit cards, a "Super Snacking" Baby Alive doll that bears a disturbing likeness to one of those blow-up sex toys, the latest Barbie in "Rainbow Unicorn Princess" flavor. Behind him is a small mountain of misshapen presents that he apparently wrapped before falling asleep.

"You know, the girls don't really need more toys," I say. I pull the cash register closer to me and cover it in glittery snowflake wrapping paper. "In the end, it's memories that matter, not material objects."

"Thanks for that great advice," Sam responds. "Next year, when the girls wake up to an empty Christmas tree, I'll be sure to tell them that. 'Hey, girls, welcome to the year without a Santa Claus! How's that for a Christmas memory?'"

My cheeks flush hot.

"What's up with you, Sam? Why the sudden outburst?"

"You don't know what it's like for me. You think you do, but you don't."

"So why don't you tell me about it? Talk to me, Sam. Tell me what's going on." I reach over to put my hand on Sam's shoulder, but he withdraws.

"Everyone talks about how hard it is to be a single parent, but you don't really know how hard it is until you've done it. I mean, I love them and all, but damn, they're a shitload of work, the endless cycle of baths and meals and homework.

"Meanwhile, I work my tail off every fucking day but can't catch a break. A week doesn't go by without some creditor or lawyer beating down my door for money. And to top it off, the fucking Lindstrom family shows up on my door every fucking holiday and expects me to play the happy host.

"'It's the memories that matter,'" Sam says, mimicking my high-pitched voice. "Well, memories cost money—money that I don't have—so pardon me if I'm not in the mood for your sermonizing."

"Sermonizing?" I splutter, "I wasn't sermonizing. All I was saying is that if you spent less money on things like stupid plastic toys or pretentious private school, you'd be able to live within the budget I gave you instead of racking up more debt. Oh, and by the way, I don't think you've been raising the girls entirely by yourself. Most single parents don't have the luxury of both a full-time housekeeper *and* nanny." I deliberately leave myself out.

"You know I let Maria go months ago," Sam responds. "You were the one who forced me to do it."

"Yeah, because you couldn't afford it. Speaking of which,

I just ran into Jorge and Maria in town. They said you never gave them the bonus or recommendation."

"They quit before I had a chance to fire them," Sam yells. "What could I do? I wasn't going to track them down and say, 'Oh, and by the way, here's a bonus and recommendation from Hannah.'"

I'm not sure how to respond. I hate when Sam makes sense.

"Well, you could have given me my money back," I say lamely.

"Seriously, Hannah? You want your money back?"

"No, I don't want my money back. I'm just saying…" My voice drifts off.

"What, Hannah? What are you 'just saying'?"

As Sam stares at me, my pulse races, and I'm instantly pulled back into that Tiffany store, the glare of the bright lights bouncing off all the glass and chrome surfaces.

"What I'm saying is I just found out the Tiffany earrings you gave me for my fortieth birthday are counterfeit. They're not diamonds, and they're not from Tiffany's. So, when you said that I was the diamond of the family, what did you really mean? Some cheap and shiny imitation?"

Sam's face goes blank for a moment, as if he's searching his memory banks for what I'm talking about. I can't tell if he's pretending, just buying more time to defend himself, or if he honestly doesn't remember. How could he possibly forget the happiest moment in my life?

"Oh yeah, those earrings," he finally says. "God, Hannah, what a disaster. Fucking Alex somehow got involved in this wholesale jewelry scheme. He convinced me to join him as a minority partner. It turned out the jewelry line was started by Donald Trump's ex who named it for their daughter, Tiffany. It had nothing to do with the actual Tiffany's. And then to top it off, we were sued by the real Tiffany's for trademark infringement."

"Why would you give me the earrings pretending they were genuine?"

"I didn't pretend anything. It was your big fortieth birthday, but I was broke and didn't want to mooch off Beth. Alex gave me the starter set as consolation for losing my investment. The earrings were the nicest piece in the set."

"But why?" I ask, although I'm not sure what I'm really asking.

"Why what?"

"Why would you give me fake diamonds? After everything I've done for you?"

"Hannah, I just told you. It was the best I could do."

"It wasn't the best you could do," I whisper, choking back tears. "You could have done so much better."

"Didn't you just say to me a minute ago that material objects don't matter? That it's all about the memories?"

I close my eyes, as if I could blot out the memory of that night by the fire pit when Sam presented the earrings to me. As if I could blot out the years of sacrifice and disappointment and loss. Yes, it's the memories that matter, but now I don't know whether any of those memories are real.

And whose fault is that?

I watch my brother fumbling to put the gift-wrapped cash register on the teetering pile of toys. He reaches for the Baby Alive and looks confused, trying to figure out how to wrap the oddly shaped object. A part of me wants to finish wrapping all the gifts for Sam so we can go out together to meet the girls for caroling. It would be the generous thing to do, the adult thing to do. But right now, a much larger part of me just can't stand the sight of his drunken face.

"I'm going to drive into town to see if I can catch up with

the family," I say. I stand up slowly, my poor hips aching more than ever. I head down to the great room. The space is darker now, the cold winter moon having slipped behind a shroud of clouds. The only light comes from the cranberry-scented votive on the table and the Christmas tree candles that continue to burn down.

For a moment, I just stare at the candles, the flicker a reflection of the anger I feel inside. I think for a second that I should douse them before I leave, but remember Sam is still upstairs. He can do it. It's about time he took some responsibility. I stride toward the door, eager to join the girls in town, but stop for a moment at the threshold. I turn around to cast one backward glance and admire the trees.

It really is the memories that matter.

It doesn't take much time for me to spot Eva, Alex and the girls huddled toward the back of the group caroling at the quaint inn in the center of town. Eva's daughters are particularly easy to identify in their candy-colored down jackets.

"Where's Sam?" Eva asks.

"He's staying behind to get some last-minute stuff done," I reply.

After a rousing rendition of "God Rest Ye Merry Gentlemen," the gracious innkeepers invite the carolers inside for some refreshments. Claire and Ally are thrilled with their Santa-shaped ceramic mugs of steaming cider and homemade gingerbread cookies with gumdrop buttons and raisin eyes, while Alex, Eva and I are content to warm up with a cup of the inn's famous mulled wine. It's so delicious that I have two.

Driving back to Le Refuge, I'm surprised to see traffic backed up.

"Do you think there's been an accident?" Eva asks. She knows how much I hate driving alone at night and agreed to ride back with me. I reflexively look at my rearview mirror but don't see Alex's car. The girls wanted to ride together in the same car, so we said goodbye at the church parking lot. I'm almost positive they left after us. It takes forever to get the little ones buckled into their booster seats. Still, I say a prayer under my breath.

The sound of a fire engine siren echoes from the opposite direction. Up ahead are the distinctive blue lights of police. I feel mildly panicky. Perhaps it's a Breathalyzer stop. I cup my hands around my mouth and breathe, reach down to find my purse and fumble around for the tin of Altoids. A police officer is walking down the middle of the street with a superbright LED flashlight, peering into the cars as drivers roll down their windows to ask what's going on.

Up close, I can see that the police officer is young, probably no older than twenty-five. Maybe he'll be lenient with me, someone old enough to be his mother. "I thought most of the alcohol was burned off in mulled wine," I imagine myself explaining. Perhaps it would be good to add that we were caroling with the church. That must count for something.

"What's going on, Officer?" I ask.

"There's a fire at one of the houses on Water Street."

Eva and I look at one another.

"Which house?" Eva asks.

"The fancy one," he says. "I think they call it the refuge."

The officer's words hit me hard. I rush out of the car and start vomiting into the trench by the side of the road. The mulled wine comes out looking like blood. Eva parks the car on the shoulder before coming over and wrapping me with her woolen jacket. The young police officer leads Eva and me into his cruiser and drives us slowly past the twisted snarl of traffic. All heads turn as the annoyed drivers try to make out our faces.

Eva and I sit silently in the back seat. There is a bulletproof glass separator between the front and back of the car. Sitting in the rear of the cruiser with strangers staring at me through the tinted glass windows—it feels somehow appropriate.

After all, I'm the one who should be in prison.

As we approach Le Refuge, I see the fiery orange outline of the main house's roofline against the dark night sky. The wrought-iron security gate has been taken apart, and a hook and ladder fire engine is getting set up on the lawn. Eva and the police officer stand by my side as we watch the flames destroy everything Beth worked so hard for. My eyes sting from the smoke as they scan the devastation, hoping to see Sam's silhouette emerging from the wreckage. The fire chief takes a moment from his official duties to ask me and Eva if anyone is in the house.

"My brother," I say, fighting the urge to run into the flames. "My brother's in there."

As a roof beam falls with an explosive bang, I rush forward, but Eva pulls me into an urgent embrace. I can't tell if she's holding me back or holding me together—maybe both. The police officer glances over at me, unsure of what to do next. Even in the flickering light, I can see how young he is. He looks like he barely needs to shave, and his unlined face still bears the hints of baby fat. I suddenly feel protective of his innocence. I turn away from the burning house and walk toward the gravel driveway.

"Where are you going?" Eva asks.

"I need to find Alex," I shout. I start running through the blinding sea of headlights.

The roads leading up to Le Refuge are a nightmare. One lane of traffic is completely closed, the other is barely moving. Motorists stand outside their cars, craning their necks for a view of the inferno, taking photos with their cell phones or speculating among themselves about what might have happened.

"Alex!" I yell, spotting Eva's husband standing next to the familiar Volvo station wagon.

"Hannah! What's going on? Where's Eva?"

I ignore him and peer through the car windows. Stevie is sitting in the passenger seat, her feet propped up on the dashboard and her eyes glued to her iPhone. In the back seat, Ally is fast asleep in her booster, snoozing along with her two younger cousins.

"Alex, where's Claire?"

"Claire? She's in the back. In the jump seat."

Sure enough, there she is, my precious niece, lying down on the jump seat. She's got her oversize headphones on, staring up peacefully at the car ceiling, singing along to a song that only she can hear.

I don't know if I can do this. It's almost more than I can bear. How can I tell my nieces that their beloved father is dead? Claire and Ally have already suffered so much in their young lives: the loss of their mother to prison for nearly a decade, and now this, the loss of their father forever. As I gather up my courage, I'm reminded of those long-ago cold mornings in Buffalo, when I had to get Sam ready for school. I'd stand there in the doorway, gazing at my brother's small body as he lay in his bed, dreaming whatever it is that little boys dream, and wondering to myself how much longer I could delay waking him up.

beth

thirty-five

"What're you gonna have for your last meal?" Charlotte asks.

It's one week before I have to leave for Alderson, and the two of us are lying in bed at the Four Seasons in Georgetown. I reach over to the room service cart and pull the bottle of Perrier-Jouët champagne from the ice-filled bucket. It's empty.

"Hey, you're dripping water on me," Charlotte complains.

I put the bottle back on the cart and lick the droplets off her belly.

"You should order sushi," Charlotte continues. "They won't have sushi in prison."

"I don't know. Maybe the puttanesca from Osteria Bellagio?"

"You know they call it puttanesca because the anchovies and capers taste like a whore's cunt?"

"Well then," I reply, "at least I'm consistent in my tastes."

"Whore," Charlotte whispers into my ear.

"Guilty," I whisper back.

Later that night, I find myself staring into the darkness and crying.

"What is it?" Charlotte asks wearily.

"The same old shit," I reply.

By now, Charlotte's gotten used to my periodic emotional breakdowns. They always happen at night, usually after I've had a few too many drinks. And they all revolve around Papa.

The first time I broke down in front of Charlotte, I told her about the snowy night of my tenth birthday, seeing Mother sprawled naked on the bed while Papa stood by.

"Oh my God, this is like a Psych 101 exam," she laughs. I've always loved her throaty, no-holds-barred laugh. "How many Freudian issues can you spot? Masturbating mother equals Madonna/Whore complex. Sexy father equals Oedipal—or in your case Electra—complex."

"He's not my father," I protest for the umpteenth time.

"Yeah, technically he wasn't your father, but c'mon, who's kidding who? He made you call him Papa. Anyway, where was I? Oh yeah—the pipe's a classic phallic symbol but also an oral fixation. Was it Magritte—or maybe it was Freud—who said, 'Sometimes a pipe's just a pipe'?

"Let's see, what else? The naughty girl peeking through the door, what could she stand for? Transitioning from the latency stage to the genital, maybe?"

I feel a flush of shame mixed with a wave of relief.

The second time I broke down in front of Charlotte, I told her about the night after Mother's funeral.

"Father was passed out on the living room couch, and Martin and Eva were taking turns checking on his breathing to make sure we didn't lose two parents in one week. I was sitting alone in my bedroom when Papa walked in.

"I remember he was wearing his nicest black suit, the one with the subtle herringbone texture. He came in and sat next to me on my bed. I still remember the delicious smell of his cologne—an expensive mixture of sandalwood and citrus.

"We stared out my bedroom window at the streetlights on Nebraska Avenue. I loved the way they went on automatically, as if Tinker Bell was flying from light to light and touching them with her magic wand.

"As I sat there, Papa told me about the things he loved about Mother—the subtle spray of freckles on the bridge of her nose, the tiny golden sparkles in her crystal-blue eyes, the way her soft pink lips turned up in the corners.

"And then I realized he wasn't just talking about Mother. He was talking about me. Before I knew what was happening, he leaned in to give me a kiss."

"How old were you?" Charlotte asks.

"Fourteen."

I expect Charlotte to turn away. Instead, she holds me all night.

The third time I broke down, I confessed my relationship with Papa didn't end with that kiss.

"Martin went back to Dartmouth to start his senior year, so I didn't have him to talk to. Eva channeled all her grief into school and trying to get into a good college, meanwhile eating everything we had in the house and throwing up afterward. Father drank himself into oblivion. And then there was Papa, who seemed like the only person who understood what I was going through.

"I was fourteen, and my girlfriends were losing their virginities left and right, so it didn't feel like a big deal. But instead of getting screwed by some hormonal boy in his stained twin-size bed, I was made love to by a grown man on imported Frette bedsheets."

"A grown man who made you call him Papa," Charlotte interjects.

Okay, yeah, I guess that part was kind of fucked up.

The fourth time, I had just gotten a call from the hospital informing me Father was dead.

"After Mother died, Father had no one to keep his drinking in check. You can do a lot of things and still be a drunk, but you can't be a driver. Fortunately, Papa was reassigned to work at the UN, so we moved to New York, and Father was given a new job as the doorman at our co-op apartment. A job he kept until the day he died."

"When did it end with the Ambassador?" Charlotte asks.

She can't bring herself to call him Papa. "Too creepy," she says.

"I was still adjusting to life in New York and my new friends at Brearley. Papa and I were hanging out in bed when Martin decided to visit. No advance warning or anything. When Martin saw us together, he went ballistic. I swear, he beat Papa to within an inch of his life. Papa never forgave him, and Martin's had to make it on his own ever since.

"After that night, Papa never slept with me again. I don't know if Papa was scared of Martin or maybe he just realized it was wrong. Anyway, even after our relationship ended, Papa continued to take care of me. He paid for my trip to Europe, my college tuition, even gave me an allowance. And then the day after I graduated from Barnard, I found him dead on the floor of our Park Avenue apartment. Papa had killed himself."

That time, Charlotte not only held me all night, she called in sick the next day.

Charlotte has always been super understanding about my fucked-up life, but there's one thing that I never told her.

Going back to that fateful night in my parents' bedroom, Charlotte always assumed that I identify with Mother, that I saw myself in her, the object of another person's desire. That makes sense, right? I mean, why else would I place myself literally in my mother's position after she died?

The reality, and the thing that I haven't told anyone, not even Charlotte, is this: seeing Mother's naked body, her full breasts and spread legs, was the first time I felt sexually aroused. It was the first time I understood the connection between sex and power. And it was the first time I wanted to be in power.

Yes, I wanted to be her, but I also wanted to be him.

beth

thirty-six

It's the last day of the Lindstrom family reunion, and I'm trying to get as drunk as I can. I don't want to think about what lies ahead. Besides, starting tomorrow, I've got nearly ten years to go cold turkey.

"I can't believe you think it's Eva," Sam says.

He pours a healthy glug of Grey Goose into the mixing glass and shakes up another batch of dirty martinis.

"I mean, she's your own sister. Sisters don't betray one another."

Sweet, unsuspecting Sam.

"What about Martin?" Sam pours the faintly green liquid into a chilled martini glass and drops in two jumbo olives, just the way I like it. He hands me the drink, and I take a sip.

Damn, he's a good bartender.

"I know he's desperate for cash these days," he continues.

"Ever since Chaz got diagnosed with cancer, he hasn't been able to bring in any new clients. EMC is on the verge of bankruptcy. And Karen keeps spending money like there's no tomorrow."

"There's no way Martin's the one," I say. I scoop out the olives with my index finger and pop them into my mouth. I bite down and savor the brine.

"He would never do that to me," I say with conviction. As if conviction in my tone could cast away my lingering doubts.

"No, I'm sure it's Eva. She's hated me ever since I slept with her first boyfriend. And the three boyfriends after that. Anyway, Eva's the only one I can think of beside you and me who knew about the photos."

"Well, there's no way to know for sure," Sam says. "It's not like Eva's going to have a come to Jesus moment and confess."

I throw back the rest of the dirty martini and hold my glass out to Sam for a refill. He obediently pours me another.

The alcohol lubricates my imagination, and my Spidey senses are tingling.

How would I feel if I had turned in my own sister to the federal authorities, sending her to prison for nearly ten years? Even if I hated her, wouldn't I feel just the slightest bit of guilt, if not for my sister, then at least for my two young nieces who'll be left without a mother?

Wouldn't there be a part of me that wanted to confess?

"I know what we'll do," I say.

I look at Sam with a mixture of love and pity, knowing he'll do whatever I say.

Sam returns my gaze expectantly.

"You need to fuck the truth out of her."

I sit and wait in my bedroom for Sam. The pasta puttanesca is sitting in my stomach like a brick. It was a stupid choice for a last meal. There's going to be lots of pasta in prison. What I really should have ordered is sushi.

I look over at the clock on my nightstand. It's been about

an hour since I left Sam and Eva in the great room alone to-gether. I heard the sound of footsteps coming up the stairs a while ago, so knowing Sam, it shouldn't be much longer.

To kill time, I walk over to the bookshelves and look at the Shutterfly photo albums I've amassed over the years. My eyes are drawn to the album I created for Eva's fortieth birthday.

I bring the album back to my bed and feel a strange lump in my throat as I pore over the photos of Eva and me over the years. The ones from Sweden, when we were both very young, show the two of us in matching little-girl outfits that Mother had sewn herself. We are smiling broadly, without a trace of artifice, thrilled to be together, two peas in a pod.

Things change when we move to the US—not immedi-ately, but very clearly. We stop wearing matching outfits. Eva embraces the Laura Ashley look, while I'm more of a Calvin Klein jeans type. My parents start calling Eva "the smart one," and me "the pretty one," as if determining our destinies. I suppose in some ways they did.

There aren't many photos from our teen years. After Mother died, there was no one to document our lives. In the few pho-tos of those sad years, Eva and I stand stiff and apart, forcing smiles for the camera. Eva's college-aged face gazes mournfully at me, her eyes distorted by her thick eyeglasses, the blurry images of forgotten freshman roommates in the background.

I reach for the bottles on my nightstand, which have be-come a fixture in my life ever since I learned I was headed to prison. I take a swig from the half-empty Evian bottle to choke down the pills. I'm startled when Sam walks into my room.

"Mission accomplished?" I ask.

"God, Beth, you can be so cold sometimes," he says.

"Don't get soft on me now, Sam."

"Yeah, mission accomplished," he says, sitting on the edge of my bed.

"And?"

Sam takes a moment to observe the scene. I can't tell if he's worried by the prescription bottles on my nightstand or if he wants to take a couple himself, like a social smoker bumming a cigarette off a stranger.

"I did everything you said," Sam says. "Told her how lonely I've been ever since Lise left. How you spend all your time with Charlotte. How it's too bad she's happily married to Alex because I've always found her so attractive."

"And?"

Sam looks pained.

"Sam, what happened?"

"Like you said, Eva fell for it. She practically threw herself at me."

"And then what? What did she say?"

"You know, the same stuff she always says when she's shitfaced. That she should have been a better sister and should have been there to protect you. From the Ambassador. And from yourself."

"Anything else?"

"Nah, she just pulled on her clothes and ran back to her room."

"You were that good, huh?"

Sam looks hurt.

"Geez, I was kidding," I say.

"Any other brilliant ideas?" Sam asks.

"Nah, that's enough for now. You did good. Now get some sleep."

Damn, that didn't turn out the way I thought.

A part of me is disappointed that Eva didn't confess, but another part—a tiny ember deep inside of me—is relieved. Maybe she didn't betray me after all.

I give Sam a consolation kiss and send him to bed. He doesn't even beg for sex the way he usually does. Ever since that nymphomaniac Lise left, Sam's been hornier than ever. I can thank Eva for giving me the gift of a night off.

I look around my beloved bedroom. The walls painted the perfect shade of soft blue; it took me forever to decide on Benjamin Moore Forget Me Not. The one-of-a-kind crystal lamp that Charlotte and I found tucked in the corner of that antiques store in New Hope, Pennsylvania. The astonishing collection of seashells that Claire picked up on Sanibel Island that spring I was huge and pregnant with Ally.

It took me so long to create this space. Will it still be here when I get out of Alderson? As the saying goes, you can't take it with you.

Feeling justifiably sorry for myself, I stride to the other side of my bedroom, pull down the rest of the photo books and pile them up on my bed.

I linger over the photos of the girls as they went from mouse-like infants to plump and juicy toddlers to bright-eyed little girls. I always thought Claire took after Sam's Korean side, but now I see just how much she looks like Hannah. Her Cupid's bow lips. Her shiny black hair. The way her cheeks glow when she's excited.

My brain starts to get fuzzy as the Ativan and Ambien kick in.

It's the next morning, the day I'm supposed to self-surrender at Alderson. I'm in the steam shower with the water turned up to the hottest setting. The heat feels good against my skin. I turn the color of a medium rare Kobe steak, and my mind turns back to the last time Lise stayed at Le Refuge.

It was a few days before Martin and Eva were due to arrive with their families for the annual Lindstrom family reunion. Lise, Hannah and I take the girls to the U-Pick berry farm in the morning. Hannah wants to make individual strawberry shortcakes for dessert, and Claire and Ally are excited to explore the open fields.

Lise forgets to put on sunscreen, and she comes back from

the day trip as red as a lobster. Hannah researches home remedies for sunburns on the internet and makes a concoction of iced green tea, fresh mint leaves and aloe.

Lise sits on the shady veranda, her chest, arms and legs covered in white gauze strips soaked in the soothing solution. Claire and Ally are glued to Lise's side, fascinated by the sight of their former nanny and favorite playmate sitting there like a Zen-scented mummy.

"Does it hurt?" Hannah asks.

"A little," Lise replies. "This is helping," she says, indicating the gauze. "And this, too," she adds, taking a long sip of her mojito.

"I remember when you got a sunburn on Maui," Claire says.

"Wow, Claire, you remember that?" Lise asks. "You were just a tiny girl when that happened."

"How tiny?" Claire responds. "Tiny like Ally?"

Ally looks up from the veranda floor. She's naked except for her diaper. Her pale brown hair is still just growing in and stands up in a shock, like a mini Billy Idol.

"Claire, come upstairs with Mommy," I say, "and we can get the photo album I made about that vacation." The whole point of making those damn photo albums is to preserve—or maybe even create—happy memories for the girls. Thankfully, Lise is a whiz at doing shit like that.

"Uppy," Ally says, raising her dimpled arms. Of course, she wants to join us. She can't stand to be separated from Claire. I hoist her to my right hip and take Claire's hand with my left hand.

"I want to be carried, too," Claire pleads.

"Claire, your mommy has her hands full with Ally. Why don't you let me carry you?" Hannah suggests.

Claire starts crying, "No, I want to go with Mommy." She squeezes her eyes shut, as if by blocking the sight of Auntie Hannah, she can make her disappear.

I don't blame Claire. We only see Hannah once or twice a year. She's essentially a stranger to the girls.

"Don't worry about it, Hannah," I say. "I can handle both girls. You stay here. It looks like Lise needs a change of gauze anyway."

I schlep the two girls up to my room, where I scan the shelf for the Maui vacation photo album. As much as I love my housekeeper, Maria, she always puts the albums on the shelves willy-nilly, so it takes me forever to locate anything. But on that particular day, I am pleasantly surprised: all the photo albums are in perfect chronological order.

A couple weeks later, Lise quits her job as my personal assistant and disappears from our lives. Without notice. Without explanation. And without apology.

At least she learned one thing from me.

A few months after that, the whistle-blower suit lands on the God Hälsa doorstep with a heavy thud, and my world implodes.

My mind returns from that long-ago day to today—my last day of freedom before going to prison. I've been standing in the shower so long that the air is thick with steam. I can't see a thing. I won't be getting many hot showers in Alderson, I fear.

I emerge from the steam shower, and the air clears. I grab a towel for my hair. When I open the door to my bedroom, I discover Hannah waiting there, startled as a fawn, my bed made and the room tidied up. And then I notice all of the Shutterfly photo albums have been returned to the shelf.

My brain starts to itch. The pieces slowly come together. I reach for Charlotte's jar of Guerlain body crème sitting on the makeup table, and I open the golden lid. I stand there, stark naked, and apply the emollient all over myself, knowing that Hannah will be so uncomfortable that she'll leave me alone.

And when she does, I'll go to the shelf and confirm what I already suspect.

hannah

thirty-seven

I've always been a planner. When I was a young girl, I used to plan my daily outfits, my homework study schedule, even what I'd pack for school lunch. My life was a well-oiled clock.

When Sam came along, I did my best to plan for him as well, but things didn't always work out as planned with him. Sam was constantly screwing up. Playing tackle football during recess and staining his brand-new button-down shirt on class photo day. Losing his take-home algebra test and forcing me to walk across town to his best friend's house to make a copy. Sneaking off campus to buy pizza for lunch and wasting the perfectly good ham and cheese sandwich I packed for him.

I can't blame Sam for the biggest mistake of my life, however. I have to take full responsibility for that. I thought I knew what I was doing. I thought I had done my legal research. I thought I knew how to fix Sam's life.

I was wrong.

It was a cold and wet Sunday, almost three years ago. Sam called to say that he was feeling cooped up, tense. He said he wanted to come visit me at my condo. I had just seen him a few weeks earlier at Le Refuge for Christmas, so I knew something was wrong. Sam was not one to stop by for a casual visit.

When Sam shows up on my doorstep, he's shivering wet. He forgot to wear an overcoat. He isn't dressed for the weather. His thin cotton sweater and khaki chinos are plastered against his body. His face is ashen, and he breaks down in tears as soon as he sees me. I've never seen him like this before.

"What is it?" I ask, running to the bathroom to get a towel to wrap him up in. "Is it the girls? Is something wrong with the girls?"

"Yes, it's the girls," he sobs, and then he shakes his head. "No, it's not the girls. The girls are fine. It's Beth."

Sam allows himself to be led to the oversize armchair in my living room. I walk to the kitchen to pour two glasses of whiskey. I hand one to Sam, take a sip of mine and wait patiently while Sam collects himself.

"Beth wants a divorce," Sam explains. "Last night, we had dinner, put the girls to bed and in the middle of *Flip or Flop*, she tells me that she wants a divorce. A fucking divorce."

I feel a strange sense of anger mixed with relief. I think about Sam's life with Beth: lavish homes, expensive cars, luxurious vacations, closetfuls of brand-new designer clothing. I think about my sweet, young nieces growing up into entitled brats like the vapid characters they watch so intently on the Disney Channel and Nickelodeon.

"Sam, I know this isn't what you want to hear, but let Beth have the divorce. And then move on. I never wanted to interfere with your life, but I don't think Beth is good for you. The only thing Beth cares about is money. Money and all the things that money can buy."

"That's not fair," Sam says. "And it's not true."

"Yes, it is," I insist. "And worse, over the years, you've become just like Beth. I barely recognize you anymore. Do you remember how we grew up? How our parents raised us? We went to public schools. We ate at home. We were grateful for the little things. You and Beth live like awful reality stars."

Sam doesn't say anything. He takes a long swallow of the whiskey. I can practically feel the burning sensation in my own throat. It feels good to be speaking my mind, and I hope Sam is open to seeing things my way.

"That's not the point, Hannah. I don't care about that stuff, the houses and the schools and the clothes. That could all disappear tomorrow and it wouldn't matter. All I care about is Beth—and the girls."

And then it occurs to me: the girls—of course, the girls— nothing is more important.

"So, what happened?" I ask, relenting.

Sam tips back the last drops of whiskey. He walks to the kitchen and brings back the bottle of whiskey and fills up his glass.

"Sam?"

"Well, it all started when the St. Michaels police department called Beth to report an intruder at Le Refuge."

"An intruder?"

"Yeah, only it wasn't actually an intruder. It was just this producer from HGTV scoping out the property. Alex has been trying to convince Beth to let them do a feature piece about Le Refuge, and the producer jumped the gun."

"Okay...so there was a misunderstanding. Why would Beth blame you for that?"

"Well, I sort of gave Alex permission to talk with the guy. Alex said he would split the money from the producer with me. I needed some cash to buy Beth an anniversary gift, and I didn't want to use Beth's own money."

"I could see why Beth would be annoyed, but it's hardly grounds for divorce."

"Beth's a really private person," Sam explains. "She blew a lid when she heard a stranger was poking around Le Refuge without her knowledge. Particularly a stranger with a camera."

It's ironic to me that Beth, who has framed copies of her puff pieces from the *Wall Street Journal*, *Time* and *Fortune* displayed on the walls of her Princeton study, should be so protective of her privacy. She's always struck me as someone who craves attention.

"Well, that's just crazy. There must be something deeper at issue. Have you two tried marriage counseling?"

"Beth doesn't want marriage counseling," Sam says. "She wants out, and she wants full custody of the girls."

Now I'm angry. How dare Beth threaten to take the girls? My nieces are the only blood relatives Sam and I have left.

"She can't do that," I say. "She doesn't have any right."

"Actually, she does. She made me sign a document before Claire was born."

"What are you talking about? Why would you do that?"

"We had a different relationship at the time. It was before we got married."

"Okay, well then I'm sure it won't hold up in court. You've been faithfully married for almost five years."

A cloud crosses Sam's face.

"Sam, you have been faithful, haven't you? Because adultery would be legal grounds for divorce."

Sam takes another gulp of whiskey, and then refills the glass before it's even half-empty.

"Hannah, I know this'll sound strange to you," Sam explains, "but Beth and I aren't so hung up on the monogamy thing."

"You mean, you have an open marriage?" I try not to sound judgmental.

"Not open, exactly. More like...partly open."

"Partly open?"

"Yeah. You know Beth's always complaining about being too tired for sex," Sam says. "Well, once when we were fighting about it, Beth said she'd be fine if I found someone else to satisfy my…uh…my needs. I thought she was kidding until one day she told me Lise would be interested."

"Lise? You mean your nanny, Lise? Isn't she a teenager?"

"She's not a teenager, and she's not a nanny anymore either. She's twenty-one and Beth's personal assistant."

"So, you and Lise—how long have you been…doing it?"

"God, Hannah, you make it sound so sleazy."

I glare at him.

"I don't know how long exactly. Beth hired her after Claire was born, so what's that? Four years? Five?"

I do the mental math. Lise would have been sixteen or seventeen when she first got hired as Claire's nanny. I don't know what the age of consent is in New Jersey or Maryland or the places they've vacationed together, but sixteen or seventeen is awfully young. Then a terrible suspicion comes over me: perhaps Beth has been setting Sam up all this time. Maybe she's been taking advantage of his ignorance and sexual desires to use as blackmail in case she ever needs it, and poor Lise has been the innocent pawn.

A couple weeks after Sam's visit, I'm working late at the office, proofreading an article for the firm's monthly newsletter. We send it out to our roster of clients in the hopes of rustling up new business.

"Fair Hannah," a voice trills from behind me. It's Thing 1— the former Supreme Court clerk from Indiana who shares my love of *Masterpiece Theatre* and Hugh Grant movies. "My computer crashed, and I need to finish editing my piece for the newsletter. Might I borrow Tracy's?"

"Of course," I reply. I walk over to Tracy's computer and

flick the power switch on. While we wait for the computer to boot up, I ask, "So, what's your article about?"

"It's a fascinating piece, if I do say so myself. One of those thrilling 'ripped from the headlines' cases. It involves a twenty-two-year-old receptionist who received a fifteen-million-dollar government bounty for blowing the whistle on her employer."

"Huh, that sounds interesting. What did the employer do?"

"The employer was a Florida mortgage company who pressured appraisers to inflate home values for properties with federally insured loans. For a while, these guys were making money hand over fist and living the high life off their ill-gotten gains. Vacations on St. Barts. Italian sports cars. Bottle service at Las Vegas strip clubs. The whole nine yards. But when the economy tanked, so did the mortgages, causing hundreds of millions of dollars in losses for the federal government."

"And then what? How did the receptionist get involved?"

"She filed a lawsuit against her employers under the False Claims Act."

"I read an article in this morning's *Wall Street Journal* about a False Claims Act case," I respond, "but I didn't really understand how it works."

"There have been a number of high-profile whistle-blower cases in the news lately," Thing 1 explains. "Most of the cases involve pharmaceutical companies or defense contractors, but with the recent financial meltdown, banks and financial institutions have come under focus, as well.

"Basically, anyone can blow the whistle on their employer if they believe they're defrauding the federal government. So, here, the receptionist knew her bosses were faking the appraisals for the federal loans. She worked with an attorney to file a whistle-blower lawsuit. The US Attorney prosecuted the miscreants, who agreed to pay a hefty settlement, and then bingo—Little Miss Receptionist gets a cool fifteen million dollars."

"Kind of like hitting the lottery."

"Indeed," Thing 1 concurs. "Most of these False Claims cases involve billions of dollars in government revenues, and whistle-blowers can get up to 30 percent of the proceeds. Even with the legal fees, it's a nice chunk of change."

"I suppose the corporations settle because they don't want their executives to go to prison?"

"Alas, no. The False Claims Act is a civil statute, not a criminal one, so the government can't seek jail time. The theory behind the act is that the most effective way to deter corporate malfeasance is to go after what these companies really care about—money."

"Sounds reasonable, I guess."

"Perhaps," Thing 1 replies. "They say cheaters never prosper, but it seems to me that there are plenty of cheaters who are prospering quite nicely. Even when they get caught stealing billions, these corporate types land back on their feet. Maybe a little poorer, maybe a little wiser, but almost always in a good place. Meanwhile, under federal mandatory minimums, those poor bastards who commit minor drug offenses get sent away for years."

Tracy's computer finally springs alive, and Thing 1 sits down at her desk to type in his log-in and password. I return my attention to my own article: a bone-dry piece about changing regulations impacting longwall mining. The pompous partner who authored the article is an abysmal writer and even worse speller, which I find baffling in the age of autocorrect. Nearly every other word in the article is underlined with a red squiggle. Does he not realize what that means? But then again, the partner knows I'll be proofreading the piece. Why bother to do the work if you know someone else will do it for you?

My phone buzzes on my desk. A photo flashes for a moment on the screen. It's an email from my brother.

"Hey, when you're done with that piece, would you mind emailing it to me?" I ask. "It might be helpful for something else I'm working on."

The days and weeks following Sam's death pass in a blur. Beth gets a temporary release from prison, and the two of us alternate between taking care of the girls and taking care of Sam's funeral arrangements. The memorial service at the funeral home is packed, standing room only. There are friends from college, the country club, even God Hälsa. I'm touched to see so many of Claire's classmates and teachers from Princeton Country Day. They show up in a true circle of community.

After Sam's service, Beth and I are sitting side by side on the velvet lounging couch in their Princeton home. Claire and Ally are huddled together at Sam's desk, working on an Alvin and the Chipmunks coloring book. There's an empty box of Kleenex on the coffee table in front of me and Beth, and another almost empty one on the floor. My eyes are swollen from so much crying. I've avoided talking to Beth about the fire, the lawsuit, everything, but I can't keep it in any longer.

On my lap is the Min family scrapbook with its well-worn Naugahyde cover. I open the scrapbook to the last page, and slide it over to Beth so that the book is balanced on our combined laps. There are two obituaries pasted on the page: my parents' notice from the *Buffalo Evening News*, and Sam's announcement from this week's *Princeton Times*. I know them both by heart. After all, I wrote them. Beth rereads Sam's announcement.

"It's beautiful, Hannah," she murmurs, her finger tenderly tracing the contours of Sam's handsome photo. His face, as always, is open and devoid of artifice. Tears trickle down Beth's pale cheeks.

"No, not that one—the other one," I reply. I watch Beth's

bloodshot eyes as they slowly make their way down the yellowed announcement.

Professor Nick Min and Mrs. Nora Min of East Amherst died on December 10, 1994, in a fatal car crash with a drunken driver. They were both 54.

Professor and Mrs. Min were born and educated in South Korea. They emigrated to the United States in 1964 for Professor Min to pursue graduate studies at SUNY Buffalo with Albright Distinguished Professor of Linguistics William Schugart. Professor Min received his PhD in linguistics in 1970, and has served on the faculty of SUNY Buffalo since that time.

Professor and Mrs. Min are survived by their children Hannah and Sam, and were predeceased by their beloved daughter Doori.

A funeral is scheduled for noon on December 15 at Amigone Funeral Home in Amherst, with a reception to follow at Lee Chu's Restaurant, also in Amherst.

"I didn't realize you had a younger sister," Beth says. "Sam never mentioned her."

"He had no reason to," I say. "He never knew her. She was born when I was three, and she died just two years later." Beth takes a closer look at the page.

"Her name was Doori?" Beth asks.

"It means *two* in Korean. *Hannah* means *one*."

"And *Sam*? Does it mean…"

"Yes, *Sam* is *three*," I say. "What can I say? My dad was a linguist."

"Tell me about her," Beth asks. "Tell me about your sister."

I'm overwhelmed by Beth's words. No one has ever asked me to talk about my sister before. The story spills out of me.

I tell Beth about the little sister who came into my life and left it suddenly and far too soon.

"My parents told me Doori was a gift from heaven. That my job as a big sister was to take care of her. In retrospect, I think they wanted to make sure I wouldn't feel jealous of her, to make me feel like I had a special job. Even when I was young, I loved to have a purpose."

"Claire takes after you that way," Beth says. I'm surprised how much it warms me to hear Beth acknowledge that.

"I took my job very seriously," I continue. "I loved holding Doori and giving her a warm bottle of milk. I used to lie by her side on my parents' bed, watching her sleep and making sure she didn't kick off her blankets or roll off the edge. My mother said I even potty-trained myself because I didn't think it was right to change Doori's diapers if I was still in diapers myself."

"I could totally see you doing that."

"And then one day, when Doori was almost two, she died."

It's shocking to me how, nearly a half century later, Doori's death still pains me.

"I'm so sorry, Hannah. What happened?"

I've never had this conversation with anyone before: not Sam, not Owen, not even my parents. It's a conversation I've always needed to have.

"My parents never talked about it, so it was a mystery to me for a long time. I remember finding Doori in her crib, limp as a dishrag, ugly purple bruises up and down her legs. I ran as fast as I could to tell my parents that Doori was hurt. They rushed her to the hospital. The nurses wouldn't let me into her room. I sat by myself in the hallway, holding her favorite teddy bear. I remember telling the bear, 'Doori will be fine, don't worry.' But Doori wasn't fine."

I catch myself as a sob bubbles up from my center. Over forty-five years of sorrow that I've tucked away find the light of day at last.

"No one ever told me what she died of," I say. "I figured it had something to do with the bruises. Years later, after my parents died, I found Doori's death certificate. And it was only then that I learned Doori's actual cause of death—something called meningococcal septicemia."

"I've never even heard of it," Beth says.

"I know, I hadn't either. I looked it up after I found the death certificate. Apparently, it's very rare. It's caused by some kind of bacteria that most of us have in our bodies, but babies and young children are especially susceptible due to their immature immune systems. Mothers can transmit the bacteria just by giving them kisses."

"I'm so sorry, Hannah."

"Doori's death hit me hard. It hit all of us hard. Like Sam used to say, I was a lonely child who did everything I could to make my parents happy. The only quibble I have with his story is that my parents didn't wait all those years because they had trouble conceiving—they waited all those years because they were still in mourning.

"When Sam was born, my parents didn't tell me I was responsible for taking care of him. They didn't need to. The moment I saw Sam's perfect little face, I vowed to myself I would do whatever it took to keep him safe."

"And you did that his entire life," Beth says. "Until you couldn't."

When I look up from the Min family scrapbook, I see something in Beth's eyes that sends a chill through me. Beth knows the truth, and she understands.

"It's okay, Hannah," Beth says. "You did what you thought was best. For Sam. For the girls. I'm not mad at you. Not anymore." I am both frightened and relieved. My entire life, all I've ever wanted was for someone to accept me, faults and all.

Never in my wildest dreams did I imagine that person would be Beth.

beth

thirty-eight

"What gave me away?" Hannah asks.

Hannah's face is drained, and her tiny hands are shaking. But she also looks curious. Like she can't believe she's been outsmarted.

I nearly laugh. What didn't give her away?

Claire and Ally have finished their coloring and come over to me and Hannah, begging for another activity.

"Claire and Ally, go downstairs and find your cousins," I say. "I bet they'd love to play Ping-Pong with you."

The girls yelp excitedly and run off. As soon as they're out the door, I turn to Hannah and tell her what she wants to know.

That the photographs from the Shutterfly photo albums were the prosecution's strongest evidence against me, proof of my personal knowledge and responsibility for the Metamin-G ads at the heart of the government's case.

That Maria never put the albums in any kind of order.

That Hannah's heart beat like a rabbit's when I hugged her goodbye at Alderson.

That she has a terrible poker face.

"If anyone else had conspired with Lise, they would've asked for their share of the whistle-blower reward," I say. "Only you would let Lise have the whole thing."

"I hope you know I never intended for it to go so far," Hannah says. "When Sam told me you wanted a divorce, I was fine with it. Good riddance, I thought. But when I saw how upset he was, and then he said you wanted sole custody of the girls...well, I panicked. Those girls are the only family Sam has. That I have."

I sit there and let Hannah talk. I can tell she needs to let it out.

"Something in my brain just flipped, I guess," she continues. "I thought maybe if you lost your job, you wouldn't be able to afford to divorce Sam. That you'd focus on rebuilding your life rather than ripping it apart."

"It's okay, Hannah," I say. "What's done is done."

"The False Claims Act is a civil statute," Hannah continues, "which means there's no possibility of jail time. None of the pharmaceutical cases I researched resulted in anyone going to prison. And believe me, I researched all the pharma cases, not just the FCA ones. They were all resolved with monetary penalties. But then the Deputy AG came out with the Yates Memo, and the Justice Department wasn't content to limit their efforts to just the corporations. They started to go after the executives themselves."

I assure Hannah I believe her.

Hannah may be misguided, but she's not cruel. She just underestimated how much public pressure the Justice Department would feel after the financial meltdown to bring white-collar criminals to justice. How the case against me would snowball once the feds started to really dig beneath the surface. How no one could have imagined how much shit was going on around me.

First, there were Martin's extravagant gifts and dinners with his cronies in the federal government. The low-quality foreign goods that he marketed as US-made. His sloppy books and failure to pay import tariffs. The laundry list of federal violations that Martin could have been charged with made my indictment look like child's play.

And then there were Sam's emails to Alex about my work at God Hälsa. Alex's stock trades based on Sam's insider information. The way the two of them gave out stock tips to their golf and tennis buddies like some kind of friends and family discount code.

"The worst-case scenario would have been for all of us—Martin, Alex, Sam and me—to get serious prison time," I explain. "Those poor guys wouldn't stand a chance in federal prison. Given that overhang, my plea didn't seem like such a bad deal."

"It seems I'm not the only one who sacrifices herself for her family," Hannah says.

"Hey, don't let that get around."

We sit together in silence for a while.

"If you knew it was me, why didn't you confront me right away?" Hannah asks.

Good question. How do I explain the workings of my warped brain?

"What did I have to gain by confronting you?" I begin. "Nothing. It wouldn't get me out of prison. It wouldn't undo my plea. All it would do is turn everyone against you, which wasn't in my best interest.

"I knew Sam couldn't take care of the girls on his own, and there's just so much I could control from prison. I needed someone on the outside to help hold the family together. Charlotte wouldn't do it. I had hoped Eva might step up, or maybe even Martin and Karen, but in the end, you were the only person who was there for Sam and the girls."

Although she averts her eyes, I can tell Hannah is touched. I'm tempted to tell her I also enjoyed watching her squirm, like a worm on a hook, but that seems unnecessarily cruel.

"Why pretend you wanted me to find Lise's conspirator?" Hannah asks.

"That was my bunkie's idea. As you can imagine, I was pretty pissed at you when I first got to Alderson. Juanita and I thought we'd play a little mind game. See how far we could push you before you cracked. But you never did crack. You're a surprisingly tough cookie."

"And the wrongful death lawsuit?" Hannah asks. "The girl who died?"

"That part was actually true, but I wasn't particularly worried. Plaintiff's lawyers only go after deep pockets. Sam and I were up to our ears in debt—as you eventually learned. God Hälsa paid the girl's family an out-of-court settlement. It's chump change for the company. The cost of doing business."

"When I found out you were going to prison," Hannah says, "I felt so guilty that I tried to do everything a real sister, a loving sister, would do. It started out like acting, like playing a role. But after a while, something happened. I actually started to look forward to our time together."

"Ditto," I hear myself saying.

Damn, when did I go soft?

The truth is Hannah was my connection to the world outside. I grew to depend on her. Not just the magazine subscriptions and Danielle Steele books, but also her weekly letters, the photos of the girls, the in-person visits.

In the end, Hannah was the only one besides Charlotte to

visit. Neither Martin nor Eva ever bothered. Even Sam didn't take the time to come on his own. He only ever visited with Hannah and the girls.

"I know the judge who sentenced you has a reputation for being tough on white-collar criminals," Hannah says, "but is there any chance you could stay out of prison? Would he grant you an early release? Have your lawyers tried invoking the minor-child extenuating circumstance provision?"

I have to laugh. Even after Sam's death, Hannah insists on doing her research.

"Nah, that guy's not called the Coldhearted Snake for nothing. My lawyers say there's no chance he'll give me a 'get out of jail free' card. Not when I have family who can raise the girls for me."

"Eva's going to have her hands full with five girls," Hannah says.

"I'm not asking Eva," I reply.

It takes a moment for Hannah to understand my meaning. I can tell by her terrible poker face that she's simultaneously sorry for me and overjoyed for herself.

"It's okay to be happy, Hannah. As much as I can't believe I'm saying this, you're the only person I trust to take care of the girls. Claire and Ally both love you, and I know you love them. But don't you go and get any more crazy-ass ideas. It's just until I get out of prison. After that, you'll have to settle for being the world's best auntie."

Hannah starts laughing and crying at the same time.

"Have you read *Charlie and the Chocolate Factory*?" Hannah asks.

"No, but I saw the movie," I say.

"Do you remember the final scene where Willy Wonka tells Charlie he's won the rights to the entire chocolate factory?"

"Claire and Ally are a lot sweeter than a chocolate factory, I think."

Hannah nods in fierce motherly agreement.

The Min family scrapbook feels heavy. I lift the book off our laps and place it on the floor. Hannah and I sit together silently and gaze through the streaky glass windows. Outside, the thick, gray clouds swirl and shift.

The torrential rain comes down like ecstatic applause.

hannah

epilogue

It's been three years since Sam died. We buried his ashes at
Forest Lawn Cemetery in Buffalo. There's a modest memorial
marker for him, right next to the ones for my parents and Doori.
I think Sam would be happy to know his final resting place is
just around the corner from Rick James. "Super Freak" was the
first song he danced to at his very first middle school dance. He
wore a white linen blazer and pink cotton T-shirt in tribute to
his favorite TV show, *Miami Vice*. I'd like to imagine Sam and
Rick in heaven, best friends forever, dancing and singing at the
top of their lungs.

Charlotte finally decided to quit the pharmaceutical rat race
and moved to New Hope, Pennsylvania, where she opened
her own boutique. Charlotte's Web specializes in expensive
ladies' accessories and European beauty products. Wolford
and La Mer are among her most popular brands. She's even

in talks with the people at Agent Provocateur to become an exclusive retailer.

Beth and Charlotte are planning to get married when Beth gets released from Alderson, which should be just a couple years from now if Beth gets full credit from the BOP for good behavior and completing her drug rehabilitation program. Claire and Ally will be the flower girls, and Eva and I will be co–maids of honor. Beth asked me to get her a subscription to *Modern Bride* magazine for inspiration. Both Beth and Charlotte plan to wear white.

As for me, I left Drinker, Barker and Horne, and accepted the position of head librarian at one of the Princeton public library branches. I love my new job. The library patrons appreciate how well I maintain the shelves. Everything's always in the right place. While I don't earn nearly as much money as I used to at the firm, that's fine by me. I made a tidy profit selling my condo in Hoboken. The new owners are an entrepreneurial young couple who run a stylish but homey cat café featuring artisanal small–batch coffees and gluten-free, vegan pastries. It's *Zagat*-rated and earns 4.7 stars on Yelp.

The girls and I live in an updated three-bedroom bungalow not far from the library. Claire and Ally share a bedroom overlooking the leafy backyard—it was their choice, the inseparable, dynamic duo—and Beth convinced me to take the master. We use the third bedroom for guests.

Eva and her youngest daughter come to visit us in Princeton quite often. Eva's two older girls are growing up so fast they barely have a free weekend, but they're good about catching up with Claire and Ally on FaceTime. Eva asked Alex for a trial separation, but Alex is staying in the garage cottage until he can find a job to support himself. I hear he's trying to get his place featured on one of those tiny-house programs on HGTV.

Martin and Karen and their kids live in Nebraska now,

where Martin works at a plumbing supply company owned by one of Karen's brothers. I still can't eat fish without thinking of him.

Beth and I are fighting with the insurance company over coverage for Le Refuge. The insurance company claims that the antique candleholders on the Christmas trees—which the fire inspector determined was the cause of the accidental blaze—are illegal in all fifty states, and the homeowner's policy contains an express limitation of coverage for any damage caused by illegal activity. Old Man Barker assigned Things 1 and 2 to handle the case for me pro bono, and we're hoping to settle out of court.

We had no such troubles with Sam's life insurance policy, however, which paid up within months of his death. You can imagine my surprise when I saw the insurance check made payable to me. "Of course, you're the beneficiary, Hannah," Beth said. "Sam adored me and the girls, but he felt most loved by you."

I received a sympathy card in the mail from Owen about six months after Sam died. Apparently, he read in the news about the fire and Sam's death, but it took him months to track down a mailing address for me. He finally found my name online in an old issue of the Drinker, Barker and Horne client newsletter, and the firm forwarded his card to me in Princeton. We've talked by phone several times and exchanged Christmas cards. He's offered to come out to the East Coast to visit me, but I've held him off. I don't think I'm quite ready.

It's still hard for me to accept Sam's death. There's a lot of guilt I'm working through. How I might have prevented the fire if I had stayed at Le Refuge rather than gone out caroling. How I should have forced Sam to join me instead of leaving him alone. How I could have helped Sam more—or less—

throughout h life. My weekly therapy sessions are helping, but I don't know if I can ever forgive myself.

The best thing I can do is keep busy. At the library, I read my favorite children's books aloud to wide-eyed toddlers and their overeager parents during my daily lap-sit sessions. I take Claire and Ally grocery shopping on Sunday mornings and cook them a home-cooked dinner every night. Their favorite is chicken tetrazzini and spaghetti with meatballs. I have a regular slot every Wednesday to volunteer at their school, and I try to chaperone as many field trips as possible. My absolute can't-miss trip is The Cheesecake Factory.

Hey, don't judge me.

In the end, I couldn't bear to pull Claire and Ally out of Princeton Country Day.

After all, the girls are thriving there.

★ ★ ★ ★ ★

acknowledgments

"One too many chocolate martinis."

That was the prompt Christopher DeLorenzo read aloud in his warm and inviting living room in 2015—the prompt that inspired the opening scene of this book. To Chris and my fellow Tuesday evening Laguna Writers, Carol Harada, Chris McClean, Daniel Raskin, Iris Fluellen, Kate Nitze, Ken Linton and Sharon Smith: thank you for telling me to "put a sticky on that one" and keep writing. Eternal gratitude to Merijane Block (miss you) for making the introduction.

As the random bits of writing came together into a messy manuscript, I was lucky to have a group of insightful readers (and gifted writers) to provide encouragement and feedback. To my manuscript group, Lisa Hills, Bill Manheim, Lily Rubin, Gargi Talukder and Debbie Weissmann: thank you for reading those awkward early drafts, highlighting the parts you loved and remembered, and telling me in the gentlest possible way how I might make the story even better.

To Alice Kim Blake, Adrian Blake, Seung Oh, John Kim (miss you, Ope), Erin Edmunds and Aichi Daniel: thank you for reading my book in progress and helping me believe it wasn't tripe. Your love and friendship nourish me.

As many aspiring writers will confirm, trying to get an agent is a maddening, ego-destroying process. To Kirby Kim, my awesome agent and brother from another mother: thank you for seeing the potential in my manuscript, working hard with me to transform it into a novel and guiding this first-time author through the thrilling but unfamiliar world of publishing. Thanks also to Brenna English-Loeb, the staff at Janklow & Nesbit, particularly Eloy Bleifuss and Michael Steger, and Lia Chan at ICM Partners for all your efforts on my behalf.

While getting an agent might have been the most frustrating phase of publishing, the most mysterious to me was editing. After all the work it takes to get a manuscript ready for publishers, what's left to be done? In my case, it turned out the answer was "Plenty." To Brittany Lavery, my wise and wonderful editor: thank you for your keen intelligence and clear-eyed guidance that helped tighten the story, give it more heart and amp up the suspense. Thanks as well to the team at Graydon House, especially Roxanne Jones, Laura Gianino, Pamela Osti, Ana Luxton, Susan Swinwood, Margaret Marbury and Amy Jones, for bringing *A Good Family* into the world.

When my friends hear that I'm going to be a published author in addition to my full-time job as a corporate lawyer, they inevitably ask, "Where in the world do you find the time?" Too often, writing time comes at the expense of family time. To my husband, John, and beloved sons, Jonah and Theo:

thank you for pushing me to keep writing when I wanted to give up, letting me know how proud you are of me and being the very best supporters anyone could have. You give me infinite joy.

Finally, to my parents, Yong and Yongboon Kim: thank you for everything. I love you more than I can say.

A GOOD FAMILY

A.H. KIM

Reader's Guide

GRAYDON
HOUSE

1. The two primary narrators, Hannah and Beth, are a study in contrasts. In what ways are they different? In what ways do we discover they are alike? What do you make of the relationship between the two?

2. Hannah and Beth start off the book with distinct narrative voices. In what ways do their voices differ? Do you find that their voices change over the course of the book? If so, how and why? Whose narration do you find more enjoyable to read?

3. The book opens with Hannah observing the luxurious details of Le Refuge—everything from the Carrara marble countertops in the kitchen to the memory foam mattresses in the dorms—and she continues to mention such details throughout the book. How do you think Hannah feels about these extravagances? How do you feel about them? Do Hannah's feelings change over time? Do yours?

4. Both Hannah and Beth face conflicts working in white, male-dominated environments. How do Hannah and

Beth respond to such conflicts? Have you faced similar conflicts in your life? Whose approach do you find more relatable?

5. Both Hannah and Beth come from modest immigrant backgrounds, although Hannah was born in the US and Beth was born in Sweden. What role does immigration play in each character's life? What about race? Do you think it's easier for an immigrant to "blend in" when they are Swedish versus Korean?

6. The three main male characters in the book—Sam, Martin and Alex—share a number of common traits. Discuss the commonalities and differences among the men. What forces or events do you think made them the kinds of men they are?

7. Sisterhood is a key theme underlying the book. How is Hannah shaped by her role as older sister of Sam and Doori? How are Beth and Eva shaped by their roles, respectively, as "the pretty sister" and "the smart sister"? Do you have a sister? Do you relate to any of the sisters in the book, and if so, how?

8. Both Hannah and Beth use language as a way to mislead without outright lying: for example, calling Alderson Prison "Mommy's camp." Are there other examples in the book—whether in the form of language or actions—where the characters mislead without outright lying? Are there examples in your own life where you've used language or actions to mislead without lying?

9. In the end, we discover both Hannah and Beth have sacrificed themselves for the ones they love. What did Hannah sacrifice? How about Beth? Reflect on a time that you've sacrificed something for a family member or friend.

Do you think Hannah gave up too much for Sam? That Beth gave up too much for her family? Why or why not?

10. The story ends in tragedy, but the epilogue hints at better days. What do you imagine the characters are doing after Beth is released from prison? Does Hannah stay with the girls or does she have her own "happily-ever-after"?